HIDDEN MICKEY₄

WOLF!

HAPPILY EVER AFTER?

BY

[signature]

NANCY TEMPLE RODRIGUE

2011
DOUBLE-R BOOKS

DOUBLE-R BOOKS ARE PUBLISHED BY
RODRIGUE & SONS COMPANY
244 FIFTH AVENUE, SUITE 1457
NEW YORK, NY 10001
WWW.DOUBLE-RBOOKS.COM

HIDDEN MICKEY 4 WOLF!
HAPPILY EVER AFTER?
VOLUME 4, 1ST EDITION 2011
FOURTH BOOK IN THE HIDDEN MICKEY SERIES

PAPERBACK ISBN 13: 978-0-9749026-8-5
PAPERBACK ISBN: 0-9749026-8-3
EBOOK ISBN 13: 978-0-9749026-9-2
EBOOK ISBN: 0-9749026-9-1

COVER DESIGN BY JEREMY BARTIC
WWW.JEREMYBARTIC.DAPORTFOLIO.COM
COVER COLOR BY CHRISNA RIBEIRO
WWW.JUHANI.DEVIANTART.COM
COVER COPYRIGHT © 2011 DOUBLE-R BOOKS
WWW.DOUBLE-RBOOKS.COM
PENDANT DESIGN BY NANCY RODRIGUE
COPYRIGHT © 2010 NANCY RODRIGUE
WWW.AWESOMEGEMS.COM

PRINTED IN THE UNITED STATES OF AMERICA

This is dedicated to my support system:
My husband Russ.
His on-going efforts to support me and
promote this series of books are
unending, untiring and tremendously
appreciated.

Nancy Temple Rodrigue

Disclaimer

While some of the events and persons contained herein are historical facts and figures, other persons named and the events described are purely fictional and a product of the Author's imagination. Any resemblance to actual people is purely coincidental. The actions depicted within the book are a result of fiction and imagination and are not to be attempted, reproduced or duplicated by the readers of this book.

Dear Readers,

I am pleased to present to you the fourth book in the Hidden Mickey Series: *Wolf! Happily Ever After?* There have been a lot of wonderful comments about my new character Wolf who was introduced to you back in Hidden Mickey 2: It All Started…. and then given his own story in *Hidden Mickey 3: Wolf! The Legend of Tom Sawyer's Island*. Thanks to all of you who embraced my time-traveling leading man and who loved the fantasy element that I introduced into the series.

As with all the fun-filled adventures you have experienced in the Hidden Mickey series, I think you will enjoy this last, exciting episode just as well. You will encounter quite a few familiar characters and faces along the way.

As always, the real Leader of the Pack, Walt Disney, is seen throughout this story. Without his dreams and hard work, these books would not have been possible. There would have been no Disneyland and no inspiring animation from which to draw. I hope the gratitude and admiration we have felt for Walt and his creative genius has shone through in each and every novel.

I have been asked—quite often, actually—if any of the stories will take place in Walt Disney World in Florida. At this point in time, I haven't been to WDW in many years. As I am not that familiar with the Park, I couldn't do it justice—yet. I hope to get out there soon and start doing "research!"

So, enjoy this "time" you will spend with my wolf! Hopefully, all your dreams will come true.

Best Wishes and Thank You,
Nancy Temple Rodrigue

PROLOGUE

"That's not my castle."

The two male voices that had been quietly arguing about the best way to proceed stopped mid-sentence. Hidden under the curved arch of the stone bridge above them, standing in knee-deep water of a moat, a confused pair of green eyes and a frowning pair of sapphire blue eyes turned at the anxious words of the speaker.

"What did you just say?"

The blond head, catching all the moonlight from the crescent high above them, pulled back into the dank shadowy niche under which they were hidden, the golden glow abruptly dying from view. After the terror of their arrival through the swirling vortex had receded and being anxious to get back to her family, Rose Stephens had ignored her two male companions and peered upwards at what she hoped would be a familiar sight. Her own deep blue eyes reflected the disappointment and concern that was flooding through her. "I said that this is not my castle," she repeated, her heart pounding as the

11

meaning of the words sank in.✒

"Are you sure?" Wals Davis asked her, turning from the third member of their party, Wolf. Rose had been so silent all this time he had forgotten her role in all this—how much this would mean to her.

Hands on her hips, she just stared back at him, her mouth in a firm line.

"Okay, okay, you're sure," Wals conceded, half smiling with his hands up in front of him in mock surrender. "Then, whose castle is it? Do you recognize it?" He was hoping the jump through time had just put them in the wrong neighborhood. The other possibility—that this could perhaps be the *wrong* time period—made his blood run cold.

Even the darkness surrounding them didn't conceal the fact that her face had blanched. She grasped her hands together only to keep them from trembling. "It's awfully dark, but, no, I didn't recognize the castle or the flags that I could see on the turrets."

Wals turned back to the leader of their group. The wolf had waded to the edge of the bridge and was looking upwards, nose in the air. He counted on the fact that his black fur would blend into the night, rendering him nearly invisible to the casual eye looking down from the guard posts. Anxious to get out of the dark water lapping around them, he now knew it was time to fall back and regroup. "Where are we, Wolf? Did we end up in Florida? Is this the Cinderella Castle?" Wals, knowing Rose wouldn't recognize the Florida icon, offered that possibility as a more hopeful outcome than what he knew, deep down, was the truth.

Sniffing the air, Wolf could get no sense of the familiar scents of humanity, an amusement park, or even anything industrial. The smells were a mixture of earth and nature and animals, mostly horses and cattle, he thought. Eyes closed, he imagined it was similar to his father's home along the River, before the age of the steamboat. Similar—but older. Much, much older. "I don't know, Wals. But, I do know this isn't Florida. This is by far older than Florida."

Wals was distracted from this troublesome statement by the appearance of a small, sparkling blue dot that flew under the bridge and settled on Rose's shoulder.

"Oh, Merri! You made it through with us! I thought we lost you!" Rose was genuinely happy to see her friend, the Blue Fairy.

"Yes, yes, dear. I have been out having a look-see. This isn't what you planned, wolf," she said in a surprisingly loud, disgusted voice from such a small figure.

"I am beginning to realize that, fairy," the wolf growled, going to the edge of their arched hiding place and lifting his sensitive nose one more time. "What else can you tell us? Anything that might actually be of use?"

Merri ignored the barb in his words and popped out into her normal size, hovering inches over the water so she didn't get her slippers wet. "I cannot help you, wolf. I can only observe and offer suggestions. Until we get my girl back to her proper time, I cannot utilize my special talents. You should realize that by now."

"A fog is coming in, Wolf," Wals observed, ignoring the animosity between the fairy and the wolf and trying to get their leader back on track. "That might help us get out of here. Rose is starting to shiver from the cold and the wet," taking her in his arms as much for warmth as for his own reassurance.

Turning his attention back to the needs of the moment, Wolf's superior eyesight came into play. "I can see what looks like sentinels on the curtain wall, over there behind those battlements. If you look closely, you can just make out their spears." He broke off and silently observed for a couple of minutes. "It appears there may be more movement than when we first arrived. It could be that dawn is near and they are getting ready for the new day," he raised one shoulder in a shrug. "Or it might be because our voices are carrying further than we thought and we are being heard. So, we need to either whisper or not talk at all until we know what's going on. Agreed?" Wolf asked quietly, looking back over his shoulder.

Wals' whisper was at a slightly higher pitch than he normally used, betraying the effect Wolf's words had on him. "Spears? Why would there be spears? Even when we went back to Fort Wilderness they used long rifles. Where in the world are we?"

"'When' might be better to figure out first," Wolf muttered, getting only a nod of agreement from the Blue Fairy who was waiting patiently for them to get moving. He shook his head as he looked away from her, hoping she would be of more use. Right about now he would like her to use that wand of hers, not just offer up an observation. "Ah, good. The fog is getting thicker, Wals. It might be better if we made it to that forest and hid. We can figure out what to do from there. If dawn is coming, I don't want to wait it out here and possibly be seen. All right?"

Ducking his head back out in the open, he quickly checked the position of the sentries again. "Rose," he commanded, "throw your cloak over your hair. It's like a beacon even in this fog. Wals, you help her to keep her footing. We don't know what's in this water. Merri, you're awfully bright…."

The fairy gave a small sniff. "Humph, nobody see me unless I want them to, wolf."

"Fine. I'm not trying to start an argument, just trying to keep everyone safe from a hail of flaming arrows…."

Feeling Rose tense up, Wals turned on his friend. "Was that necessary, Wolf? We're all on edge as it is."

His huge head turned back to Wals, his eyes narrowed. "Yes, it is necessary. Those spears don't appear to be made out of plastic, and any arrows they use wouldn't have red suckers on the ends of them. This is real. Just like Fort Wilderness was deadly real when you went back there. Understand?"

The reminder of the dangers he had faced when he was taken back into the 1800's was like a bucket of cold water thrown on his anger. Resolutely nodding, he took Rose by the elbow and

made ready to leave the relative safety of the un-
derbridge.

When the sentry on the walkway completed
his last pass and had turned away, Wolf slowly
led them from their place of concealment. Trying to splash as little as possible, they all hoped
the late hour and the mist would make the
guards drowsy or inattentive and less likely to
see the expanding ripples in water that, by all
rights, should be perfectly still.

Now encased in a cushioning layer of fog,
the companions made their way as quickly as
possible through the close undergrowth of the
forest. Out of any possible sight from the high-
est tower of the castle, Wolf called a halt and
held his nose in the air, trying to get a feeling for
the place in which they found themselves.

Due to the late hour, birdsong was noticeably absent as those denizens of the forest
would be sound asleep in their nests. The
creaking of branches and the occasional drip of
water off of the leaves mixed with muted sounds
of scurrying mammals fleeing from the scent of
something new, something that didn't belong,
something that was deadly. Louder noises that
came to their ears from a distant crash might
have signified a dropping branch giving up its
tenuous hold or, more disturbingly, the sound of
pursuit—the hunter and the hunted.

Knowing the sounds were moving away
from them, Wolf ignored those unimportant
noises and fell back to relying on his training

from birth. Being a Lakota brave of the wilderness, he would need every trick he knew to help his friends survive.

"Do you think it is safe enough now to start a fire?"

Even though the question was whispered, the sound seemed overloud in their perilous condition. "Shh, Wals. Not so loud. I can hear you just fine. No. I know we need the warmth," *and the false sense of security it would provide*, he silently added to himself, "but it isn't a good idea just yet. We still don't know who or what is around us. Sorry, Rose." He had refrained from shaking the water off of his thick black coat. It would have just reminded them that he was impervious to the cold and dampness that they were feeling.

Whatever else Wolf was going to say died in his throat when he realized they were not alone in that small clearing in the misty forest. A different, unique smell came to his nose. Unable to place it, his head jerked upwards when a soft rustling noise settled on a limb high over their heads. Eyes narrowed and teeth bared, he saw they were being watched by a pair of frowning golden-yellow eyes.

The hair on the scruff of his neck stood and he took a defensive posture in front of his friends. Head down and front feet wide apart, Wolf's back legs were tense, ready to spring at a moment's notice. Wals placed a steady hand on the sword hanging at his side, his fingers wrapping easily around the elaborate hilt. Eyes trained upwards, he pulled the steel blade a few inches out of the scabbard and waited.

They all watched in silence as a dark shape dropped from the tree and headed straight towards them.

CHAPTER ONE

Burbank — 1963

"How do you make cartoons, Walt?" the National Geographic interviewer asked next.

"Well, if you'll come this way, I'll show you the animators at work," Walt replied after picking up the phone and making the arrangements.

As his troop filed in, Walt smiled, pleased with himself. The interview was going really well, and the editor seemed interested in every facet of the workings of the Studio.

The first stop they made was the Story Department. There was a prominently displayed wall of sketches showing the feature-length cartoon that was currently in production: *The Sword in the Stone*. As Walt explained, the main ideas were drawn out and pinned to this large wall and then used, rearranged, or discarded as the storyline progressed.

In the Sound Department, the large empty

room was filled with chairs and music stands patiently waiting for the orchestra to arrive for the next session. Here voices, sound effects and music were recorded after just the right songs and background music were written and the perfect voice was auditioned and chosen for the characters.

An animator was next on the list for a visit. Walt continued talking while the interviewer scribbled furiously in his notebook. Walt explained that the animators needed to be actors themselves to be able to portray and then draw the movements they see in the mirror that was mounted next to their desks. Once the director has told the animators how the scene will play, they would get to work drawing the assigned character. In the next cubicle, Walt introduced an animator named Shirley who was drawing the outline of Merlin. She pointed out that the drawing would later be painted on the reverse side and then photographed over a woodland scene deep in the forest.

The layout man was an artist too. He provided the visually stunning backgrounds that were a favorite feature of the full-length cartoons. Next, the inkers and painters traced the animator's drawings onto clear celluloids, or cels as they were more often called, and would then they'd refer to a color guide to get the correct, pre-determined colors for the characters.

Once the cameraman was delivered the finished, dried cels, they would be placed, one at a time, over the correct background and then he would shoot them. "It requires sixteen different drawings for just one foot of film," Walt pointed out, indicating the cels on the table. "What we are working on here, *The Sword in the Stone,* will end up with something like two hundred twenty-seven thousand hand drawings!"

The film editor was then introduced and he gave the interviewer a sample of the film he had just edited out, explaining it took eighteen drawings for the owl in that part of the film to flap his wings one time. Holding the piece of film up to the light, the National Geographic man could see the brown, round face of the owl. "May I?" he eagerly asked his host. At Walt's nod, he smilingly slipped the piece of film into his pocket.

The projection room, Walt explained, came with many moods depending on the progress of the film on which they were currently working. If it was going well, it would be a light, joking atmosphere, as it was that day. If not, well, it was "back to the drawing board," Walt said with a chuckle. He knew, all too well, how often that could happen and how months of work would be scrapped in the desire to have a perfect finished product.

Clearly enthralled, the interviewer shook his head at all the things he had just seen. "This has been amazing, Walt! Our readers will love to get this behind-the-scenes glimpse into your world. So, tell me something about Disneyland."

"Tell you?" Walt laughed, a twinkle in his eye. "How about if I show you! You have time?"

"You bet," was the enthused reply. He hurriedly jammed his hat on his head as he saw his host was already halfway to the door.

Disneyland — 2008

"**W**ho so pulleth out this sword of this stone and anvil is rightwise ruler born of England." The words were mounted on an elaborately shaped shield and attached to a large rock in the courtyard of Fantasyland. Sitting on the rock was a golden anvil and embedded in the anvil was a golden-handled sword, mere inches protruding from the anvil, tempting all those who pass to test their strength and worth. With the backdrop of the King Arthur Carrousel, it was a fitting reminder of Days of Olde when knights pursued their glorious quests and fair maidens awaited in their castles.

"Hear Ye! Hear Ye! By proclamation of Arthur, the right and true king of the land, it is time to choose a temporary ruler of the land."

Coming out of thin air, the voice of the unseen speaker, preceded by an energetic blast of trumpets, settled over the guests in Fantasyland as a tall, blue-robed figure strode majestically through them. "Merlin!" was the cry from knowing youngsters as they flocked around him, following his circuitous route to the embedded sword.

"Yes, it is time," Merlin declared, glancing at the huge wooden hourglass hanging from his belt. "You're late," he called upwards to the hidden voice.

"A new ruler is needed to keep the kingdom safe while our good King is…."

Merlin interrupted, "Is what? What is King Arthur doing that requires a temporary ruler?"

"On vacation. Hey, every ruler needs a break…," the voice sounded put out that he needed to defend the rights of the King.

"Oh, get on with it. We understand," Merlin chided, his arms waving to include the entire, growing crowd gathered outside the thin ropes he had quickly set up around the sword and the stone.

The grand, invisible voice continued, "Presiding over this most sacred ceremony and selection is the royal prestidigitator, the royal wizard, and the official temporary royal ruler selector…Merlin!"

Arms out, Merlin accepted the applause around him. "That's me!"

"Let the ceremony commence," declared the voice.

"Thought it already did," Merlin mumbled as if to himself. "You can go now, Voice. I am Merlin, the most humble adviser to good King Arthur, and I must find amongst all of you delightful subjects of the realm the one who is most qualified to be the temporary ruler while Arthur is, er, sunbathing in Bermuda. Now, in order to find a good candidate, it takes a little extra…." Pointing to the nearby entrance to Peter Pan, Merlin opened his large soft-sided bag and reached inside. Pulling out a pair of red long johns, he hurriedly stuffed them back inside, red of face and embarrassed. "Oops, wrong bag…. Oh, wait, here it is." Throwing a cloud of sparkles into the air, he continued, "A little extra help. Now, who feels confident that they can provide the needed protection and direction this realm needs? Any volunteers?"

A sea of hands shot into the air. Merlin walked around the rope barrier he had erected earlier and approached a large, smiling man. "Ah, I can see courage, strength, moral charisma, and a definite fashion statement," as he pointed to the pair of Mickey Mouse ears on the man's head. "You…you are the choice. Come with me."

The fanfare of trumpets could be heard from speakers above as the chosen guest was led to the backside of the waiting sword.

"What is your name?"

The man, getting into the spirit of the moment, threw out his arms as if in greeting. "I am Jeff," he declared to the answering hoots from his family in the audience who had their cameras ready for the fun to come.

"You are correct! You have passed the intelligence part of the exam. Sir Jeff," Merlin continued, "Before I can allow you to ascend the throne of Arthur, according to tradition, only the right and true king can pull the sword from the stone. You look like a strapping young man, so don't get carried away here. Just pull the sword about halfway out. Now, place your hands on the handles of the sword. Are you ready, Sir Jeff, to take your rightful place in history? Are you ready to pull?"

Jeff looked like he was straining. "I already

am," he admitted as his face turned red.

"What? You couldn't possibly be pulling. Put your back into it, man!"

Jeff tried again and it was obvious the sword wasn't going to budge.

"Hmmm, I'm not sure what is wrong…besides you, of course…. Perhaps I should try another fellow and proclaim that you are the Official Royal Bodyguard. Stand to the side, Sir Jeff, over there," Merlin pointed.

Adjusting his tall, cocked hat, Merlin looked out over the audience again. "Well, I'm going to lose my credentials if I don't get this right. Usually this is so simple even a child can do it! Ah, that's it!" Merlin stopped in front of a small, smiling boy of about eight years old. He could see the pleading twinkle in the boy's eyes. "You," as he laid his hand on the child's head, the boy's mother busy snapping pictures and laughing. "Come with me. Your name, young squire?"

"Kyle!" the child giggled, nervous and excited at the same time, bouncing up and down on his toes.

"Sir Kyle." Merlin led him back to the position behind the sword and had him face the audience. Merlin next went to the waiting Jeff and positioned him behind the boy, his arms outward towards Kyle. "Now you guard him, Sir Jeff…. Perhaps you can get that right," Merlin mumbled out of the side of his mouth, eliciting a chuckle from the audience. "Sir Kyle, how old are you?"

"I'm, uh, eight."

"Are you married? No, never mind. Now, I want you to think of a wonderful place…. Oh,

wrong story, sorry. I want you to think coura-
geous thoughts and then pull the sword. Can
you do it, Sir Kyle? Are you ready?"

Kyle chuckled uncertainly and shrugged his
shoulders.

"Oh, your confidence is so assuring! Now,
get in position…."

The sound of trumpets came from the
speakers as Kyle tugged upwards on the sword.
It slid easily from the anvil and stood gleaming in
the afternoon light as the audience clapped their
approval.

"You did it!" Merlin declared, and wiped the
nonexistent sweat from his brow. "Whew." He
pulled a red cape out of his bag and fastened it
around Kyle's neck. "Our new temporary ruler,
King Kyle!"

The audience broke out into applause again
as Kyle waved to his parents.

"Now, Your Majesty, it is time for your first
official business of the land, your first proclamation. You can make any law you want. Anything
you can think of, it will come true. Anything at all.
Ice cream for dinner. Free FastPasses for Indy
for all. Anything you want. So, think carefully,"
Merlin continued, pulling up his hourglass and
checking it. "Oh, I'm sorry, your time is up." He
removed the cape from the youngster's shoulders and stuffed it back in the bag. Holding up
a golden medallion he had just retrieve from his
pocket, Merlin looked at the confused boy.
"Since the joy of the day has been somewhat di-
minished, I would like to present you with this
royal medallion that commemorates your time

as our ruler and kind King. Now, return to your family and think of your rule fondly." Merlin turned to Sir Jeff, who had just now thought to lower his arms, and stood awaiting his reward. Fumbling around in his bag, he turned to the guest empty-handed. "And, for you, Sir Jeff, you will always have this wonderful memory!"

As the audience continued clapping, Jeff laughed and went back to his wife Jean who was still snapping pictures.

With a grand flourish of his robes, Merlin turned and purposely strode towards the Cast Member Only door and vanished from their sight.

England — 589 C.E.

A small fire blazed in the arched stone fireplace, a well-used, blackened cooking pot hung from a crude metal hook and bubbled contentedly off to the side. The cheery light of the flames did little to brighten the rest of the small cottage, nestled as it was in the depths of the dripping quiet forest, surrounded by a cozy gray blanket of fog.

Sitting in a comfortable overstuffed chair—one that looked somehow too modern and out-of-place in the rustic thatched dwelling—was an old man who was currently staring into the flames, the bent pipe that dangled from his relaxed fingers having gone out hours before. To a passerby, the old man would appear to be perhaps thinking back over his long life, the look of contentment on his lined face signifying that it had been a good life, one filled with more happiness than sadness.

But there were no passersby at that late hour to peek in through the wavy, yellowed glass in the window. And this was no old man. Oh, he looked to be of great age—and he was—but his appearance could change as often as his many moods. This appearance did well for him now. It served his purpose. This was the look that was expected of someone in his position, his authority. And he certainly aimed to please.

The shaggy gray tufts that formed his eyebrows narrowed as he gazed into the flames. Leaning forward and impatiently shoving aside the footstool on which his slippered feet had been resting, his countenance altered as he looked deeper into the dancing flickers.

"What's this? What's this?" he muttered, his beard coming alarmingly close to the burning embers. "What kind of foolishness is this?" Curiosity and interest filled his green eyes as he stared intently at the figures seen deep within the flames. The small smile tugging at the corners of his mouth was unseen behind his flowing gray beard. *This could prove to be an interesting day after all*, he thought to himself. Head turned slightly to the left, his eyes not leaving the sight in front of him, he added out loud, "It looks like we are going to have visitors this night, Ar…." He broke off when he fully turned and realized he was alone in the room. "Hmmm, gone

already. Figures," he mumbled, his attention returned to the fire, and idly wondered where his
footstool had gotten off to. As if an afterthought,
he raised his face and said aloud towards the
ceiling, "Bring them to me when you can."

With the sound of fluttering wings, the
black, indistinct shape slowly materialized out of
the fog. As it got closer, all the eyes below
strained to see through the misty air, trying to determine what it was that was coming at them.
Taken aback, they finally could make out a
brown and white owl that hovered, it sincerely
hoped, just out of reach of the possible snapping
jaws of the wolf. As it slowly flapped its wings,
the owl kept one eye on the defensive stance of
the wolf. His blue eyes narrowed as he glared
upwards, the huge black wolf didn't look too
happy to see the bird.

"Who...."

"It's an owl!" Wals exclaimed unnecessarily, his sword lowering as he looked back at his
companions with a mixture of relief and humor
on his face. "Kinda scruffy-looking one, too."

"...are you?" the owl finished his interrupted
sentence, choosing to ignore the insult to his appearance that the man had given him. Turning
his head away from them at almost one eighty
hundred degrees, the owl then added shortly to
someone else unseen, "Yes, yes, I know. I'm on
it." His head swiveled back again to face the
newcomers in the forest. The wolf had eased
his stance a little, the man still seemed amused,

and the beauty had relaxed enough to smile up at him and seemed to want to chat.

Wolf chose to remain silent and, catching that, Wals took over as their spokesman. "A talking owl! How is that possible? What's going on here?"

Wolf groaned and was rethinking his decision not to talk. Wals heard him, and knowing Wolf's not-so-subtle meaning, cleared his throat and tried again. "Who are you and where exactly are we? We seem to be lost."

The owl seemed to find that amusing. "A talking human! How is that possible?" he mimicked and chuckled to himself. "Yes, I think you are very lost, considering how you are dressed. But, first, let me introduce myself," as he settled on a low-hanging branch just in front of them and cleared his throat. "I am Archimedes." He grandly stopped, wings spread outward, and was only rewarded with silence as three pairs of eyes stared at him. "Ah, I take it that you have not heard of me," he sighed, refolding his wings with a shake of his feathers. "Well, then, I suppose I should take you to my master. Let him straighten this mess out. Follow me, please," he directed, flapping into the air and immediately heading deeper into the forest.

Not hearing any sounds that would indicate he was being followed, Archimedes turned and looked back. He could see the group clustered together now, whispering. His sharp hearing picked up an extra male voice—unless the lovely blond had an incredibly deep voice for one so fair….

"What other options do we have? He seems friendly enough."

"I think he is adorable," Rose added. "I think we can trust him."

Merriweather, who was concealed in the hood of Rose's cloak, agreed with her charge. "I have heard the name before. It is an old name, a distinguished one."

"I can think of nothing else to do. I don't want to call the vortex again until we know for sure this isn't the right castle."

"I think I would recognize my own castle, Wolf," Rose stubbornly insisted. Glancing up, she became aware that the owl was coming back. "Shh, he might hear you," she warned the wolf. Turning to face the impatient bird, Rose adjusted her hood slightly to keep the Blue Fairy hidden. "We will follow you, Sir Owl. Lead on," she commanded with a regal gesture of her hand.

"Yes, milady," Archimedes briefly bowed his head, recognizing something unmistakably royal in her tone and words. "If you please. There is a hidden footpath this way. Keep alert. There are worse things in this darkness than a talking owl."

The deer path they had been following for some time suddenly widened out into a pebble walkway. The first hint of dawn was tinting the eastern sky pink as they emerged into a small clearing in the forest. They could hear the sound of running water off to the north as the river Astolat made its way towards the castle. As the fog mysteriously vanished from this clearing—yet left the forest deep within its misty grasp—they could see a rock well with a wooden bucket perched precariously on its side. The smell of wood smoke came to their noses and drew their attention to a small, thatched cottage nestled into the gnarled roots of a huge oak tree.

At Rose's startled gasp, her companions turned to face her. She broke off her stare at the cottage. "Oh, for a minute there, I thought it was the woodcutter's cottage where I stayed as a girl! Merri, don't you think so?" she whispered out of the side of her mouth.

Suddenly a slight movement near Rose's hair caught their attention as the fairy peeked out, still careful to be unobserved by the hovering owl. "Why, yes, my child, it is similar! What a lovely setting." She went back out of sight. "But, take care, dear. There is more afoot here," she softly warned.

Wals looked over the small house before them. "It's so tiny. It looks more like part of Fantasyland than where someone would actually live. Don't you think so, Wolf....oh, sorry. Never mind," he trailed off when he saw the wolf roll his eyes and slowly shake his head.

Their contemplations were halted when the door suddenly swung open. They waited, but no one emerged. In fact, they couldn't even see who it was who had opened the door.

Archimedes went ahead of them and glided silently into the door and banked to the right, out of their sight.

After a moment more of staring at the doorway, a kindly voice called out. "Well? Mustn't
let the night air in. Enter. Enter."

Wals shrugged his shoulders at his companions. Wolf took the initiative and padded
slowly to the door, nose down, trying to get a
grasp on who, or what, was inside. Smelling
only avian, human, and some kind of food cooking, he slowly entered the cottage, followed by
Wals and then Rose. As she stepped over the
threshold, the door quietly closed behind her.

Their eyes adjusted to the semi-darkness
inside, and looking around at the size of the
rooms in front of them, Wals whispered wonderingly to Rose, "How big was that tree outside?
These rooms seem to go on and on! Look at the
size of that library! Is that a pool table? How…."

"What a perfectly lovely house," Rose broke
in, not really hearing Wals as she looked around
at all the cozy furniture and the piles of dusty
books that covered most of the surfaces.

"Why, thank you, my dear. I like it myself,"
came the voice that had invited them inside.

Turning towards the speaker, who was now
silently chuckling at them, the mouths of each of
them fell open as one. Speechless, they could-
n't, wouldn't put the name out there for all to
hear. Doing so might make the impossible come
true.

The old man stood from his chair and
walked over to the perch where Archimedes
waited, the same look of amusement on his
round avian face. "I see you brought me an interesting group, Archimedes. I trust they gave

you no trouble."

The golden eyes took in the gawking guests still standing in the hallway. "No, no, no trouble once they decided to follow me. Shall I make the introductions?"

The owner of the cottage turned to face his guests and took a step towards them. Wolf instinctively went into protect mode and took a position in front of Rose, head slightly down and his back legs braced. He didn't bare his teeth, but his intent was obvious. Rose, however, put a calming hand on his head. "I think it is all right, Wolf. I think we are in a distinguished presence." She stepped around the animal and regally held out her hand. "I am Rose. Most know me as Aurora. I am delighted to meet you, Merlin. I have heard many songs from the minstrels."

The wizard took her hand and lightly kissed its back. "Princess. Welcome to my humble home. I hope the songs were pleasant ones. One never knows…," he trailed off with a mischievous twinkle in his eye.

"Merlin!" Wals muttered, sinking down onto a wooden stool next to an overflowing desk of some ancestry.

"Yes? And you are?"

"I…I am Walter Davis. My friends call me Wals," he managed to croak out, and then blurted, "How can you be Merlin? He was just a matter of fiction. Wasn't he?" he finished wonderingly, as he turned to get confirmation from his friends. Seeing only looks of acceptance and belief on their faces, he closed his mouth and could only stare.

The blue robes turned and headed further into the living area, closer to the fire. The room seemed to grow longer with each step he took. As the day dawned around the cottage, the forest was still deep into midnight. Light crept in through the windows making the necessity of the fire obsolete. So, it extinguished.

"Come in and be comfortable," Merlin called as he settled back into his chair with a small grunt of pleasure.

Rose happily complied, taking a seat very near his chair. Wolf padded silently next to her to sit on a small rag rug, careful to keep his tail away from any popping embers. Wals, still stunned, remained where he was.

Merlin looked pointedly at the wolf and green eyes met blue in an unblinking stare. After a moment, the man smiled. "Taŋyáŋ yahí. Welcome. You may talk freely here, wolf. None will bother you. But," he added as a warning with an upraised finger, "only here and only with me. Do not forget that."

In that moment of connection, Wolf had sensed something familiar, something long ago. Or, was it something far in the future? He couldn't put a name to it. Only that they had met before. "Philámayaye. Thank you," Wolf said quietly, silently wondering just how this had happened. "Owákaȟniğe šni. " In his confusion, Wolf reverted to his native tongue. He didn't even wonder how this Merlin was able to know his language. He just knew he would.

"What is it you don't understand?"

"What is it I do understand?" Wolf slowly answered back. "Perhaps if you could tell us the year that would help pinpoint where we are."

"The year?" The request stumped Merlin. Confused, he looked over at his companion. "Archimedes, would you please check the calendar for these good folk?"

Archimedes sniffed. "I don't need to check the calendar, Master. I always know the date, the time, the season...."

"Very well," Merlin broke in with a tired sigh. "Just the relevant facts, if you please."

The owl looked put out that he couldn't regale them with more facts and figures than that. "It is the year 589 and in the rule of good King...."

"Thank you, Archimedes. Does that help you, wolf?"

The newcomers stared at the bird as if waiting for a more complete figure than that. He had to have left off a number....

"Hmm, I guess not," Merlin decided at the stunned looks on their faces. He noticed a movement under Rose's cloak, one that she had refused to take off even in the warmth of the room. "And, you, madam, you may come out as well. We are all friends here."

In a dash of blue sparkles, Merriweather appeared and settled comfortably on the mantle of the fireplace. "Oh, that's better. Thank you, sir. I don't care for the darkness."

Merlin bowed his head in her direction. "Welcome, madam. Where are your other two companions?"

Merri glanced somewhat irritably at the wolf who was intently watching the proceedings. "They await us in our proper time. Which this does not seem to be."

Chuckling at her remark, their host turned to a small table at his side, set with a sturdy tea set. None had noticed it before. "Can I offer you a spot of tea? My manners are quite atrocious. Not used to company, you know. Well, I guess you wouldn't know, would you?" he chuckled at his own joke as he poured.

As the delicate cups were handed around, Wolf briefly shook his head at the offered saucer.

"Well, now that we are all refreshed and up to date on, well, the date, perhaps we can get on to more important details," Merlin announced as he stood and walked over to Wals.

Wals, having been silent since his previous outburst, held himself back from visibly shrinking as the wizard approached him. He had an unsettling urge to stand and thrust out his chest, which he, thankfully, suppressed.

"Perhaps, young man, you would like to tell me why I feel the presence of something quite familiar to me, something special, something I made for another which has been gone for a long time. Do you know about what I am speaking?"

Wals did stand now, his sword banging against his leggings. Dressed as he was as a prince, in an outfit 'borrowed' from the Costume Department of his employer, Disneyland, he wiggled the left big toe in the brown knee-length boots he wore. His toe connected with the item he had stashed there, wrapped in the remnants of an old sock. In the other boot were four pieces of gold he had taken from the not-yet-buried pirate chest he had discovered deep in a cave on Tom Sawyer's Island. With a swallow, he nodded, knowing Merlin wasn't talking about the gold.

Rose, who had previously been wearing the item under discussion, had been turned into a white swan during the transfer from the eighteen-hundreds to Wals' time period of the twenty-first century. Wals had taken it from her long, graceful neck, promising to keep it safe for her until such time as he could return it. She stood in her surprise, almost stepping on the wolf. "So, the rumors were true. It was yours!" she whispered, her hand going to her mouth.

"Yes, my dear. I made it myself. It was a gift for someone dear."

Wals wasn't sure what was expected of him. "Did you want it back? Or do you want to see it again? We were wondering how the surrounding band of gold got to be shaped like a Hidden Mickey."

"Hidden Mickey?" Merlin stopped and thought back. "I know not that term. The setting is something I saw before that was indicative of the circle of life and love. I sense the pendant has had a long, eventful journey. If it is here again, it has truly come full circle," he chuckled. "How amazing life can be. What have you seen in the red diamond? Have you touched it?" he eagerly asked, leaning towards them as he spoke.

Archimedes gave a small laugh. "Who cannot touch it when they see it? A gem such as that makes men want to hold it, possess it."

"It does not work for me," Wolf admitted.

Merlin looked at him closely. "Either now or as a man?"

Wolf shook his head but said nothing.

"Ah, that is most peculiar," Merlin murmured, stroking his beard as he looked intently at the animal. "Nor does it work for me. Perhaps we are much alike."

His heart pounding, Wolf again remained silent.

"Did you make it for the lady?" Rose wanted to know, walking over to Wals and putting a hand on his shoulder. She hoped it would have a calming affect on him as it did with Wolf. Wals' cold hand covered her warm one.

Merlin smiled warmly. "Yes, my lady apprentice, Nimue. I expect her later in the morn for another lesson."

At the name, Wolf and Rose exchanged an anxious look. Both knew the name as the one who would later betray Merlin after she learned all his secrets. Apparently she was still a student, a fond student, if the valuable necklace was any indication of Merlin's feelings for her.

"Did you want the diamond back, sir?" Wals tentatively asked, still not sure where he stood in all of this.

Head down, Merlin began pacing, apparently debating with himself on the question Wals had just asked. "Do I want it back? Haven't I already made it and given it to Nimue if they have it? Has it come back to me for a reason? Is it to fulfill its journey with these good people? Do you still require the gem?" he asked, suddenly turning to Wolf.

Wolf hesitated for a moment and then answered. "I need to give it to a friend again. He is very discouraged and could use the vision of the future that it will give him."

"You said 'again.' If the future is the same, it will come to you again," Merlin pointed out.

"I'd rather not wait."

Merlin's face broke out into a wide grin. "Perhaps I will be around then and I can meet your distinguished friend."

Wolf's mouth opened as if to answer, and then he abruptly snapped it shut. How could he tell Merlin that he wouldn't be around, that he would be betrayed by the one he loved the most?

Merlin saw the look of sadness that swept through the wolf's eyes. The wizard already knew. With a silent sigh, he let that pass and asked instead, "This friend of yours. Is he worthy of the pendant?"

Wolf gave a single nod. "Yes. You would like him. He is a true visionary."

"Then I must be content with that knowledge." Turning back to Wals, he then said, "No, Sir Wals, you must keep it safe for now. It has already done what it needs to do here." With his head down, deep in thought, Merlin returned to his comfortable chair. The fire had sprung up again and was cheerfully hissing over the logs that never burned. Hands steepled in front of his face, he again stared into the flames. Archimedes came and landed on his master's shoulder, and heads together, they debated quietly between themselves.

At the other end of the room, a whispering Rose had just finished telling Wals the legend of Merlin and Nimue, the story of which he was not familiar.

"Then it really is Merlin, THE Merlin," Wals still tried to wrap his head around the impossibility.

"Yes, Wals, we are apparently in the sixth century, the time of knights and kings and dangers beyond what you can imagine. We have to get back to our time and figure out what went wrong," Wolf stressed.

"Then you are saying that the castle we saw was Camelot? You know, King Arthur and Guinevere?"

Wolf looked surprised. "I guess it must be. I never thought of that."

Merlin roused himself and looked over at his guests. "Yes, the fair castle on the hill. King Arthur and his Knights are in a time of peace now. It is a good time for the land. A nice change," he mumbled to himself.

"You can say that again," Archimedes sighed and went over to Merriweather who had busied herself with some of Merlin's books. It looked like she was memorizing some of the passages. "Anything particular I can help you find, madam?"

She looked up surprised at the interruption. "Oh, owl. I didn't hear you there. No, no, this is all quite amusing. Amazing what two centuries of progress will correct."

Taken aback by the veiled reference that they were in a backwards time, Archimedes and Merri got into quite a spirited arm-waving, wing-flapping debate that was largely ignored by the others in the room.

Wals was still enthralled that he was so close to Camelot and King Arthur. "Oh, I would love to see King Arthur!"

"Ah, but you do not want King Arthur to see you," Merlin commented dryly, crushing Wals' enthusiasm as his meaning sunk in.

"We need to keep a low profile until we can get back through the passage, Wals," Rose reminded him. "I would love to see the ancient castle, too, but it is best we do not."

"Ancient!" Merlin echoed, affronted. "There has never been, or will be," he added, stiffly, "another castle as grand or as beautiful as Camelot. Ever!"

Rose, thinking of her own castle and her own well-appointed suite of rooms, said nothing and diplomatically smiled a charming apology.

Getting back to the needs at hand, Merlin turned to Wolf. "What needs you to get back? Anything I can do to help?"

"No, thank you. I know where the portal is...."

"And that is where?" Merlin wanted to know. "Just out of curiosity," he averred to Archimedes who had broke off his argument with Merri and was watching his master closely, his yellow eyes narrowed in suspicion.

"Under the first arch in the stone walkway leading up to the castle," Wals told him. "It is a matching portal from where we entered in my time."

Merlin seemed to be thinking, his eyes unfocused and seeing what they could not. "Ah, so that is what that feeling is. I wondered why I felt like that whenever I crossed over the bridge. Interesting," he muttered, stroking his long beard, deep in thought.

As the day progressed, the cottage welcomed another visitor. The Lady Nimue came as expected for her lessons from Merlin. Surprised to find so many strangers—and ones dressed so oddly—in with her teacher, she lapsed into silence, pretending shyness when she was, in reality, studying them as if they were bugs under a magnifying glass.

The moment she had stepped into the room, all were curious at the startled intake of breath from Merriweather. She seemed extremely upset and her blue dress and cape seemed to shake in rage. "You! You!" was all she seemed capable of saying. "What are you doing here in this time? Be…." Her words were immediately cut off by an unseen movement from Nimue's hand.

Merri, made incapable of speech now, could only glare at the beautiful gray-eyed woman who cozied up to Merlin's side, drawing the attention away from the angry fairy. Merri knew her somehow. She knew the presence of this one, her essence, the feeling she exuded. She was as familiar with her as she was with her own two dear companions. This one was evil…. And she could do nothing to warn them.

Merlin, always distracted when his pupil was around, hadn't seen or felt the quick spell aimed at the Blue Fairy. The owl knew he could do nothing and gave a silent apology to the sputtering woman.

Nimue gave another quick gesture and Merri calmed and quietly sipped the tea that Merlin had served earlier. Her irritation and agitation was forgotten in a cloud of distant, lovely memories that had suddenly filled her mind.

The apprentice had had another feeling when she entered the house, one that was much more intriguing than the insignificant fairy. It was the feeling of power from something stolen from her in the past. And that feeling swirled, inexplicably, around the plain, mortal man that hung close to the regal one. Nimue couldn't put her finger on what it was. Her training wasn't complete yet. She only knew that the power came from Wals, and she needed to keep track of him. *Shouldn't be too difficult, seeing he was as naïve as a baby*, she chuckled to herself.

She also kept glancing at the dark wolf that hovered near the golden-haired woman. Eyes narrowed as she surreptitiously stared at him under lowered lids, she could feel a menacing *something* emanating from him. She knew this wasn't an ordinary wolf. She had too many of them at her command deep in the forest. She kept expecting something *more* from him, but he stayed on the floor, now pretending to be asleep. *I'll find out what it is, wolf, just give me time*, she thought.

Wolf's eyes shot open as the woman's thought suddenly entered his head. Covering the movement with a sneeze, he looked around until he saw Nimue's gray eyes staring right through him. He let his tongue loll out of his mouth as if he were panting, and let his mind go blank.

The woman gave an unladylike, silent snort, not fooled for a minute. She would wait. She had the time and, looking over at Merlin's many books, soon she would have the means.

As night slowly approached once more and the high coastal fog began to slowly roll in over the land, it was nearing time for the visitors to leave. The apprentice had given up hours ago on trying to crack through the surface of the wolf and had left, delighting Merlin with a meaning-less peck on his cheek and a promise to return the next day for another lesson.

Merlin himself led them through the forest, the trees falling back to allow a wider, easier passage and receiving thanks for their efforts. When they came to the edge of the clearing on which sat the magnificent castle, Camelot, they halted to wait for the full covering of darkness and mist that might, hopefully, mask the profu-sion of light and color and terror that the vortex would bring when Wolf called for it.

Even though it was still just evening, dusk

had taken hold of the sky, turning it all the colors of the pastel palette. Soft yellows blended into oranges and into a pink that itself changed to a bright bold red as the sun set further in the west. As the needed darkness began to settle, torches on the castle walls were lit one by one until the high rim of the curtain wall was a solid flickering line.

"What's this? What's this?" Merlin muttered. "Archimedes? Is it that time already?" Receiving no answer, he frowned as he looked around. "Where is that bird? Never there when you need him," the wizard sniffed as he turned back to the spectacle.

Across the stone bridge came a lively procession of people and horses, all armed with torches and lanterns. The large group made for the meadow on the opposite side of the castle from where the friends awaited the midnight hour. Soon the flat plain was alight as if it were the middle of the day. The hidden onlookers could see that the horses were gaily bedecked with colorful ribbons and trappings that wove through their manes, tails and covered their saddles. These white horses of Arthur's, usually outfitted for war, were led into a large circle, a knight dressed in his best tunic, his sword hanging by his side, held the bridle of his own charger.

When all the horses were in their places, the First Knight raised his sword toward the castle. There, on the battlement, ablaze in light, were the King and Queen. Arthur signaled back with his own sword and a score of trumpets blew a loud blast.

As the strangers across the meadow watched, a happy, running, screaming hoard of children now came across the bridge from Camelot and headed for the horses. The musicians who had accompanied the first group of adults now began to play their flutes and harps in a happy, light melody that floated over the land. The children obediently slowed as they neared the horses. They knew what surprised hooves could do. As they waited eagerly at the fringe of the circle, a knight in half armor approached and chose a child for each horse. The music played louder as the children hung onto the manes of the white steeds as they were led in a continuous full circle, and the laughter of the young ones easily carried over the distance.

Merlin looked on, a pleased, serene look on his face, his feet tapping time to the music.

Wals looked over at Wolf. "Does that look familiar to you?" he muttered wonderingly.

Wolf could only nod, speechless as the children on the horses were set down and a new group was placed on the back of the patient horses.

"Hmm?" Merlin asked, turning from the festive scene. "This? This is a small summer festival Arthur throws for the young ones of the castle. It always takes place at dusk. Too hot during the day, you know. You've seen this before, eh?"

Wals nodded, smiling now at the pictures, both in front of him and in his mind of the King Arthur Carrousel that makes up the heart of Fantasyland. "Yes, but in a slightly different form. The horses there are also prancing and galloping but are made of wood and painted to look like these steeds."

Making a noise of recognition in his throat, Merlin added, "Well, the knights do train on wooden horses in off times. Perhaps it is the same principle."

When all the children had been given their turn, the musicians led the happy throng back into the castle walls. When the last lantern had flickered over the walkway, and the torches on the wall had been extinguished, the friends knew it was getting to be a safer time for them to leave.

Merlin turned to Merriweather, who by now had been released by Nimue and had no recollection of her distress. "Madam, give my well wishes to your companions when you get to where you should be."

"Thank you, Master Merlin. Your name is honored in our time."

Hand on his heart, he bowed his head briefly to her. "Master Wolf, take care of these, one and all. You have a heavy weight on your shoulders. You carry it well. Taŋyáŋ ománi yo." *Bon voyage*.

Turning to Wals, Merlin simply said, "Protect her well. Protect *it* well."

"Thank you. It was…it was amazing meeting you!"

Making a subtle gesture with his hand, Merlin spoke to Wolf. "You needn't fear being seen now. Do what you must."

Merlin and Archimedes moved back into the covering trees as the friends headed towards the bridge. A fog, thicker than the one on their arrival, now covered the region. The huge castle, gleaming white even in the darkness, became a shadowy, vague object in the mist.

"We won't be able to see," the owl complained, straining his neck forward. "I want to see what the wolf can do."

"Look again, friend owl."

"Ah, thank you, Master!"

Within moments, a lingering howl drifted through the fog. The misty vapors seemed to pick up the sound and waft it in all directions. People who had been snug in their beds behind the thick castle walls heard and now pulled the covers higher to their throats, glancing nervously at their open windows. Looking this way and that out over the darkened plain, the sentries on the towers were glad of the height of their assignment as they murmured to each other just to hear any other sound than that.

The wolf's howl triggered the vortex, as it always did. The still water of the moat began to be agitated, slowly at first, barely ripples, and then building into a swirling whirlpool. The foursome moved quickly towards the maelstrom, their hearts pounding even though they had gone through many times before. It never got easier.

The water slammed against the side of the stones that formed the chosen arch. When the lightning struck the water and the air was filled with electricity, a shower of pink sparkles fell from the arch and a black darkness opened in front of them.

"Now!" yelled Wolf over the sound of the tumult. "All together, jump!"

Eyes closed in fear, they jumped, the water engulfing them and, instantly, they disappeared from view.

Content that they were safely on their way home, Merlin and Archimedes turned and headed to the small cottage tucked securely in the forest.

As the pink glitters began to fade and the waters began to calm, another person could be seen struggling against the waters, trying her hardest to reach the vortex. The waters seemed to push against her, forcing her back inch by inch away from the core, rejecting her.

Nimue cried out in frustration. She needed her pendant back for she understood the value of being able to touch the stone and see into the future. Once you knew what your future would be, you had the power to either change it for the better, or profit by the foreknowledge. To her, that power was worth more than any mere fortune the red diamond itself could bring.

She was still struggling against the current when, suddenly, the pink light subsided and the waters calmed. She was too late. Her pendant was, once again, gone.

CHAPTER TWO

Copenhagen — 1951

"This is it, Lillian! This is how the park should be!"

Walt and his family had been touring the Tivoli Gardens in Copenhagen, Denmark for most of the day already. Walt was clearly enthralled by the beautiful gardens, different types of architecture, and the band stands and cafés that filled out the property. They even rode on the wooden roller coaster that had debuted in 1914.

"This park opened back in 1844 and you know what the founder Georg Carstensen said?" Walt asked as he led his wife past a beautiful garden surrounding a giant weeping willow that was dripping with tiny white lights. Not even waiting for Lillian to reply, he enthusiastically continued, "He said 'Tivoli will never, so to speak, be finished.' Isn't that something? He knew the gardens would keep growing more beautiful, the trees would get taller and more full, more rides could be added, different concerts and shows could be presented in that Chinese-styled Pantomime Theatre! That's vision, Lillian! That's wanting to make something that will last forever!"

He led them back to the Pantomime Theatre. "I want to see that curtain again. That was really neat. Do you think they would let me go backstage?" A marvel of its time, the curtain was a mechanical wonder that took five men to operate and was painted and decorated to look like a brilliant peacock's tail as it unfolded.

After watching the workings operate another four times, Lillian thanked the helpful workers for their time and led Walt back outside into the warm, fairy-lighted night. Knowing her husband, she offered, "Do you want to go see the train and the merry-go-round again?"

Talking mostly to himself, as if making mental notes, Walt murmured as they walked along the winding path, fireworks going off overhead. "A happy and unbuttoned air of relaxed fun. Yeah, the fireworks are a nice touch. The crowds seem to love them. Could use a castle, though. Yeah, a fairy castle, but not too big. Don't want it to overshadow the park. And a bigger train. Say, Lillian," he suddenly stopped and turned to face her, a big smile on his face, "Remember that castle we saw in Germany?"

Used to her husband's rapid change of thoughts, she shook her head. "Which castle, Walt? There were so many. Which trip do you mean?"

"You know, when we took the train through the Alps in 1935 with Roy and Edna. That huge white castle on the hill. Remember? The Neuschwanstein Castle, in Bavaria. Its name meant New Swan Stone, I believe. You think we should go look at it again?" he asked, his eyes sparkling with excitement.

Knowing Walt was thinking about his own park that he had been talking about so much, Lillian reminded him of the reason they were in Europe in the first place. "What about *The Adventures of Robin Hood and His Merrie Men*? Don't you need to go back to the studio in England again for supervision? Do you really want to take the time to go all the way to Germany?"

Treasure Island, back in 1949, had been Walt's first British all-live-action film and had been both a critical and financial success, bringing the studio over $2 million in profit. Now they were tackling the impressive story of *Robin Hood*.

However, as usual, the idea of his own little park somewhere in Los Angeles was in the forefront of his mind, and he was always tinkering with plans and architecture and adding this element or that kind of ride to his mental vision. "No, I think the boys at the studio are doing a fine job," Walt skirted. "I was just merely giving them suggestions, anyway, you know."

Lillian smiled in the darkness. She, as well as anyone at the studio, realized the boss's "suggestions" were as good as engraved in gold.... "So, when do you think we should leave for Germany?"

Walt put a fond arm around his wife. "I was thinking Thursday would be soon enough. Does that work for you and the girls? We don't have to be home until August!"

Burbank — 1954

"**W**hat are you working on, Herb?"

Walt had just wandered into the Model Shop at the Studio. Herb was, at that moment, pondering the large model of Sleeping Beauty's Castle in front of him. For instant comparisons, his artwork had been tacked onto the wall and was also lying on the table next to the beautiful, highly detailed model. Acting on a spur-of-the-moment impulse, he had removed the top half of the castle and flipped it around just to see if that would make it look "different" enough from the Neuschwanstein Castle photographs that were next to his drawings. He was just ready to set it back the way it had been built, like it was in the myriad of drawings and sketches he had done, when Walt walked in. Saying nothing in response to Walt's question, Herb just waited to see how his boss would react, his hands still hovering above the model.

Walt cocked his head to the side as he stared silently at the new perspective. "I like it that way," he stated before turning to leave the room.

October 27, 1954 marked the debut of Walt's newest project, the television show on ABC that was called *Disneyland*. Walt looked at ease as he stood in front of a large, pristine model of the Sleeping Beauty Castle. Its top was now firmly reattached—and backwards.

Disneyland — 2008

Sleeping Beauty's Castle was now being seen from an even different perspective—from the middle of the moat at half-past two in the morning.

"We've gotta quit doing that," Wals tiredly muttered as he slogged his way towards the firm ground surrounding Swan Lake. "Rose, are you…." His words were cut off when an angry white swan paddled up next to him and bit him on the arm. "Aww, Rose, I was hoping you would stay human when we came through. I'm sorry, sweetheart."

A miniaturized Merri was sitting on the swan's back, holding her own head and groaning. "That's quite a ride, wolf. Perhaps next time you can get it right…. There, there, my dear," she murmured, stroking the agitated swan's neck, "We'll get you home. Then we can figure out this strange enchantment you are under. If the century hadn't been all wrong, I would have guessed it was that evil woman we just met."

Wolf had swum to where his clothes were hidden and quickly dressed himself, his own head pounding from the tumult of the passage. He glanced up to survey his charges and saw that they were all accounted for. None of them were happy, but they were all in one piece. He, too, was disappointed Rose had reverted into the shape of a swan. It appeared that was to be her lot in this time period, he mused, just as it was his lot to turn into a wolf whenever he jumped into the past. *My head hurts too much to try and work through that again*, he muttered to himself as he waded back out to retrieve Rose's dress and cape, silently wondering why he didn't grab them when he was out there.

At a loud honk and hiss, all turned to see what was bothering Rose. She was flapping her wings, trying to fly up with the departing blue sparkle that was now Merri. Finally giving up, the dejected swan slowly swam to the small cove and waddled up on the shore next to where Wolf was now standing. She leaned her head against his chest and gave an almost-human sigh.

Knowing why Rose was agitated, he looked upwards, frowning. "Where are you going, Merri?" Wolf called to the departing fairy who was heading towards the topmost tower of the Castle. Realizing their vulnerable position, he quickly lowered his voice and glanced around, letting his acute hearing take over to see if anyone else was around at that late hour. There should be cleaners and painters and gardeners at work readying the Park for the next day's guests. However, the Castle and the surrounding areas were thankfully dark. He could see activity at the other end of Main Street, near the Train Station, but those workers were too far away to either hear or see them.

At his call, Merri stopped her ascent and responded shortly, "Well, wolf, since you have failed and have brought us back here again, I must get ready for work tomorrow. Apparently I am still to be the Park's Animal Handler so I can continue to look after my girl…as I have been for *way* too long."

At Wolf's answering growl to her rebuke, she turned her back with a "Hmph" and continued on her way to her rooms hidden in the Castle's turret. There she would again hide her robes and her wand and continue living as a human until such time as they could really go home.

Wals was holding in his hands the ruined flat velvet cap he had been wearing, the feather long gone in the swirling waters of the vortex. Staring at it, he vaguely wondered how he would explain the mistreatment of his outfit to the Costume Department. He wouldn't be sorry to lose the tights, though. With a nod, he accepted the pile of Rose's sodden clothes that Wolf handed him. Using her black cape, he carefully wrapped his sword to get it out of sight lest they run into someone on their way to the lockers. "What now, Wolf? Any ideas?"

Wolf was staring at the curved arch under

the Castle's walkway. It was almost identical to the one at Camelot, only somewhat smaller. "We were so sure it was the right portal," Wolf muttered as if to himself. "What?" he asked, shaking his head to clear the fog and bring his thoughts to the problem at hand. "Ideas? Not at the moment. Rose?" he gently lifted the head of the swan so he could see her tormented blue eyes. "Do you know of any other possible passage? I know you had a bad feeling about that archway, but I think we know now it wasn't the one that brought you here."

Rose looked towards the bridge that led to the Castle. She had never swum through that passageway in all the years she had been stuck there. It just felt *wrong*. She hadn't gotten that feeling anywhere else in the moat, or in the other parts of Disneyland that she had been able to explore when she could escape the confines of Swan Lake. Unable to speak in this form, she just shook her head no. She would have to rely on her friends to find the way home.

Wolf just nodded that he understood. He would have to think this one through. Wishing his father was there to talk to, Wolf gave a silent sigh and looked over towards Frontierland. Within a few minutes walk was the Friendly Village where the Shaman was animatedly telling the seated braves the story of how the flute came to their people. All it would take was one little howl next to the Frontierland River and he could go back to his family in 1817.

Wals saw Wolf's gaze, and, after his own adventure back to that time period, he turned a sickly shade of white. "No, man, not now! We just got back! Don't make us go through that again!"

Wolf gave a small smile. "Who said you were invited? I was just thinking about my family."

Calming down once he realized Wolf wasn't serious, Wals conversely began considering the other ramifications, thinking out loud, "Well, Rose would be human again if we went back. Maybe we can stay together in your father's tent until you figure it all out."

Rose was looking one to the other as the men talked. When Wals mentioned actually going back to 1817, the memory of the hardships she encountered there in the small settler's cabin on Tom Sawyer's Island came flooding back to her mind and overshadowed the closeness she and Wals had attained. She gave a loud grunt and made a swipe at Wals' leg with her beak. She wanted no part of that. With a definite gesture of her head, she pointed upwards to the spires of the Castle above them. It was obvious she wanted the men to work on the problem at hand here so she could finally go home.

"Okay, okay," Wals capitulated, jumping back from her sharp beak. "We won't go back to the Village. I don't know if they are still having problems with the pirates, anyway, and don't relish having to get in the middle of another fight."

Thinking about his family and his past, Wolf had remained quiet as the two frustrated companions worked it out between them. He hadn't actually said *he* wasn't going anywhere....

One of the peculiarities of that time period was that everything that happened in Disneyland at the current time affected what happened in the past. Tom Sawyer's Island in Wolf's family's time had been overrun by pirates—just as it had happened in the Park the year before in 2007. Fort Wilderness in 1817 had been looted and closed and the soldiers either pressed into service by the pirates, run off the island, or possible killed. Rose had been in terrible danger alone in what used to be called the Burning Cabin and it had been up to Wolf to bring her home—or as close to home as he could get her for now.... Wolf had taken the unknowing Wals back with him and had been alarmed when the Island of that time drained him of his real memories. It finally took Wals' Disneyland name tag to bring him around.

The men still didn't understand why Rose had turned into a swan during the transfer to Wals' real time period of the twenty-first century, and why the ancient sword Wals had found in a cave on the island had fit his hand like it had been made for him. Wolf knew the story behind his own transformation and the mysterious wolf that had tracked his mother when she was pregnant with him. The rogue wolf's bite had proven to be lethal for his mother, but gave Wolf the strange ability to jump into the past through the terrifying portals his howl summoned—and a seemingly long lifespan. Rose, however, was still a mystery. It might not be solved until they could get her home and Merri's friends, Flora and Fauna, would finally be able to use their powers to help the woman.

"Wolf, we need to find a calendar and find out *when* we came back," Wals reminded the security guard, as Wolf was now dressed in his work outfit. "We don't know for sure what is going on now in this time. You agree?"

Given more to action than words, Wolf silently nodded and made his way to the small, hidden gate built into the metal fence that encircled the moat. Wals gave Rose one last hug and promised they would be back to fill her in on whatever they found.

Exhausted, Rose found her nest hidden in amongst the tall reeds. Nestling her head under her wing, she promptly fell asleep, dreaming of another fairy castle, one she called home.

After the tenth ring, the phone was finally picked up.

"It's three o'clock in the morning, Wolf. This had better be good, dire, or important," Lance grumbled as he tried to keep his eyes open, carrying the portable phone into another room so as not to disturb his wife.

Wolf gave a silent chuckle. Lance hated to be awakened from a sound sleep. "I just wanted to chat."

There was an expected silence on the other end of the phone. "You're kidding, right? That sounds like something *I* would do, not you," Lance pointed out.

"Yes, I am kidding. I just wanted to let you

know we were back."

"Back from where?" Lance asked, sounding confused.

Wolf gave a snort. "I guess you didn't get enough beauty sleep.... Wals and I went through the portal to take Rose home. Remember?"

"Wolf, you just had Kimberly shut down Fantasyland two hours ago."

Now it was Wolf's turn to be speechless. "I...I thought the calendar just hadn't been changed. We were gone at least twenty-four hours."

"What happened? Did Rose get safely back to her time?" Lance was fully awake now, his curiosity pushing aside his desire for sleep. He still didn't fully understand this strange ability of Wolf's; it was more terrifying to him than anything else, but, he knew it was part of Wolf's make-up and he had to accept it as something over which neither of them had any control.

Wolf gave a small growl as he shook his head. Realizing Lance couldn't see the gesture, he had to explain, "No, it turned out that portal was to the wrong past. We came out right under Camelot, though we did get to meet Merlin. Nice chap. You'd like him. His owl, Archimedes, found us in the forest...."

"Whoa, whoa, wait a minute! What do you mean Camelot and Merlin?"

"Merlin? The wizard? What about Merlin?" Kimberly asked, pulling a robe closed as she came into the study where Lance was sitting on the edge of his leather chair.

"What are you doing up?" Lance asked, smiling as he always did when his wife entered a room. Pulling her onto his lap, he wanted to know, "Did I wake you? I was trying to be quiet."

A shrill whistle could be heard coming from the phone that Lance had forgotten he was still holding. "Sorry, Wolf…. It's Wolf," he explained to Kimberly, who was grinning at him.

"I know," she mouthed loudly.

"How would you know that?" Lance asked, pulling the phone away from his ear again.

"One: who else would be calling at this late hour? Two: who else would be using that phone? And, three: you just called him by name," she counted off on her fingers.

"That's why I married you. Brains and beauty," he declared, giving her a kiss on her cheek.

They heard another shrill whistle and what sounded like the phone being pounded on a hard surface. "Yes?" Lance calmly asked.

"Does he growl like that a lot?" Kimberly wanted to know as Lance had to hold the phone away from his ear again.

"Only when he is *really* pissed," Lance explained, giving her a wink that he was glad Wolf couldn't see.

"What about Merlin?" she prompted when Lance seemed happy enough to leave Wolf hanging there.

"Oh, yes, what were you saying about Merlin and Camelot? You guys watch a movie instead of doing what you were supposed to do?"

Wolf contemplated snapping the phone in

half, but thought better of it. He would wait until he could do it to Lance's neck. "No," he slowly said through gritted teeth. "We went back in time to the year 589, if the owl was correct. Then, when night had fallen again, Merlin brought us back to Camelot and gave us a covering of invisibility so we could get back to our time. Rose is back in the moat and Wals is probably home in bed by now."

"Oh, so it was just another day at the office for you," Lance commented lightly, trying to figure out if Wolf was actually kidding or was serious. He sounded serious. Wolf wasn't known for his sense of humor.

Kimberly took the phone from Lance. "Wolf, Kimberly here. You…you really went back to the days of King Arthur? It is so far before your time. Is that possible?"

Glad to hear the voice of reason, Wolf gave a relieved sigh. "Yes, that is what I have been trying to explain to that wooden-headed husband of yours. It…it was quite interesting."

Knowing he was telling the truth, Kimberly was stunned. "Wow, that must have been amazing. What was he like? I always thought he was just a…a fictional character, not a living, breathing man….uh, wizard, whatever!"

"Wals thought that, too, and voiced it to the owl. Archimedes didn't think it was too funny."

"Archimedes? The owl from the movie? He was there?"

"What movie?" Lance was asking. "Ha! I knew they didn't go through any portal."

"*Sword in the Stone*," Kimberly said as an

aside to Lance, who was now smoothing her messy hair with his fingers. "No, he was actually there with Merlin. How fascinating!"

Wolf ignored the comment of Lance's he could clearly hear through the phone—as Lance had intended. "I guess I should add that Nimue wants her pendant back. She could tell it was somewhere near us, but her powers weren't strong enough yet to determine exactly where."

That made Kimberly sit up, her eyes wide with concern. "Oh, Wolf, she's the one who learned all Merlin's secrets and then entombed him in a tree, isn't she? This is terrible! She didn't get it, did she? That could have severe repercussions with Walt!"

"What about Walt?" Lance broke in, suddenly concerned.

"Tell Lance I'll fill him in later. Is he going to work tomorrow? Or, I guess, later today is more accurate," Wolf amended.

Kimberly was still thinking about the red heart-shaped diamond pendant that had the mysterious ability to show you your future. It had first come into Walt's possession in the Columbian jungle in 1940 by means of the Guardian Wolf. Stolen in the 1960's by Tom Bolte when Walt was working closely with her father, the Blond-Haired Man, it had been recovered and put in a secret chamber above Main Street where she and Lance had found it at the end of their Hidden Mickey quest. It had subsequently disappeared when her uncle Daniel Crain took it and vanished with Wolf into a vortex on Tom Sawyer's Island. She thought it was safe with Wolf until she heard this revelation. She well knew who this Nimue was. Kimberly had held the pendant herself and been over- whelmed with the vision that streaked through her mind—parts of which had already come true with Lance…. While she had no desire to touch the mysterious gem again, she knew it could not fall into the wrong hands. "We need to talk about this, Wolf," she stated seriously.

"I know, Kimberly. We will," Wolf promised. "I just need to figure out where the correct por- tal is to get Rose home. Merri is back, by the way, too, and will keep on as the Animal Han- dler. Where do you have Wals assigned?"

Kimberly tore her thoughts from the pen- dant, her mind still going over the vision that was still so real she could reach out and touch it. "Wals? Oh, yes. We had already changed him from the Westside Ops into Fantasyland so he could be near Rose and keep an eye on her. Is that still good?"

The security officer gave a very wolfish grin. "Assign him to the Casey Jr. Circus Train for now."

After a moment of amused silence, she wanted to know, "Are you sure? Why?"

"Keeps him humble. Tell Lance, who must be asleep if he has been silent this long, that I will see him on the job in the morning."

Kimberly chuckled as she pictured Wals, who had become quite physically fit working the canoes, sitting on the small colorful engine of the train going around Storybook Land over and over again. "Good night, Wolf. I'm glad you are all right."

All she heard was an answering grunt as the phone went dead. She pushed the End Call button and turned her attention to her husband. Far from asleep, he was, at that moment, nibbling on her neck.

Three days later, the disgusted Wals, dressed in the faded olive green slacks and puffy white shirt uniform of Fantasyland, was slumped in the bright orange engine of the Casey Jr. Circus Train. The blue smokestack puffed white vapor as the train waited in the station. Too tall for the confines of the small engine room, he had to hunch over to see the walls of gauges set in the bright stainless steel facing. The black microphone was up on the side of the tiny cabin, the green stop button below the green speed lever. He hadn't once rung the shiny gold bell perched on top of the cabin.

The cheerful young women who also worked the ride were busy assisting the guests into their chosen ride vehicle—whether it was the pink Monkey cage, the orange Wild Animal cage or one of the open air carriages that were brightly painted and trimmed in gold.

As the train filled, the ladies reminded the sullen Wals to smile and wave to the Storybook Land canal boats that would be slowly gliding by below them in the waterways. Biting back a retort, he checked the gauges and prepared to start the train. The recorded voice of Timothy the Mouse cheerfully reminded everyone to stay seated.

The guests could hear the train cry, "All aboard! Let's go."

Timothy seconded that by saying, "Here we go!"

Staring off into space, Wals missed his cue as Timothy kept up a steady stream of narration about the homes of Mr. Toad and Cinderella and Snow White. The train started with a neck-jarring jerk as the girls happily waved good-bye to Wals.

The happy circus tune from the movie *Dumbo* played over and over during breaks in the narration as the train rolled along through and around the hills of Storybook Land. Wals gritted his teeth as they approached the hill and the train chugged out, "I think I can. I think I can. I think I can."

Wals had forgotten to slow down and they barreled over the hill and into the next turn, throwing the guests to the side of their cars. "Oops," he muttered, shoving the speed down to its correct place.

As the train came around the last bend, Wals, again lost in thought at the disgrace of his situation, came to a screeching halt. Wide-eyed, the women waiting at the station quickly ran to the cars to see if everyone was all right, throwing disgusted looks at their sullen conductor.

Not really caring, Wals checked the gauges again as the train cooled. *If I do it just right, I can carve three minutes off the run*, he was thinking as Anne, the lead on the ride, stormed up to the gaily painted engine. Even though she had a pleasant smile on her face, her eyes flashed as she dressed down the unrepentant Wals, reminding him this was a children's ride and not the Bobsleds. Pushing the blue and white conductor's hat that he had swiped from Costuming off of his forehead, he was about to tell her what she could do with the ride when a smiling mother and her six-year old daughter approached and asked if they could take a picture with the engine.

Anne flashed a quick warning at Wals, but he put on a big smile—the first one in three days—and gently set the little girl on his conductor's seat. All smiles, the cute girl waved as her mother snapped a couple of pictures and then handed the camera to Anne. "Do you mind? I'd love to have a picture with Timothy here," indicating Wals who had just backed away.

Heaving an unheard sigh, Wals put his arm around the brunette and smiled as Anne took a second picture. Muttering nothings about 'thanks' and 'have a magical day.' Wals smile faded as the gate was opened and the next batch of guests climbed aboard. Wals was about to switch places with the handlers, as the cast members who helped the guests were called, when Anne called him back.

"Since you were having so much fun driving, I think you should go another round. This time YOU do the narration. That isn't a request. Have a magical trip!" she called as she went back to make sure everyone was properly loaded and seated, smiling smugly to herself. She got a high-five from the other cast member,

Ruth. "He deserved it," Anne muttered, a big smile on her face.

The people in line wondered why the two women burst into laughter when the conductor began in a flat monotone, "Ok, Casey, let's get this show on the road. All aboard," and the train sedately chugged out of the station.

Disneyland — 1956

"Here is the world of imagination, hopes and dreams. In this timeless land of enchantment, the age of chivalry, magic and make-believe are reborn—and fairy tales come true. Fantasyland is dedicated to the young and young-at-heart, to those who, believe when you wish upon a star, your dreams do come true."

Walt words showed he loved his land of Fantasy, but he detested empty spaces. Standing just outside the high arched façade on the back of the Castle, looking up at the forced perspective that made the castle look taller than its modest seventy-seven feet, he pursed his lips as he thought about the Opening Day just last July.

Everyone had been frantically working to get Disneyland finished and everything in order for the live broadcast. Movie stars had been invited. The press would be there. Special tickets had been printed and mailed out. The builders and workers—and Walt himself—were desperately going over every detail they could think of to make it all ready for the Grand Opening. There was just one little thing they had forgotten to check: They hadn't locked the doors that led to the inside of Sleeping Beauty's Castle.

Walt smiled as he thought back. He knew there was nothing to see inside the Castle. It was basically an incomplete shell full of rigging and construction platforms. But, that didn't stop some curious, inventive guests who wanted to see the Opening Day ceremonies from a better, more unique vantage point.

Inside the Administration building, he was told later, a usually calm executive buttonholed another key man and yelled. "We've got to get to the Castle! There's people up inside! Go get them before they kill themselves!"

The handful of guests were disappointed to lose their prime viewing spot at the top of the Castle, but they allowed the wide-eyed, yet still smiling, cast members to carefully lead them down from the scaffolding.

Knowing whom he wanted, Walt made a call to one of the Imagineers, Ken. Another man, a friend of Ken's named Emile, heard the call and decided to go along with them.

"Hey, you guys come with me. There's nothing in here, no rooms at all, but I want you to take a look," Walt told them as they stood in the back courtyard.

Nodding to their boss, the three men went inside the dark interior and followed Walt up a ladder to get to the first floor. It was about eighteen feet up and they could see the scurrying around of some of the wild cats who lived inside the castle.

Walt was telling Ken, "I want you to put Sleeping Beauty in here. There's room and I know you can do it." Emile listened to the two men talking for a few moments and then he wandered away since he wouldn't be involved in the project. Going over to the side of the room, he noticed a big box. Inside the box was a gunny sack which made up the bed where many of the cats slept.

Emile loved nice clothes and he always dressed in white. His suit was all white and his shoes were also white. Curious, he tapped the gunny sack with the toe of his shoe and then leaned over to pick it up, wondering what might be in the sack.

Within mere moments, his white suit had turned gray. At Emile's franctic yelling, Ken and Walt turned to see Emile jump over the railing to get away from the thousands and thousands of fleas that had been hiding in the sack. Ken turned to look at Walt, but before they could move, the fleas had covered them as well, turning them gray.

Slapping and jumping around, Walt told them, "Don't panic, guys! I'll get someone right away!" Picking up a phone, he called for a car to come get them. "Don't go out into the crowds!"

A motorcycle with a sidecar came up to the entrance of the Castle, and Walt got in. The cycle roared off and took Walt to Wardrobe so he could shower and change clothes.

Ken and Emile were on their own.

In the days that followed, Walt received many recommendations on what to do with the cats. Most of them would prove to be lethal. Instead, he arranged for the "castle cats" to be bathed and groomed and found homes for them.

Disneyland — 1957

April 19, 1957 came and Walt's desire to "plus the show"—to make it even better—had occurred within the dark, unused interiors of the Castle. After much debating, the team of Imagineers had decided to do a walkthrough inside this iconic landmark. One would think that the Castle itself would be enough of an attraction, but Walt had wanted more—and he got it.

Hosted by a popular former child-star, dressed in a royal red robe and a golden crown on her dark curly head, Sleeping Beauty Walkthrough opened with much pageantry and fanfare. Memories of the feral cats and fleas that had inhabited the sealed rooms of the castle were just that—a memory. Located on the west side of the castle facing Fantasyland and near the "secret" Frontierland exit, the entrance was protectively guarded by a canopy shaped like an elaborate golden crown that matched the medieval faire theme of Fantasyland. For a cost of ten cents, guests were allowed to set their own pace as they climbed the narrow, winding stone steps that were cast in a low, flickering light, just as Sleeping Beauty herself might have seen them. Greeted by an elaborate leather bound storybook in the first alcove, the guests began their journey by reading the opening of the classic tale.

There were eleven dioramas in all, each in the style of the beautiful artwork that would fill the animated feature when it was released two years later. Children were both thrilled and scared by the evil-looking eyes of the castle's gargoyles that actually blinked at them when they peeked through keyholes. The adults admired the elaborate stained glass windows that dotted the attraction as they continued their journey up and down the countless steps deep within the castle. Enthralled, they could see the three good fairies who appeared to float over the cradle of the newborn princess.

As they exited into the bright sunlight, the guests were each handed a commemorative souvenir book, its fanciful cover depicting a fairy-tale castle high on a hill.

"Imagination is the mold from which reality is created. Sleeping Beauty's Castle has now been completed. Behind these grand walls, in these tall towers and courts, are the joys and tears of the beautiful princess. Share her great adventure with the powers of good and evil. May the sights and sounds stir your heart to see your own most precious dream—the dreams from which all fairytales are made!"

It was a hit. They had been handed a gauntlet and the boys had once again come through for the boss.

Disneyland — 2008

Wolf stood with his hands on his hips, glaring up at the charming pink icon of the Park. He had just gone completely around the castle. Again. Every so often he would pause, eyes closed, and try to summon a portal, attempting to find the way Rose had come into the Park so long ago.

Nothing. Not even a ripple of the force that usually started deep within his body that signaled the change that would come over him and open the mysterious vortex that still terrified him.

Just off duty, Wals located the security guard in the back of the castle near the entry to Snow White's Scary Adventure. "Anything?" he asked hopefully.

Not having heard his friend come up to him, Wolf turned and immediately had to bite the inside of his cheek to keep from laughing out loud. Wals was still dressed in his Casey Jr. outfit. He might have been able to hide a smile but his eyes betrayed him. "You look…you look cute, Wals. I like the floral suspenders. Nice look for you." He couldn't help but add, "I even like it better than your Prince Phillip look."

"Once I figure out the combination to your

locker, I'm going to hurt you with my sword that you hid there," Wals promised with a glare. "Then I am going after Lance."

"You'd have to get past Kimberly first," Wolf muttered, only half-kidding.

"Like I asked earlier, did you find anything yet?"

Wolf gave him a wolfish grin. "My, where is that devil-may-care wicked sense of humor you are so known for? Don't like your new job?"

At the dark look on Wals' face, Wolf held up a hand. "Okay, just kidding. No, in answer to your question. I've been around this entire building three times and have sensed nothing! Not even a ripple."

Wals looked up at the three shields on the next level, not really seeing them. "Are you sure the castle would be the entrance to Rose's world?"

Wolf grunted. "I'm not sure of anything. That's why we got to meet Merlin...," he admitted, drifting off. "But," he finally continued, shaking his head at what had initially seemed simple, "This should be the perfect portal. If you remember, when you were on Tom Sawyer's Island with Rose, the only thing that was familiar to her was the castle on your nametag."

Silently, Wals nodded and looked away. He missed the warm, female human body Rose had had in that time period. He was anxious to find a way to get her home and human again. "Yeah," he answered vaguely, his head tilted as he glanced at the new, unobtrusive blue and gold striped entrance to the Sleeping Beauty

Walkthrough that would reopen in a couple of months. After its remodeling in 1977, it had quietly closed again in 2001. Surrounded by much speculation and with the promises of the latest technical advances, the new dioramas promised to be quite stunning.

But Wals wasn't considering the attraction itself. He was thinking about the castle. He had to wait while Wolf answered a call on his walkie-talkie. When the security guard didn't suddenly go running off to fix an urgent problem, Wals suggested, "Say, Wolf, here's a thought: What if the portal was *inside* the castle?"

Wolf just stood there, silently staring at him.

Becoming defensive, Wals got a little flustered. "Hey, I don't know how it all works with…whatever you do…. I just had a sudden thought…," he drifted off, unsure of what Wolf was going to say.

Wolf held up a placating hand. "No, its okay, Wals. That's actually a good idea."

"Don't act so surprised," Wals commented dryly.

That brought a small smile to Wolf's face. "Didn't mean it that way. I always assumed the portal had to be outside somewhere for Rose to end up in the moat. How else would she, as a swan, get out there?"

Thinking back on the history of the attraction, Wals shrugged. "Well, since we don't know exactly *when* she got here, I suppose it could be possible the Walkthrough was open and being used at the time. It has been open twice before. If that was the case, she may have just waddled outside and found the water. Or, could it be possible that Merri helped her?"

Wolf was slowly, silently nodding all through Wals' explanation. It did make sense. It wasn't a highly guarded entrance or exit, for that matter. There might be just one cast member assigned to it at various times during the day. As for Merri's help, he gave a low growl. *She hadn't been much use so far.*

"So, what do you think?"

Wals' question brought Wolf out of his speculation. "What? Oh, you might have something here." He glanced over at the entrance, located in the same place as in 1957. There had been a few construction workers and designers coming and going since Wals and he had been standing there, but he hadn't seen any movement for a while. He looked back at his waiting companion. "Well, there's only one way to find out."

Without another word, Wolf strode over to the entrance and dropped the small rope that served as the barrier for the public. Followed by the now-curious Wals, he entered the brightly lit stairway and looked around. "We're not alone."

"Yes, we are. It's as quiet as a tomb in here. I think everyone left," Wals commented, his words fading as he looked at the colorful gem-encrusted storybook in the first alcove, leaning closer to the glass to read it.

Wolf knew they weren't alone inside the castle. He could hear, as well as smell, the few workers still busy higher up. With his usual silence, Wolf continued up the stairs, ignoring the working animation that was being tested in some of the dioramas. He knew Wals would figure out he was gone in due time and follow; not that he needed Wals' help for what he was about to do.

Making sure one last time that he was relatively alone when he reached the next level, Wolf closed his eyes and reached out with his strange power. Feeling no reaction at all, he strode up the next flight of stone steps.

Knowing the other men inside were just up one more level, Wolf decided to clear the way before he tried again. The workers gave the security guard a pleasant nod and figured he was just doing a perfunctory sweep through the attraction. As Wals finally joined him, Wolf was saying, "I need the place cleared. Get out."

Wals gave a surprised, "Wolf, that was rude."

Wolf looked back at the men. "Sorry. Please. Get out."

Knowing the reputation of that particular guard, the men nodded quickly and gathered up their few tools. They didn't like it, but they weren't going to argue. "We'll be right outside. We have a lot to finish up, so let us know when you're done with…whatever…," the foreman grumbled to Wolf. "Okay, guys, break time. You heard the man."

Voicing their various feelings about being summarily dismissed, the men made their way down the stairs. Wolf waited until he could no longer hear them and he knew for sure that they were completely outside.

"Little heavy-handed, don't you think?"

Wolf barely glanced at Wals. "We don't have time for all the pleasantries. I'll have Lance and Kimberly give each of them some kind of bonus later. Now, let me concentrate. You can go back to playing at the windows if you want."

Letting the remark slide, Wals was far more interested in watching Wolf "at work" than he was in the fire-breathing dragon animation in one of the dioramas. He was slightly disappointed when Wolf just closed his eyes, moved his hand towards the far wall, and then moved up the next flight of stairs.

"That's it?" Wals ventured to ask when Wolf performed the same action with no visible result.

Wolf cocked open an eye and peered at him. "What would you like me to do? Tilt back my head and let out an ear-splitting howl?"

Wals snapped shut his mouth. That was exactly what he would have liked to see. Knowing better, he gave a small shrug. "Umm, no. Just wondered," he finished lamely.

They had reached the apex of the stairs and were now heading downwards again.

"Sound echoes through these corridors," Wolf decided to explain. "It wouldn't be too easy to explain to the guys waiting impatiently and listening at the door, now would it?"

"Oh." Wals fell silent and decided he had better just watch. Until…"Wolf! That cast member door just had a faint pink around it! Did you feel something?"

Wolf immediately pulled back his questing. Yes, he had felt it, his blue eyes snapping open to find the source. He put a hand on the locked door. It had already begun to fade, but he knew that this just may be the location of the portal.

Looking around, he memorized exactly where they were. There was no diorama in this section and it would look very different when the bright lights were out.

Wolf gave a curt nod to Wals, who was grinning broadly. "Yes, I think this is it. I can tell it is a portal. Let's just hope it is the *right* entrance this time."

That reminder of the previous failure dimmed Wals' smile a little. Still, it was more than they had a few minutes ago. "Let's go tell Rose and Merriweather," he suggested as they ran down the rest of the steps and exited into the courtyard of Fantasyland.

"Merri already knows," Wolf stated flatly as he gave a wave to the workers who rolled their eyes and hurried back inside to finish up as much as they could for the day. Seeing so much activity near the exit of the coming attraction, a few of the guests strolling past on their way to Snow White's grotto slowed down and looked curiously at the two men. They wanted to ask what it was like inside and when it would be open, always hopeful that they might be invited inside early. However, the two cast members looked way too preoccupied and unapproachable, so the disappointed guests just continued on their way.

"She does? How do you know? Why didn't she say anything?" The fairy's role—or nonrole—in all this was becoming more and more confusing.

"That's her room."

"Then, why didn't she tell you? Shouldn't she have known the first portal was wrong?"

Wolf paused before they reached the curve of the walkway. "There are many portals all around the Park, Wals. They all go to different places. She must realize this. But, as she has said many times, she can only watch and make suggestions. She hasn't much power here, not that she would admit that…. I figure she doesn't know where exactly any of them lead, just as I don't until I actually try it."

That was as good of an explanation Wals would get as the men walked around the side of the castle to Swan Lake where Rose was swimming in circles, bored out of her mind.

"Lance, we found the portal. I'm going to need the Walkthrough shut down until such time as we get back."

His security partner and fellow Guardian of Walt gave a small grimace that was unseen over the phone. "You sure, Wolf? The Imagineers are working overtime to try and get the thing open. They were put out enough by your interruption earlier."

Wolf was unconcerned about the workers. "I am trying to get Rose home, Lance. It can't be helped. We can't risk jumping back into the middle of a group of workers. Or even guests if it takes longer than we think and the attraction is actually open. You know my clothes don't make the jump going in, and I don't wear any as a wolf.

So, coming back…," he broke off.

"Naked as a jaybird. Yeah, I've heard," Lance laughed. "Yeah, that would be a little hard to explain to a family with teenage girls walking through when you landed at their feet. You might get a date out of it," he offered as a possible good outcome.

The answering growl got Lance to laughing again. "No, no, we'll take care of it somehow. Kimberly will make the call as soon as we hang up. You sure this is the right one, Wolf?" Lance asked, becoming serious.

"No," was the quiet response. "But, it felt right. As did the portal under the drawbridge," he reluctantly added, giving a deep sigh. "There's only one way to find out."

"Well, hope it goes well," Lance told him and then had a sudden thought come to his mind. "Hey, Wolf, to change the subject a little, I have a trivia question for you."

"This isn't the time for your little game, Lance."

"No, no, it will take your mind off things for a minute. Listen to this. It stumped Kimberly, by the way." When Wolf started muttering in Lakota, Lance hurried up. "Okay, don't bite anything. Here it is: Which is the only Park to have both Sleeping Beauty's Castle and Cinderella's Castle?"

Smiling expectantly, Lance was disappointed to hear only silence at the other end. "Not even a guess?"

"Lance, we *really* don't have time for this."

"Fine, I'll tell you since you are in such a bad

mood all of a sudden. It's Disneyland!"

"Fascinating."

"Do you know where the two castles are?" Lance prodded, being actually glad he wasn't face to face with Wolf right then.

Silence again was his answer.

"Okay, be that way, but I am still marking it down on our running score. One is the obvious big castle, and the other is Cinderella's castle on that little hill in Storybook Land."

"Can I go now?"

"Fine. Be that way. But I'll bet you use it on Wals before your trip is over."

"Don't bet too much," muttered Wolf.

Lance knew when to stop his games. "So, do you think you are all ready to go? You'll have to be prepared for anything. You don't know what to expect back there."

"Yeah, I know." Wolf sounded relieved to be talking about the trip again. "Wals will use the same costume as before, and we already have Rose's dress and cape wrapped. "

Remembering his and Wolf's adventure in Columbia when they were following Walt's second Hidden Mickey quest, Lance was torn between wanting to go along for the adventure and being glad he was safe and warm in the mansion in Fullerton. He still didn't know what he would do if Wolf offered to let him go, but he then realized his partner had already hung up.

Kimberly would have killed him if he went.

Hidden by the bright lights from the overhead firework spectacular going on, no one noticed a bright pink light radiating out from the upper castle windows. The roar of the vortex's thunder as it swept through the darkened hallways was muted by the *BOOM* of the rockets as they burst into a dazzling display of yellows and reds, the accompanying music rising to a soul-stirring crescendo.

No one noticed that the swan was no longer swimming in the fern-encircled moat or, had they peered deep in the black confines of the castle, that two men—one dressed as a prince and one unselfconsciously naked—were there one moment and gone the next. Had they noticed the small blue trail of pixie dust that had followed the swan, they would have seen that it, too, vanished in the angry, swirling whirlwind. That conical wind had bounced off one wall and then careened into another, violently shaking the colorful pennants that flew high above the elaborate windows of the dioramas. When its use had been fulfilled, the whirlwind blinked out of existence in a shimmering curtain of pink glimmer.

CHAPTER THREE

England — 1289

Water lapped at Wals' feet, threatening to soak through the thin boots he had again 'borrowed' from the Costume Department at Disneyland. Tucked securely into the tips of the brown boots were the well-wrapped pendant and a few of the gold coins taken from the pirate chest on Tom Sawyer's Island. Eyes closed against the pain throbbing in his head, arms stretched out in front of him, his fingers opened and closed. His white lips frowned as he imagined he was grabbing handfuls of sand. Prying open one eye, he slowly came to realize he was lying on a beach, the placid waves lapping against the bottoms of his feet.

Hearing a feminine groan somewhere over to his left, his eyes shot fully open, remembering that he had not been alone in the terror he had just experienced. Pulling his arms closer to his chest, he managed a shaky version of a pushup and got his feet under him enough to stand. "Rose?" Wals thought he had said it out loud, but it only emerged as a croak out of his dry mouth.

Glancing up, he was rewarded with the sight of a crescent moon peering brightly over the serene beach. To his left, the groan was re-peated. With a loud pop coming from his neck, he turned to see Merri helping Rose lace up the back of her dress. He wasn't sure which of them had groaned. The fairy was back in her flowing cape and light blue gown, but her pointed hat was slightly askew and her hands were slightly shaking as she helped her friend get dressed. They had all been affected by the violence of the time shift.

As Rose wrung some of the excess water out of her long lavender skirt, Wals came over to her and held out his hand. Going into his arms for a quick embrace, she gave him a trem-bling smile. "Are you okay?" he tried again, the words coming out in a hoarse whisper.

Finishing her dressing, she tied her flowing blond hair back into place with the black ribbon Merri handed her out of the parcel Wolf had packed before they made the jump. Nodding, Rose looked around. "Where's Wolf? Did he make it through with us?"

Wals' eyes widened as his head jerked around. Remembering when he had gone back with Wolf to the 1800's to rescue Rose, Wolf had somehow ended up in a different year. He paled even further when he didn't see the huge black wolf anywhere, his hand unconsciously going to the hilt of the unproven sword hanging off the belt of his Prince costume. Not knowing where, or when, they were, Wals hesitated to call out for their missing companion, his consternation growing. It had also registered into his brain that there was no castle within sight, not the familiar castle of Disneyland, nor any that might signify their location. Only, inexplicably, a sandy beach. *Where are we?* he wanted to shout.

Merri ignored the two humans as their heads came closer together, anxiously whispering in the night, trying to decide what to do. Reaching inside her flowing dark blue cape, she smiled contentedly as she pulled out her wand and tapped it against her palm. "Wake up, dear," she muttered to it and tapped again. A shower of blue sparkles fell over her fingertips. "There you are! I missed you, too" she told the glowing wand as it belched out another array of glimmer. Shaking slightly, it settled and the glow receded. "All back to normal," she said happily as she approached the two humans. "Ready to go, dear?" she asked Rose, ignoring Wals.

Rose reached out and straightened the fairy's tall conical hat for her. "Go?" she repeated with a confused frown, "Merri, we can't go anywhere until we know what happened to Wolf." At the stubborn look on the fairy's face, she could tell Merri didn't agree. "It's only right, you know. I'm sure he's doing everything he can."

Wals had been watching the fairy, stunned silent by her transformation and the animated wand in her hand. "You...you really are the Good Fairy?"

The short plump figure turned impatiently back to the man. "Who did you think I was?"

His mouth opened and then clamped shut. Who *did* he think she was? He just feebly shrugged his shoulders and shook his head.

Merri turned back to her charge. "He's not very bright, dear. Are you sure he's the one?"

Rose was saved from answering by the silent approach of the wolf. In the darkness, with only the moon for light, he was reduced to an eerie dark shape moving over the shimmering sand, the gray tips of his black fur glowing silver in the light. Head down, he moved slower than his usual brisk pace. Obviously the passage through the vortex had taken its toll on him as well. Exhausted, he dropped into a sitting position next to Rose, her hand automatically going to rest on his head as she had done so many times before on Tom Sawyer's Island. "Are you all right, Wolf?" she asked, worried as she rubbed the soft fur around his ears.

His eyes closed briefly as he leaned into the soothing feeling. Nodding, he glanced to the right and held his nose a little higher in the air. He knew they weren't alone on that seemingly deserted stretch of beach. Briefly standing, he turned his back to the source of the smell and, head down to hide his moving lips, quietly told them, "We have company. Fairy, you take Rose home. You know the way. Wals, you stay with me. You all must remember this: I *will not* talk again while I am here. It is too dangerous. You are my mouth, Wals. No, don't interrupt. We don't have time. Merri, go now. I will find you all later, Rose," he promised. He then hissed to Wals, "Draw your sword and stand at ease."

The Blue Fairy stiffened suddenly and her wand almost leaped out of her hand. "It's *her*. I can feel the evil is near. How did *she* get here, wolf?" she demanded, glaring suspiciously at the animal, her knuckles white around her wand.

The huge black head turned sharply to the fairy. "Do not address me directly again, fairy. It is not safe! She is always near. The pendant draws her. She has been waiting for it to come. Now, go!" he commanded and snapped his mouth shut.

Merri drew a circle around the confused Rose with her wand. Holding off any arguments the girl might offer, she simply said, "You must come with me, dear. Your mother must be worried by now. Come quickly. Draw your cloak over your hair."

With an anxious parting glance at Wals, Rose reluctantly did as she was told, and the two disappeared through a small cleft in the shadows of the huge boulders that lined the edge of the beach. Finding a narrow deer path, the Blue Fairy led the worried girl briskly through the dark woods. No soothing beams of moonlight found their way through the dense, dripping trees of this forest. Holding her straining wand under the concealing folds of her cape so it didn't inadvertently tell *her* where they were, Merri led the princess unerringly through the night, each quiet with her own thoughts.

After the women were safely away, Wolf stood and faced the unseen, dark presence. Far enough away to insure its anonymity, it had stopped and was quietly observing the two remaining figures on the beach. Head down, Wolf planted his stiff front legs wide apart, the hair on his back rising as he bared his fangs. Wals was startled into taking a step back when the wolf snarled and snapped at the darkness that faced them. Pawing the sand in front of him, Wolf lashed out one more time with his lethal teeth, his tail straight out, ears alert. The message was sent: I know you're there. Leave us be.

His fingers easily gripping the elaborate hilt, his back straight, Wals raised the tip of his sword in the direction Wolf was facing. Whatever was out there, the wolf didn't like it, and he would back the animal. He knew not to speak. The wolf's actions spoke clearly enough.

For a full minute Wolf kept his defensive stance. He finally backed slowly to Wals' position. Deliberately turning his back on the unseen danger, he proudly walked along the shoreline in the opposite direction. Keeping his sword out of its sheath, Wals let his grip relax as the blade hung down by his side as he followed the wolf. Silently wondering what was going on, he had figured they would follow the path the fairy and Rose had taken. It was becoming obvious, however, that Wolf had other plans.

Once they came to the curve of the shore-line, the man and the wolf disappeared from her sight. Safe now from detection, a large gray wolf padded to the spot where the group had just emerged from the sea. Her sharp gray eyes narrowed as she sniffed the ground where each individual had been. Seeing the indents in the sand, it would be easy enough to follow the direction the man and wolf had gone. But the other two.... The vixen's ears twitched as her head swiveled this way and that. She wasn't able to get a sense of them. Thinking it odd, she lifted her nose one more time.

Going to the spot where the black wolf had taken his stand, she used her hind legs to contemptuously throw sand over the clear line he had drawn.

Easing into a sitting position, she let her mouth loll open into a wolf's imitation of a smile. She already knew which path she would follow.

"Fools," she muttered to herself.

Rose gave a small cry of happiness when she saw the familiar turrets and walls of her castle. "Oh, Merri!" she tugged on the arm of her companion, "It's been so long! I'm actually home!"

With a silent sigh of relief the Blue Fairy by-passed the drawbridge and the imposing gatehouse. She headed for a secret door known only to the three Good Fairies. The last time she had used the entry was to bring Rose back to her family after raising her for sixteen years in the hidden cottage deep in the forest. *If only we had waited one more day*, she mused to herself, thinking back on the disastrous consequences when they had left the princess alone in her room for just a moment.

Shaking off the memories, Merri was met at the door by her long-missed two companions. They shed many tears of happiness that the princess was finally back.

When Merri—the Blue Fairy—and her friend Fauna—the Green Fairy—started an animated conversation on all that had gone on in that strange place where Rose had been sent, Flora—the eldest, the Red Fairy—interrupted them. "I know we are all anxious to hear the tales, but we must think of the poor child!" She broke off when she realized Rose had run on in ahead of them and was already out of sight. She smiled fondly as she shut the wooden door to the outside world. "That's my girl!"

"Where'd she go?" Fauna asked, looking around, anxious. "She didn't run off again, did she?" the fairy fretted, her green hat unable to keep up with her swiveling head.

"No, no, I'm sure she is on her way to see her mother." Flora popped out of sight for an instant. In a red burst of light, she was back and nodding wisely. "Yes, just as I expected. She's up in her room in the upper tower now, changing her dress first, thank goodness." Eyes narrowed, she glanced suspiciously at Merri. "She looks pretty worse for the wear. You had said you could handle anything when we decided to send her away."

The three fairies continued arguing as they flew to their brightly decorated sitting room. Merri's wand tapped out a tea service, and she handed the fragile cups to her waiting companions. Sighing contentedly again, she glanced around the familiar room, the tapestries on the wall moving slightly in the night air coming in from the open windows. "Oh, I missed this room!" she told them as the tea and remaining biscuits winked out of existence.

The ladies got down to business. "So, Merri, did you know Prince Phillip disappeared the same time you did? Was he with you?"

Merri's small, round mouth fell open. "He did? Oh, that's terrible!" She shook her head at her memories of the few happy days after the Evil One had been vanquished. "No, he wasn't with us. At least, I don't think so," she frowned, thinking back on the man Wals and his unknown role in all of this. "I'm not sure."

That wasn't what Flora wanted to hear. "Perhaps you should tell us where you and the princess went. My, after all this time, I still just want to call her Briar Rose," she admitted with a smile.

"It was your idea," Merri muttered under her breath, getting her feathers ruffled at the suggestion that she might not have taken care of her charge as well as she should. She pointed at Flora. "You were the one who said she should go to another castle for safety."

"How was I to know the Evil One was still

alive? We all saw the dragon fall. But, there's no use harping on the same old tune. It happened, and we did what we thought was best. Their Majesties agreed again, if you remember." Flora refused to take the full blame for whatever it was that had happened to Rose.

Stepping in between the two, the gentle Green Fairy held up her hands. "Now, there, there. We mustn't get all upset. All's well that ends…or something like that!" She turned to the red-faced Blue Fairy and clasped her hands together eagerly. "Now, Merri, dear, tell us where you went. I'm dying to hear the tale!"

"Hmph." With a last glare at Flora, Merri settled more comfortably onto her invisible cushion and prepared to relate her experiences as a human. A patch of embroidery appeared in each of their hands, and they automatically started weaving the colored floss in and out of the white cloth. "As I am sure you will remember," she started, then broke off and changed the color of her pink thread to blue. "That's better. Now, where was I?"

"Nowhere," Flora mumbled.

"Oh, yes, if you remember, *you*," she stressed, glancing at the Red Fairy, "decided it would be better if Rose went to another castle to be protected. King Hubert's was too obvious, so we needed to find another place that would be safe. Just as we were weaving the spell…."

"I said she would make a lovely swan," Fauna broke in with a contented sigh, and then her eyes widened as she clapped her hand to her mouth. "Oh, no! Did that make a difference?"

"And I mentioned what a sleeping beauty she had been just days earlier," Flora injected shortly. "What, if anything, did that have to do with our work?"

Merri crossed her arms over her ample bosom. "You see? It wasn't just me," she pointed out. "You should have just concentrated on where you were sending her. But, no, you let your minds wander. And look at the mess you got us into!"

Chastised now, Flora's embroidery dropped into her lap. "Oh dear. I am so sorry, Merri. Go on, tell us where you went."

"It was just awful," Merri groaned. "We came out inside of a beautiful castle all right, but it wasn't a real castle!"

"Not real? How could it not be real?"

"It was a make-believe castle in a large park. There were trees and flowers and rides and buildings and boats and a snow-covered mountain and people everywhere," arms waving as she tried describing everything all at once.

Fauna's eyes got all dreamy. "It sounds just lovely! But I still don't understand the 'not real' part if there were people all about."

"And I had to be a...a human again! The whole time I was there!" she sputtered. "My poor wand almost didn't forgive me. Did I mention the part about Rose being turned into a swan and having to live in the moat?" she broke off, looking at her two companions.

"Oh, dear," Fauna muttered to herself, realizing that had been her doing.

"Were you in a different part of the country?"

Merri shook her head. "No, we ended up in a place called America. No, don't try so hard to figure out where that is, Fauna, dear. You'll hurt yourself…. It hasn't been discovered yet. It was over eight hundred years…," she drew it out to build the suspense. Fauna looked intrigued. Flora looked as if she wanted to turn her into a toad. "In the future!" she finished, pleased with the startled expressions on their faces. "The castle was quite lovely, actually, but humans don't live in castles then. This one was in the middle of a large place they call an amusement park and it is actually called Sleeping Beauty's Castle!" She glanced at the Red Fairy to see if the implication sunk in. It had.

"I…I sent our dear girl into the future!" Flora's shocked expression slowly changed into one of smugness. "Didn't know I had it in me!" she declared, smiling as she looked at her two friends.

Merri was trying to decide if she should include the part about Rose accidentally going through another vortex with the wolf and ending up back in an even more dangerous time period…. No, she figured she would save that story for a stormy winter night when they could use a good yarn.

"You've been gone for a good many years, Merri, dear," Fauna was pointing out as Merri's thoughts turned back to their current situation. "Rose is probably meeting her brothers about this time."

"Brothers! There are princes now?"

Fauna sighed and thought about the handsome lads. "Yes, they helped Her Majesty the Queen with her great loneliness after you left with Rose. They were quite the handfuls until they got bigger." She lowered her voice and added, "At least the Evil One didn't seem interested in them," worriedly glancing at the open windows. You never knew who might be listening.

"You will meet them later, Merri," impatient Flora cut in, wanting to figure out the rest of the story. "You didn't seem positive about Phillip. Are you sure he wasn't there? He's been missing this whole time."

"Perhaps he is on a quest to find Rose," the Green Fairy suggested, pricking her finger on her sharp needle. "Oww! That happens a lot in this castle," she muttered to herself.

Merri got up to pace the floor nervously. "I'm not sure about the Prince. The human I was with says his middle name is Phillip," she shrugged. "When we tried coming back the first time, there was the wolf, the man Wals, Rose and myself. Of course, the wolf got it wrong and we ended up back to Merlin's time." She still hadn't forgiven Wolf for that.

"A wolf!" cried Fauna. "Oh, they can be such evil creatures! There seems to be so many more of them prowling around in the woods these days!"

"This one isn't evil," the Blue Fairy conceded reluctantly. "He has some kind of power that lets him—and whoever is close to his side— travel through time. He doesn't understand it any more than I, so don't ask. He is a human in the time of the pretend castle but turns into a wolf when he travels backwards." She wandered over to the window. The faint pink of dawn was tinting the eastern sky. Another day was at hand. *What dangers would this one hold?* she wondered with a heavy sigh.

"Where are this wolf and the human you mentioned? Are they close? I think we need to talk to them."

"I don't know where they are, Flora. The wolf told me to bring Rose back home. There was something out there in the darkness, an evil force I could sense." She broke off and shuddered. "It's a familiar feeling. I've encountered her before," she ended quietly.

"The dragon?" whispered Fauna as she hurriedly closed the wooden shutters and sealed the room.

Slowly shaking her head, Merri didn't know how to explain it. "She is and she is not," she began. "There are many layers to this one. She is very ancient. Just as old as the red diamond pendant she follows. The wolf is determined to keep it from her."

"And where does your human man fit in with all of this? Does he have any extra abilities that we need to know about?"

"He is in love with our Rose," Merri simply stated.

"Oh, dear," sighed Fauna. "That is a problem, isn't it?"

All three heads nodded slowly in unison.

The problem was becoming more apparent as day after day passed. At Rose's insistent urging, the three fairies finally went looking for Wals when he failed to show up at the castle. Struggling to fit in this foreign environment, he had taken a room in the small village just outside the castle walls. Pushed back near the edge of the encroaching forest, Wolf was able to come and go from this establishment without being noticed and alarming the inhabitants.

It was in these dismal rooms that the three ladies found Wals. Looking around, it was obvious they were comparing it to the opulence of the nearby castle. Gritting his teeth, still dressed in his now-shabby-looking costume, Wals waited. Unused to the harsh conditions of the time, his patience was growing thin.

The Red Fairy, whom he instinctively pegged to be the leader, looked him over when she was done inspecting his sparse furnishings. "You have been missed at court," Fauna told him when she was done with her scrutiny. "Our lady has been awaiting you."

Knowing he had fallen short in their estimations, Wals held back from growling—a habit he was picking up from the missing Wolf. "I haven't been able to get *to* court," he frowned. "I seem to be barred from the king and queen's presence."

Walking around him, the Green Fairy asked in a kind tone, "Is that what you were wearing when you tried, dear?"

Liking this gentle one, he smiled at her. "It

is all I have. I didn't figure I would be here this long."

This brought up three sets of eyebrows. "Oh? And what were you planning on doing?"

He stammered and ran a hand through his brown, messy hair that was overdue for a trim. "I…I don't know. I didn't have any plans! We just wanted to get Rose home safe. I didn't think past that."

Realizing he had been thinking only of protecting Rose, the fairies relented a little. "She wants to see you," Merri told him, though it was obvious from her tone that she wished he would just go back to his own time and leave the princess be.

Ignoring the inflection in her voice, Wals' eyes brightened. "You'll take me into court? Will I finally get to meet her family?"

The three visitors glanced at each other. He seemed so optimistic that they hated to dash his hopes. Flora shook her head slowly. "No, I don't think that will happen. You see, you might be dressed…somewhat…like a prince, but that doesn't make you one. You would not be let near a princess. Surely that hasn't changed so much in your time."

Not really knowing too much about royalty and their doings, Wals shrugged. "It wasn't part of my life," he said simply.

"There is another problem we need to relate." Merri decided it was best to lay it all out in front of the human before any decisions were made.

"Go on." Wals leaned back in the plain

wooden chair when he found he had been perched on its edge. His excitement to see Rose was beginning to fade as the discussion continued.

The Blue Fairy mouthed the words, "The pendant."

Steadily holding her gaze, Wals didn't even look down at the boot that hid the precious stone. "What about it?"

Looking to see if anyone was listening at the open window, Merri lowered her voice before she spoke. "It is whispered that you hold an item of great value."

Wals held out his empty hands. "Who would know to start that rumor? I surely haven't told anyone about it. I doubt that Rose would, either." He looked plainly at the Blue Fairy, his meaning obvious.

She sputtered, "I...I...would not! How dare you, boy!"

Always the calming influence, the Green Fairy stepped in again before Merri thought to pull out her wand and do something they...well, Wals...might regret later. "Now, I am sure that isn't what he meant," as she looked to Wals for confirmation. As he folded his arms stubbornly over his chest, frowning, she murmured, "Oh, dear. Well...I'm sure he meant it in the nicest of ways."

"We are getting nowhere," Fauna declared, throwing her hands up as she stepped into the fray. "Merri, we know you didn't utter a word. We also know Rose would not place this...man in danger," waving a vague hand in his direction.

"Who do you think that leaves, Merri?"

Taking her glare off of Wals, she relented and answered, "The Evil One. It has to be her." She stopped and shook her head sadly. "Merlin had no idea what he created."

"Do you mean the pendant or his apprentice?"

"Yes."

Wals pulled his sword. In the small room it seemed overlong. "Well, I have this and find I am quite good with it," he declared with a smug smile, swishing the blade side to side.

Unimpressed, the ladies said nothing. They knew it would take more than a fine sword to battle what was coming.

"Put that away, dear, before you hurt…someone," Fauna patted his arm with a smile. "Are you ready to go see Rose?"

This surprised the man. "Now? You mean it? I thought you would make me jump through some more hoops first."

"Amusing as that sounds," Merri chuckled at the thought of him dressed with a ruffle around his neck and sitting atop a prancing pony, "Rose is waiting for you in a secret location. One that I hope remains more of a secret than that pendant…."

"Hey, I…." Wals started to say.

"Come along before the day is too far spent and Rose is called to her duties," the Red Fairy interjected and led the way out of the room.

Not knowing where they were going, Wals had no choice but to follow.

After losing the men who were following

Wals' every move, the fairies stopped in a brushy area near the curtain wall of the castle that surrounded and protected the bailey within. Releasing a hidden level cleverly concealed in the rockwork of the wall, the wooden door swung inwards. Rose immediately rushed out of the doorway, almost knocking Wals over in her excitement to see him.

"Come, dears, we must get inside," Fauna counseled, glancing nervously around. "The forest has many eyes."

Entering the darkened doorway, Wals had the distinct impression that was as far as he would ever be allowed within the castle walls. But, after their lips briefly met and Rose began an excited recital of all that she had been doing since she got back, Wals forgot his displeasure and enjoyed the stolen moments.

When the three chaperones finally gave them a moment alone, Wals told her of another place where they could meet and have some time together, one outside the castle walls. He had had plenty of free time to roam the countryside and had found the perfect spot. Chaffing at the confines of the castle and always ready for another adventure—even one that would incur the hint of impropriety—Rose readily agreed and a date was set for their rendezvous.

When the fairies came back to escort Wals home, they were a little surprised at the ease of the parting. They had expected a lot of drama and tears from the two frustrated sweethearts. Eyes narrowed, they observed Rose's serene face and were suspicious of her calm kiss and wave good-bye. Wals, close-lipped all the way to his lodgings, gave them no further clue.

After the secret door had closed, Rose turned to ascend the stone steps to her suite of rooms in the tower. She did have a calm heart now that she had finally seen Wals again. Smiling smugly, now all she had to do was lose the vigilance of her brothers and the eyes that watched her every move—for she had heard the whispers about the pendant too, and knew there were others who seek it.

A cold fog had rolled in over the coast, dimming a nearly full moon and obscuring the stars that would otherwise be seen in abundance. The sound of the ocean's waves crashing against the rocky shoreline was muted into a pleasant distant roar. Night sounds from the surrounding dense forest were heard only as ghostly whispers through the swirling vapor.

The surrounding blanket of gray and its sound-restricting presence was a welcome cloak to the two people nestled together on that small strip of sand. Standing, facing each other on a lichen-covered boulder, their foreheads touched as they whispered. A crescent strand of black rocks formed a natural wall, blocking their view to the south and east. The only approach to the young man and woman was from the north, along the stretch of sand that sloped gradually from a forest of pines and vine-covered shrubs down to the foamy waves of the sea. Unless the hunters who sought the pair could somehow miraculously emerge from the waves crashing upon the sandy beach as they themselves had done, the two felt they were safe enough. Should they be wrong, however, he knew they would be able to detect any impending approach in time and be able to melt deeper into the shadows of the fissures in the boulders behind them. If that failed, he had his sword at his side.

They talked in low, earnest whispers—the whispers of those who should not be meeting together, nor as others would righteously insist, should be meeting alone at all. Theirs were quick exchanges of heartfelt passion and pent-up desire. They used stolen kisses when words failed, their hands clasped by the necessity to be always touching. Her blue eyes brimmed with happiness at their time together. Their lips murmured promises they hoped they would be able to keep while their hearts filled with love.

As if disobeying some unspoken promise of obscurity, the brilliant moonlight momentarily broke through the shroud of covering fog. The silver light shone down on the two sweethearts, illuminating them as if they were lone performers on an empty stage. Her unbound blond hair glimmered in that light; the regal golden circlet settled over her forehead shone like a band of fire. His brown shoulder-length hair was tipped by the silver light, his green eyes lit only by the deep love he felt for the woman held in his arms. Neither paid notice of the play of light being fashioned by the moon. Too intent were they on each other and the gift he had just pressed into her hands.

As the moonlight did its magic, the gift glowed and throbbed in the light as if it was a living, breathing thing. She caught the glimmer of this large heart-shaped object, recognizing it to be the beautiful diamond. What else could throw out colors of the rainbow even in the dim light of the moon? As she held the diamond by its golden setting in her hands, the moonlight caught each facet and flung out reddish blaze like either the glowing embers of a well-stoked fire or the glowing pits of Hades—where some had insisted it sprung. Surrounding the diamond heart, almost too heavy for its blood-red glow, were circlets of gold. The three golden circles had been set by cunning hands as the creator of the piece unconsciously pictured something far in the future and smiled as the fire forged the metal. The heart hung from a heavy golden chain that would soon be placed once again around her fair neck.

Shaking her head, she tried to press the gift back into her sweetheart's hands. "I can't wear that! It's too precious. Too many are looking for it."

But he was insistent. "You must wear it. Think of this gift as my heart that you already possess," he pleaded. "You must remember me until I can properly come back for you."

"I have no need of jewels to remember you. You are already etched in my heart," was her answer, her blue eyes flashing the truth of her words.

Smiling at her response, he kissed her fair neck as the moon slid into obscurity once more.

"Take my gift. You know it's a powerful heart," he claimed, smiling at her frowning, dubious look. "It's true!" he exclaimed. "You remember what Merlin himself said."

"King Arthur…," she started to say.

He put a finger against her lips, holding it there. "Shh…Yes, *that* Merlin. We mustn't say it out loud," he whispered back. He replaced his finger with his lips, issuing an assuring kiss. With a grin on his face, he leaned back watching as she brought the precious gemstone up by its chain between them, feeling extremely proud of himself that he was finally able to give it to her once more.

"Do you remember what it does?" she asked, looking at the object in her hand with a wary scrutiny, its fiery radiance now subdued into a blush of red by the gloomy fog.

"It shows you things. Are you sure you want to see them again? It frightened you last time." He refrained from adding that what *he* had seen in *his* mind's eye was likewise frightening—and the fact that half of his vision had already come true.

Her lips smiled and created a little dimple in her cheek. "You mean my future? Then it all must be true because you are my future." She had seen him in the depths of the pendant's vision, plus a fire-breathing dragon.

Noticing the dimple, he kissed it. "We know I can't stay much longer. Your brothers will kill me unless I can prove myself to them."

She gave an unladylike grunt. "My brothers can go…."

Her sharp retort was cut off by the approaching sound of muffled footsteps crunching on the sandy beach in front of them. His fingers again went to her lips to silence her, this time unnecessarily as she was very aware of the footsteps and the clink of armor moving closer and closer to their location. Momentarily using the imminent danger as a distraction, he slipped the golden chain over her head. Knowing their perilous situation, not taking the time to argue, she carefully tucked the diamond into the blue bodice of her dress. The pair pressed back further into the sheltering darkness of the boulders, the shallow niche providing temporary concealment. She slipped the hood of her black cloak over her head, hoping she hadn't been too late in hiding her radiant blond hair.

The intruders were as silent in their approach as they could be on the sand. There was no talking amongst them. They knew where they were going, and they knew who was hiding there. They had followed their quarry's tell-tale footsteps in the sand; the two pair of side-by-side depressions that appeared from a path in the dense foliage had betrayed the pair's direction as well as any signpost could have done. Beyond the footprints across the beach, just as they had emerged from the forest, the hunters had seen a flash of movement deep within the natural jetty of boulders running from the land out to the sea. Swords already drawn, it was now just a matter of steps. Like a pack of wolves that had trapped their prey, the men picked up their pace, triumphant smiles already on their unshaven faces.

Armed only with his sword pulled silently from its leather sheath, the young man stood resolutely in front of his love. His heart pounded with anticipation. Fear never once entered his mind. He would take as many of them as he could before…. He couldn't finish the thought. He would take them all.

The insulation of fog became their enemy now. They couldn't tell how many were coming or how far away they actually were. He felt her hand on his shoulder, squeezing, encouraging, reassuring, and then, suddenly, the intruders were upon him.

His sword flashed and bit, plunged and parried. The clanging of metal against metal echoed along the rocks. The sounds of the battle were fierce and loud. The sounds from the men, however, were eerily quiet with only a grunt or a moan issuing from their determined mouths. Glints of metal flashed as blade collided on blade and recoiled. A muted blow of one blade evading another and finding flesh, sinking deep; one attacker fell back bleeding at the hip, another eager to take his place in the confines of the boulders. Try as he might, there were too many for him. His sword was straight and true, but it was no match for their many longswords. The woman watched in dread as one skilled attacker, his sword circling in an elaborate flanking move, caught her sweetheart's hand at an awkward angle. His sword was flung to the ground, clanging against the rocks and then silenced in the sand. Disarmed now, the point of an enemy blade aimed at the hollow in his neck, he could only watch in mute fury as his woman was roughly pulled out of the shadow of the boulders behind him. The moon betrayed them and came out of hiding once again as her hood was yanked off of her head. The golden chain, just so recently bestowed on her, glowed and shimmered around her neck, its heavy links parading down the front of her dress. And, at its end, the beautiful diamond heart radiated its red glow like a crimson beacon. Rough hands followed the chain down the bodice of her dress. With an outraged cry, she bit the hand that dared to touch her. Her assailant ignored her outburst and the bleeding gash on his hand as he brought out the prize—the gold-encircled red diamond—into the light. He tried to yank it off her neck, but the chain was surprisingly strong. He tried again, but she held her head high and gave no indication of the pain it was causing her.

Sensing his confusion, her quick mind took a chance. "Beware. It is enchanted by Merlin. He told me himself," she loudly whispered. "You cannot harm us."

Within the moonlight, at the sides of her vision, she noticed the point of the blade that was aimed at her sweetheart's neck began to waver with superstition, a sliver of light danced along the blade in its slight tremor. Her man wisely said nothing, moving a step away from his woman, lest his captor decided to test the theory. Another man standing beyond the group, a bloody hand pressed against his injured hip, forgot his pain as he listened in fear and began slowly, silently backing away.

The leader of the assailants looked from the fire of the gemstone to the fire flashing from her blue eyes. There was no fear in those eyes—only hatred and unwavering faith. He had felt his heart suddenly start to pound at her whispered words. Now it was threatening to burst out of his chest as the implication echoed around in his mind. He had heard the rumors, of course, the whispered talk of her brothers in the village. Everyone had heard the rumors, but he had scoffed at their words of warning and had wanted the gem for himself—regardless of who it was that had hired him to find it. The brothers had known her sweetheart would eventually give the fabled stone to her; they had been told the stone was in his possession. The leader of this group of marauders had heard of the legend and the power that this stone was said to possess. In his mind, such mystery was a myth. He had only been interested in the wealth the gemstone would bring and the power such wealth would ensure once he was far away from this part of the country. Now he was not so positive and silently cursed the one who had sent him.

In those few moments of hesitation, another sound came to their ears, one that instantly struck fear in all of them. It was a low sound, one they usually heard in the dead of night when they were safely in their beds, covers pulled high to their chins. It filled their ears and rumbled around deep inside their chests causing their hands to shake of their own accord. The growl came again, louder this time, closer, but, closer to which one of them? Who would be its first victim? One by one the assailants slowly turned in full circles where they stood in the sand, swords drawn and ready, aimed low. Another snarl sounded. It seemed to echo around in the swirling fog coming from nowhere and everywhere all at once.

A black blur wove between them faster than their eyes could follow. Ankles were suddenly bleeding; feet were knocked out from under them. Ignoring the weaker minions, leaping, the huge paws landed in the middle of the chest of the leader, pushing him; the force knocking him away from the woman and onto his back in the sand. The golden chain broke from around her neck and his fingers tightened around the prize as he fell. As the chain broke, he thought he heard a muttered curse come from the wolf that now stood on top of him, teeth bared, inches away from his unprotected neck, his sword dropped in the suddenness of the attack and out of his reach. As his fingers touched the fiery red surface of the diamond, he forgot the wolf that was hovering over him and the fact that he was now unarmed. His eyes rolled away from the wolf as his mind clouded and whirled, and he could see himself in a different place, inside an opulent castle. The man with him was a king who had raised a sword before him. The sword was held in the position for knighthood. Pride swelled in his chest as his head bowed before the king. Then the vision changed, and he saw everything in the castle growing larger before his eyes.

Seeing the huge beast pinning their leader, unaware of the vision he was now witnessing, his men broke from their defensive positions and ran down the beach towards their frightened horses. In a frenzy of screaming horses, cursing men and blinding sand, they threw themselves onto the backs of their mounts and plunged away. Knowing the assailants were now gone and the two sweethearts safely clinging together, his sword in hand once more, the wolf inexplicably stepped off the leader. His head remained down, teeth bared, front feet wide apart. They recognized the position of attack.

As the confusing vision continued to assail the leader, his hand involuntarily jerked and the pendant fell into the sand, the gold links of the chain still entwined in his fingers. Once the gemstone broke contact with his hand, his mind instantly cleared and he remembered the black wolf. Shaking his head back and forth he tried to understand what had just happened to him, what he had just seen. Not sure why the animal had let him go, he backed away slowly, the chain still clutched in his white knuckles. He never dropped his eye contact with the wolf. Forgetting his lost sword, he didn't stop backing until he, too, was at his frightened horse. With a curse, he found he had been abandoned by his men. Vaulting into his saddle, he viciously spurred his rearing, snorting charger. Unarmed and knowing how far a wolf that size could jump, he galloped away into the swirling gray of the fog. Only when he was far enough away did his mind begin to function normally again, and he was able to remember those startling blue eyes. They had been on the golden-haired girl…and they were on the black wolf! He tucked the cursed heart into his shirt and rode after his men, all the while his mind still spinning.

As the assailant's departure grew more distant, and his horse's hoof beats faded into the night, the defensive posture of the wolf relaxed. He sat and listened, ears forward, hearing the horse far longer than the two people left behind were able to. Assured the men would not be back, that they had gotten what they had come after, the black wolf turned and faced the couple. Panting after his exertion, he seemed to be waiting.

"Thank you, Wolf," Wals said when his own heartbeat returned to normal. He hadn't even noticed his arm had been ripped open and that he was bleeding. "I can't tell you how glad I was to see you. I couldn't have held them off much longer."

Knowing he wouldn't speak to them, Rose crouched down, her gown bunching onto the sand. "You saved me yet again, Wolf," as she hugged his neck. "Thank you seems so little to say."

The wolf leaned into her caress, his eyes momentarily closing in pleasure. He took a chance and barely whispered, "We are still being watched. I have to go."

Breaking free from the woman, he tilted his head to the sky and letting out a piercing, linger-

ing howl. This was a different sound than before. There was no menace, no warning threat
to this sound. It was a haunting, lingering call.
Rose was filled with inexplicable sadness as her
eyes filled with tears. As the wolf looked pointedly towards the unseen ocean, they turned to
look as well. Suddenly a streak of lightning
across the sky caught their eye. Knowing what
was coming, they stepped far away from the
wolf. Their senses alerted, they could now hear
the sound of the roaring sea, no longer was it
muffled by the thick fog. The ocean now
sounded angry, the waves rising, and then almost pausing before thundering down against
the shoreline.

Just then, a bolt of lightning from the sky
collided with another flung up from the sea. The
blaze of jagged bolts then combined into a bright
ball of pink fire which came hurtling towards
them from the center of the collision.

The wolf stepped onto the firm white sand,
stopping just before the ebb of waves that
pounded onto the beach. The pink shimmering
light that had grown out of the sky moved
through the air over the water towards them.
The bright light ignited the shoreline and then
suddenly burst apart, dissipating before them in
a dazzling shower of twinkling pink sparks that
emanated outward in a widening circle.

"What about the pendant?"

Over the noise of the storm around him, the
wolf heard the question. His head suddenly
spun towards them as he had forgotten the gem
in the fury of the battle and in the knowledge that

they were not alone. Ears flat, he stared at the pair who was still standing closely together. He then looked in the direction that the leader of the marauders had gone in his flight. His brilliant blue eyes closed as his head shook slowly side to side as if in disbelief.

The couple watched as the wolf hesitated on the edge of the hovering inferno—for it did seem to be waiting. They could see his black lips part and only they could clearly hear his disgruntled comment, "Here we go again."

When the last of the sparks died out, the sea was again peaceful and the moon played its silver light across the calm waves and the sand. It was so lovely that it was as if the sea and the moon were apologizing for the moments of sheer terror. The couple, however, wasn't looking at the charming scene around them. They stared only at the quiet, lapping waters of the sea.

The wolf was gone.

CHAPTER FOUR

Burbank — 1956

"How about if we do a special all about villains, Walt?"

"What do you mean? A movie, a cartoon, or
part of the *Walt Disney Presents* show?" the
boss asked, setting down the itinerary for his
and Roy's upcoming trip to their boyhood home
of Marceline, Missouri. The town was dedicating
a park to him and he was looking forward to the
train trip as well as seeing the old farm once
more.

"Yeah, part of the weekly show. As the
main prop, I was thinking we could use something like the Magic Mirror from *Snow White*.
You know, hanging on the wall behind you and
either talking to you or interrupting the show as
it goes along."

Walt quickly turned his attention to this new,
intriguing subject. He thought over the Mirror as

it was animated in the movie. He nodded slowly, his eyes getting that familiar far-away look in them. "Yeah," he murmured, tapping his pen on top of the forgotten train schedule. "It would be easy to build a really ornate frame. Lots of gold and shiny gemstones all over it. Have some actor's face in it, lit from the bottom to make him evil looking. Smoke and lightening swirling around inside the glass."

The aide was making notes on his sheet of paper, his lips pursed as he wrote. "We already have a working title," he added, encouraged that the boss liked their idea so far. "We came up with *Our Unsung Villains*. What do you think?"

"I like it! It's a good idea. I've always believed a good film needs a really good and evil antagonist. That way the stakes are high enough to make the audience care about the hero of the film. Why, all the way back in 1928's *Steamboat Willie* we had Peg-Leg Pete. Without a good villain it's just…it's just singing and dancing!"

"Well, we have a lot of choices for the show," the aide nodded. "We were thinking maybe you and the Mirror could get into an argument over who was the worst villain of all time and introduce them that way."

"Who did you have in mind?" Walt wanted to know, his own ideas already formulating.

"For the villains? Well, it's just a one-hour show, you know, so we figure we can fit in only four or five of them. Captain Hook is really popular, Lady Tremaine or Lucifer from *Cinderella*, the Big Bad Wolf, Stromboli, the Evil Queen—

since it is her mirror." He broke off when he saw Walt's attention wasn't on what he was saying. Used to this common occurrence, he waited patiently next to the large dark-wood desk, his eyes roaming over some of the many awards and statues Walt had been presented over the years. He idly wondered if he would be allowed to pick up the Academy Award—just to see how heavy it was, of course….

With his thoughts already on Marceline, Walt really wasn't paying attention to the aide just then. A small smile filtered across his face as he thought back to an odd event that had happened when he was, oh, probably eight years old. He and his little sister Ruthie had been left alone at the farm and were playing in the yard under his Dreaming Tree. She had spotted a huge, black animal lying over in a ditch. "Oh, Walt, I'm afraid of the big, bad wolf," Ruthie had cried, hiding behind her older brother for protection when the beast had stood up. Injured by a well-aimed rock to the head, it had whined and limped towards them. Terrified, the girl had gone running back into the house…. But it hadn't been a dog, like Walt had first thought. That was what the wolf had suggested Walt tell his sister to calm her down, to make her feel better. He had wanted the wolf to stay, but the animal had said he couldn't. That odd memory—dream?—had remained buried deep inside Walt ever since.

"Not all wolves are villains," Walt mumbled, not realizing he had said it out loud.

"True, boss, but that one in *The Three Little*

Pigs sure was. That's why we wanted to use him...."

Walt's head snapped up. The memory of that warm afternoon in Marceline faded as the aide continued talking about the wolf in *The Three Little Pigs*. The cartoon had been the thirty-sixth *Silly Symphony* they had produced and went on to win the 1933 Academy Award for the best animated film. It became so popular that there were not enough prints to meet the demand and sometimes two or three theaters had to share a print, running it back and forth between showings.   One theater in New York played the film so long that the manager took the lobby poster and added beards on the pigs. Week after week, as the cartoon kept playing, the beards got longer and longer.

Walt had felt he was trapped with the Mickey cartoons. The audience expected Mickey to act one certain way and would not take kindly to him branching out. The *Silly Symphonies* had been an experiment in different formats of cartooning.   The success of the *Symphonies* had eventually led to the studio being able to produce *Snow White and the Seven Dwarfs*.

In the original tale, the wolf had eaten the first two pigs after destroying their houses, but ended up being eaten by the third pig. Walt himself revised the tale and made sure that none of the particulars—especially the wolf—got eaten.

In the United States, the main song, "Who's Afraid of the Big Bad Wolf?," played constantly on the radio, relaying hope to all the people affected by the Great Depression. The story became so popular that Walt was asked if his four characters could be used in a dream sequence in a live-action movie being produced south of the border in Mexico. Half of the proceeds of the feature went to a special charity that provided poor children a free lunch every day of school.

"…and people are still humming that song!"

"Right," he hastily said and gave a small cough to cover his discomfiture over losing track of the conversation. Quickly getting his bearings back, Walt suggested, "How about if you take out Lady Tremaine and Stromboli and put in Br'er Fox and Br'er Bear. They could add a little comic relief. I think adding them to The Wolf, the Evil Queen, and Captain Hook should make it a good line-up."

The aide nodded, scratching out some lines and adding others. "We'll let you know when we have a script."

When the man had just reached the door, Walt called to him. "You know, maybe it would be a fun idea to have the Mirror steal the show from me and make me disappear in a huge puff of smoke. That way I can make this grand entrance later when it's time to end the show."

Nodding as he made more notes, the aide remembered to close the door behind him.

Walt sat back in his chair, thinking about all the villains they had introduced over the years. "I am called by many names," he muttered and then frowned, looking out the window over the sprawling, busy Studio. "Which movie did that come from?" It sounded like it should have been uttered by one of his evil ones. Making a mental note, he smiled, knowing it would resurface just when it was needed in a film.

England — 1289

When the last of the pink sparkles extinguished themselves in the lapping foam of the ocean, the wolf was gone. Wals and Rose knew it was time for her to get back to the castle before she was missed. There would be too many awkward questions to answer if they were found alone together so late at night. Wals would probably be thrown into the dungeon and forgotten for about, oh, a few hundred years or so, Rose figured, if she knew her father.

Throwing her hood over her hair, Rose picked up the marauding leader's forgotten sword. Now they would be doubly armed, she thought, as she hefted the steel blade, trying not to wince at the sheer weight of it. Wals smiled in the darkness. After living by herself in the frontier wilderness for so many years, he had no doubt she would be quite able to take care of herself. Gritting his teeth against the pain from his wound, they started off, retracing their steps to the castle wall and the secret entrance.

Back in his dreary rooms, Wals wrapped a torn rag around his bleeding arm after cleaning the wound the best he could. It was a long sword cut, one that would probably leave a scar he would have trouble explaining once he got home to the twenty-first century. Battle scars here in this time were a mark of honor. In his time, not so much. Thinking of germs and bacteria and possibly even gangrene, Wals idly wondered why Wolf had gone home without staying to help them or even mentioning the trip to him at all. As he saw the blood slowly seeping through the coarse fabric of the rag, all he could do was hope that the wolf would come back and at least bring along some antiseptic cream....

Using the violent storm of the vortex as a diversion, Wolf didn't actually go through the waiting blackness this time. He knew he had a pendant to recapture and didn't want it known that he was still around.

Running hard through the dark, angry surf and avoiding the brighter sand, his black coat had immediately blended into the darkness of the fog and the night. Once he was far enough away from the couple on the beach—and anyone else who might have been hovering on the fringes watching—he put his nose down and was easily able to follow the smell of the frightened horses.

From the winding, confusing trails the horses had trampled, he could tell that these riders had completely lost control over their frantic animals. Once that control had been regained, the horses and riders had finally all come together at the edge of the forest. It then became obvious to their tracker that the men were not in agreement about which way they should go. After a short distance, the hooves had churned up the mud in multiple directions showing they had simply scattered like roaches in the light, going back into whatever dark hole from which they had emerged.

Wolf, though, was only interested in one horse and one man. The leader's horse had been the last one to leave the beach and had the strongest stench of fear—both from the horse and from the rider. This was the path Wolf was following, nose down, still running and gaining ground. He might not be able to outrun a galloping horse under normal circumstances, but this stallion was scared out of its mind and running erratically. While many horses of this time were trained to face the terrors of war, the sounds and actions of battle did not usually include the smell of a full-grown angry male wolf.

Wolf caught up to the leader and his horse sooner than he anticipated. In fact, because of the swirling, misty gloom, he almost ran right into them. By then, the man had finally gained control of his beast, but the temptation to again gaze upon the pendant he had successfully stolen from the princess was too much to resist. Finding a small clearing deep in the woods and out of sight of the tallest spire of *her* castle should the fog suddenly dissipate, he reined in his heaving, lathered horse. Dismounting, he negligently threw the reins into a nearby bush and walked over to a stream of moonlight that found its way through the ever-changing fog. Reaching into his filthy shirt with his left hand, he carefully pulled the pendant out by its broken chain.

Glancing up as he heard the sound of breaking branches from some creature running through the thick underbrush, the man merely grunted, quickly turning his attention back to his prize. He wasn't interested in or worried about some fearful hind or timid rabbit fleeing from his presence. Turning the stone this way and that in the moonlight, he smiled greedily at the glittering show of red light and fire. Reaching out with a finger, he wanted to touch the blazing stone to see if what happened before would somehow, miraculously happen again.

His horse, still skittish from the terror on the beach, suddenly neighed and reared again, pulling free the loosely placed reins. With a wide-eyed snort, the stallion pivoted and broke into a frenzied run, mindless of the scratching tree limbs and brush.

Cursing at his temperamental steed, the man angrily turned. Immediately he froze. The irritation that marked his face changed into a look of terror as his hand instinctively dropped to his side. Reaching for his sword, a sinking feeling began in the pit of his stomach as he remembered it was no longer there. It had been dropped on the beach. He knew he was still armed, but it was only a short knife hidden in the top of his right boot.

The wolf, the same one that had attacked him on the beach, sea water still dripping off his black coat, slowly shook his head side to side as he saw the man's hand start to edge down toward his boot. The man's eyes widened. It was almost as if the wolf was saying no, telling the man not to even try it. Without breaking eye contact, the wolf started walking toward the man, his fangs bared in a silent snarl. Confusion play over the man's face when the animal didn't immediately leap at his throat as expected. The leader's head unconsciously followed the wolf's in a slow side to side movement and the downward motion of his right hand stopped as if he was mesmerized or in a trance. Not daring to move, he just stood there, waiting, watching as the wolf got closer and closer.

Right in front of him, feeling the animal's hot breath on his bare arms, the man closed his eyes and braced his body for the attack, knowing it was now too late for any means of defense. In that instant, he felt the hot air and a tug on his left hand and then…nothing. No sound. No heavy panting. No pain. Even the dank wet animal smell that had filled the clearing was gone.

Prying one eye open, fully expecting to see the wolf taking his final lunge, the man's mouth dropped open. He slowly came to realize that he was alone in the little meadow. He was still alive and the wolf was nowhere to be seen. "What kind of spell be this?" he murmured as he jerkily turned in a full circle like a puppet suddenly deprived of its strings.

Heart pounding and starting to hyperventilate at his miraculous escape, he ran a sweaty hand over his clammy forehead. It was then that the man realized something else—something that terrified him even more than the sudden reappearance of the wolf.

The pendant was gone. The wolf had actually grabbed the pendant from his hand. That's all the beast had wanted.

Wondering if this could possibly be what had just happened, he quickly spun side to side, checking the ground to make sure he hadn't simply dropped the gem in his fright. Falling to the floor of the forest, frantically throwing aside handfuls of leaves and dirt in an ever-widening arc, he found nothing.

She wasn't going to be pleased. His heart, which had not returned to its normal beat, pounded even faster in his chest now as he contemplated how he would explain the loss of the pendant to *her*. Even though he had secretly entertained deep, unspoken plans of keeping the cursed stone for himself and riding far, far away, he now realized that this dream, this delusion of his would never have come to pass. *She* was everywhere.

Quickly working himself into paranoia, he began imaging noises where there were none. Leaping to his feet, his mouth hanging open, the man's head jerked around the dark clearing. Yellow eyes that blinked open and closed seemed to be watching him from the dark corners of the forest. Phantom voices teased at his ears but never formed complete words. Fingers in the branches of the trees and bushes were touching his arms and his sweating face, reaching for him.

With a high scream, he broke into a panicked run, following the wide path of broken brush his horse had left behind. He ran until he was exhausted and dropped in a dead faint onto the rocky ground.

Coming to hours later, when his eyes forced themselves open, he snapped them shut again and wished for the darkness of oblivion. He found he was at the drawbridge of the Dark Castle.

There was no escape for him now. *She* was waiting.

"**D**id you have a nice rest?"

The question was pleasant enough, uttered in a voice almost kindly to indicate the concern the words should have conveyed.

Staring at the beautiful face before him, framed by a dark two-horned hat and tinted an eerie shade of green by the flaming torches surrounding the dais on which the ostentatious throne sat, the leader of the marauders knew not to be fooled. The eyes that stared through him were a clear, emotionless gray, her cheekbones high, the nose and chin sharp.

"Madam Male...," he started to explain, his hand on his heart—a heart that he sincerely hoped would still be beating within his chest when this interview was over.

On her feet faster than his eyes could follow, those gray eyes flashed at him and a narrow, tapered black fingernail pointed straight at him. "Do not call me that," she hissed. "Do not ever call me that again!"

The air crackled around him, pricking his skin in too many places to count. Wide-eyed, his bravado faltered. "I…I am sorry, Majesty. I thought that was your name."

"I am called by many names," she spat at him, her robes billowing in the sudden gust of stale air that burst through the castle, whipping up the shreds of banners high in the smoke-filled rafters above their heads.

"By which would you care to be addressed?" He was aware of a few titles that she would not know. Wisely, he kept his face devoid of any humor.

She glared at him, trying to determine if it was impertinence or stupidity that made him ask the question in such a way. Deciding it was typical of the stupidity that she always faced, she retook her throne, the winds instantly subsiding. As the tattered tapestries and pennants on the walls fell back into place, she inexplicably gave him a charming smile, one that might have been bestowed upon courtiers in a more civilized place and time.

The leader didn't know which was more terrifying—her anger or her smiles.

"I think," she started slowly, as if the question required deep thought and meditation, "I think you shall now address me as Nimue." Through her lowered lashes she watched the re-

action on the man's face. She wasn't disappointed by the look of shock as the implication
sunk in. "It is a fine name," she continued, her
fingers tracing a circle over the orb that nestled
on the arm of her throne. "A name that has been
too long absent. What do you think, Leader? Is
that satisfactory for you?"

His head briefly dipped. "Yes, madam. As
you wish." *You can call yourself Merlin himself,
but that doesn't make you so*, he dared to think
to himself.

Seeing the subtle change in his expression,
she smiled placidly again. *Let the fools think
what they want. They will know soon enough.*
"I believe you have retrieved something of mine.
It has been out of my possession far too long."
She held out an elegant hand in his direction.
When he did not advance toward her, she added
dryly, "You did do what I asked, did you not?"

Ok, this is where it gets tricky, he swallowed. "I did, Madam. My band and I tracked
the princess and the newcomer to the secluded
beach where we knew they met. He put up a
fierce resistance, more than we expected of
him."

"Let me see if I have this straight. There
was an unarmed, cowering female and an un-
tried, unknown man against...how many of you,
did you say?"

The collar of his tunic seemed to close in on
his windpipe. "We were six."

"And you had them trapped in the rocks?"

"Yes, Madam," he whispered.

"Go on with your fascinating narration. I

should be writing this down."

"We quickly disarmed the man...."

The corners of her mouth tilted slightly upwards at the change in his story, but she said nothing.

Seeing the small smile, the leader cleared his throat. "And took the pendant from the girl."

"Did she put up a fierce resistance as well?" was the next question, dripping in disdainful sarcasm. "Where was the pendant at the time?"

"Down the front of her bodice. "

"And you went after it?" The evil one suddenly gave out a loud, croaking laugh. "Oh, that must have really upset her delicate sensibilities! Wonderful! Wonderful!" She wiped a tear from the corner of her eye. "Wish I could have seen that closer," she sighed, confirming the man's idea that she did, in fact, see everything. "Well, then, hand it here, Leader. You've played with it long enough."

Her eyes narrowed at the sudden, nervous shifting of his feet and how his glance wouldn't meet hers.

"You do have the pendant, do you not?"

"Madam Nimue, you see," he started, and suddenly decided to just get it all out there and take what was surely coming. "There was this black wolf that suddenly attacked my men! They scattered like rats and left me alone to face the demon. He jumped me and my sword went flying."

"As you are standing whole in front of me, I fail to see what this has to do with my pendant. You obviously got away and...," she encouraged, the impatience starting to come through her voice.

"I made it to my horse and thundered off. I was coming straight back to you…," he broke off at the malicious look on her face.

"Then hand…me…the…pendant."

"My stallion went lame," he had a sudden inspiration and blundered on, "and I had to stop to care for him. As I was looking at his fetlock, the wolf attacked again. My horse ran off," he stopped again as she slowly descended the stairs of the dais, her face livid.

"I am happy to hear your horse recovered so quickly. I was worried." She stopped immediately in front of the man, leaning down slightly to stare into his white, sweating face. Her breath smelled of death and decay as she slowly whispered, "Where is my pendant?"

"The wolf took it."

That cursed wolf! I knew I couldn't trust him when he came to Merlin's with the girl that night. But, how? How did those two fools come to be here with the princess? I've followed that pendant through perdition and still he *keeps it from me!*

The leader of the band stood still, afraid to move or breathe. The Evil One still stood in front of him, their noses almost touching, yet she said nothing. She didn't even seem to see him any longer.

In a split second, her eyes snapped back to his. "I want that wolf."

"Yes, madam. Shall I regroup my men?"

Standing upright, she gave him a warm, unexpected grin. It froze his heart. "Yes, you do that."

She turned from him and regally climbed the stairs to retake her seat.

As the man turned, wondering at his miraculous delivery, he began to notice something odd as he walked the length of the throne room. It could have been his exhaustion, but everything around him seemed to be getting…taller and bigger. Brushing a hand across his eyes to clear them, his steps slowed. As he blinked them rapidly, he kept his eyes on the far door and the fresh, clean air outside. It should have been only a few more steps until freedom. The doorway was farther away now, the broken tiles on the floor were looming larger and larger. The columns next to him that held up the darkened ceiling were now immense in height and circumference; the ceiling itself beyond the scope of his beady black eyes.

His scream of terror turned into a high-pitched squeak as the large brown rat on the floor of the throne room scurried to the nearest, darkest hole.

"Not to worry, Leader," Nimue smiled pleasantly at the departing tail of the rodent. "I've made other plans. Oh, and that vision you saw when you dared to touch my diamond? That knighthood being bestowed *would have* been yours, had you not failed me. But," she sighed deeply, "you did."

Dark clouds gathered and swirled over the top of her decrepit castle. Lightning flashed in an otherwise clear sky. Knowing the warning signs, the villagers, far away near the fair castle of the kind King and Queen, put their heads together and murmured quietly, wondering what evil doings were next to come.

The petulant weather matched Nimue's mood at the moment. She had seen the brilliant pink display—pink of all the disgusting colors!—centuries ago when the wolf's group had disappeared under Camelot. She knew Merlin had nothing to do with it. She would have gotten that out of him at some point before she entombed him. Then, that showy entrance had happened again on the nearby shoreline. But how? She had detected something *different* about the wolf back then, but she just hadn't been able to put her finger on it.

Unable to figure out how the black wolf was able to transport himself through time, she wanted to take out her frustrations on her castle's serving minions who were always cowering at the edges of the room—only they had been smart enough to flee when they saw the bold leader reduced into a filthy rat.

Glancing around at the huge, dismal, empty room, she observed, "Perhaps they aren't so stupid after all." With a half-smile, she sighed, "It's getting harder and harder to find obedient minions these days. The forces of evil aren't what they used to be in the good old days."

Turning her attention back to the problems

at hand, Nimue looked deeply into the greenish orb glowing at her fingertips. "I see you, man," she muttered to the image of Wals practicing with his sword behind his lodging place. He had just gracefully pivoted and struck off a branch of the nearby tree. "Yes, keep practicing. I think you just found out that real swords fight back much better than trees and bushes," she chuckled. "Now, where is your companion? Ah, there he is, sitting and watching you. My, he does look amused, doesn't he?"

The image faded as her slender finger left the orb. "Now that I know where you are, wolf, I can proceed."

She swept out of the throne room and headed for the barracks of her men. Stepping over and around the broken pieces of furniture and fallen masonry, Nimue muttered, "I really need to get a maid in here."

A crockery jug was hastily hidden from view when the door of the barracks suddenly burst open. The thick smell of ale hung in the air. Nimue surveyed the blurry eyes and stupid grins on the faces of the dregs of society that faced her. Her gray eyes rolled briefly. "Well, you get what you pay for." She raised her glowing staff and banged it sharply on the stone floor of the room. When the inhabitants groaned and held their hands to their ringing ears, she said quietly, "Now that I have your attention, *men*," she smiled, knowing some of them were and some of them were not, "I have a job for you. Perhaps you have heard about the recent failure of the leader to perform admirably?" She broke off and looked around at the faces that had lost some of their drunken stupor.

Realizing she was expecting an answer, they all nodded slowly, wary now.

"Ah, yes, bad news does travel fast, does it not? Well, I have a wolf to catch—and, I have found, if I want something done, I need to do it myself."

A small sense of relief seemed to flow from one man to the next. It sounded as if she would be gone for a time and they could finally relax.

She turned to go and smiled to herself as she heard the collective sigh behind her. "Oh, yes, I forgot," she claimed, turning back. "You," she pointed at one large, oafish brute. In front of their eyes, he instantly reverted to his original form—a mottled timber wolf. "And you and you," she continued around the room until only a few humans were left standing, surrounded as they were by a pack of lean, snarling wolves. As the pack eagerly circled her, she cried out delightedly, "Now there is a beautiful sight! Come with me, my pets! We have a wolf to catch." She gave a grand, dramatic gesture with her hands, her robes flowing around her. When the robes settled, the largest wolf of them all stood in the middle of the pack. Beautiful gray fur covered her muscular body and sharp gray eyes looked around the room. "To the forest!"

She led the group in a dead run out of the castle and down the steep mountainside. Tirelessly they all ran, fueled by the spell and the spirit of evil. Straight towards the village they headed, scattering frightened denizens of the woods and stampeding cattle as they continued through the inhabited valley nestled under the protecting walls of the fair castle.

Nose in the air, Wolf had sensed the approach of the pack. He knew they were wolves and that they were coming fast. And…he knew they were coming for him. With a parting warning yell, "Get in the house!" to Wals, he turned and plunged into the thickest part of the trees.

When the following pack easily picked up his trail, Wolf tried to lose them with a twisting, erratic path. He leaped to the tops of huge boulders in an attempt to end his scent. From there he would jump onto a large tree branch and crash into the nearby river, swimming to the opposite side. But, whatever he did, they followed—unceasingly, unerringly. She seemed to anticipate his next move and follow his every step. Even when Wolf did a sweeping turn and doubled back on his own trail, she followed.

For hours the chase continued. Wolf was beginning to feel the effects of the long run and the strain. But, he knew she and her followers would never tire.

He was thinking about opening a portal, any portal that might be near, and escaping that way. He could always come back. But, that would leave Wals and Rose to face her anger alone. They didn't know where he had hidden the pendant. Nimue would not accept that answer, he knew. No, he couldn't leave them.

In his contemplation, he got careless and

missed the turn he should have made. Caught in a narrow ravine, the surrounding boulders were too tall for his leaps and the sides were too steep for his claws to get to the top. Hearing the sounds already behind him, Wolf slowly turned, head down to face the onslaught of fangs and claws that would be on him in an instant.

Only he didn't face a pack of wolves. Nimue stood behind four of her strongest men as they hurled a weighted net over the snarling wolf. With nowhere to escape, he crouched down to lessen the impact as the heavy ropes and stone anchors landed on top of him. It was so heavy he couldn't even lift his head to snap at the hands that slid long poles through the mesh. The men grunted at his sheer weight as the poles were placed on their shoulders and the wolf hung swaying in defeat between them.

In silence they trod back to the Dark Castle, their triumphant leader, the Evil Fairy, ahead of them all.

Flanked by a row of sharp spear points, the net was removed from the exhausted Wolf. He had not been allowed to sleep or eat for two days. Knowing his defenses would be at their lowest, Nimue had finally called him into her presence.

"Welcome to my humble castle," she smiled broadly, throwing her hands out. "I am so glad you could join us, wolf. May I offer you some water?" She clapped her hands and a terrified lad of about fourteen scurried out of the darkness with a bucket.

Wolf saw the look of fright on the boy's face and refrained from snapping at him. He could tell the boy was here about as willingly as he himself. Turning his head away from the much-needed water, the wolf stared defiantly back at the woman as the boy vanished back into the depths of the shadows that lurked everywhere in this castle.

Nimue appeared shocked. "What? You aren't thirsty?" Her eyes narrowed and she spat at him, "Then perhaps this is more to your liking!"

The green orb glowed and the water in the bucket was changed into bubbling, spitting acid. Wolf snorted at it and kicked it away with his hind leg. The acid spilled out of the bucket and ran towards his guards who screamed and backed away from the red, hissing flow.

She looked surprised at the insolence, and then began to chuckle. That chuckle quickly turned into full laughter. Her men looked at each other, unsure of what they should do. A couple of them gave a nervous laugh at their mates who were still dancing away from the spilled acid.

"Oh, wolf," she sighed, when she got control of her emotions, "I can see that we would get along famously if you would just let us. You see," she added confidentially, leaning away from her throne, "I know you are more than just an ordinary wolf. I also know you can talk, only you have been too stubborn, or perhaps afraid to do so. So, I give you permission to speak freely," she waved a regal hand in his direction.

Wolf sat on his haunches and tilted his head at her, his blue eyes steady. *No chance, lady*, he thought to himself.

"Come now, it is all right. We all know it is true, wolf." She waited for his mouth to open; she was watching the muscles play around his face. When she saw his black lips part, she smiled triumphantly.

Only, Wolf just let his tongue loll out of his mouth. Rather undignified, but that was all she was going to get.

He could see her gray eyes change in anger. "Very well," she snapped, "if that is the way you want to play it." Her index finger stroked the waiting orb as her eyes closed.

Seeing the gesture, the sword points around him wavered as the guards fell back a few steps. They would have fled the room, but they didn't dare.

Coming warily to his feet now, Wolf's eyes narrowed as he waited. He saw a streak of green light curl upwards from the throne and slowly snake its way over to him. Around his body it swirled. Tensed, waiting, Wolf felt nothing. He slowly relaxed his stance. Thinking quickly about his options, he decided it would be better for all if he let her think the spell actually worked. He figured, correctly, that the next attempted spell might be a lot worse. He closed his eyes so she wouldn't see them rolling upwards in derision.

"What is it you would like me to say, madam?"

The deep voice coming from the beast

shocked the guards surrounding him. The spears were quickly lowered into place as their eyes widened in fear. They apparently had no memory of their own transformation just days before.

Nimue, on the other hand, was delighted. "I made an animal talk! Oh, imagine the possibilities," she crowed. "I should have tried this years ago with my poor Diablo." She glanced out the glassless window at the frozen, stone raven that used to be her pet. Stuck forever on the turret, it was frozen as if in mid-flight, its mouth open for a warning that never came. That malicious Blue Fairy had done that.

Whatever you want to think, witch, Wolf thought to himself. He would like to be around when she tried it again, over and over, and failed each time! But, then again, perhaps it would be better if he wasn't.

She turned back at his amused chuckle. "Something you would like to share with the group, wolf?"

"No, not particularly. But, thank you for asking."

Her gray eyes narrowed. "Do not push the limits of my good temper, wolf!" she warned. "I can just as easily turn you back into a common brute."

"My apologies." *When pigs fly.*

"I think you know why I brought you here, wolf. I want what is mine. It has been out of my possession far too long. You know that of which I speak?"

"Yes, Nimue."

"Ah, you do know who I am. Interesting. And you will take me to it?"

"No, I shall not."

There was a grunt of "ooh" that went through the surrounding men at his words. Again they held themselves back from leaving their posts. *At least her anger won't be directed at me this time*, was each of their thoughts.

Nimue calmly stood from her throne and descended the four steps. She seemed to be in deep thought. Her men unconsciously leaned away from her as she paced back and forth in front of the waiting wolf. "Well, I see we are at an impasse. I want my pendant back and you do not wish to give it to me." She stopped directly in front of Wolf and looked down at him, grudgingly respecting the fact that he did not cower. "Is that how you see it as well?"

"Yes, madam. That is a succinct summary."

She snorted. "You sound more and more like that blasted Archimedes. But, yes, that is where we stand. Unless," she stopped, and tapped a finger on her black lower lip, "unless you decide to join my happy little group here," she declared, waving a hand around the men-at-arms, each of whom winced as her fingers flew past their position. "Think of what fun we could have together! The pendant would be shared equally with all."

Wolf bowed his head briefly. "Again, I must decline the honor."

She spun on him before he had time to react. Her specter pointed at him, its tip glowing with prickling heat. The black lips formed soundless words as Wolf was bombarded with unseen forces. Too much for him, not even knowing how to resist, the evil penetrated his body and his mind. Scenes of darkness and pain played through his brain, overshadowing his memories and thoughts of friendship and love and family. Try as he might, already exhausted, he just couldn't fight off the intrusion. He couldn't regain his own self. Flung to the cold stone floor, he lay panting from the exertion.

Seeing a film darken his blue eyes, Nimue smiled smugly. "Now, let's talk about my pendant," as she retook her throne and settled into its depths.

Wolf staggered into the small room at the back of the tavern. "There you are," Wals smiled. "I wondered what happened to you after that pack ran you off. You've been gone for days." He broke off at the lowered head and narrowed eyes. "You okay, Wolf? You look a little beat up."

Fighting every new instinct deep within him, Wolf could only snap out, "Come with me. Quickly, Wals."

"You don't sound very good, Wolf. What's wrong?"

A growl forced itself out of his mouth and he had to snap his mouth shut. "I can't explain it. Just come."

The wolf blended into the darkness of the forest and followed the path to the sea. Wals looked around. "Hey, this is where I met with

Rose. We haven't been back here since we were attacked."

"Quit talking!" Wolf yelled at him.

At the surprised, hurt look on Wals' face, Wolf shook his head. "I'm sorry. I can't help it. I...I'm supposed to kill you now, Wals. That's what I've been sent to do."

Wals gave him a big grin. "Who sent you? King Stefan? I know Rose's father wasn't too happy with her sneaking out like she did that night."

Wolf picked up a piece of driftwood in his mouth and snapped it easily in his jaws. "This is supposed to be your neck. No, it isn't the King. It's Nimue."

"What?" Wals was shocked. "That...that was centuries ago! How did she get here?"

"She follows the pendant. She will always follow the pendant until she gets it back."

Wals held up his empty hands. "But I don't have it. You know that. You saw that burly guy take it from Rose. I tried everything I knew to stop him," he broke off, shrugging his shoulders, angry at his failure to protect Rose.

"Wals, Nimue forced me to join her side. I...she put me under some kind of spell. It is taking everything I have to keep from leaping at you as I have been commanded."

"You're serious." Wals' eyes got big as the truth of the situation began to sink in. Wolf was acting far too different for him not to believe. "What do you want? Why did you bring me here? You can't kill me. I'm your friend."

Wolf snarled and snapped at the darkness.

He was obviously fighting a powerful force attacking him from the inside. "I know you are, Wals." The film covering his eyes wavered for a moment as Wolf tried to do the decent thing, the right thing. "That's why I brought you here. You have to go back."

"Back to the castle or my room?" Wals was confused. He didn't know what Wolf meant or what he was capable of doing.

"No. Back to the twenty-first century. You have to bring back help. I...I just can't fight this off by myself. I need help."

"Who? Who can help with this?"

"Mato," Wolf said, almost in a whisper as the evil in him surged against the thoughts of family and friends.

"Your brother? How can I get to him? He is back on Tom Sawyer's Island in 1817!"

"There is a way."

"How? The portals only open with your howl. That much I do know."

"In my locker. In the back there is a recorder. Get Lance to help you. Use that recorder, or I am as good as dead," he panted, hopeless.

"Wolf, I can't leave you here like this. There must be something I can do."

"If you stay, I won't be able to fight this spell any longer and...I...will...kill...you."

Wals looked quickly about. He was unarmed and only the piece of broken driftwood was near at hand. He had no delusion that the wolf was joking. He knew Wolf was totally serious. Trying to reach out to touch his friend, he quickly jerked his hand back when he saw Wolf starting to snap at him, the dark film coming back to cover his blue eyes. "Call the portal. Now, Wolf! You were always there for me and I will do everything I can to come through for you. Remember this: I will be back," Wals promised, torn by the knowledge that he wanted to help his anguished friend, but, to do so, he had to leave him in this condition.

Head back, Wolf let out an angry, anguished howl. It was different than any Wals had ever heard before. Stepping back from the divided animal, he could see the ocean start to change. The fog came very quickly this time, as if sensing the urgency, the desperation of the summons. Falling over themselves, the waves became a swirling whirlpool as lightning split the sky above them.

The electricity in the air somehow sparked the new evil deep within the wolf. In a sudden frenzy, he snarled and bit at the waves crashing onto the sandy shore. Just as the whirlpool neared the beach, Wolf began to turn on Wals, setting himself to jump at his throat. Seeing the legs bunching, Wals took the initiative and had already thrown himself into the gaping darkness.

Wolf sailed through empty air where the man stood only moments before. Turning quickly he bit at the edges of the water. Once Wals had fallen through, the yawning pit closed and sparkled out, its job was done.

Seeing he was alone and his prey had vanished, the wolf dropped into the placid, lapping water, his energy totally spent. "Hurry, Wals," he gasped, his sides heaving. "I don't know how long I can hold out."

CHAPTER FIVE

Disneyland — 2008

"**M**ommy, look! It's Prince Phillip!"

"Where, honey?" the mom asked as she peered closer through the window of wildly turning spindles inside the Sleeping Beauty Walk-through diorama. "I don't see him in here. Hey, where are you? You're supposed to stay right next to me."

Her daughter, Kyla, pulled on her arm. "No, not in there. Over there." She was still tugging on her mom, Rhea, with one hand and gesturing with the other.

Immediately reaching for her camera, Rhea's hand hesitated when she saw where her daughter was pointing. "Are you sure that's Prince Phillip?"

"Yeah! Look at the red cape and hat! Can I have a picture with him? Please!?" as she clapped her hands and jumped up and down in her excitement at seeing a real prince.

"Umm, he doesn't look very…umm…happy…. I think he's…he's sleeping, Kyla. Let's go back outside. Your dad is waiting for us with little Daisy. I…I think I hear her crying," as she looked back at the figure sprawled out on the floor and quickly grabbed the seven-year-old's hand. "Let's not bother the prince right now, sweetie. Come on, we need to hurry."

Pulling the disappointed Kyla down the last flight of stairs with the girl's mumbled, "I don't hear Daisy crying," they exited the Castle and practically ran to their waiting family. Standing in the shade near the Castle Heraldry Shoppe, casually pushing a huge stroller back and forth in a soothing rhythm to keep the baby asleep, Rhea's husband wondered about the concerned look on his wife's face. He had just been watching the "virtual" tour of the Walkthrough in the special room on the ground floor. This room had been set up for those who aren't able to navigate all the stairs—like the disabled guests and those with baby strollers—and showed each of the animated dioramas as it told the story of the Sleeping Beauty. He couldn't remember any scene that would have alarmed either his wife or his daughter. However, after another quick glance at the look on Kyla's face, it was apparent she was pouting rather than upset. After the mother's disgusted whispers of explanation—most of them centering around the word "drunk"—the dad glanced upwards at the towers of Castle, the ghost of a guy-smile playing across his face. Leading the way, Rhea hoped to divert her daughter's attention by getting them all around the far corner of Fantasyland as quickly as possible. Once in the line for the Alice in Wonderland ride with its colorful caterpillar-shaped vehicles and elevated track running back and forth over huge Wonderland-style leaves, there were plenty of distractions—from the towering peak of the Matterhorn with its shrieking bobsled riders and the occasional Monorail gliding by to the neighboring lantern-covered, twirling Mad Tea Party. When Rhea pointed out the laughing costumed characters of Alice and the Mad Hatter as they spun by on the teacup ride, Kyla, whose attitude at that point was mirrored by the expression on the face of each caterpillar as it loaded the next group of guests—that of arm-folded obstinacy—quickly forgot the sleeping prince.

"Ooooooh, I've gotta quit doing that," Wals grumbled as he felt to see if his head was still attached to his body. When he remembered the sight of the leaping wolf, his hand quickly dropped to his neck. Only able to get one eye to open, he checked his fingers for blood. Seeing none, he gave a deep sigh of relief and tried to get into a more comfortable position to go back to sleep.

As Wals irritably shifted his body this way and that, he began to realize he just wasn't able to get comfortable. As a matter of fact, his bed was quite hard and cold. He thrust out a hand

and encountered only a cold stone floor and what felt like a solid wall instead of the scratchy woolen blanket that covered his rush-filled bed. The sound of voices, soft feminine voices, now came to his ears. *The women in the tavern never sounded like that.* These soft sounds overshadowed the distant echoes of the maelstrom that had unceremoniously spit him out into the darkness.

Alarmed now, his head shot up and an instant wave of vertigo brought his knees up to his chest. Fighting against the feeling, he knew he had to figure out where and *when* he was—for he knew he wasn't alone.

"You'd think I'd be used to this by now," he muttered in a voice too low to be heard clearly. Footsteps could clearly be heard running away from him. "Get a grip, Davis," he told himself, placing a steadying hand on the cool, solid surface of the wall. "Bricks, they feel like bricks. Okay, I'm in something made of bricks," he tried talking himself through the confusion swirling through his mind. "Hope it's not the castle oven.... Open your eyes," he had to command himself.

A soft green glow welcomed his glazed eyes and soft violin music he hadn't heard before permeated the background. He looked upwards at the limp colorful pennants. "A castle. Ok, focus." Relief surged through Wals as he finally realized he was in the Sleeping Beauty Walkthrough at the Park, and, from the depth of details within the glowing windows, he knew it was in his proper time period. "I'm home."

At the sound of more voices coming up the stairs and approaching his location, he also came to realize that the Walkthrough apparently was now open to the public. "How long have I been gone?" When the shaky hand he ran through his hair encountered a felt hat, he tore it off his head and then looked down the length of his body. His borrowed costume was quite torn, filthy and bloody, definitely not up to the dress-code standards of a cast member being seen by the public.

Straightening out his legs and wincing, he could only guess that he must have tumbled down a flight of stairs when he came out of the time vortex. Getting slowly to his feet, his only thought was to get out of the Castle and out of sight as quickly as possible. Knowing there was a cast member-only door just around the corner from the exit to the Walkthrough, he hurried down the rest of the stairs, hoping all the time that he would not encounter any guests eager for a picture. Since it was rare for one of the Princes to come out for Meet-and-Greets so they could pose for pictures and sign autographs for the guests, Wals understood the need for him to keep a low profile in his current condition and go find Lance.

Holding the tattered cape tightly against his blood-stained, torn shirt, he emerged out into the bright sunlight.

And straight into the waiting arms of Security.

"**K**eep smiling, Wals, that's a good prince," Lance muttered through his own smile. "Wave," he encouraged the dazed Wals as they briskly walked from the side exit of the Castle, past Snow White's Grotto, and across the entrance of Tomorrowland—the shortest distance to the backstage area where the cast members' lockers were located behind the eastern side of Main Street. Unlike their sister Park in Florida, Disneyland had no underground tunnels in this section. Protectively surrounded by a force of security guards led by Lance, Wals managed to smile and wave while keeping his damaged arm hidden by the disreputable cape.

When Security had gotten a call from a guest alerting them of an apparently drunk Prince Phillip sleeping it off inside the Castle, Lance had immediately sprung into action, figuring at least part of the missing group might be back from wherever it was that they had gone. Choosing three other security guards known for being able to keep a confidence, they literally ran to the Castle, knowing whoever they would find would need to get out of sight as quickly as possible. Since there had been no mention in the call of any naked man, Lance silently wondered what had happened to his friend and security partner, Wolf. There would be time enough for questions once Wals was safely out of sight and cleaned up. He looked like he had been on the losing end of an intense fight.

Once the whitewashed cast member only gate just past the First Aid station nestled behind the Star Tours attraction closed securely behind them, Lance gave a dismissing nod to the other men. Without so much as a curious look or question for Wals, they told Lance they would see him later and headed back to their previous patrols.

Now sitting alone in the cast member lounge, Lance handed the returned traveler a cold bottle of water. Taking it, Wals looked perplexed as if he was trying to decide whether he should drink it or pour it over his head. After a few moments of staring at the clear bottle, he decided to drink it and, eyes closed, sighed deeply as the cool, clean liquid poured down his parched throat. *Ah, now that's how water's supposed to taste*, he thought with a small smile. *And there's nothing floating in it.*

Lance patiently waited until Wals finished the water before venturing to ask any questions. "Are you all right?" seemed an appropriate place to start.

Wals could see the security guard eyeing the blood on his shirt and the long, jagged rip in the fabric. "Not sure how to answer that," Wals answered with a small, mirthless laugh. His own eyes kept roaming around the familiar break room as if he couldn't believe he was actually back. The calendar on the wall kept getting a fair share of his attention, as well.

Seeing the man's worried stare at the date, Lance nodded. "Yeah, you guys have been gone for over a month. Wolf had asked us to keep the Walkthrough closed until you all got back, but," he shrugged and held up his empty hands, "time kept going by and they needed to get it finished and open in time to meet the deadline. I know Wolf was trying to prevent just the type of scene you created, but…," he finished by way of apology, bringing his hands back together as he leaned forward in his chair, "we just didn't know when you'd be back."

Wals briefly nodded that he understood. "We didn't know, either," his voice lowered, thinking back on the condition of Wolf when he had left. Realizing he couldn't just spring that on Wolf's best friend all at once, he began in a different place. "Rose did get back to her family," he explained to the patient Lance, who nodded slowly. Wals looked away and tried to figure out the words he needed. "It seemed like we came back to her time *after* the events that we are familiar with from the story. You know, the animated fairy tale…." He broke off, not knowing how much Wolf had filled his partner in regarding the details of the swan in the moat. When Lance indicated that he knew the particulars, Wals continued. "Apparently, it became known back then that the Evil Fairy hadn't died like everyone thought. Since Rose had been her initial target, the three Good Fairies took it upon themselves to send her to another place for protection. Through a couple of…umm, well, I guess they were errors on their parts, she ended up here at the only 'Sleeping Beauty's Castle' their magic spell could find, and—thanks to a kindly suggestion by one of them—she arrived here in the body of a swan. What we all *don't* understood is why their Prince Phillip disappeared at the same time Rose did." Wals held out his arms as he looked down at his costume. "And, apparently, I am not the prince. My...uh...affection for Rose wasn't taken too kindly by her family back there...." He broke off again as he gazed into the distance, thinking about the beautiful princess he had to leave behind.

Lance, immersed in the tale, was fascinated. For his own clarification, however, he backed Wals up a bit. "You said the Evil Fairy hadn't died like was portrayed in the film. Remember when you went back to Tom Sawyer's Island? Of course you do...," when Wals nodded and shrugged. "Sorry. Wolf had made the statement that the things that were being changed in Disneyland in our time were affecting the past. When pirates invaded Tom Sawyer's Island here, pirates were also invading his family's time period in the 1800's. Right? Well, could it be the same with the Evil Fairy?" He pointed in the direction of the Castle. "When the Walkthrough reopened here, that evil presence was introduced again. Could that have been what happened in Rose's time? Just like when you went back, everyone thought it was normal. Before you all left, Wolf had mentioned Rose was worried about her family."

Nodding thoughtfully, Wals silently went over the implications. "I don't know, Lance," he finally admitted. "We were so caught up in our lives trying to just survive in those primitive surroundings and time, I hadn't thought about that aspect. Well," he added with a wry smile, "*I was* trying to survive. Everyone else in the group seemed to be doing all right. That could possibly be the case. The townspeople back then *were* acting like it was just normal circumstances. I noticed that Nimue seemed to be well established in her Dark Castle, as it was spoken of in whispers. From what else I heard, it seemed as it was a distance away from Rose's castle and sounded as if Nimue had always been there. No one said anything about her coming back."

"Wait a minute. I don't know that much about the whole Sleeping Beauty time period, thing, story, whatever…, but I do know *that* name is associated with Merlin, not the princess. Wolf told us about her when you all came back from Camelot. If I remember what Kimberly told us about the Arthurian legend, she is the one who turned on him and entombed him in a tree, right?"

Wals nodded. "Tree. Crystal cave. Bottom of the ocean. Take your pick. But, yeah, she was there when we tried to take Rose back the first time and landed too far in the past at the wrong castle. It turned out to be Camelot, in King Arthur's time." Again he stopped to see if Lance knew what he was talking about.

Even though Lance had heard the same story from Wolf, he thought it was important to get Wals' version as well. There might be something extra Wals had noticed that Wolf had missed.

Getting the go-ahead from Lance, Wals continued, "Now I've seen her in both time periods and although her features seem to be altered a little, this much I know for sure—it was her. She even wants to go by her name of Nimue again and not the one usually associated with the princess. Which leads us up to the big problem I need to tell you about concerning Wolf."

By the disturbed look on Wals' face, Lance could tell something was very wrong. "Is that why he's not with you? What happened?"

Wals ran a hand through his hair and abruptly got up from his chair, limping slightly and getting more agitated as he paced back and forth across the floor. "Well, I don't know the full story. Only that Wolf came to my room at the tavern today…uh, last night…heck, I don't know when it was…but he came to my room and told me to follow him. I hadn't seen him for a couple of days, but, from what we both know about Wolf, that isn't too unusual."

Lance had to agree with that.

"He looked, well, he looked *different*," Wals grimaced, looking at the far wall for some kind of inspiration on how to describe it more clearly. He unconsciously rubbed the long scar on his arm, Lance's concerned glance following the movement. "His eyes are, you know, so weirdly blue. But then they seemed to be dull, scary even. He told me, commanded me really, to follow him to the beach where we had come out of that time thingy. He acted so *different*." Wals paused and took a deep breath before adding, "It was then that he told me he was supposed to kill me and rip out my throat."

Lance's eyebrows shot up. "Yeah, that's a little different for Wolf," he muttered, indicating for Wals to go on with his explanation.

"Yeah, at first I thought he must be kidding, but, well, you know Wolf isn't actually known for having a keen sense of humor…and I really knew he wasn't joking. Anyway, he told me Nimue had gotten to him." Wals' pacing had taken him to the far end of the break room, but he turned to face Lance before he continued. "I think he said something about being in some kind of a trance or something. I'm not sure. It's kinda a blur…. But he made it very clear that she wanted the pendant, Lance, and she knew I had it both times she encountered us. She even sent a gang of thugs to waylay Rose and me the one night we finally got to spend some time together." Wals broke off and grimaced as he rubbed the scar on his arm again. He would tell Lance about that another time. "They got the diamond, but Wolf told me later he took off after them and apparently got it back and hid it somewhere. That's when it all started to go downhill." Wals dropped heavily into a chair and impatiently waited until a fellow employee on a break got something out of the vending machine, nodded hello and left again. "I'm sure now that Nimue put some kind of spell over Wolf. It seemed like he really had to wrestle with himself to keep from tearing me apart. He had to put up an internal fight just so he could send me back here for help. Even then, he…he actually leaped at me right when I was going into the whirlpool," he stopped and ran his shaky hand over his eyes. "The last thing I heard before it all went black was his jaws snapping shut."

Lance sat back in his chair, his mouth slightly open. "Wow," he exclaimed, tapping his foot in his agitation. "That definitely isn't like Wolf. So that's why you are alone. Rose is still there, back in her own castle, right? And with her family as she should be?" To each question he received a simple nod from Wals. "And the Evil Fairy is really from decades...."

"Centuries," Wals corrected automatically.

"Centuries in the past. And when you left, Wolf was under her control. You said he asked for help?" Lance asked, holding out his hands in a futile gesture. "What help can we possibly provide for the kind of trouble or spell or whatever it is he is under? I have no idea what I can do to help him. And how did he expect you to rescue him? How are you even supposed to get back there? I assume you know where the entrance is, but we don't know how to open it. Only Wolf can do that...."

Wals just continued nodding his head. He was beginning to feel like one of those bobble-head Mickeys that were sold in the Emporium, just a little ways away on the other side of Main Street. These were all the same questions running constantly through his head, and he had no idea on how to answer any of them. "Wolf just told me to get you to open his locker and to use something in it...I think it was a recorder...to go back and get Mato, his brother. Wolf was in pretty bad shape, but I think he knew exactly what he was saying. I just don't understand how it would work, either."

Leaning forward again in his own chair, Lance frowned as he tried to piece this all together. "Okay, I do understand the 'open his locker' part. But, I don't get the rest. What recorder? Tell me again exactly how he said it," he requested.

Understanding Lance's confusion and deep concern for his missing partner, Wals again walked him through that last, mystifying encounter with Wolf. When he finished, Wals looked at the security guard and shook his head. "The way I understand it is that I am supposed to use something in Wolf's locker to open a portal—it sounds like I'll have to use it at least three times—to go back in time to Tom Sawyer's Island and get his brother, open it again to bring him back here, and then take Mato through the Castle portal to where Wolf is," as he ticked them off with his fingers.

Lance let out a low whistle. "Yeah, that's how I see it, too." It was Lance's turn to run a hand through his hair, pushing his white security hat off-kilter. "Unbelievable. Wow, what do you think? Do you think you can do it?"

"I *have* to, Lance. There's no way I can leave Wolf back there like that. I saw that it was going against every grain in his body to act the way he did. I *have* to help him. And, if I have to go through that nightmare three more times and bring a Lakota brave with me, I am going to do it! That's all there is to it!" Wals declared, pounding a frustrated fist on the tabletop.

The two men sat silently for a couple of minutes, each with their own troubled thoughts on their missing friend. When Wals started talking again, it was as if he was picking up the threads of a previous thought. "It's a good thing I already have a history with Wolf's brother. Mato and I traveled together to what was left of the mining town, Rainbow Ridge, to bring the doctor back to camp with us. But, with his limited English and my very limited Lakota…," he broke off, shaking his head slowly side to side. He didn't even seem to be talking to Lance any more, just voicing the many thoughts that were spinning through his mind. "Even if I *do* make it back there in one piece, I don't know how I can convince Mato to come with me."

Lance just nodded as Wals continued talking. "I want to go with you." The decision came out of the blue and Lance's words surprised both of them.

With a worried look on his face that was etched so deep it seemed to be normal now, Wals just silently stared at him.

But, thinking back over what he had just said, Lance knew he meant it and added, "I want to help my partner. I have to do something, Wals."

It hit him with a feeling of relief that he wasn't in it alone, and Wals really did appreciate his offer. "Thanks, Lance, but I don't think you should. You're a family man now, with another one on the way. You…you don't know what it's like. It isn't safe—in either time period I have to go to. Besides," he suddenly grinned, "you look more like the real Prince Phillip than I do. You

might end up having to fight a duel for Rose—
with real swords, I might add!" rubbing his arm
again.

Lance gave a half-grimace. "Yeah, I don't
see that going over very well with my wife."

Wals went over to the other man and
slapped him on the shoulder. "Thanks for the
offer, though. I know Wolf would appreciate it,
too. Can you open his locker now? I'd like to
see what the heck it is that I'm supposed to find
and work with. Maybe after that we can think
about what we have to do and make some definite plans."

Being one of the Guardians of Walt and
having access to literally every part of Disneyland, Lance was able to use his master key to
open the missing security guard's locker. As the
gray metal door swung open, both men just
stood there, silently staring at the insides.

"How can a man who has worked here for
over fifty years have so little in his locker?"

Wals slowly shook his head in disbelief.
"I've been here for only about six years and I
need a shovel to get to the back of mine."

"Yeah, I know," Lance laughed. At the
sharp look he received, he held up his hands.
"Hey, Wolf told me. He said he had to go
through your locker to bring back something to
jog the memory you lost on Tom Sawyer's Island. He mentioned he had lots of choices."

The nametag Wolf had chosen had done
the trick and had proven to be a touchstone for

Wals to help keep his tenuous grasp on his real identity. Thinking about the confusion, his hand went up to stroke the oval tag that should have been attached to his shirt. Not finding it, he made a mental note to retrieve it before the day was over. Now, just as importantly, he needed to find something in this almost-empty locker that would likewise help their friend and co-worker.

"What's his apartment like?" Wals asked out of the blue. "Is it like this? Or does he live in a house? I've never gone over."

Lance indicated the sparse locker with his chin. "About like this. Wolf isn't given much for collecting."

"Well, unless I can somehow use one of the uniforms hanging here, we'd better see what else we can find. You're taller. You take the upper shelf and see if there is any kind of recorder up there."

Lance counted off the things he went through. "Comb, one extra nametag, pen, flashlight batteries, and a rock. What are you finding?"

"Did you say rock? Umm, shoes and socks," came the muffled answer. "Unless there is a secret door…."

"Do you see any initials, like **W E D**?" Lance gave a secret, unseen smile.

"No, let me check over here. Am I supposed to?"

"No, just asking. Keep looking. There's nothing of use here on top."

"Well, there's nothing down here either. Wait a minute, I knocked over one of his shoes."

Wals stood up with a highly polished black shoe in his hand. "This was in the back corner and felt heavier than the rest of them when I moved it. Look what I found inside." He held up a small tape recorder.

Lance took it from him as a smile lit his face. "So, let's see what words of wisdom our mutual friend thought to leave us." He handed it back to Wals. "You do the honors."

With a nod and a glance around to see that they were still alone, Wals hit the Play button. After a few seconds of static-filled silence, a lone howl played over the speaker. Another one, only slightly different, sounded next.

The two men looked at each other. "Wasn't expecting that. Do you think that will call the portal? Is that how he does it? I've never heard him do it."

Wals nodded and sounded far away. "Yeah, that sounded like it usually does. Only, the last time? When he sent me back? It…it sounded like his heart was broken and bleeding."

Lance was silent for a few moments. When he spoke again, his voice was quiet. "If he was going through what you said he was going through, then it probably was."

Nodding again, Wals slid the little recorder into the pocket of his jeans. He had gratefully taken a shower and hastily patched up his arm in the men's locker room. After changing clothes, he was again in his normal street clothes. "There's only one way to find out if this will work. I'll have to use it on the Frontierland

River and see what happens."

Lance looked him over. "Well, even though you look better than you did when you got here, you still look exhausted. You should get that arm looked at and you need to rest."

Stubbornly shaking his head, Wals told the Guardian, "Wolf wouldn't rest if I needed help. I'm going tonight. We'll need to make sure I have enough time for this thing to work, if it does work. Do you have any idea when the workers will be clear of the River?"

"Don't worry about that. Kimberly will shut it all down for you. Go rest!" Lance urged.

Wals stared at him for a minute. He was beginning to see more clearly how it had all worked for Wolf, how they always seemed to have an empty part of the Park in which to do what they needed to do. There was more of a connection here between Lance and Wolf than just friendship and partners. Looking down at his clothes, he sighed. He had just felt clean again, human again. "Last time I went back to Wolf's time, I was working on the canoes and hadn't changed out of my costume. It seemed to be accepted back then just fine. I'll need another canoe costume…and I need to remember to bring this nametag with me."

Lance was picking up his walkie-talkie. "Anything else?"

"Some quick lessons in Lakota would be helpful," he only half-kidded. "Mato didn't know much English when I was there last."

Giving a quick laugh, Lance told him, "You should take my son Peter. Uncle Wolf was teaching him quite a bit. Really pissed off my mother! Which, of course, was a bonus all in it-self."

"How old is Peter?"

"Six, going on twenty-three."

Wals grimaced. "Again, I don't think it would go over too well with your wife."

Lance sighed. "Probably not. Even though Peter would love it. He's always begging Wolf to take him on an 'adventure,' as he calls them."

"I'll leave that between you and Wolf," Wals was smart enough to recognize. "Tonight around ten, then?"

Lance checked his watch and nodded. "I know you won't sleep before you go, but at least get something to eat first. I'd offer to take you to the house until you are ready to leave, but we don't have enough time."

When Wals headed off to the Costume De-partment, Lance made a couple of calls. He knew Wals would neither rest nor eat before he tried to open the mysterious portal. His own stomach knotted with worry, Lance's last call was to his wife Kimberly to apprise her of the lat-est situation. He wisely didn't mention the fact that he wanted to go along with Wals to help and that he had actually offered to do so.

Standing alongside a bobbing canoe, Kim-berly and Lance Brentwood watched as Wals untied the small boat and pulled it to the end of the wooden dock. They were at the far end of the Hungry Bear Restaurant in Critter Country, on the lower level near two canoes that always waited behind a locked gate. These were smaller canoes than the ones used by guests on the Davy Crockett's Explorer Canoes. Those larger, thirty-five-foot-long fiberglass crafts held a total of twenty people and required the guests to paddle the canoe themselves as the only means of propulsion. The canoe that Wals was taking was reserved for personnel for any emergency or need that might come up along the River.

It was quiet now in that frontier-themed part of Disneyland. The nine o'clock showing of *Fantasmic!* was already over, so the rafts and ships that were used in the show had already gone past their location and were now docked until the next day started anew. Tom Sawyer's Island had closed at dusk as usual. The Canoe ride hadn't run that day at all. Kimberly had to close the popular Splash Mountain because the exit of the ride came out above their location, higher up in Critter Country at the furthest western point in the Park where guests could walk. The steam train was also shut down for approximately another half hour. The one section of the River Wals needed would be visible to any alert passenger when the train puffed past that part of Frontierland just after leaving the New Orleans Station.

"You have everything you need?" Lance asked as Wals tossed another paddle—hopefully for Mato to use—into the canoe.

"I have the recorder. There isn't much else," he told them shortly, betraying his nerves.

Kimberly, who had been quiet as the prepa-
rations were made, spoke up. "What if the
recorder gets wet on the way back? How will
you use it later?"

Both men turned to stare open-mouthed at
her. They hadn't thought of practical things like
that. At their silence, she held up a second
recorder. "Maybe we should make a back-up?"
she offered with a small smile.

Lance gave her a quick kiss on the cheek.
"That's why you make the big bucks, sweetheart.
That's a good idea. Toss me the recorder, Wals.
I can do that easily enough."

As he pushed the button, the wolf cry was
easily heard. Even before he could push the
Record button on the second machine, the water
in the River started to change.

"Lance!" Kimberly pointed, intrigued.
"It's…it's working!"

Seeing the fog start to creep over the far
trees and feeling the wind pick up, Wals jumped
into the small canoe and held out his hand.
"Throw it back! Lance, hurry! I've got to get out
there! It's…it's coming too fast."

Lance started running towards the end of
the dock even as the recording was being finished. With a careful toss, he sent the original
player over to Wals.

Jamming it in his pants pocket, Wals aimed
the canoe towards the center of the River. He
knew the drill. He had to line the little boat up
with the center of the swirling waters that were
getting more and more agitated. He could hear
Lance yelling something out to him, but couldn't

hear it over the wind that was now blasting across the water and the distant thunder that was getting closer and closer. Head down, he dug the paddle in with all his might and closed his eyes as the all-too-familiar, terrifying blackness opened up in front of him.

Back on the dock, Lance and Kimberly huddled together, drenched by the waves flying over the usually placid dock.

"Well, we know it works," he smiled gamely as another wave crashed over them. "You should have stayed back, Kimberly. You're soaked!" Lance had to basically yell into her ear.

"No," she shouted back. "I wanted to see this. My father told me all about the time Wolf went back to take Doctor Houser to safety. He and Walt were watching the lights of the storm from inside Walt's apartment. From what he said, it must have looked just like this!"

Lance had known her father, The Blond Haired-Man, only briefly before he died at the hands of Daniel Crain. He kept forgetting the long history the family had with Walt and his Hidden Mickey quests. The second quest Lance had gone on had begun with that man's daughter as his helper and had ended with them falling in love. Her father had seen something special in the troubled Lance and had known he could be the next Guardian to work alongside his daughter and Wolf to protect the legacy Walt left behind.

Giving her a small smile as they were assaulted by the wind and water, he told her, "I keep forgetting Wolf is that old."

Whatever his wife would have answered him was cut off. He saw her eyes widen and his head whipped around to the River in time to see the canoe—and Wals—completely swallowed by the whirlpool. One moment he was there and the next moment he was simply gone.

Lightening flashed all around the twisting vortex and a blinding array of pink sparkles surrounded the dark opening.

Fascinated, Lance and Kimberly watched open-mouthed as the pink cloud hovered over the emptiness until, suddenly, it broke away and headed straight at them.

With a scream that could have come from either of them, Lance threw his arms around his wife and pushed with his legs, trying to leap out of the way of the rapidly nearing fireball. Five months pregnant, Kimberly instinctively wrapped her arms around her stomach as she turned in Lance's arms, causing him absorb the brunt of the fall.

In less than a heartbeat, its job accomplished, the pink fizzled and went out. The waiting hole in the River filled with placid green water and the fierce winds died. As the mysterious fog finally cleared, the small wooden dock with the missing canoe was again shrouded in the night's darkness.

CHAPTER SIX

Disneyland — 1956

"**D**isneyland has become a Southern California institution and an international attraction. To keep our promise that Disneyland will continue to expand, there will be new attractions and new enjoyment so people will continue to find happiness and knowledge."

With this statement, Walt Disney began the second year of his theme park. The guests were thrilled that there were so many new additions in that second, pivotal year. Main Street U.S.A. got a new motorized Fire Wagon and a bright red Horseless Carriage that carried guests to the iconic Castle. The new Skyway opened to give people a birds-eye view of Fantasyland and Tomorrowland—and a rest for their tired feet. In Tomorrowland, the bright, individually controlled AstroJets provided a thrilling spin through space in the area once occupied by the flag-filled Court of Honor. If the speed of that new ride was too much for junior astronauts, the Junior Autopia was now open near Fantasyland. Frontierland would expand to include another train ride—the Rainbow Caverns Mine Train through the charming mining town of Rainbow Ridge, the Rainbow Desert and the beautifully-colored and, aptly-named, Rainbow Caverns.

Just past Swift's Chicken Plantation House, the Indian Village was expanded and moved farther out along the Rivers of America, as the Frontierland River was more commonly called. The lonely Settler's Cabin over on the sparsely decorated Tom Sawyer's Island was now ablaze in fire as the alleged perpetrators watched from the opposite shore. The Indian War Canoes, with an authentic Native American as the front bowman and back sternman, allowed guest to experience an exciting adventure along the churning rapids of forest waterways. These first canoes were thirty feet long and made out of varnished wood. The warlike risings that were added to the front and back, and then covered with canvas, gave the canoes a textured birch bark appearance.

The Native American village was a grouping of tan and white decorated teepees with sawed-off logs spaced around the painted dance area on which the dancers sat waiting for their turn. These tribal performers led the watching audience—and any children who wanted to help participate—through six different dances: The War Dance, The Shield and Spear, The Eagle, The Zuni-Comanche, The Mountain Spirit, and The

Friendship Dance. The dancers' beautiful beaded costumes and feathered headdresses swayed and fluttered in the breeze, while the silver bells attached to their ankles sounded out the stirring beat. Displays and practice rituals that had been passed down generation to generation were also shown through the village, all watched over by a huge stuffed buffalo penned at the entrance.

Even with the opening day having had so many problems—so many that it was dubbed "Black Sunday"—guests continued to pour into the Park. By the summer of 1956, the Park welcomed its four-millionth guest.

The Island — 1817

The Shaman looked up from the four braves that were seated on the rocky ground in front of him. He had been telling them the time-honored story of how the flute had come to their people when a sudden, familiar blast of wind nearly pushed the wolf headdress he wore off his head. Clutching the worn skin closer to his body as the air suddenly turned cold, he quickly dismissed three of the curious men and called the fourth, his son, to his side. Mato, his blanket—painted with his guide The Bear—threatening to fly into the nearby River, remained behind. Standing a little closer to the back of the rocky overhang, they were somewhat more protected from the elements as they waited for what they knew was coming.

"Misukala ki." *My brother.* Mato smiled as an empty canoe floated by on its side. The turbulent weather had abated as quickly as it came and now they were anxiously watching its after-effects.

The Shaman merely grunted as he watched the canoe flounder on the far bank of the River. It wasn't the same one in which he had sent his son and friends through the storm. He had really liked that canoe.... He gave a toss of his chin, indicating the small boat which had sunk almost out of sight. "You'd better go find him. These passings are taking more of a toll on him each time." As Mato turned to go, his father called after him, "He might not remember who he is. Beware the teeth."

Mato didn't need the reminder. His brother Wolf sometimes lost some of his identity when he was transformed into a wolf in the swirling storm. Wolf had turned on him more than once.

The Cooking Woman looked up from the lesson she was giving one of her daughters as Mato ran by at a steady pace. *Wolf has been gone too long*, she thought with a smile. *It will be good to have Tahca's son back again*. She instructed the girl to add more vegetables to the ever-bubbling pot over the fire.

Stopping every now and then to listen, Mato couldn't hear any movement in the forest that should not be there. Sumanitu Tanka, or Wolf, was usually groaning by now as he regained consciousness. Plus, Mato could normally locate his brother simply by the smell of his wet fur. Chuckling to himself, he passed the log that jutted out over the flowing, green River. A fishing line was always attached to that log. He and his brother—and now his own son, Igmutaka, or Otter—used to come out and squat down, peering into the water to see if any fish took their bait, the village dog watching over them.

Across the wide River, a lone cabin stood. It was empty now that the wiya Rose had left with Wolf and his friend Wals. Her brown mare Sukawaka still stood patiently in the small paddock next to the two-room cabin, waiting for his mistress who would never return.

Getting closer to civilization and the huge, empty white mansion along the River, Mato slowed his pace and stopped again to listen. Now he could hear a low, expected groan, and he sincerely hoped he wouldn't have to swim across the wide River to help Wolf. His smile faded when he saw a figure dressed in mustard yellow clinging to a low-hanging bush in the water. Recognizing the odd costume, Mato waded out to help someone he had figured he would never see again.

"Hau kola," he greeted Wals as he slipped a strong arm around the man's back and pulled him to shore.

"Hello, friend," Wals mumbled back, surprised he could remember any of Mato's language after what he had been through—again.

After quickly determining that Wals wasn't hurt and in no immediate danger, the brave went back to the water's edge and looked both ways.

Seeing nothing, not even any ripples, he asked the water-logged man, "Sumanitu Tanka?"

Wals grimaced and sat up, running those words around his mouth. He looked at Mato and frowned, shaking his head that he didn't understand. *Great*, he sighed to himself. *Just like I thought it would go*.

Mato looked away and rolled his eyes. *Great, just like it usually was with this one*. He pointed to himself and said slowly, "Mato.' Pointing at Wals, he said, "Wellz." Pointing at the River he repeated, "Sumanitu Tanka," and held out his empty hands.

Both of them were visibly relieved when Wals finally understood and nodded, "Wolf." His companion held back from happily slapping him on the back. He didn't think Wals could take the force right now.

"Oh, gosh, how do I tell him?" Wals mumbled out loud. He simply shook his head and indicated that they should go by pointing in the direction of the village. "Can we go see the Shaman?"

Mato understood the word for his father and cast a last, worried glance at the River, hoping to see his brother swimming to shore.

Seeing Mato obviously searching the riverbank, Wals reached out and touched his arm, getting the brave's divided attention. "No Wolf," Wals told him, looking as miserable as he felt.

Mato felt his heart clench as he turned and silently led the way back to his village.

"**W**hat did you drag out of the River, Mato?" the Shaman asked when the dripping Wals was led into camp and handed over to the women by the fire. "Where is my son?"

His face reflecting his worry, Mato told the Shaman the extent of their conversation as far as he understood it. The portion of his father's face that was visible under the wolf headdress noticeably paled.

Looking over at the equally miserable Wals, the older man remarked quietly, "This is what I always feared would happen. That one day he would not come back."

"But how did this one get here? Only my brother calls the osiceca."

With only a grunt as a reply, the older man looked out over the wide River towards the barely-seen clearing where the small log cabin stood. He knew it wasn't fair, but he blamed the woman, the wiya, for whatever trouble his son was in. Things had been fairly normal around the village until the blond had been found lying face down on the River's edge, obviously blown in by mistake in the same osiceca that his son had used. The village had nursed her back to health and then placed her in the small cabin just before she regained consciousness. She—and Wolf—had never even known she had been in one of their tipi for days. The Shaman had later told Wolf to watch over her, to guard her—which he immediately had taken to heart and practically never left her side whenever she had to deal with the akicita, the soldiers, at the nearby

Fort Wilderness. It had been a dangerous time then.

Turning back to his waiting son, the Shaman asked, "How much of our language does this one," indicating Wals with a tilt of his head, "remember? He hadn't learned much last time he was here. He was too busy with the golden-haired wiya."

Mato gave a small snort. "Either he was still shaken by the storm or he forgot almost all of it. It won't be easy finding out what happened to Wolf."

His father gave him a shrewd, sideways glance. "You've been back to the small mining town a few times. You must have learned more of their words."

Knowing not to meet the sharp black eyes, Mato gave a one-shoulder shrug. "A little," he admitted.

Giving a small smile that went unseen by the brave, he suggested, "Well, let's go see what, if anything, we can learn. At least he looks dried off."

As the two men approached, Wals looked up from the wooden bowl of stew he had been handed by the Cooking Woman. He never could properly read the expression on the leader's face. He couldn't tell if the Shaman was glad to see him or ready to toss him back into the River.

"Taŋyáŋ yahí," *Welcome, I am glad to see you*, the older man greeted, holding a hand up.

Thanking the gray-haired woman, he handed back the empty bowl and murmured to her, "Philámayaye," and, hoping he understood that it was a greeting, again said, "Hau, kola."

Mato gave a small groan. *That only goes so far, Wals.*

The Shaman gave a small cough to cover the amused look on his face. *I should go into a long speech just to see if his face can get any more white.* Instead, he imperially motioned for his son to try and take over the floundering conversation.

Mato pointed to the sheltered overhang. Wals knew from his past experiences in the camp that this was the place used for important occasions or ceremonies. Favoring a bruised leg, Wals took a seat on the hard ground and looked expectantly at the two natives. As he waited for the men to begin, he noticed more of a family resemblance than when he had been here before. At that time, he had been more concerned with Rose, her comfort, and their budding relationship. He noticed both men use the familiar one-shoulder shrug Wolf often used and the subtle twinkle in their eye when they were vastly amused at something, while their faces showed no emotion at all. Mato was a larger man than Wolf, wider in the shoulders and at least half a head taller. Wolf had told him Mato's name meant Bear, and he believed it was a good match for the brave. Even though Wals didn't consider himself much of a judge when it came to a man's look being considered handsome or not, he could see that Mato had the same chiseled, sharp features as his younger brother. He knew Wolf caused quite a stir amongst the female population at Disneyland

and had no doubt that his brother would do equally as well.

As he watched the two men, he felt a familiar feeling begin to pass through him—a contented feeling of belonging and familiarity. He glanced at the nearby green water running past the encampment and thought about the canoe runs he used to make on the River. His mind drifted to the nearby town of New Orleans and the supplies he would need to take to the settlement. Looking up at the sky, he tried to estimate how much daylight he still had and if he could make the run today…. With a sudden gasp, he knew what was happening. The Island was beginning to take over his memories again. He had to think of…what was it he had to think of? His room at Fort Wilderness. No, the Fort was closed now. His horse. No, he didn't have a horse. Rose did. No, it was his car…. Breathing quickly, Wals reached up to his chest where his plastic nametag was pinned. As his fingers ran over the engraved word Wals, he could feel his mind begin to shift again, to settle. *I don't belong here. I belong in the future, at Disneyland. I am here to help Wolf. I can't let my mind drift again.* He unpinned the badge and held it tightly in his hand. Before, it had served as his touchstone to keep him grounded in reality and now he could see he would need it again. Wals decided he had better just hold onto it until they were ready to leave. Whenever that would be, considering how difficult it had been to converse so far.

One memory did return to him, the reason

for his trip back with Wolf in the first place—the coming of the pirates to Tom Sawyer's Island. Once the pirates had been installed at Disneyland in Wals' time, they had likewise shown up here, as well. As a matter of fact, the inhabitants of this village had been engaged in a heated battle with the pirates when Wolf had called the storm to take Rose, the doctor, and himself to safety in Disneyland of their time.

Glancing sharply over at the Island, wondering if they would be attacked any time soon, he interrupted the on-going conversation between father and son and tried to ask Mato about the invaders. He still had some of their gold hidden at home.

With a series of gestures, Mato seemed to know what he was talking about, which relieved Wals greatly. In a mixture of English, Lakota, and sign language that Wals had trouble following, Mato told him with an amused chuckle, "Pirates? Yes, they were a superstitious lot. Once they saw your canoe disappear in the storm and they saw their friend, the idiot, try to follow, they lost some of their zeal for fighting. Then, when they saw my brother bring back the dead idiot, they have never returned to this part of the River."

As Wals tried to absorb what he could understand, Mato described to his father what he had just related. "That was my favorite canoe," his father muttered in an undertone. Wals' contemplation was cut short when the son and father ended their resumed private discussion and turned to face him. It was obvious they wanted to get down to business and determine what happened to Wolf.

"And, here we go," Wals mumbled to himself, running a finger continually over the name tag held in his hand.

Mato noticed the tight grip on the oval plastic. Wolf had explained Wals' confusion before, so he knew what was going on in their visitor's mind. Also realizing his brother somehow worked at the same place, he pointed at the badge and asked, "Wolf there?" in English.

Wals frowned as he looked his name tag. He figured Mato was asking if that was where his brother was. He shook his head and said, "No." Pointing in the direction of the Fort and around the village, he repeated, "No." Waving a hand as if over the trees and hoping to indicate something far away, he added, "In the past. Back in time."

In low voices, Mato and the Shaman discussed what Wals might have just said and the implications. "Apparently my brother is not where they go in the future. I think his arm waving means that Wolf is not around here, either. Where else is there? Wolf never said anything about traveling further."

"Do you think this one is smart enough to understand a timeline?"

They both turned to closely observe Wals. He had the distinct impression that he was being evaluated—and coming up short.

The Shaman shook his head slowly and gave a deep sigh. "Give it a shot."

Glancing around, Mato picked up a short

twig. Squatting down next to Wals' position, he drew a long, straight line in the soft dirt. In the middle of the line, he drew a tipi. Pointing at it, he said, "Mato," and looked to see if Wals understood so far.

"Okay, that's where you live," and pointed at one of the nearby conical tents.

Mato nodded and returned to his line. About a foot to the right of the tipi, he drew a shaky representation of the castle on Wals' nametag. Now he indicated Wals, saying, "Wellz and Wolf."

Wals again nodded. "Yeah, that's where we live," as he showed Mato his nametag and pointed at himself.

Mato jabbed the stick in both locations, one after the other. "Wolf?"

Understanding what the brave was doing, Wals shook head and took the stick from Mato. Far to the left of the tipi, at the start of the line, Wals drew another, bigger castle. "Wolf and Rose. Wiya," he remembered the word they used for the woman, pointing at the larger drawing and again waving over the tops of the trees. "Way back."

When the eyes of the two men watching him got wide, Wals knew they understood where Wolf had gone. Perhaps not precisely, but they knew he was back further in time. *Now the fun part*, Wals groaned to himself, wishing he had done better in his art classes at school.

Using the twig, he scratched out a picture of what might be either a pony or a large dog next to the castle he had just drawn. Identifying it as Wolf, he saw the amusement flicker through their eyes again. Next to Wolf he drew a tall stick figure in a horned hat that set on top of long hair, wearing what might have been a cape. In her bony hand was a long stick with a round blob on top. Wals then drew a lightening bolt from the round blob to Wolf. "And now we get to play charades," he told them dryly as they frowned at him. Whatever he had done to Wolf didn't look very encouraging.

Wals pointed at himself and said, "I'm Wolf, okay?"

"Okay," the Shaman repeated in English, earning a small smile from his son.

Wals let his eyes roll up into their sockets and staggered backwards, holding his head. Then, holding his fingers like curved claws, he approached Mato and growled, taking a swing at him. He did the same to the Shaman. Turning back to his drawing, he pointed at the figure in the tall hat and pretended to bow down to it.

When he returned to his feet, he could see the two men were in shock. He assumed the message was properly delivered—Wolf was under the power of someone else and was turning on people.

Now he had another message to convey. Going back to the timeline Mato had drawn, Wals pointed at himself, then at Mato, and then at the castle he had drawn. "We have to go there and help Wolf. You, me, go back," as he repeated his stabs with the stick.

Eyes even wider, Mato knew what he meant, but he had no idea how they could get back in time to that place. He didn't even understand how Wals got *here*, let alone how he would get back to his own time without Wolf. He pointed to the River and made a twirling motion with his fingers and then did a startlingly-good imitation of a peal of thunder. Holding his shoulders up and hands out in front of him, he was obviously asking Wals how they would get back.

Remembering the forgotten recorder in his pocket, Wals' solemn face suddenly lit with a wide smile. Pulling out the small device, he was obviously pleased of it as he held it out for the two men to see.

"Oh, great. Another one of their worthless things. Remember that silver one that was supposed to make fire?" the Shaman half-laughed, half-groaned, thinking of the Zippo lighter that had belonged to Doctor Houser. It had made one little spark and, because the fluid was all gone, had never worked again. And the doctor had been so proud of it, just as Wals was evidently proud of this new thing.

Mato grunted his agreement. Wolf had tried to explain to them the many different inventions over the centuries, but he hadn't had much success. These people lived off the land and had everything they needed from the forest and the River.

Seeing the dubious expressions on their faces, Wals gave them a smug grin. "Fine, just wait until you hear this." He made a great show of pushing the Play button and the two men leaned in closer. They heard some static and the first note of Wolf's howl when the tape stopped. "What?" Wals mumbled. "Come on," as he pushed the Stop button and then tried again, shaking the little machine. Opening the clear plastic lid that protected the cassette tape, a stream of water spilled out. "Oh, great, it got wet. No wonder it broke." He slapped a hand to his forehead as the realization of what he just said sunk in. "It broke! How am I supposed to get home? How could we forget to wrap it? I wonder how long it will take Lance to come looking for me…. How would he even know that I didn't just come back and immediately leave again?" Wals was starting to get panicky. His head shot up and he looked at the two braves. They were just staring at him, waiting skeptically for whatever miracle he was going to show them. With an angry yell, Wals threw the broken recorder as hard as he could over the trees and into the surrounding forest.

"That's the first intelligent thing he's done since he got here," the Shaman mumbled out of the side of his mouth to Mato.

"Agreed," his son said, trying desperately not to laugh, "but did you hear that sound it made before it stopped? It sounded just like Wolf."

"I heard something," was all the Shaman would admit.

"That must have been what Wals used to call the storm. How else could he get here?"

"But how will he—and you, if that is what he meant—go back?"

Mato stared at his father for a long minute. "I think I can call the storm," he finally told him in a quiet voice.

Hoping his expression didn't convey the sudden pounding in his heart, the older man asked, "What makes you think so?"

"If that...thing Wals just threw away had the call of Wolf on it, then it appears that Wolf doesn't need to actually be there. It must be the essence of his howl that the storm hears.... I can imitate his call," he insisted. "I've done it before."

Not knowing what they were saying, Wals could only look back and forth at the two men who were now apparently arguing. Mato had just said something that his father obviously did not like at all.

Eyes narrowed, his father demanded, "So, you *have* tried to call the storm? Why have you not told me?"

"Because you would have reacted just as you are now. It was many years ago, after one of Wolf's visits," the brave went on to explain. "I...I was intrigued after he had gone and wanted to see if I could do it, too."

"Did you go through the storm?" The question was asked in a calm voice, as if they were discussing the next hunt. But, the dark eyes behind the wolf headdress were wide, expectant as he awaited the reply.

"No, I did not. I had no need or desire to see what Wolf had told us about. My life is here. With my family," he stressed.

"Ah, so the storm *did* come on your call."

"Yes," he admitted. "I can imitate the calls of all in our camp."

Satisfied for the moment that his oldest had not done something foolish, the Shaman just grunted. "You always did have the gift of mimicry." He looked away, torn between the desire to help his one son who was obviously in some kind of grave danger and the desire to not lose his other son to possibly the same fate. However, it was not his decision to make. His son was a grown man. But, that admission did nothing to still his fears. "What do you want to do, my son? You have always been able to calm your brother when he forgot who he was."

Mato took his time before he answered, looking over at his own tipi where his wife and son were patiently waiting for him to share their evening meal. It would be a lie to say he had no curiosity about Wolf's other life—no matter what he had just told his father. He had to admit to himself that he wanted to see his brother's world. And, now that he realized Wolf was in danger and that his brother had to have taken a big chance by sending Wals, he felt he had to do something. This was his misun, his little brother. He had protected Wolf from the taunts of the other children as they grew up when it was realized Wolf was different—starting with his vivid blue eyes and ending with his scary ability to turn a placid River into a raging whirlpool and then disappear through it for years at a time. His responsibility as the older brother had not ended when Wolf vanished from sight the first time when they were teenagers. Yes, he would help his brother, however he could.

His father could see the decision in his

son's determined eyes even before Mato spoke. His heart beat with pride at the same time it sunk with fear within his chest. Without the word being spoken, he gave one regal nod and walked over to Wals who had been ignored all this time. Putting a kindly hand on the man's shoulder, the Shaman thanked him, "Philá-mayaye. Inahni!" *hurry!*, and, head erect, slowly walked over to the Cooking Woman for a bowl of stew that he knew he wouldn't be able to eat.

Mato approached Wals and pointed at the picture of Wolf. Putting his arm around Wals' shoulder, he said—much to Wals' relief—in a mixture of English and sign language, "We go see Wolf. I call storm." He then indicated Wals should wait where he was. He had some things he had to do before they left.

Going to his tipi, he gathered his family in his arms. In a calm, unhurried voice, he told them what was going on and where he had to go. His wife had tears in her eyes, but she understood the bond between the two brothers and simply nodded. Young Igmutaka saw it as a grand adventure to share with his beloved uncle Wolf and wanted to go along. Mato held him close and whispered that they would have a different type of adventure together when he got back. They all hoped that the time would come for him to fulfill this promise he had just made to his son.

Gathering his weapons, Mato belted on a sharp dagger and took up his bow and arrows. Slinging the quiver over his back, he went to say, "Doka,"—*see you later*—to his father and asked him to watch over his family while he was gone. Their people did not say goodbye. With a nod of respect to the Cooking Woman, he went to rejoin Wals. The small canoe that had brought Wals had been fetched earlier by some of the tribesmen and the small hole repaired.

Both men looked back when the Shaman called over to Mato. "When you see your brother, tell him I want my canoe back. It was my favorite."

The tension broken, Mato tilted his head back and gave a perfect imitation of Wolf's cry. A collective shudder went through the village when they heard it. Mato called again and was rewarded by the slow approach of the familiar fog bank as it crept towards them from the Beaver Dam. When the clouds gathered overhead and began to collide, they all knew it had worked.

As Wals climbed to the front of the canoe, two other braves clasped forearms with Mato and then readied themselves on each side of the small craft to push them off when Wals gave the signal.

Lightening forked above and streaked down to touch the agitated River, sending up waves of green water and pink sparks. When the fury mounted to a peak, Wals gave the yell and they were pushed into the rapid current, aimed straight at the heart of the chasm.

Now standing back at his rocky platform, the anguished Shaman couldn't tear his eyes away from the spectacle in front of them all. At the end, he had to reach out and weakly grasp the side of his enclosure in the effort to stay upright when he saw his last son vanish as if into the thin air and the water close over the top of him.

CHAPTER SEVEN

Disneyland — 2008

Wals came to in front of the small cabin on Tom Sawyer's Island. This time he was thankful he hadn't bashed his head on one of the rocks in the Keel Boat Rapids. Remembering that he had not come through the nightmare alone, he quickly located Mato.

He saw the brave standing in front of the brown, motionless horse set in its place next to the Settler's Cabin. Mato reached out a tentative hand and touched the horse's nose. Getting no reaction from the familiar-looking beast, he ran his hand over the hard material that formed the fiberglass animal. Wals knew he would never be able to explain the two-part cloth and resin process that had made the horse.

Glancing up at the sun, he noticed it was past its zenith and knew it was sometime after noon. He had left in the darkness of night and vaguely wondered how many days had passed. As he eyed Mato, he decided they wouldn't attract *too* much attention. Mato's native garb of deerskin trousers, moccasins, and the blanket that had been repositioned around his shoulders would blend in well enough with their location in Frontierland. Just as long as he kept his dagger and arrows out of sight they should be fine until Wals could advise Lance that they were back.

The canoe fared better on this trip as Wals tipped it to empty out the water from the vortex. Mato walked over to him, shaking his head disgustedly, and grumbling in Lakota. Wals didn't even want to know what he was saying. Hearing the steamship, the Mark Twain, whistle as it passed the canoe dock, Wals knew they had to get off the small clearing pretty quickly. They would have to paddle all the way around Tom Sawyer's Island, following the proper flow of traffic.

Pulling the canoe into the water near the entrance to the Keel Boat Rapids, Wals motioned for Mato to get in front and he took up the position as sternman and gestured for his companion to wait. The Mark Twain was almost at their position and they had to let the bigger boat have right-of-way.

He could see Mato look over in amazement as the pristine white boat slowly chugged past their location. There was an almost-identical Mark Twain in Mato's time. Only the boat in the past was much larger and was actually a working boat that took cargo and supplies up the River to the settlements. Occasionally there were passengers on excursions from the neighboring New Orleans if the pilot had room on deck and allowed it.

Mato didn't know what to do about the oddly dressed people who were waving at him and pointing small boxes at him that looked like more of those worthless things Wals and the doctor had shown his tribe. He didn't understand that the guests floating by were merely snapping pictures of "something new" on the Rivers of America. His head whipped around to Wals who held out a calming hand indicating him that is was okay and he needed to be patient. Uncomfortable and feeling like he was on display, Mato turned his head away from the boat and mumbled under his breath. Wals smiled as he recognized a few words Wolf had used occasionally but would never translate for him.

Once the Mark Twain was far enough in front of them, Wals knew it was safe for him to push off. With a call to Mato, he dug in with his paddle and the canoe surged ahead. Wals figured Wolf had told, or tried to tell, his family about Frontierland and its different scenes around the River. He angled the canoe over towards the Friendly Village and heard a sharp breath as Mato recognized his Father standing in his familiar spot, his wolf headdress covering most of his face, gesturing as he told a familiar story. The encampment was way too small, but it definitely gave him an eerie feeling of home.

Wals got the canoe in motion again and they followed in the choppy wake of the steamship. The next bend of the River had no elements of civilization, just nature and the Beaver Dam. The broken-down yellow mining train caught Mato's eye as the marmots popped their heads up and whistled to him. The amused brave gave an answering, identical whistle, but they dropped down out of sight and wouldn't come up again.

The Mark Twain was already alongside the white dock and unloading as they slowly approached its location. The various features of Tom Sawyer's Island—the barrel bridge and the suspension bridge—earned a long stare as countless children and adults ran over the Island, climbing in and out of caves and obviously having a grand time. He saw a huge, familiar-looking pirate flag, but could tell it elicited no alarm from any of the visitors on the Island. In his time, the pirates had taken over the Island and even attacked his village. Since their dismal defeat, however, the pirates had left them completely alone and kept themselves to the backside of the Island.

Once past the steamship dock, Wals dug in with his paddle and got them moving faster. They were gliding past the main walkway in the ornate New Orleans Square/Frontierland area filled with families, couples and children coming and going. Mato spied the Haunted Mansion and recognized it as the empty house near the River in his time and shook his head in amazement.

Wals was glad the Davy Crockett Explorer Canoes were not running that day. He had worked there until he had been ignominiously sent to Fantasyland and the Casey Jr. Train. He had to listen to a lot of derision from his friends on the Canoes and he wasn't in the mood to hear any more of it today.

Right after the empty Canoe dock was the Hungry Bear Restaurant. Just past the two decks of people enjoying a meal, was the small dock where he would stash this small canoe and hurry backstage—or behind the scenes where the guests were not allowed—so he could put in a call to Lance.

Whenever a cast member did something that was "different" than what the guests usually saw, there was always some interest and attention. Wals noticed that everything he and Mato were doing was being closely watched and quite a few pictures were being taken of the two of them in their respective costumes. Always a cast member, he smiled and waved, putting a friendly arm around the irritated brave, hoping he would take the hint. He did not. But, the guests were just as happy that the Native American was proud and aloof as if he had broken into a wide grin and waved back.

Wals sighed with relief when the cast member-only door slammed shut under the restaurant and they were out of sight. Going over to the phone on the wall, he asked the operator to patch him through to Lance, whom, he hoped, was on security detail.

"**W**als, I can't do anything about it! You know that. There's going to be thousands of teenagers running around Fantasyland tonight and we just can't take the chance."

Wals glared at Lance, but he knew the security guard was right. He had forgotten about Grad Night, when thousands of high school seniors were bussed in from all over California and Arizona for an all-night party at Disneyland before their graduation. Given full run of the Park, the seniors were known to get into all kinds of mischief that their school chaperones and undercover security guards tried in vain to stop. Wals knew he and Mato would have no chance of sneaking into the Castle and calling the portal without being seen—and possibly interrupted or, even worse, followed—by scores of teenagers looking for "something exciting and different." There were two more nights of Grad Night until the Park returned to its normal schedule.

Mato came over to where they were standing after examining the vending machine. Lance had gotten him a bag of potato chips, but he didn't seem too enthused by the greasy crisps. His expression clearly asked, "Well?"

Wals held up two fingers and told him, "Two nights before Wolf."

With rolled eyes, Mato stalked off to the window overlooking a busy backstage thoroughfare. Costumed cast members, wearing everything from the Jungle Cruise's safari gear to Princess Belle's golden ball gown, casually walked to their lockers or back onstage after a break. He stared at the few trucks that were in view, waiting to deliver some boxes to different stores around the Park. His brother had mentioned his Mustang that was not a horse and could carry five people and wondered if those trucks were anything like that.

"What am I going to do with him for two nights? He almost pulled his knife when Goofy walked by!" Wals hissed to Lance when Mato was far enough away. "It's not funny, Lance!"

The security guard thought otherwise. His eyes betrayed the laughter he didn't allow to show on his face. Knowing how proud Wolf was, he didn't want to insult his brother.

"We'll think of something, Wals. We just need to get him away from here for now. This is probably overwhelming."

Nodding in agreement, Wals asked, "Should I take him to Wolf's place? Do you think he would recognize anything that would feel like home?"

Lance scrunched up his face for a moment. "I don't think so," he said slowly, thinking about Wolf's barren apartment. "I know what you mean, but I can't remember anything in there that might be familiar to him," with a tilt of his chin towards Mato. "I can't even imagine what he must be thinking now," as he spotted the characters from *Peter Pan* getting ready for a parade down Main Street. "Why don't we take him to my place? My son Peter would love to talk to him. Wolf taught him quite a bit of Lakota. Maybe that would help the situation. Wolf's car is still in the parking lot. Take that. Mato might enjoy knowing it belongs to Wolf."

Wals' eyes lit up. Even though he had a powerful Nissan 300ZX, he had always admired Wolf's classic 1967 Mustang GT Fastback and would love to drive it. He tried to hide the excitement in his eyes. "If you're sure your wife won't mind us coming over."

Lance gave him a wide, knowing smile. "Kimberly loves surprises."

Mato's eyes grew wide as they approached the bright red car. Seeing all the similar-looking 'things' sitting there motionless in the parking lot was one thing. Being expected to climb into it and realizing it was going to 'do something' is another. He saw Lance disappear inside the darkness inside and could feel waves of heat come from the opening that had swallowed him. When Wals cheerfully dropped into the other side of the car, he knew what was expected of him. Banging his head lightly on the doorframe, he muttered something sour in Lakota. Glancing over at Wals again, he saw him tug on a silver piece of metal, closing him in. With another unheard curse, he mimicked Wals' action and silently braced himself for whatever was to come.

After the men were settled into Wolf's car, Lance had a question for Wals. "You're pretty much known as a Disney expert, right?"

Wals was more interested in settling into the soft leather driver's seat than testing his Disney knowledge at that moment. "I guess. Why?" he asked, only half listening as Wolf's 427 roared to life, his hand on the shifter, ready to goose it and drop some rubber in the parking lot to show Mato what this kind of Mustang could do.

Lance could see the gleam in Wals' eye and ignored it. "Tell me this: When did Walt drive a De Soto?"

Their heads all jerked back in unison as Wals' blasted out of the parking space. "Walt never drove a De Soto," he grinned as the car shot forward, kicking up a cloud of dust behind them.

Deciding it would probably to prudent to buckle his lap belt, Lance had to wait a moment for the centrifugal force to end as Wals' pulled a hard right onto Harbor Boulevard, and, thankfully for all, had to slow down. "Then tell me why he did a photo shoot in 1939 for De Soto."

Silver Lake — 1939

The photographer from Life Magazine was ready for one more shot. "All right, Mr. Disney, how about if you remove your jacket and change into this striped shirt? I'd like you to settle down onto this yard chair. This one's also going to be titled 'Walt Disney, You've Got Another Hit.'"

As Walt got comfortable in the bright yellow chair, a man dressed like a butler stood at the front of the red 1939 De Soto S6, holding a tray in one hand. Walt smiled broadly for the camera, his red socks matching both the car and the hubcaps set into the whitewalls. In the background were the large trees that lined his street.

The first set of pictures had been with the car backed into his driveway. He had been told the photograph would be shaded differently so the car would appear brown in the ads. Standing in the same light blue trousers, he had worn a tan jacket and matching hat, holding a square brown case in his left hand. The vine-covered arch entry of his house was just behind him.

Glad that his subject was so cooperative, the photographer was happy to see the natural, broad smile on Walt's face. Little did he know about the conversation days earlier.

Walt had been discussing the request from the De Soto people with his mother. He refused to pose for a car ad and have it sound as if he drove that particular car. Even the offer of giving him one of their cars was not incentive enough for Walt to make a false claim. When he told Flora of his decision, she asked him why not and told him he could always give the car to them.

His parents love that little car and Walt was happy to be able to provide it for them.

Fullerton Hills — 2008

The Mustang roared to a sliding stop in the curved driveway of Lance and Kimberly's mansion in the Fullerton Hills. Originally built by Walt Disney as a gift for his right-hand man, it had passed to the next generation of Guardians—

the Blond-Haired Man's daughter and her husband. Wals knew nothing of the Guardianship and the impressive, high-tech War Room on the third floor. It was in that room that Lance and Kimberly kept their eyes on the goings-on at the Park in their efforts to protect Walt and his Hidden Mickey quests and legacy.

"So, that's the story of Walt's De Soto," Wals smiled as he finally let go of the red steering wheel and got out of the car.

Lance unfolded his six-foot-two frame from the tight backseat and shook his head. "Sorry, I didn't hear a thing you said after you passed that police car on the hill."

Dropping the keys in his pocket, Wals was unrepentant. "Hey, he was going like ten miles-per-hour. He didn't pull us over, did he?"

"Probably still in shock," Lance mumbled.

Uncaring of the ongoing conversation around him, Mato emerged from the passenger side, a huge smile on his face. He slowly walked around the car once more, now with a whole different admiration for the strange Mustang.

The front door banged open and a small boy came running out yelling, "Unka Wolf! Unka Wolf!" He skidded to a stop when Mato turned to face him. "You aren't Wolf."

"Who is it, honey?" his mother, a stunning blond, asked as she followed him out into the bright sunlight, her hand resting easily on her stomach. She instantly recognized the car, but not the passenger.

Going up to his wife and giving her a quick kiss on the cheek, Lance told Kimberly, "I brought someone home for you to meet."

"In Wolf's car?" she asked, confused as Wals motioned for the stranger wrapped in a blanket to come forward. "Welcome back, Wals. Glad you are all right."

Wals was pointing at the house and explaining, "Lance's tipi."

Mato craned his neck to see up to the third floor. "Big tipi," he muttered back.

"This is Wolf's brother."

"He did it," she whispered unbelievingly to Lance, "Wals actually brought him back!"

Peter had walked all the way around the new visitor, holding back from touching the deerskin quiver of arrows and the bone handle of what appeared to be a knife stuck into a beaded belt. "I'm Peter," he said, looking up at the brave and pointing at his chest. "Táku eníčiyapi he?"

Smiling at the miniature version of the tall man Lance, Mato answered his question. "I am Mato."

"Wíyuškiŋyaŋ waŋčhíŋyaŋke ló," *pleased to meet you*, the six-year-old grinned back, obviously pleased with himself that he remembered the words Wolf had taught him.

Wals had wandered over to Lance. "This was a good idea of yours. Mato looks more relaxed already."

"Yeah, I think he and Peter are going to get along just fine." Lance looked over at Kimberly. "Do you think we have anything he can wear? I'm sure he's going to want to do some sightseeing while he is here."

"Lance, he didn't just fly in from Nebraska

for the weekend," his wife reminded him flatly. "Does he realize it will be two nights before he and Wals can leave?"

They looked at Wals, who nodded. "Yes. Well, I think he does. Maybe Peter can find out for sure," he suggested with a grin.

Peter, clearly delighted with their guest, was leading Mato inside the mansion. "Taŋyáŋ yahí," *welcome*, as he had been instructed was the polite thing to say.

"I guess we're all going inside," Lance told the others, holding out his hand so his wife could go on in ahead of him. "Wals, why don't you plan on staying here, too. It might be a good idea for Mato to have someone familiar at hand. Even though," he paused with a laugh, "I don't think Peter is going to give him any rest!"

Wals looked around the large foyer, his eyes traveling up the polished hardwood walls to the second story landing. He noticed all the antiques that sat on shining pedestals or within lighted nooks in the walls. "Well, if you think you have the room," he kidded, glancing into the formal sitting room off to their left.

Lance clapped a friendly hand on Wals' shoulder and then wiped the resulting dust off onto his pants. "I think we can manage. We might have to set up a cot in Peter's room, if that's all right." To his wife he said, "There might be some of Daniel's clothes still in the room over the garage. I'll go see if there's anything that might fit Mato."

Grimacing at the mention of her abusive uncle, now dead and buried in the past, Kimberly nodded and unconsciously rubbed the scars on her arm. Now, as she felt them, it all flooded back, unwelcome, to her mind. Daniel had kidnapped her and used a knife to hold her captive, inflicting a series of unnecessary cuts on that arm just to keep her in line. He had even succeeded in stealing the red diamond Hidden Mickey pendant from Kimberly and Lance until Wolf had interceded, opened a vortex, and then both Wolf and Daniel had disappeared from Disneyland's Tom Sawyer's Island. Her memory then turned to Lance and how Daniel had bashed his head with a rock that day. Not only did she have a few scars—both mental and physical—from the upsetting incident, but her husband also had his own scars. His, though, were in the form of infrequent headaches that still bothered him to this day.

Seeing her pause in thought as she looked down at her arm and then back to Lance, he realized what she was thinking. Lance gave her a gentle, reassuring hug. "He's gone, sweetheart," he whispered to her, kissing her ear. "I'll be right back."

Glad to turn her wandering attention back to her guests, Kimberly idly wondered what she should fix for dinner. She now had three grown men in the house to feed. Kimberly gave a light laugh as she thought about Wolf's rare appearances at their dinner table. He would just stoically shove anything placed in front of him into his mouth. She never knew if he liked it, loved it, or hated it. Now Wolf's brother was here and she figured more than likely Mato would be exactly the same way.

She was still laughing about this as she went upstairs to make sure everything was tidy and in place in the guest rooms.

Sitting in Lance's comfortable study after Peter had been put to bed, the three men were sitting back, staring into the sparkling crystal Waterford glasses that Lance had just passed around. The single-malt Scotch inside the glass was unfamiliar to Mato. As he looked over at Wals, Mato noticed that he was enjoying the sparkling effects on the walls and ceiling of the room from the lamplights hitting the multi-faceted glass now filled with this amber liquid. As Wals took a satisfying sip of the thirty-year-old Balvenie, Mato put his nose to the glass and pulled quickly away as the potent liquid overpowered his nostrils. He then pointedly set his glass aside.

"I really think we need something else, Lance," Wals was saying as Kimberly came into the room, smiling her hello to Mato. As she settled herself comfortably in Lance's lap, he continued. "I told you about the memory loss the Island had on both Rose and myself, right?"

Lance nodded. "The doctor, too, if I remember correctly."

"Yeah, right. I keep forgetting about him for some reason. Even when I just went back to get Mato, I could feel the Island working on me again. I had to take my name tag off and continually hold it in my hand just to stay in the reality of the moment."

Mato spoke up in his deep voice. "My father's place of speeches. That place puts many to sleep. You stare off in the distance until you touch it again."

Nodding, Wals continued. "That's what I am worried about with Wolf. I know he is under some kind of powerful spell, but I noticed that his eyes started to clear—a little—when he said his brother's name," indicating the interested warrior now pacing the room. "I know he probably wants Mato as a recall of reality, but could it be possible that he may also need some other kind of a touchstone, too, besides the obvious one of his brother? Something he can see or touch?"

"We have access to his Disneyland name tag," Kimberly pointed out. "Do you want to take one of those?"

Wals sighed and looked out past them toward the darkened window behind Lance. "I don't know if his name tag will be big enough, and then there's the problem with getting it to him. If he is capable of lunging at me like he did, I'm afraid something that small might not be enough."

Lance looked at his wife. "Is there something from Walt's Hidden Mickey quest that we might use? What all was there?"

"You have a stock certificate from the railroad and some animation cels," she said, frowning as she thought about the treasures Lance and Adam had found with Walt's clues. "The key that opened the telephone and…and the other place," she hesitated, not wanting to tell Wals about the secret room above Main Street where they had first found the pendant. "No, that is all small stuff, too. What else was there?"

Thinking back, Lance said, "Adam and Beth have most of the other things we found." He paused as Kimberly got up from his comfortable lap and joined Mato as they started pacing back and forth across the ancient Persian rug. "Was it something I said?"

"No, no. I just needed to walk," she waved him off.

Lance tried counting off what he could remember. "Let's see. Adam has more animation cels, more stock certificates, an engineers hat and that Disneyland flag from the locker in the Marceline school, the deed to the Golden Oak property—we really need to go out there again soon," he broke off as that random thought suddenly came to him. At their blank looks, he muttered, "Never mind. Oh, there was also the broken gold piece from Tobago, and Walt's Number One name tag. And whatever it was Adam and Beth found on their own search," he finished, following his wife's lead and not revealing more than Wals needed to know.

Wals had just shaken his head as each item was listed. Most sounded like things that would not survive the trip through the water very well, or were kind of valuable. He really didn't want to attempt taking anything like that unless it was absolutely necessary. "Wait a minute, what flag did you say? Some kind of Disneyland flag? What does it look like?"

At his question, Kimberly went to the

shelves behind Lance and pulled down a brightly colored book on the history of Disneyland. Flipping a few pages, she showed it to Lance who nodded. Holding the book out to Wals, he could see a bright orange rectangle-shaped flag with the face of Mickey Mouse in the center. Only, this Mickey was very different than the current version. This flag had to be decades old. The caption under the picture read: "The only flag to fly over Disneyland and Marceline" and, in the photo, school children were holding the flag out from the flagpole, showing Mickey's face.

Wals frowned as he looked at the picture. "I've seen this flag before."

"Yeah, there is one flying over Walt's apartment, and two smaller ones over the train station on Main Street," Lance told him, tapping the book with his finger. "This flag was taken down from Disneyland and given to the school children in Marceline. It's the only place Walt allowed that official flag to be flown other than at Disneyland."

"And did you say Adam has it now?"

Lance nodded. "It was part of our find in Marceline. So, yes, I'm sure he still has it. Adam is quite the collector," he smiled, remembering how Adam's face had lit up when they discovered Walt's first name tag hidden in a secret compartment of the diary that had started it all for them. Yes, he was positive Adam still had the flag.

They could see Wals hesitating. "Do you think we could, you know, borrow it from Adam? It sounds pretty valuable, historically speaking.

But, it is large enough and that flag just might do the trick."

"What are you thinking, Wals?"

Looking at Mato, Wals explained, "Whenever knights of old went into battle, they always had a flag, a banner, if you will, flying in front of them, to lead the way and give them courage. This flag sounds like it would be pretty easy to see if we set it up in front of us." He looked back at the couple, thinking about the violence of the vortex. "I don't know if it would get ruined, though. I can't make any promises one way or the other. Do you think it is worth the chance?"

There was an immediate answer. "Yes, if it will help Wolf."

"What do you think? Do you think Adam will give it to us, then?"

That was the million dollar question for Lance. When that first Hidden Mickey quest had ended, he hadn't parted still friends with Adam and Beth due to his own stupidity, as he called it. It had taken literally years before Adam had spoken to him again—even after Adam's silent attendance at Lance and Kimberly's wedding. Now, at this point, tensions had eased, but Lance still was not sure he had totally regained his friend's confidence. The couples split babysitting and play dates between them and seemed to be on good terms—at least from appearances.

"I can ask," was all Lance could promise, glancing at the clock. "He should be off the construction site by now," as he went over to the phone and dialed the well-known number.

At the end of the second day, Wals found Mato on the edge of Lance's property, staring out over the brightly lit valley below. Situated high in the foothills of Fullerton, the house had a stunning view.

Mato didn't seem impressed, but sad. He gave a sweep with his hand. "People. All people." Used to his small village, there had been only the few soldiers that used to be posted in Fort Wilderness, and he had rarely gone to the outskirts of the town of New Orleans. Mato had a hard time picturing so many people living together like that, seemingly crammed right next to each other. He had likewise been unimpressed with Wals' apartment in Huntington Beach where people were literally living on top of someone else, each in their own box. The ocean had awed him, having never traveled to the far side of New Orleans where the ships came in. But the fast pace of all the cars, buses, trucks, and trains, with the people always on the move and always in a hurry, frustrated him. While it had been somewhat interesting at first, now all he wanted to do was go home to his family.

But, he realized he couldn't. They still had to help Wolf. With a sinking feeling, he knew there would be more new sensations and locations with which he would have to deal. Wals had shown him drawings, highly detailed pictures of what he might expect in the time where Wolf was waiting for him. There were no noisy machines there, he was relieved to see. Horses provided transportation. But men wore shiny metal over their body for protection. He recognized the spears and arrows and knew he could hold his own against those. But the huge, towering castles looked intimidating. How could one escape from there if locked inside? The wooden doors of Wals' time seemed pitifully inadequate for protection. The castle, however, looked fortified by thicker walls and doors.

As the night sky deepened, Wals told Mato it was time to go. Kimberly would have Sleeping Beauty's Castle shut down around nine. With the firework show going on overhead, that would give them the perfect diversion.

Going into the house, Mato said to his hostess in English, "Thank you for the food," as Peter had coached him.

"I want to go!" Peter whined when he saw the men were leaving for good.

Remembering the fireball that had swept over their heads when Wals left, Kimberly clutched him to her side. "Sorry, sweetie. Not this time. Say good-bye to Uncle Mato."

"Lakota men do not say good-bye," he told her seriously. "They say doka."

Hearing the familiar word, Mato turned back and held his arms out to the boy. Peter ran to him for a final hug.

"You go get Uncle Wolf!" Peter told him. "You bring him back safe!"

"Yes, I will."

"Aŋpétu wašté yuhá po."

To the surprise of all, Mato burst out laughing. He put a kind hand on Peter's head. "I will try to have nice day, little one." He nodded to Kimberly and silently followed Lance and Wals to the waiting Mustang.

Dressed in his security uniform, Lance had no trouble getting the two men, curiously dressed as princes, into the closed Castle. Mato had balked at the tights and puffy shirt that was handed to him in the Costume Department, but knew he had to comply. Scowling, he was lead into the small castle and up the stone stairs. Not even glancing at the animated windows of the Walkthrough diorama, he kept his mind focused on what he would do to help his brother Wolf. That was all that mattered to him now that the time was at hand.

When Wals stopped in front of a door that looked like all the others they had passed, he simply nodded, knowing what was coming and what he had to do.

Lance gave them a hurried good-bye and ran down the stairs to be safely out of the way of the vortex. It had been too close for comfort on the edge of the River. He would rather take his chance outside with the raining residue of the fireworks than what he knew was going to happen inside.

Only Lance heard the plaintive howl that drifted down the stairwell. Only he knew that the pinkish glow in the upper windows didn't come from the brilliant displays bursting overhead.

And only he, out of all of the hundreds of

people filling Main Street watching the fireworks, silently wished the two men inside the Castle a safe, successful journey.

CHAPTER EIGHT

England — 1289

"Nata mitawa yazo."

"I don't know what you said, but I agree with all my heart...that is, if I could just get my heart beating again," Wals muttered, rolling over onto his back in the sand, one arm resting across his eyes. "Oh, my head hurts."

"That's what I said," Mato groaned, picking up the green velvet hat that had fallen off his head when they were dumped onto the beach by the vortex. Looking at the limp white feather that was now bent in half, he said something unpleasant in an undertone as he crammed the worthless covering back on his head.

"And I don't even want to know what you just said." Wals managed a small smile when he saw the rakish angle of the hat. As an afterthought, he gingerly reached up to his head for two reasons. One: to see if his own hat had made the transition to this time period. And, two: to see if his head was actually still attached to his body. Based on the way he felt, he wouldn't have bet any money on either one.

Walking a few steps off, ignoring Wals for the moment, Mato had already started to let his keen senses take over. Closing his eyes and blocking out the groans next to him, he could distinguish no sounds other than the ebb and flow of the waves lapping on the shore, a few sea birds overhead, and the distant, usual noise of a busy forest at midday. Wishing he had his brother's sharp eyesight, he gave the deserted beach a long stare in each direction. His glance lingered on the darkened coves hidden between the huge boulders that divided their part of the beach from the forest, but, seeing no movements other than a crab scuttling for cover, he turned back to his companion.

"Wašté?" Wals asked when it looked like Mato was done with whatever it was that he had been doing.

"Yes, good." He suddenly broke into a broad smile when he realized Wals had actually used the correct word in his language. The smile transformed his whole face from the serious, stern warrior he was into the handsome prince he was dressed to portray. "You spoke well."

Pleased by the compliment, Wals suggested, "Maybe I should try talking to you only in Lakota from now on."

"Tókhi wániphika ní," muttered Mato, hiding a smile. *Good luck with that.* "No, here I speak like you. Better for you. Maybe they think you misun!"

"Your little brother?" Wals looked up at the dark brave who stood at least a head taller than him and was much wider in the shoulders. Mato's raven hair and eyes were no match for his brown hair and green eyes. Giving a light laugh, Wals nodded and held up two fingers that were intertwined. "Yeah, it's just like looking in a mirror!"

"You have orange wowapi safe?"

If Mato hadn't used the word orange, Wals would have had no idea what he was talking about. "The flag? Is that wowapi?"

Not wanting to get into a discussion of language right now, Mato curtly nodded. "Safe?"

Wals felt underneath his embroidered doublet and the puffy-sleeved shirt beneath it. Protected by a plastic bag, the valuable flag was securely tied to Wals' chest with twine. Lance had at first suggested duct tape, but Kimberly had stepped in, reminding Lance that the plastic bag might be difficult enough to explain if seen in that time without the modernistic, gray vinyl tape adding to the potential problem. Plus, she—and Lance—well knew what the effect would be of pulling the sticky duct tape off a hair-covered chest.

"Go to Wolf now." Now that Wals seemed to be recovered from the time shift and he knew the flag was safe, the time for pleasantries was over. Mato wanted to get moving. He was more worried about his brother than he had let on— either to Wals or to his father. In the times Wolf had come back to their village disoriented, he had snarled and snapped at Mato, even turning on him, but never, even in his darkest moments, had Wolf ever threatened to kill him. That was completely out of Wolf's being, his character. Mato knew this condition of his brother's was more serious than any he had ever faced before. Picking up his bow, deep in thought, he went to collect the arrows that had been scattered over the beach. He had the sinking feeling he would need every one of them before this trip was over.

Brushing the sand off his blue tights and tunic, Wals adjusted his red cape, attempting to drape it neatly over his shoulders. He reached down to make sure he still had the small dagger he had tucked into one of his boots. While he was repositioning the elaborate sword hanging by his side, he silently gave thanks that it had not pierced him when they were violently thrown onto the beach. It would have been tragic for either of them to get injured in an accident before the real fight even began.

Remembering the path to the village he had taken when he was here before, Wals started leading the way through the forest and headed to the small rooms he had let behind the tavern. As they traversed the narrow, almost invisible path, the bright midday sun became more and more obscured the deeper they went into the forest. Now trudging through deep shadows and thick underbrush, Wals failed to notice any of this. Watching only his feet on the trail in front of him, he was silently wondering how he was going to let Rose know he was back. Then the thought struck him that she probably hadn't even realized he had been gone, let alone returned. He gave a sudden dry chuckle. *I wonder what would happen if I just went up and knocked on that secret door into the castle.*

Following a few steps behind, Mato heard the laugh Wals had given, but paid it no heed. He was trying to keep fully alert as they walked. This forest was in some ways similar to his woods back home, but yet, it was very different. He could hear small common noises like the birdcalls from one tree to another, and the familiar chirping of squirrels as they shook their tails at the intruders and dove out of sight into their protective holes in the trees. Then there were larger noises, like a deer crashing through the brush, fleeing from the frightening scent of man. However, it was another, softer sound he detected that made him pause just for a mere moment. Eyes narrowed, he recognized this also as a sound familiar to him—the careful placement of pawed feet as they were trying to avoid snapping twigs or clusters of dried leaves and acorns. This almost-silent movement, however, was not gaining on them, nor was it falling back. It was keeping pace with the two men, a little off to their left. Mato tried to catch their scent, but the followers—for he could now tell that there was more than one—were downwind. Instinctively knowing it was not his brother, Mato kept from turning his head in that direction. He didn't want to give any indication that he knew the two of them were being shadowed. Glancing at Wals' back, he decided to refrain from alarming his companion at this point. Not knowing for sure how many were in the pack following them, Mato knew the lack of aggressiveness on the part of these predators was to their benefit for the time being. If they would just stay at bay for a little while longer, Wals would hopefully arrive at their destination. There would be another, better time to face this unseen enemy than here and now.

Yes, this wilderness was much like the one at home. Yet it felt older, much older. He sensed an eerie presence wafting in the light breeze, one that made the hairs on the back of his neck tingle. There were also secrets here. Deep, dark secrets—ones he wasn't so sure he wanted to uncover.

"Ah, I see your little friend is back, Wolf," Nimue purred as she stroked the huge black head sitting next to her throne. "And it looks like he brought a playmate. How delightful!" She glanced up at the frozen, grotesque faces of the gargoyles that capped off the columns holding up the roof. The open-mouth expressions on all their faces betrayed the terror of their unexpected demise. "I can always use a few more ornaments once you bring me their heads."

His eyes now totally glazed over from her ongoing powerful spell, Wolf merely sat, allowing her touch. In this entranced state, he didn't even glance over when she spoke to him to see what she meant or who it was that she could see. He just sat there, numb, as he waited for his next command.

Chuckling smugly at Wolf's docile compliance, she turned her head to gaze deeper into the green orb on her armrest. Through the eyes of one of her wolves as they kept pace with the steadily moving pair, she had a clear view of Wals and this newcomer as they made their way through the forest. Wals seemed to be his usual blundering, unseeing self. But, the other one.... She leaned closer to the glowing sphere, staring at the broad back of the tall, dark one. Ignoring the fake trappings of a prince that he wore, she studied the man, the way he moved effortlessly through the trees. She thought she could detect a sort of tenseness about his shoulders, the way his head moved slightly towards the location of their followers and then immediately back again. It was then that she let out a small, delighted gasp. *He knows. He knows the two of them are being followed!* "This could be more fun than I imagined. A worthy adversary, perhaps, my pet?" she murmured to the uncaring wolf.

"Shall I go kill them now, Madam?"

"That's a good boy," she cooed, patting the top of his head. "No, no. We don't want to do that just yet. I want to see what they do once they get settled and are able to relax a bit in the village. Let them get off-guard, you know. I think the best time will be when they are with the girl again. Yes, then we shall strike."

"Yes, Madam."

"I've seen enough for now," she declared happily, removing her tapered fingernail from the orb. "Call the pack to return, wolf. I don't want those mindless beasts of mine getting caught up in the hunt. The idiots could spoil all my fun by carelessly attacking before we are ready."

Wolf, pulling himself to his feet, obediently trotted to the entry of the throne room and turned to face the unseen endless forest below him. Tilting his head back, he let out a commanding howl. This call was different than the ones he used to summon the portals. The spell over him picked up the howl, causing it to be relayed on a sudden, stiff breeze and echoed to the four corners of the kingdom. Loud enough, all creatures under the Evil Fairy's control would hear and obey that ungodly command.

Deep in the forest, Wals and Mato paused as an eerie, haunting, disturbing sound drifted over them. Quickly putting a determined hand on his sword's hilt, Wals turned in a slow circle, instantly alert and ready. But, there was nothing different for him to see. No movement, no other sounds. Even the birds had gone silent There was nothing except the sound of his heart pounding violently in his chest.

Mato's eyes narrowed as he listened, carefully looking back over his shoulder to see if their followers were now making their advance. As the last note faded into the distance, he came to realize that their trackers were gone. Turning back to his companion, he muttered that the howl must have called them off.

Confused by Mato's statement, Wals looked

back at him and asked, "Called who off?"

"Oh." Mato hadn't realized he had said it out loud. "Followed by wolves. Sorry."

Surprised, Wals' mouth dropped open as he fully drew his sword, his eyes scanning the shadows around them once more. "What? You didn't tell me? I need to know these things!"

Mato merely looked at Wals and grunted, giving him a one-shoulder shrug so like his brother. There was no need for any explanation at this point as he indicated for Wals to put his sword away and get moving again.

Head up and alert, Mato silently followed. He had other, more important things to worry about than Wals' feelings.

His own heart now beat heavily in his chest, but for a different reason than Wals'. Unlike his companion, he had recognized the call that had floated over and around them. It was one that he hadn't heard in a long, long time. Commanding, powerful, and angry, it was the sound he had heard just before Wolf had appeared out of nowhere and turned on him, lost in the effects of the time vortex and out of his head. This howl had been tinged with the madness Wolf had battled before.

"Where is witch?" Mato suddenly demanded at Wals, impatient and unable to keep silent any longer.

"What?" Wals spun to face Mato, his sword coming halfway out of the sheath again. "Do you see her?"

Mato held up a calming hand. "No," he said, managing to keep the anger and worry out of his voice. He pointed all around them. "Which way her tipi?"

Wals shook his head at this request. "No, we aren't ready yet."

Eyes narrowed in anger, Mato repeated his question without having to use any words.

Recognizing the same stubborn trait that was in Wolf, Wals reluctantly told him, pointing off to the north, "That way. A few miles off. Once we get out of the trees, you can usually spot the castle's location by the nasty storm clouds circling her towers."

Satisfied that this was the same direction from which the summoning howl had come, he now knew where his brother was being held. Mato grunted and, once more, indicated Wals should continue the way they were previously going.

Relieved that they were not going to head into a fight so soon, Wals gave a single nod. Turning back to their original course, head down, Wals trudged on, following the narrow, shadowed path through the woods.

Answering a timid knock on his door later that night, Wals opened it a crack to see a tall black-robed figure standing on his sill. Before he could say a word, a swoosh of black fabric pushed the door open and rushed past him to enter his room, slamming the door shut.

Before he could even protest, the dark hood was thrown back to reveal beautiful golden hair and happy blue eyes.

"Rose!" Wals cried, opening his arms to welcome her.

As she embraced him, she spied the silent warrior crouched in a dark corner, ready for attack with his knife in his hand. "Mato?" she gasped in surprise, pulling away from Wals. "Is that you? I'm so happy to see you! Oh," she broke off as he recognized who she was and put his blade back in its sheath, "can he understand me?" she loudly whispered to Wals, who wasn't very happy to have his reunion interrupted.

"Hau wiya," Mato nodded to her, giving a half-smile at her confused expression and coming fully into the dim candlelight that illuminated the room. "Yes, understand. Part."

There was some movement around her hair and a blue pointed hat peeked out. "All clear, dear?"

"Yes, Merri. You can come out. We're all friends here."

Mato's eyes opened wide in surprise as the Blue Fairy unexpectedly popped full size into view, quickly followed by her two companions. That small room was now suddenly quite full.

Rose introduced her friends to the stunned, silent warrior.

Seeing the expression on his face, Fauna tried to put him at ease. "Taŋyáŋ yahí," she told him. *Welcome*.

That simple greeting started a lively discussion amongst the three fairies. "Why, Fauna! I didn't know you could speak other languages!"

The Red Fairy huffed, "Well, why couldn't I?"

"That sounded just lovely, dear. What did you say?" Flora wanted to know.

"Do you even know what you said? You might have insulted him, for all we know!" Merri pointed out.

"I did not insult anyone! I told him he was welcome."

"What a nice thing to do, Fauna. Could you teach me some words, too?" asked the smiling Flora, her eyes wide and her hands clasped eagerly in front of her. "What else do you know?"

"I…I just learned that one phrase so far for the wolf," the Red Fairy stammered, wishing Flora hadn't asked that. She had been so proud of herself and that took some of the wind out of her sail.

"Ha! I knew it," Merri exclaimed, a wide, triumphant grin on her round face. "You don't know what you're saying!"

Fauna pointed at the confused Mato who took an involuntary step backwards from her finger. "Does he look insulted? No, he does not!"

The three humans in the room looked back and forth in silence as if watching an odd three-player tennis game.

Remembering the fiasco with her dress when she had turned sixteen, Rose decided she had better step in before their wands were pulled out and the trouble really started. "Now, Fauna, that was just lovely! I'm sure Mato appreciated it very much. You do know who he is, don't you?"

With one last contemptuous look at her two companions, Fauna huffed, folding her arms over her bosom, "Of course I do. He is brother to the wolf. That's why I said what I said to him. I am assuming he is here to help with the problem."

"Problem?" Rose repeated, her eyebrows narrowing in suspicion as she realized that something was being kept from her—again. "I haven't been told of any problem. What is wrong, Wals?" she asked, turning back to him, figuring—correctly—that she would get more out of him than out of her three stubborn companions.

"Oh, I thought you knew and that's why you were here."

Her worried expression changed into an unexpected, lovely smile, one tinted with shyness that so many others were witnessing it. "I came because I have not heard from you in a quite a while and because I was worried about how you were getting on."

Knowing now was not the time to take her into his arms and kiss her—especially with her three watchful chaperones so near at hand and glaring at him as if they knew his intentions—Wals had to settle on giving her hand a tender squeeze.

"So, how does Wolf's brother come to be here?" Rose asked, smiling encouragingly at him when all the tempers had settled and they all had finally seated in the few chairs and onto the plank floor. "The last time I saw him was when we were living in his village. What is this problem you mentioned?" The fairies whipped up some refreshments for everyone and were amused by the close scrutiny Mato was giving the dainty rose-covered china cup that suddenly appeared in front of him.

Mato indicated for Wals to take over the explanation as he tried another teacake from the tiered plate suspended in midair next to the teapot. He had decided early on—agreeing with his father's advice—to just accept anything that happened as long as everyone else seemed to think it was normal. He had no way of knowing if three brightly-dressed magical beings were considered normal in this time period or not. As they made a nice cup of tea, he let their hovering a few feet off the ground go by without comment.

"You know what's going on, don't you," Wals asked of Fauna, the apparent leader of the three fairies.

Glancing at the others, who nodded for her to speak for all of them, she cleared her throat. "Yes, we do. We keep a close watch on the Evil One now that she is back. We think it's just tragic. You did the right thing in bringing him," she told him, motioning at Mato with her rounded chin.

"Will someone please tell me what is going on?" Rose angrily pushed up from her chair, hands on her hips as she regally stared at Wals, silently commanding him to speak.

He took a deep breath before continuing. "Okay, okay…gosh, where do I start? Well, it was Wolf himself who asked me to bring his brother here. He opened the whirlpool and sent me through."

The sharp blue eyes narrowed as she listened. "Why did you need to go back and why did he not go with you? Mato is not from your time. You would have had to go through another portal. Without Wolf's help, I don't understand how this could have worked."

"Sit down, dear," kindly Flora requested, taking the young woman by the hand. "You will want to be sitting when you hear."

At the encouraging nods, Rose retook her seat and looked expectantly at Wals.

"I don't know how exactly it happened," Wals started, "but the evil fairy, Nimue, as she is now calling herself again, captured Wolf...and put him under some kind of spell." He stopped when Rose gave a startled gasp.

"That was the woman who was with Merlin! The one we met, right? I know the ballad that is still being sung about her! So that's who it is inside the Dark Castle now. I thought there something was *off* about her, but nobody else seemed to notice." Her hand came up to her lips as she thought about her friend. "Oh, dear. Poor Wolf."

Wals nodded at everything she stated and continued, "Wolf came to me here and had me follow him to our beach where we met." His mouth suddenly went into an "Oh," when he thought he might have revealed something he ought not, and glanced over at the fairies.

"We know," Merri replied flatly, staring accusingly at him. "Her brothers are even less pleased than the King."

Clearing his throat, he went on with his story. "Wolf told me he was supposed to kill me, but, instead he sent me through the whirlpool and said to bring his brother back. He knew Mato would be the only one able to help him." Here he stopped and looked pointedly at the three fairies. "Well, Mato is the only one *he* thinks can help him. Are there any others?"

"We can only do so much, Wals, as you know. When the Evil One went after the princess so long ago, we could only protect her, not change the spell. We will do what we can," Fauna promised, as the other two fairies solemnly nodded in agreement.

"Oh, Wals! This is terrible! Poor Wolf. This must be killing him," Rose cried, her hands forming fists. "We have to help him! How will we get to him?"

Merri looked upwards at the ceiling. "Oh, I think he will find us when it is time."

"*She* will know we are waiting, too," Flora whispered, looking miserable. She flew over to the silent warrior and put a kind hand on his shoulder. "You will have to be strong to face your brother."

Mato nodded his understanding. "Yes. I know."

As they were talking, Fauna had gone to the men's weapons and waved her wand over them, hoping it might somehow be enough to help. "Now we have to wait," she told them. "But, I fear it will come much sooner than we expect. *She* likes to work that way."

As the three fairies went over to Mato, who, in spite of the seriousness of the occasion, was vastly amused by their antics, Rose and Wals took the opportunity to quietly slip out the door. Going around to the back of the tavern, they were out of sight of any curious eyes. Her hood securely in place hiding her royal identity, she quickly embraced Wals. "I wanted to come before, but my brothers are keeping an even closer watch on me. They hate you, you know," she told him sadly.

"Yeah, I heard. Is it because I'm not royal and don't fit in?"

Nodding slowly, the princess confirmed his suspicions. "That and your connection with the pendant that they do not understand. But, there is something else I need to tell you, Wals." She paused before continuing, stepping back from his warm embrace, the sparkle in her lovely eyes gone. Whatever it was that she was going to say, it was obvious that it was hurting her deeply. When she started speaking again, her voice was very low. "You see, I was promised at birth to Prince Phillip. I...I thought perhaps you were he when you came to rescue me on the Island. And then, when you told me your middle name was Phillip…," she trailed off into miserable silence, slowly shaking her head side to side, hating what she was about to do—what she *had* to do.

Not liking where this conversation was going, Wals had to ask, "Has the prince been found? Last I heard he vanished at the same time you did."

Rose's head dipped, her hood hiding her face. He could barely hear her answer. "Yes, the prince is back. He was on a quest to find me. Phillip thought he might find me hidden in a neighboring country. He searched through every town and village for many years, not accepting the fact that I could be gone. It wasn't until he happened to hear a traveling balladeer singing about my return that he knew to come home."

"You were gone for many years. He must be a lot older than you by now."

Rose looked up at him now, her blue eyes filled with tears. "True, he should, but he looks just the same as when I first saw him in the forest." With a fond tilt of her head and a small smile, she indicated the three fairies still inside chatting with Mato. "That must have been their doing. He was so happy to see me...." She broke off, not wanting to tell him the rest.

"And you? Were you just as happy to see him as well?" Wals asked in a kind voice, a voice that masked the fact that he knew his heart was about to break.

She gave a slight nod of her head. "I'm so sorry, Wals," she whispered, looking back up into his dear face. "All the feelings he and I had for each other came rushing back when he first ran into the throne room. The joy we had felt in the forest when we first met when I was sixteen.... When he awakened me with his kiss.... The completeness we found in each others arms when we danced.... It was as if we had never been apart." She went into Wals' arms for a final hug. "I'm so sorry, Wals, I really am," she whispered against his neck. "I do love you, you know. You rescued me when I needed you the most! I'll always love you."

He brought her to arms length and gazed

into her beautiful face. "And I'll always remember my beautiful princess," he whispered back, giving her a look that might have been a smile. "Just remember this one thing, will you, Rose? You have to live happily ever after. It's required, you know."

She wiped a tear from her eye and gave a broken laugh. "Will you be all right?"

No. "Yes, I have another mission right now. We have to save Wolf. Do you think your three friends in there will still help me?"

She glanced towards the rooms where the friends in question were still entertaining Mato. "I don't think I could stop them even if I wanted to! They seem to be quite taken with Mato." She picked up Wals' limp, cold hand and gave it a kiss. "I have to go, Wals. Phillip and King Hubert are waiting at the castle. I have a wedding to plan," she tried to smile, but her heart was torn. Feeling so badly for Wals, Rose told him gently, "I won't ever forget," as she turned to mount the waiting white horse that pawed the ground impatiently.

Stunned at what had just happened to him, Wals mutely stood there, staring into the darkness until the sound of the hooves faded away. He barely felt the hand placed on his shoulder.

"It had to be this way, Wals," Merri told him in a kinder voice than she usually used for him. "Surely you knew that."

He looked at the Blue Fairy and could see there was no bad intent in her eyes, only truth and unexpected compassion. He had to nod. "Yeah, I kinda did. But, I was just hoping I was wrong."

"You know, they were promised from the day she was born. It's a good match. He's twice proven himself to be worthy of our princess." The hand on his shoulder tightened in sympathy. "You are a good man, too, Wals, and very brave."

He gave a small chuckle. "Bet it hurt to admit that."

"A little," she admitted, the corner of her mouth turning upwards. "You have proved worthy, as well. You took care of our girl when she needed it the most and brought her home safe to us. For that we will be forever grateful. But...," she stopped to make sure she had his full attention.

Suddenly wary, he asked, "But what?"

"But, you really don't belong here," the Blue Fairy sighed and held up a hand to stave off his protests. "Now, don't take that wrong. You know you are having a hard time of it. We have been watching all along and doing what we can to help."

He rubbed the sword scar on his sore arm. "A little help then would have been appreciated."

"Those were *her* men. It had to play as it played."

After a long moment of silence, Wals had to ask, "Will Wolf be all right?"

Merri sighed again and looked towards the Dark Castle. The lightning was flashing all around the uppermost turrets. *She* was very active. "I certainly hope so, Wals. I certainly hope so. He is lost right now. You and his brother have to help him find himself. You both need to make him remember home and family and love. *She* took that away from him. They are things she knows nothing about."

Wals just nodded as the Blue Fairy talked. It seemed so daunting to him, regardless of their offer of help. "We will do what we can. We have to."

She patted his shoulder. "You and the warrior go sleep now. You will need every ounce of your strength for what is to come. We will watch through the night."

He looked towards Rose's castle, concerned. "Don't you need to follow Rose? Will she be all right? It's pretty late."

"Her horse knows the way well and she will ride fast. She was riding astride—a bad habit she picked up in your time," she chided. "No, she won't be harmed." Merri turned to go, but, after a second thought, came back to the man. "It broke her heart to tell you what she did."

"Mine, too, Merri. Mine, too."

As Wals returned to his room, Merri's wand appeared in her hands. Humming quietly to herself, the animated stick danced in the air as she motioned in the man's direction. "You'll be fine, Wals. You'll be fine. This is my gift to you for all you've done and all you will do."

He didn't even feel the blue sparkles as they gently landed and played across his back.

"**B**last that girl! She never did do anything she was supposed to!" Nimue fumed as the princess remained day after day in her castle with her parents and that interfering fiancée of hers. He was supposed to be gone for good. The Evil Fairy had been waiting for the girl to meet up with Wals again on the secluded beach, but that seemed highly unlikely at this point. "Well, my pet, it looks like we will have to take matters into our own hands again and end this! Are you ready for the taste of blood?" she cooed into the waiting wolf's gray-tipped ear.

His dull, lifeless eyes kept their unfocused gaze on something far in the distance. "Yes, Madam."

"My," she sniffed, "I expected a little more enthusiasm. Perhaps I shouldn't have been feeding you all this time…."

The Dark Fairy left her latest pet as she stalked to the barracks. She was tired of waiting. Unannounced, the heavy oak door flung open by itself. A stale gust of wind preceded her into the room as the men inside cowered when they caught sight of her, hoping to avoid her malicious glance in the darkness of their corners.

As soon as she left the throne room, Wolf struggled to his feet and staggered to the open door. Away from her suffocating presence, he gulped in big breaths of fresh air. Breathing heavily from the effort it took, he shook his huge head side to side as he tried to still the horrible images as they swirled through his brain. Looking past the broken stones and damaged battle-

ments of her castle, his eyes cleared enough to
see the individual trees in the forest far below.
The stillness of the woods called to him and
looked inviting deep within the fog of his
thoughts. Confused, he just stood there, swaying from all the energy it sapped from him merely
to remain upright. *Why do those trees look so
good to me? Why do I have a sudden urge to
run free in any direction I choose to go? Why....*

The cloud over his blue eyes swirled and
closed in again. The forest became a mere
green blur and the faint feeling of self and of
freedom evaporated like a wispy mist in the
blinding glare of the sun.

"See something interesting, my pet?"
Nimue asked, her voice sugary sweet as her
gray eyes narrowed, watching the wolf as he
confusedly shook his furry head.

"No, Majesty," he muttered in a low voice,
head down as he slowly, obediently returned to
her side.

Her fingers caressed his head in what might
have been perceived as a loving embrace. Ever
so slowly, though, her nails moved until she
grabbed onto the tender part of his ear, squeezing until the pain caused him to wince. "That's
good, my dear one. Let's keep our mind on our
own business, shall we?" she muttered with a
barely-veiled threat as her fingers released him,
but her eyes did not.

All he could identify was relief now that the
pain was gone. Then, as his brain swirled and
dipped even deeper into darkness, his previous
memories were almost totally extinguished. As

she mentally continued to prod him, anger replaced his confusion. His breathing became shallow and gasping as the transformation continued. His eyes finally glowed red as his teeth were bared, his fangs dripping. Hair standing upright along his spine, he snarled and snapped at the rest of the pack as they slowly filed into the room, wary of this black fiend and back out of the way of his sharp teeth.

"That's my good boy," she murmured to herself, pleased with his conversion. "Here is your pack!" she cried out to Wolf as he circled the yapping animals. "You are their leader." She pointed her staff in the direction of the village, its green light raking the air and forking outwards. "Go and bring me their heads! Do not fail me!" With a swirl of her black cape, she changed back into the huge gray wolf she had been once before. "Now! To the village! Run, my pets, run!"

With a commanding howl, Wolf, fueled by her hatred, turned and ran out of the castle, the pack hard on his heels. As the last of her motley crew flew out past her, the Dark Fairy joined them, laughing in her glee to finally put an end to these last friends of her wolf. Once they were gone and the simpering princess off with her disgustingly-persistent prince, there would be no more dangers to the spell over her pet. He would be hers forever.

Then…then he would lead her to her pendant.

Wals was busy practicing his swordsman-ship with the amused Mato. Thinking he had been doing very well, Wals was slightly irritated by the thinly-veiled humor he saw in the warrior's eyes as he easily countered Wals' best moves. "You could at least pretend you're having a tough time of it, Mato," he grunted as he tried to defend himself against a forward thrust.

"What good that?" Mato smiled. "You do better," he claimed as he glanced up at the sun while Wals did a feint and lunge.

Stopping in mid-motion, Wals felt like snap-ping his blade in half. "You aren't even paying attention and still you beat me!"

"I am Lakota." To Mato, that explained everything.

"Hmmph," was all Wals could say to that as he attempted to work out a kink in his arm.

"You ready?" Mato asked, raising the tip of his sword again.

Wals lowered his blade. "How come you can fight so well with a sword? You never used one before. You used arrows when we went on our journey to Rainbow Ridge."

"I am...."

"Yeah, yeah, I know. You are Lakota. Still, it doesn't explain...."

Wals was cut off at the sudden appearance of Fauna when she flew right between them. The Red Fairy seemed very agitated as she flut-tered her wand around them, random red sparks flying off in every direction.

"Fauna! I could have run you through! You

should be more careful than that!" Wals rebuked her, flinging his blade to the side out of harm's way.

"No, no, dear, I've been watching you. No danger in that," she waved him off, looking worriedly in the distance. "You are going to have company...and it is going to be very soon." She looked directly at Wals. "They are coming."

Wals had no need to ask who 'they' were as he glanced over at Mato. The warrior merely shrugged and went inside to gather his quiver and arrows and the hidden flag.

Flora popped in next, her green robes swirling around her as she came to an abrupt halt. "I've been tracking them. They come faster than we thought they would. And, *she* is with them."

"Where's Merri?"

"Out of sight nearby, watching them."

The Red Fairy nodded as she thought. When Mato emerged, his quiver slung over his back, sword and bow in hand, she asked, "Is there a better place where you want to meet them? You do have a little time to choose."

The warrior glanced at the tavern. Villagers had been coming and going all day. These men didn't know Wals or his problem. They would offer no help in the coming battle and, even if they did get involved, they would surely be hurt or killed. He knew most had families and shook his head. It was not their battle. "Not here. Too small. Too many people."

"Where do you think would be best?"

Wals agreed with Mato's assessment.

"While we could use the tavern at our backs, there isn't enough room to maneuver. What about the beach?" he asked, looking at the brave. "Where we came in through the water? Near the boulders. Only a few can attack at a time. That might throw them off a little, if we are not where we are expected. How much time do we have to get there? It is a fairly long run," he asked the Green Fairy.

"Don't worry about that, dear," she smiled pleasantly. Working with Fauna, green and red sparks flew and the two men were instantly transported to the beach.

"I'll go tell Merri," Flora said as she popped out of sight in a green cloud of dust.

Back in less time than it took the men to realize she had gone, she was back, giggling behind her hand. "Oh, I think we made the Evil One a little angry! They just burst into your room and found you gone!"

Nodding as she thought, her companion remarked, "Good, good. They may tire out a little more by the time they realize where you went and reach this spot. That might give us a little more of an advantage."

"Us?" Wals repeated, looking at the two fairies.

They both looked taken aback. "Why, yes, us. You didn't think we would let you have all the fun, did you?"

Each with their own thoughts, the odd foursome was quiet as they awaited their fate.

The cry of a raven high overhead split the air. It was gone before they could identify its exact location.

"Ah, she has found us," Fauna commented, adjusting her pointed red hat, and shaking the kinks out of her wand. "Come on, dear, no time to get fussy," she murmured to it as red glitter spilled out over her hand.

"Oh, dear," the Green Fairy fretted, "I do so hate conflicts like this. I wish everyone would just get along like they should."

Fauna put an arm around the slender shoulders of her friend. "I know, I know. But we have faced this evil before, and we will again. We have to help these mortals. It is the least we can do after they helped our girl so much."

"Oh, that great lumbering horned toad," Merri grumbled as she suddenly appeared on the beach. "She is angry, indeed. I don't think we are going to have an easy time of it. Are you ready, Wals? Mato? We have the flag."

A drawn, waiting sword was her answer as the sound of a running pack of wolves came within their earshot. Backed by high boulders, the two men stood resolute as the fairies blinked out of sight, hopefully remembering his full instructions about the flag.

Mato gave a sharp gasp as he saw his brother at the head of the pack. Wolf was barely recognizable with the crazed, maddened look on his face and the red glare in his eyes. The warrior's eyes narrowed as a beautiful gray female wolf came up next to his brother, nuzzling him. He had no doubt who that was, especially when he clearly heard her say, "Are you ready, my pet? There is my enemy. Command your pack!"

"Spread out, men! Attack in pairs. Leave the tall one for me," he instructed as he glared unknowingly at his brother.

Wals and Mato pulled their knives from their boots, tightly sticking them within easy reach in their belts. Mato strung an arrow, aiming at the breast of the female gray wolf as they slowly advanced on the beach.

With a loud cry, Mato let the arrow fly. Straight and true it flew toward the gray wolf. With a short laugh, she easily leaped to the side at the last moment, the arrow burying itself in the forehead of the unsuspecting wolf behind her. The first fatality, he dropped to the ground without a cry as the others leaped over their fallen comrade, not even giving him a backwards glance.

"The battle begins!"

Wolf and Nimue held back while they allowed their pack do what they could in an all-out attack formation. Their plan was to let the others wear out the two men, and then they would move in for the kill. Snarling directions to his wolves, Wolf moved this way and that over the sand, always moving, always watching the fight, calling out instructions.

As he easily fought off the wolves who didn't recognize the length of his blade, Mato suddenly called out in a loud voice, "Táku eníčiyapi he?" *What is your name?*

Wolf's head jerked toward Mato's direction as the familiar language came into his ears. His breathing became more labored, but he didn't understand why. Shaking his head as he ran to the other side of the beach, he bit the leg of a pack member who was falling back. "To your place! Attack when their blade is up!"

Eyes glowing red in hatred, Nimue ran up next to Wolf, whispering something in his ear. She had noticed his slight hesitation and knew to counter it with another spell.

Wals was now forced to the ground when a mottled, ugly wolf jumped him from the top of the boulders. Pulling out his small dagger, he thrust it upwards, catching the soft underbelly. With a howl and shriek, the wolf fell to the ground as he twisted and turned in his effort to stop the pain in his stomach. Jumping back to his feet, Wals followed Mato's example of distraction and called for Merri to unfurl the flag.

Within a second the orange flag appeared on the boulders above the fighting men, snapping smartly in an unseen, unfelt wind within its own protective spell.

Wals yelled, "Wolf, remember your place at Disneyland. You need to get back to work at the Magic Kingdom." No sooner had he said that than an unnoticed brown vixen made a sudden leap at his throat. The invisible Flora came to his aide and a green arc of twinkles transformed the wolf into a spitting kitten that was easily pushed aside. Seeing her sudden change, the frightened kitty ran off into forest.

"Disneyland?" Wolf whispered to himself, staggering from the word and staring at the bright flag waving boldly from the rocks. "I have a job...."

"Your job is to attack!" Nimue screamed, as she saw the blue of his eyes return for just a second before the fog of her spell swirled it away. Nothing she could do would make the flag vanish. It was guarded and protected by the combined goodness of the three fairies as if a giant, clear dome surrounded it.

Not as distracted as she seemed, the sorceress easily dodged the next arrow that flew mere inches past her head. Turning to glare at Mato, she watched as he defended himself against the next attack. His blade flashed and twisted and another animal went to the ground, the sand stained red with wolf blood.

"Tukténitaŋhaŋ he?" he yelled again towards his brother. *Where are you from?*

"From?" Wolf gasped, jerking in his direction. "I am from...I am from...."

"Come, my pet," she cooed anxiously, frightened by the effect the two men were having on Wolf. "We must end this now. We must no longer rely on our minions. You need to go for his throat!"

Calling the pitifully small remainder of the pack to their sides in order to let Wolf attack, the two men were given a short reprieve. Taking advantage of it, they gulped in huge breaths of clean air, wiping the hilts of their swords dry of the sweat from their hands. "I don't know if we can hold them all off at once," Wals said in an undertone to his companion. "There are too many of them."

"I keep talking to my brother. He remember his tongue. Perhaps there is hope."

"There is always hope," a small voice whispered into their ears. "You are not alone."

"Good to hear," Mato murmured as the pack slowly began their second advance.

Within seconds, the beach was a churning mass of teeth, claws, swords and daggers. The men fought steadily but the wolves, attacking steadily in pairs, were pushing in hard, sensing the end and getting bolder.

With Wals' leg slashed and bleeding from the last attack, he was getting weaker, arms bleeding and aching from swinging the sword. He wondered how much longer they could keep up their front. There seemed to be no end to the number of wolves coming continually at them.

Mato, clearing his mind of the pain of his lacerations, continued to fight against the onslaught.

Suddenly, new sounds came to their ears. The noise was dimly heard over the snarling and whines of the animals. It was the sound of beating hooves on the sand, the scream of approaching war horses as they smelled the frenzied wolves and the stench blood.

Not able to take their eyes off the mad beasts in front of them, Wals could only hope it was not the return of the marauders who had attacked him before on this very same beach.

Their swords continued to aim true with blue, red, or green sparkles biting deep into their attackers as they heard another yell. Neither man knew the voice as it called out, "Attack, men! Watch the teeth!"

Wals heard a sharp gasp from the invisible Merri who called out, "Prince Phillip! Watch your back!"

Throwing himself from his white horse Samson, his sword came up in time to skewer the brute that had cowardly attacked him from behind. His shield pushed through the mass of fur and teeth as he fought his way to Wals' and Mato's side, his sword slashing to the right and left.

Arriving with four of his men, they, too, fell into the fray, attacking the outer edge of the animals. The men fought to their sides silent and sure. The wolves were falling in goodly numbers as they were killed or injured or limped silently away into the forest.

Soon there were only four wolves left—Nimue, Wolf, and two especially large beasts. The Prince dispatched one startlingly white wolf, sending it into the waves of the ocean to wash out to sea. Recognizing that the tide of the battle had turned, he called his men back to his side as Mato and Wals were left with only two.

Mato had one more thing to say to Wolf as the red eyes turned on the two last men standing in front of him. "Thečhíȟila, my brother."

The wolf stopped in mid-motion. He was about to snap Wals' leg in half. "Love?" He turned to face the dark, panting warrior. "Thečhíȟila?" he panted, his head low. "I love you? My brother!?"

He turned in confusion to the gray vixen beside him, her eyes widening as she saw she was losing her hold over him. Her evil spell wouldn't work against the strength of love and family. His eyes were by now returning to a faint blue, his teeth still bared, but now they were turned on her. "What have you done to me?" he suddenly demanded, snapping in her direction, "This is my brother!"

Shocked, Nimue's head whipped around to look at the tall warrior, his last arrow notched and drawn back. His arm quivered with the strength it took to pull the bow back to its full power. The arrow would bury deep in her heart, ending this forever.

She didn't know who moved first, Wolf or his brother. Wolf jumped at her throat and the arrow was let loose from the bow. Her leap out of the way of both of them showed her amazing agility, her paws frantically moving in Wolf's direction as the three good fairies moved in to help him with this final battle. The good that was buried deep inside the wolf now came to the surface, and, united with the good of the fairies, they moved towards the wide-eyed sorceress.

"No!" she screamed. "You will not defeat me again!" She threw a final green bolt at Wolf as she instantly changed form and took to the air. The dark black raven hovered just out of their reach. Knowing there were no more arrows, she screamed one last taunt at them, "I am not done with you yet! I will find you wherever you go and I will get back what is mine!" With that promise, she turned and streaked into the air with a powerful thrust of her wings. She vanished from their sight as the few remains of her pack slunk off into the depths of the forest, never to be seen again.

Surrounded by her green blaze, Wolf snapped and bit in every direction, trying to fight the final spell she had flung at him. Eyes just beginning to cloud again, in his agony, he turned to the nearest person—his brother Mato. With one last snarl, he hurled himself at the man, teeth bared and claws foremost.

With a sinking heart, Mato raised his sword and braced himself as the tip of the blade buried itself into the side of his brother.

CHAPTER NINE

Disneyland — 2008

"Quick, Mato, give me your cloak! The green thing on your back.... We've to get Wolf covered up before anyone comes along." Wals had already tugged off his own battered red cape and draped it over the prostrate form of Wolf, unconscious on the cold stone floor of the Castle Walkthrough. With no outer windows, he couldn't tell what time of day—or night—it may have been. The Park could be open, closed, busy, being fumigated....he had no way of knowing.

At Wals' request, Mato turned from the brightly-lit window. Inside was a pretty fair representation of the woman he had known as Rose, lying in an oddly furnished room with a man dressed similarly to Wals bending over her, apparently wanting a kiss. Not knowing the story of the Sleeping Beauty nor ever having been inside her fair castle, he couldn't make heads or tails out of the animated scene that played over and over. Knowing he wouldn't understand most of Wals' explanation anyway, he silently complied, unfastening his green velvet cape and tucking it around his brother. "Where Wolf's clothes?"

Wals had run up a couple of the steps to see if anyone was coming. He couldn't hear anything, but the soft music playing as ambience could mask subtle sounds. "What? Oh, that. When he changes into a wolf, his clothes aren't needed. When he comes back, he's always like this. There's no way for him to put them on ahead of time. But he usually plans ahead by leaving clothing somewhere close by. Now that I think of it, I think he left his uniform in one of these rooms." Wals tried the doorknob nearest him, not remembering exactly which room had belonged to Merri when she lived here to keep an eye on Rose. She had kept under wraps pretty much, presenting herself as an animal handler for Disneyland.

As he opened a door on the next level up, not even pausing to wonder how it could possibly be unlocked, he found the correct room, spotting a neatly piled stack of clothing off in a dark corner. Quickly gathering the uniform, he didn't take the time to look around. Had he bothered, he would have found the room was completely empty, devoid of any signs of habitation. Merri had made sure there was no trace of anything left behind that would raise a question about her—or her abilities. Once Wals let go of the door handle, it quietly shut and locked itself for good.

"How badly hurt is he, Mato? He usually regains consciousness by now." At Mato's blank look at his last sentence, Wals reworded it. "He should not still be sleeping."

"Ah." Seeing a handful of clothes in Wals' arms, Mato proceeded to rip the unneeded cloak into long strips, small particles of fluff filling the air like a strange green snow appearing out of nowhere. The pieces of velvet were then wrapped around Wolf's ribs where the sword had pierced him. His mouth in a firm line, Mato felt tremendous guilt over having to hurt his brother, but there simply had been no other way to stop him. Both men carefully pulled the uniform's pants on over the many cuts and scraps on Wolf's battered body. As they gently lifted him to tug his shirt on, some of the larger cuts reopened and blood immediately seeped through the clean fabric.

The sound of running feet coming up the stairs towards them caused the two men to exchange a worried look. Wals quickly repositioned the red cape over the worst of the blood stains. Mato drew his knife and stood resolute, facing the approaching noise.

Wals almost yelled at Mato, but reduced it to a loud hiss, "Put that away! We're in Disneyland, for crying out loud! You don't need that!"

Obviously not agreeing, Mato still complied, slipping the dagger back into his boot. He knew he would be able to reach it quickly enough if Wals was wrong and it was needed.

In a flash, Lance, dressed for work in his security uniform, burst into sight carrying a first-aid kit, bringing them both tremendous relief.

"How did you know we were here?" Wals asked as Lance kneeled next to his immobile partner.

"How long has he been out like this?" Lance first wanted to know, putting a cool hand on Wolf's hot forehead. "We had cameras installed in here just after you and Mato left so we could monitor it from the control room. Kimberly has been watching you all since you arrived," he hurriedly explained as he picked up his walkie-talkie.

"He like this before we came back," Mato clarified when Lance turned to face him. "It was bad fight," he murmured, hating his role in it.

Seeing the pain in the brother's eyes, Lance just merely nodded as he pushed the button to connect to his wife back at the mansion. Explanations would come later. Now, Wolf's care—and getting him quickly out of sight—were the most important things. "Yes, he is as bad as he looks, Kimberly. We need to get him out of sight. Where do you suggest?"

Looking at the huge holographic map of Disneyland projected into the middle of the War Room, she suggested, "There's some kind of empty room under the Hungry Bear. What about that? That way he will be close the portal to get Mato home."

Lance looked to Wals for confirmation, as they could all hear Kimberly's voice over the two-way radio. "I know where that is. We'll need a wheelchair or something to get him over there, though. He won't be walking any time soon."

"Yes, I heard, Lance. Give me a second." Kimberly's voice died away from the radio as she went over to the phone that went directly to the Park. Within a minute or two she was back on the radio. "Done. Lance, why don't you go downstairs and wait for the chair. Wals and Mato are too conspicuous in those clothes. I already put a call in to Doctor Houser. This isn't his specialty of cryogenics, but I'm sure he will know what to do to help. I'll also send a security detail to divert traffic for when he gets here."

"That's a good idea. We'll need a couple of escorts, too. Once we get Wolf comfortable, we'll get Wals and Mato changed into regular clothes," Lance directed as he looked over the torn, dirty costumes. He silently shook his head thinking about what they must have gone through to come back looking like that.

"All right. Peter is on a play date, so I'll probably arrive around the same time as the doctor. See you all later. Take care of Wolf!" Kimberly called out a little louder before she disconnected.

The wheelchair arrived within minutes and was there waiting for Lance at the exit to the Walkthrough. Mato and Wals carefully brought Wolf to his feet and carried him down the last few flights of stairs. Once settled in the chair, Lance wrapped Wals' red cape over Wolf a little tighter this time to hide and, hopefully, help stop the flow of blood.

"Okay, here is where it gets fun," he mumbled as they were already attracting attention, both from Mato and Wals being—sort of—dressed like princes and someone being carried out of the Walkthrough and placed in a wheelchair. The attraction wasn't known to be so exciting that a guest would not be able to take it. A few of the people standing around them were looking up at the pink towers of the Castle, contemplating giving it a go and seeing what all the fuss was about. Lance pointed towards the other side of the courtyard. "Let's take the shortcut to Frontierland. It's not as well used as the route through the Castle entry and into Main Street."

Two of Lance's and Wolf's security friends quietly appeared next to the wheelchair. They took one look at Wolf and threw a worried glance at Lance. "We need to get him out of sight under the Hungry Bear," Lance told them. He knew these two could be counted on for any emergency or problem and would never mention it again.

Nodding their understanding, the oldest, Bob, observed, "Unfortunately, as you know, there are no hidden passageways we can use. I think through Adventureland would be the best route. It would be the smoothest ride without the rough concrete in Frontierland."

Joe, the other guard, concurred. "Over the top of the Pirates entrance, then the upper level past the Haunted Mansion and down past the canoe dock. Agreed? We'll have to go double-time. Y'all ready?" He looked at all the men. Wals was nodding in agreement. Mato was impatiently waiting for them to do *something* besides talk.

Taking turns pushing the wheelchair, one of them always making sure Wolf didn't tumble out, they traveled as fast as the crowd would allow them. The guests, seeing a fast-moving wheelchair accompanied by Security, were helpful in quickly getting out of the way. It seemed to take forever before they were safely out of sight under the huge wooden restaurant, mere steps away from the small canoes Wals had used just a short time ago.

The plain white room they were in had become more or less of a storeroom with odds and ends discarded from the restaurant and forgotten broken canoe paddles and parade pieces littering the area. Cast members who had known about the little-used room had brought in a variety of "borrowed" furniture pieces over the years as they used the room for secret rendezvous and, once, a huge after-hours party that had ended with an impromptu canoe race and most of the participants skinny-dipping in the River.

Wals and Lance both cast subtle glances at each other, each wondering how the other knew about this place. Questions like that, too, would come later, when they were in private and Lance's wife wasn't nearby.

Kimberly met Dr. Houser at the special VIP entrance to the Park and rode with him to the delivery entrance for the Hungry Bear, tucked behind the Winnie the Pooh ride there in Critter Country. Once they were both in the hidden room, the doctor merely nodded his hello, showing little surprise at seeing Wolf's brother stand-ing there. After his past experience with both Wolf and Wals in the early 1800's, nothing much surprised him any longer. Opening his medical bag, he got to work examining Wolf, who by then had barely regained consciousness, but, typi-cally for him, felt no need to announce that fact.

Kimberly walked up to the silent, tense Mato as he watched his brother. Lightly resting her hand on his arm, his eyes softened as he turned to face her. "Thank you for bringing Wolf back," she told him quietly, her eyes showing her gratitude. "We don't know what we would have done if you hadn't been able to come."

"He is my brother."

She patted his arm and nodded her under-standing. "I wish I had a brother like you. I would have felt very safe growing up." She looked back as they heard a low groan coming from the patient. "Is he going to be all right?" she asked Mato.

A look of worry crossed Mato's eyes, but it was quickly gone and the warrior replaced it with pride. "Yes, he is Lakota. He will get better. He would have to answer to our father if he did not."

That brought a quick smile to Kimberly's face. "That I understand, too. We go to a lot of pains to make sure our parents don't know how badly hurt we really are!"

Seeing his partner was in good hands, Lance felt at liberty to attend to other necessary matters. "Wals, where did you leave your other clothes? In your locker or did you hide them on the Island like Wolf usually does?"

Tearing his eyes from his hurt friend, his mind filled with the fight, losing Rose, the violence of the vortex, and that final threat from Nimue, he had trouble remembering. "Oh. I think I left them here. I think.... It seems so long ago," he faded off, looking back at Wolf when he heard a muffled curse in Lakota. At least, he figured it was a curse when he heard Mato give a deep chuckle.

"I'll go check. You all stay here. I need to get you all a change of clothes. Anyone else need anything? Doctor?"

Dr. Houser, who had been silent since he started examining Wolf, looked up from his patient, distracted by the interruption. "What? Oh, no, thank you. I think I have all that I need. From the small amount of blood still seeping out and no swelling, it appears the puncture wound may have missed all the vital organs, thank goodness," he reported to the anxious group standing back to give him room, but still watching his every move. He silently eyed the long, ancient-looking sword hanging from Wals' belt, remembering seeing it during his time in the past. "The other cuts and contusions seem to be fairly minor in comparison.... Although, I am not sure where the burn marks on his arms and neck came from. At least I think they are burn marks." He looked to Wals and Mato for any information they could give.

Not knowing exactly how to describe a glowing green arc of white-hot lightning coming from a centuries-old sorceress, Wals and Mato looked at each other and just shrugged innocently. With an unbelieving "Hmph," the doctor turned back to his patient who was already starting to complain—a sign they all took as encouraging.

When he was stable enough and Doctor Houser proclaimed him able to be moved without opening his wounds again, Wolf was taken to Lance and Kimberly's place in the Hills. Wolf, of course, considered himself quite able to go back to their village with his brother. Finally listening to cooler heads than his own, he stoically resigned himself to the fact that he would have to put up with everyone's hovering for a few more days before he could go home.

"**W**als, I suggest you go back to work for a couple of days while Wolf recuperates. That way you can keep on record as an active cast member," Kimberly told him as he wandered aimlessly through their house in the Fullerton Hills. He was getting antsy with nothing to do. Not yet talking about Mato and his experiences, she wondered if work would be the answer to get his mind off whatever they had been through. Mato wasn't a problem. He never wanted to leave his brother's side. But Wals needed a diversion. It was getting harder and harder to keep him from following Lance into the off-limits War Room.

She was glad to see his eyes light up. "Back to the canoes?"

"Well, no, you had been reassigned to Fantasyland. You should go back to Casey Jr. Or," she offered as an alternative, "I can put you on the Storybook Land Canal Boats."

Wals clamped his mouth shut. He would rather go back and face Nimue again....

"Okay," Kimberly said slowly. "Casey Jr. it is," as she was unable to read the look on his face. "All right?"

"Fine," he replied in a clipped voice.

"Your lead, Anne, reported you were doing a good job...." Kimberly faltered as he plastered an obviously fake smile on his face.

"That was nice of her. My car is outside. I'd better go check in now."

Lance came into the library as Wals pushed past him, muttering under his breath something about puffy shirts and lederhosen. When the front door slammed shut, he turned to his wife. "Did I miss something?"

Kimberly looked flummoxed. "I think perhaps I missed something," she admitted with a shrug of her shoulders. "I merely suggested Wals might like to go back to work to get his mind off whatever it was they went through."

"Did you let him go back to the Canoes? He loved that position."

"Oh? Should I have? I sent him back to Casey Jr. Although I did offer to have him switched to the Canal Boats if he wanted."

Lance let out a laugh and gave his beloved wife a hug. "And he took that badly, did he? Poor Wals," he theatrically sighed. "I think we should change him back to the Canoes...but let's wait a few days! Speaking of which, I have a question for you, Madam Trivia Master, what do these names have in common: Nellie Bly, Lady Katrina, Lady of Shallot, Annie Oakley, Bold Lochinvar, Lady of the Lake, Lady Guinevere, and Gretel?"

Kimberly gave him a light slap on the arm. "That's an easy one! My father told me all about The Mud Bank Ride!"

When Lance gave her a blank look, she grinned smugly. "Ah, I have another one on you this time! I believe that makes our score 210 to 166. Well," she started, taking his arm in hers as they strolled out of the library, "It all went back to Walt's love of miniatures."

Disneylandia — 1952

After a decade of collecting and building his own intricate, elaborate miniatures, Walt unveiled his first Americana exhibition at the Festival of California Living in Los Angeles, California. Walt himself described his scene as a "visual juke box with the record player replaced by a miniature stage setting." Almost eight feet in length, the entranced audience listened to the recorded voice of the actress who had appeared in the movie *So Dear to My Heart* as they peered into the small version of her rustic cabin. They marveled at Walt's own handiwork that included rocking chairs, plank floors, a stone fireplace— the stones having come from his Smoke Tree property, small rugs, lace curtains, dishes, and even an outhouse.

The public reaction was so positive that Walt wanted to expand the exhibit to include at least two more tableaus. The most energetic display would be the frontier music hall. Titled "Project Little Man," this would feature a one-eighth scale, three-dimensional old-time vaudeville dancer. The Imagineers filmed the moves of a popular actor/dancer while others built the elaborate music box that would house the gears and mechanics of what would be come to be known as the beginnings of audio-animatronics. Walt, though, didn't like the unmovable clay face of the puppet, and wanted to do more work with pliable plastics.

The third set would be a barbershop complete with a quartet singing the popular *Sweet Adeline*. But, after another set of actors were filmed for reference, the project was stopped.

Walt was pretty sure that the audience able to view his works of art would be too limited and there wouldn't be enough income generated to pay for the ongoing upkeep of the displays. Building his miniatures had done what Walt had wanted them to do—they diverted his attention from the worries of the Studio and allowed him to become so absorbed that his cares melted away…at least for a little while. Over the years, he had even built and sold around one hundred small metal pot-bellied stoves, each about five and a half inches tall with fully-working parts, and each one decorated differently.

By now, the Disneylandia project wasn't proving to be feasible, so it, in turn, slowly morphed into Disneyland. Walt's brother was sent to New York in 1953 to begin raising funds for this larger, more complex idea. Included in the sales pitch, located between Tomorrowland and Fantasyland, was a land called Lilliputian Land. Here would be a miniature Americana village with mechanical people only nine inches tall who would sing or dance or tell you about their lives as you looked in through the windows of their small shops and houses. The tiny Erie Canal barge would take guests through the famous canals of the world.

This special section of Disneyland never got built, but the small Erie Canal barge ride eventually evolved into Canal Boats of the World that was operating on Disneyland's Opening Day in 1955. The souvenir guidebook described it as the "Boats of Holland, France, England, and America that travel through canals and see the fabulous sights of Fantasyland." With eight grandly named boats, the ride was composed of muddy water and unfinished banks of dirt decorated, part of the time, with weeds. Until the elaborate upgrade in 1956, the ride was known, out of Walt's hearing, as the "Mud Bank Ride," and the men who worked the attraction would have to tell the guests that the "miniature landscaping was so small that it could not be seen by the unaided human eye."

The new additions of 1956 were marvels of miniature technology. Doors and windows in the quaint cottages and houses could be opened. Electrical systems rivaled those of full-sized homes. Special varnishes and coatings were used so the buildings would withstand the elements year after year. One stained-glass window contained three hundred sixty pieces of cut and beveled glass. The doors of the houses were weathered with a wire brush that scraped the wood to give them an aged appearance. The doors and latches were made of lead and weathered and hammered to also look appropriately old. Toys filled the front window of Gepetto's workshop, so tiny that the passers-by in the canal boats could hardy see them.

The landscaping was another wonderful element of the ride with miniature trees, bushes, shrubs and even a mountain range that all had to be one inch to a foot in perspective. Walt wanted nothing fake, so all the plants had to be live and growing.

When a contractor complained about all the expense and work that went into things that most people wouldn't even know were there, he suggested cutting corners and lowering expenses. "Who would know the difference?" he asked. The stern reply from the boss was, "*I'll* know the difference."

One Imagineer thought it would be a nice idea for the guests to be swallowed by Monstro the Whale, just like Pinocchio had been in the movie. Lifted high in the whale's throat, the boats would hurl down the track into a pool below. Walt nixed the idea, thinking the adults might not want to go on a white-knuckle ride like that. Monstro stayed, but the steep water flume did not.

Disneyland — 2008

"Lance, we have to do something about Mato!"

"Why? Did he try to teach Peter how to start a fire in the middle of the kitchen again?"

"What? What do you mean 'again'?" Kimberly stopped and stared at Lance, hands on her hips. "When did he do that?"

"Not to worry," Lance waved her off, "it was nothing. The smoke detector went off and called the Fire Department. When they came wailing down the street, that's when Peter knew he was in big trouble. Mato hated knowing he got Peter in trouble—for some reason totally unbeknownst to him, so he said he'd never do it again. What's wrong?"

Kimberly tilted her head as she looked at her husband—the mask of innocence. Knowing she would get nothing else out of him, she continued with her previous thought. "I think he is getting too bored. Wolf is almost ready to, uhm, travel again, but still not quite strong enough. We need something to divert Mato's attention. The television sure isn't doing it."

Lance had to laugh at that. Hoping to impress the visitor by their marvelous technology, the television had proven a dismal failure—especially the less-than-accurate Western that happened to be playing when they turned the set on. Getting angrier by the moment, even after the movie had been hastily turned off, Mato could never be convinced to watch another show. Muttering to himself, he had stalked out of the room.

"Yeah, bad timing," Lance agreed, grimacing at the memory. "What if Peter and I take him somewhere? He still gets a kick out of riding in the Mustang."

"Why don't you ask Wolf what he might like to do? Perhaps he has some suggestions."

Wolf had laughed so hard about the fire incident that he had reopened his sword wound. Lance wasn't so sure the younger brother would be much help. "I'll ask," he shrugged. He knew Mato was out back showing Peter the finer points of archery. He'd have to have the holes in their new gazebo filled in later, hopefully before Kimberly spotted them.

"Why don't you take him to Disneyland. Show him where you and I work."

"Really?" Lance stared at Wolf, trying to figure if he was kidding or not. "I didn't get the feeling he was too impressed when Wals brought him through the portal."

"No, no, he really liked it," a straight-faced Wolf told him. "He was just too shook up from the passage to say much."

Lance knew Mato wasn't "too shook up" by much of anything that he had ever had to face in his life. Looking into the sharp blue eyes of his partner, he still couldn't tell if this was a joke.

"I'd go with you if I felt up to it," Wolf sighed weakly, closing his eyes as he settled back onto his pillows.

"Uh huh." Lance knew, for a fact, that Wolf never, ever admitted to being anything less than perfect. Eyes narrowed with suspicion, Lance went back to his wife. "He says to take Mato to Disneyland for the day."

Not knowing the subtle guy-things that men do to each other, Kimberly thought that was a wonderful idea. "Be sure to take him on the canoes. He might feel a little closer to home," she suggested brightly. "Besides, Peter will love it. I'm too far along to go on all the rides he likes. I wonder how Mato will like Space Mountain?"

"I'll let you know," Lance replied flatly. Still not sure he was being set up, he collected together his cast member I.D., sun block for Peter, and the large Hawaiian shirt he had found for Mato to wear that he had promptly discarded. Comfortable only in his deerskin trousers and moccasins, Mato would need slightly more covering to go to the Park. "Here goes nothing," he muttered as he headed out back.

"I want to go on the canoes!" the over-excited Peter demanded next. "Uncle Wolf said Uncle Mato would love them!"

Glancing at the set face of the silent warrior, Lance sincerely doubted Uncle Mato would "love" anything just then. They had ridden the steam train around the Park to give Mato an idea of the different areas they could visit as well as the size of Disneyland. The Grand Canyon had been mildly interesting with the stuffed animals on display as they chugged by, but the Primeval World had elicited scoffing chuckles at the odd beasts. Mato had indicated, in a few descriptive gestures, that he could easily dispatch them with his knife—which Lance had finally convinced him to leave home. Getting off in New Orleans Square, much to the relief of the parents with small children who had witnessed Mato's extensive description on how to gut a carcass, Lance hoped the graceful architecture would remind the native of the New Orleans on the outskirts of his home forest.   He was still debating on whether or not to take Mato inside the Haunted Mansion. Doctor Houser had told Lance about meeting the real Master Gracie while the house was still under construction back in 1815 and wondered how a mansion now filled with nine hundred ninety-nine ghosts would go over with Mato.

The line to the Davy Crockett Explorer Canoes was thankfully short. Grabbing an oar and quickly exchanging Peter's adult-length paddle into the proper, smaller child size, they were able to board the next canoe as it slipped into place beside them. Mato commented on the wiya who was steering in the back and recognized the costume as the one Wals had worn both times he had traveled back into the past.

Once the canoe was floating free from the confines of the wooden dock, Mato was told to watch and do what the cast member in the front was doing. Amused by the simplicity of the lesson the guide was giving, Mato looked around at the thick trees that made up the interior of

Frontierland, pleased to see finally something familiar. Once the brief lesson in how to paddle was over, the guests were invited to begin rowing.

"Finally," Mato muttered under his breath.

The canoe suddenly shot forward in the water. The guide in the front glanced back, curious to see who was actually paddling. Most guests made feeble efforts, soon tiring and then would sit back to enjoy the ride their guides had to provide. Smiling at the broad shoulders and determined look on Mato's face, he quickly turned back and matched the energetic guest stroke for stroke. The sternsman gave a war whoop as their canoe flew past another canoe that had left the dock minutes before theirs. A couple of the other passengers onboard got into the spirit of things and the canoe almost skidded around the next bend in the river.

Mato didn't lessen his pace all the way around the Rivers of America. He had seen the sights when he had first arrived with Wals. Lance finally had to tell him to stop paddling as they were nearing the canoe dock almost too fast. The cast member in back had to both steer and backpaddle to slow them down for the proper sedate approach.

"Gosh, I've never gotten around that fast!" one of the female guests in front gushed, eyeing Mato with appreciation.

"Good thing the Mark Twain was already docked," was muttered by sternsman as he changed places with the next set of guides who had been yelling and encouraging the canoe as they had shot around the final bend. "I don't think we could have stopped in time!"

"Mato, that was supposed to be fun," Lance told him as he rubbed his sore arms, putting their paddles back in the wooden bins.

"That was fun!" Mato broke out into a wide grin as they exited the ride, looking pleased with himself for the first time in days. "What next, little one?" he asked Peter who was wiping water off of his face.

"Want to go see Uncle Wals on Casey Jr.?" Lance suggested before Peter could reply.

"No! I wanna go on Splash Mountain! We're already wet," he pointed out, holding out his arms so the water could run off them.

"The line is too long," Lance told him in an undertone. "I don't think Mato would like to wait that long."

"Use your pass. You do it with Mom."

Lance stared at the innocent-looking boy. "You aren't really six, are you?" he asked Peter, giving him a half-smile.

"Can I have some popcorn? I'm hungry."

"We just had lunch at the Rainforest Café," where, again, Lance had been glad Mato wasn't armed when the gorilla suddenly came to life, angrily growling and shaking the tree next to their table.

"That was hours ago," the boy argued, trying to use his big green eyes to his advantage to sway his father.

Lance gave a loud laugh as they headed for the exit of Splash Mountain. "You are dealing with the master, my boy! That look won't work on me. I perfected it!"

As they reached the continually-moving loading ramp, Lance asked Peter if he wanted to ride the very back seat that held two people, rather than the single seats that ran down the middle of the "carved log" ride vehicle.

"Sheesh, I'm not a baby, Dad."

Mato recognized the tone of voice. His own son used it regularly on him as well. He gave Lance a knowing look as they exchanged smiles.

Mato, of course, didn't know the backstory of the log ride, but seemed entertained by the bouncing, singing animals that inhabited the sides of the flume, plus he was intrigued by the fact that the ride didn't need paddles for the log to advance in the water. As their vehicle bounced and slid through the moving current, taking them higher and higher with a series of ramps, he wasn't sure what to expect when the log seemed to stop in midair and there was nothing to see in front of them except the distant Park. The log tilted downward and he gave an excited, surprised yell as they flew down the sharp incline and splashed into the pool at the bottom. Reverting to Lakota, he yelled back to Lance that that was fun and was better than running the rapids at home.

Having no way of knowing what Mato had just said, Lance took the wide smile on his face as an indication that he really liked it. As they shook the water out of their hair, Mato now looked expectantly to see what was next. This day at Disneyland had just gotten more interesting!

"Big Thunder! Big Thunder! Big Thunder!" Peter chanted as he danced around the two men, leaving wet footprints wherever he stepped.

Recognizing those words from something Wals had said when they had traveled to Rainbow Ridge, Mato indicated that was fine with him.

"Okay, Big Thunder it is," Lance smiled as Peter led the way out of Critter Country, bypassing the laid-back Winnie the Pooh ride. Lance idly wondered how Mato would have liked the Heffalumps and Woozles scene.

Peter chose to sit with Uncle Mato, leaving Lance by himself in the car behind. He saw Mato closely scrutinizing the small buildings that formed the backdrop of the ride queue, Rainbow Ridge. Wals had described their trek and what the remnants of the small mining town of the past had looked like, and Lance wondered how much Mato actually recognized. Supposed to be a runaway train, there was no engineer in the cab as the train started with a jerk and quickly turned into the dark cave filled with bats and colored pools of water. Up they went towards a waterfall that split in half to allow the riders a safe, dry passage. Peter whooped as the train veered to the right and went into a hairpin curve. The brave next to him seemed fascinated by the mining equipment and animals lining the tracks as the train dipped and curved through the red-streaked rocks. He started laughing at the double, looping curve the train made after passing a goat oddly chewing on a stick of dynamite. He was still laughing when the train splashed down next to the dinosaur bones and sedately chugged past Rainbow Ridge and back into the station.

"I wanna go again!" Peter jumped up and down, adrenaline coursing through him.

"Me, too!" Mato grinned.

"We'll have to come back later. It's too busy to take a second trip just now."

"Aww," echoed Peter and Mato.

Lance hid his grin as he led them off of the wooden train platform and back to the textured concrete thoroughfare of Frontierland. He had the distinct feeling he had created a roller-coaster monster in Mato. "Let's go say hi to Uncle Wals."

That took care of the exuberant look on Peter's face. "We don't have to ride the canal boats, do we?"

"He's on Casey Jr., but no, we don't. I was thinking Mr. Toad or Peter Pan might be interesting for Mato."

"Space Mountain?" Peter threw out there, hopeful.

"After we say hi and ride Peter Pan."

"'Kay."

"'Kay," Mato echoed, looking around at the wilderness behind Big Thunder as they walked the back way into Fantasyland. Lance gave him a moment to stare into the green depths of the empty Bear Lake, the tunnel overhead that would have led to Nature's Wonderland being boarded over. The turkeys received a second

look as they passed by the Big Thunder Ranch.
Lance didn't think his explanation of the Presidential Pardon each year at Thanksgiving would have much meaning for the brave at this point in time. "Supper?" Mato asked, pointing at the large, white birds.

Lance glanced at his watch. These two were putting his prodigious hunger to shame! "Soon," he told Mato.

"That means later, when he feels like it," Peter whispered to his new best friend.

"I know," Mato whispered back. "I say same to my son, too."

Peter nodded sagely and smiled.

As they continued walking towards the barbecue restaurant, Mato spied something else familiar. Walking away from his companions, his head tilted upwards, he circled the last vestiges of Nature's Wonderland—two natural rock arches tinted with the familiar yellow and red stripes of the region. Wals had made the arduous, dangerous climb to the top of one of those peaks—much to Mato's annoyance at the delay—and had almost gotten bit by a rattlesnake. Now the remnants of those arches were only a few feet taller than his head. He ran a thoughtful hand over the warm rock as the changes between their two worlds that Wolf had told them about over the years suddenly made more sense.

Emitting a shoulder-raising sigh as they entered Fantasyland, Peter knew he wasn't going to get to the Space Mountain roller coaster or the Buzz Lightyear target-shooting ride any time soon. Mato noticed the instant crush of more people and especially more children in this noisy, colorful area. It hadn't been this bad when they had come out at the back of the castle. He grabbed an apple off of a snack cart as he walked by, and Lance hurried back to pay for it when he saw Mato munching away.

Wals was working the line when the trio approached up the exit ramp to say hello. He looked so envious of their day together that Lance almost felt sorry for him.

The lead cast member on the ride, Anne, came right over when she spied Wals' good-looking friends. She pushed her dark curly hair back behind her ear. "Who're you friends, Wals, and why haven't you introduced us before?" she smiled at the two men, not even looking at her co-worker.

She quickly spotted Lance's wedding ring, not recognizing him out of his uniform, and turned her dusky gaze to the tall Mato. Her interest wavered when he merely grunted some kind of hello and turned to watch the spinning carrousel.

"I'm Peter," the little boy with them chimed in, holding out his hand to her.

"Anne," she muttered, the wind evaporating from her sails. Ignoring Wals' smug expression, she turned to go back to work. The train had tooted its approach to the station and would soon unload. "You're up next, Wals," she called.

Biting back a retort, Wals plastered another fake smile on his face and muttered to the men, "I'm up next. Lucky me."

Saying good-bye, the trio walked down the exit ramp. Lance led them over to the carrousel and asked Peter if he wanted to ride it. Glancing up at Mato, who gave a quick shake of his head, Peter told his dad he would rather go on Peter Pan. Lance put the walkie-talkie he had just used back on his belt and led the way to the popular ride's exit. As their elaborate pirate ship lifted them up into the air, Lance knew another call was being made. By the time they banked past the nursery scene and soared over London, he knew Wals would soon be waiting for them at the exit to Space Mountain, already dressed in his street clothes.

Days later, Lance, Kimberly, Peter, Wals, Wolf, and Mato stood on the bank of the Rivers of America. It was late at night, far too late for Peter to be up, but the excited boy was allowed the special treat of saying good-bye to Mato and Wolf as they were now able to go back to their family. Knowing it was useless to try and keep him down any longer, Wolf had received the reluctant go-ahead from Doctor Houser and was declared well enough to make the jump again. Unable to form any concrete plans, still in a sense of shock over the loss of Rose, Wals had asked if he could go along with them for a visit.

While they had been in the Brentwood's house that last day, Kimberly brought out a small black metal box to show Mato. Rolling his eyes, he was prepared to be unimpressed by yet another one of their worthless gadgets. True, some of the wonders he had seen—like Wolf's Mustang—had proven themselves to be worth the trouble they seemed to cause. But most—like the Zippo lighter and the television—proved to be a waste of time.

"Just wait," Kimberly had promised, bringing him over to where Wolf was sitting, resting in a chair until it was time to go. She had Mato stand behind the chair and rest his hand on the tall back of the antique wingback. "Just stay there a moment," as she backed up, putting the small box in front of her face. Wolf knew what she was doing, but said nothing to his brother. "Smile," she commanded for some reason. Both men remained straight faced, as usual. "Fine," she muttered and pushed a button, producing a clicking noise and then a louder 'whirr.' A flat object was ejected from the box. Kimberly pulled this away from the box, smiling smugly as she slowly shook it back and forth in the air. Coming back to Mato she held it up for him to see.

He saw nothing. Muttering something to Wolf under his breath, Wolf just told him with a smile, "Keep looking."

In front of his eyes, he could see Wolf's face and his own slowly appear on the shiny gray surface. He took the picture by the edges as he had seen Kimberly handle it, and grunted as their image became sharp and defined. "Not worthless," he declared. "What used for?"

Kimberly looked over his shoulder at the picture. It was a good shot of the two brothers. "I thought you might like to give it to your father as a gift. Wolf mentioned that the Shaman hasn't seen his actual face since he was a boy."

Both men looked sharply at her. It was a nice idea that Wolf had never thought of. They were quite touched at her thoughtfulness. Not that they would tell her, though.

"Thank you," Wolf said. "I think he will like this. It will need to be protected," as he remembered what happened to the recorder he had so carefully prepared and hidden for an emergency just like the one that had happened. He would have to look for it in the forest when he got back.

Reaching into her pocket, she had pulled out a plastic zip-topped sandwich bag and let it swing slowly back and forth in front of his face.

That bag and the picture were now tucked securely into the waistband of his deerskin trousers, and Mato stood waiting by the small canoe while everyone said their good-byes. Peter, dry-eyed at first, dissolved into a puddle of tears as he hugged Wals and the two warriors. He was so upset that they were leaving that he could not remember any of their words—which made him even more emotional.

"Be brave, little one, we will see you again," Wolf whispered to him. Pulling away, he shook hands with Lance and endured a rib-crushing hug from Kimberly that made him grunt in pain.

Nodding to the others, Mato, Wals and Wolf climbed into the canoe. When Lance and his family had gone back far enough to be safely out of the way, Wolf called for the portal.

As they were slowly paddling out in the River that was getting more agitated by the second, only Lance and Kimberly noticed an odd blue light. Coming from the upper story of the Hungry Bear, it sparkled and glimmered over the water as it caught up to the bobbing canoe. Ignoring the two men in the back, the light settled on Wolf's head, disappearing into his gray-tipped black hair.

"Did you see that?" Lance whispered to Kimberly.

She merely shrugged as the pink of the vortex exploded and consumed the canoe and its riders. "I don't know what that was," she finally answered when the phenomenon was over.

Torn between grief at losing his friends and seeing something better than any of his video games, Peter stood silent and wide-eyed as the men disappeared right in front of his eyes.

Sitting on the top peak of the restaurant's roof, watching the storm angrily swirl the River and the canoe around, a very small Merri smiled as her wand settled down in her hand. Now that Rose was back in her proper place in time, Merri and the other fairies were now able to travel freely and come and go as they liked. Thrilled to no end that they had all their powers back, Merri had wanted to do one last thing for the wolf. "There is our last gift to you, Sir Wolf. Good journey!" Humming a lively tune, the wand now circled her own head and she vanished in a brilliant cloud of blue dust.

The Island — 1817

Standing at the edge of the River, the Shaman grunted disgustedly as a small, empty canoe floated by. It still was not the favorite canoe in which he had sent his son off so long before. "What's the use in having nice things if you don't take care of them?" he mumbled to no one in particular.

Hiding his impatience, he stood in his rocky overhang, waiting. The storm and the canoe meant at least one of the travelers had returned. A broken paddle now bobbed past the encampment, carried along by the current. There was no way of knowing who was going to be coming home. He had been shocked when the last storm had only produced the man Wals and not his son Wolf. His eyes continued to scan the banks of the River as far as he could see as some of his braves came to his side, silently waiting for instructions. Mato's wife stood anxiously at the edge of the meeting place.

"We will wait," he told them, his voice calm and not betraying his high feelings. "We will see what this storm has brought us." *Apparently it has* not *brought back my canoe….*

Nodding, the men went back to their duties around camp. Mato's wife resolutely stood where she was, her hopeful eyes following the small canoe as it floundered on the far bank.

Soon a shout went up from the outskirts of the camp. His heart beating erratically in his chest, the wolf headdress of the Shaman was held high as his face still betrayed no outward emotion. He bit on his lower lip when his son Mato emerged from the forest and he envied the joyful reunion as Mato's wife threw herself into his arms with a happy cry. He could see someone else coming behind his son and his heart beat joyfully again. His breath caught in his throat, though, when he saw it was Wals who emerged from the shadows of the trees. While glad to see he was alive, the Shaman strained to look beyond the man, hoping to see four familiar black paws bringing up the rear. His heart plummeted when he did not see the shape of the wolf. As he was about to turn away and go greet Mato, he caught sight of another man emerging slowly from the depths of the forest, one he did not recognize. This man had black hair tipped in silver and clutched his side as if in pain, a slow trickle of blood seeping out between his fingers.

The Shaman stared at the stranger, his eyes widening as the man steadily approached his position. His eyes darted over the face and the high cheekbones and finally settled on the sharp, blue eyes. "My son?" he whispered, not daring to say it out loud and possibly cause the apparition to fade from his sight.

"Atewaye ki," came from the smiling lips in a voice that he did recognize. *My father*.

Reaching out his arms, all semblance of propriety and stoicism gone, the Shaman took his son into a warm embrace. "How can this be?

I never thought to see your face again!"

He held Wolf at arms length now, staring into the face that looked so much like his beloved wife's. His hands ran over the cheeks and the chin, across the broad shoulders. He laughed when he saw the patch of white hair within the matt of black that covered Wolf's chest. "Just like when you are a wolf."

Mato came to join them, his son hanging on to his leg and refusing to let him go as he stared at the stranger in their camp. Wolf laid a hand on Igmutaka's head and smiled at his nephew. The Shaman clasped arms with his oldest son, thanking him for this great gift.

"I don't know how it happened, either, Father. But, we are happy it did."

Wals was called to come over, but he was unable to keep up with all the words the leader kept saying to him. Turning to his friend for translation, Wolf told him, "He says thank you."

Knowing that was all he was going to get, Wals nodded and chuckled. "Glad it all worked. You're welcome." He left the family alone to catch up as he went back to the fire where the Cooking Woman was holding court. Accepting a bowl of stew from one of her daughters who smiled encouragingly at him, he settled onto the ground to eat.

The Shaman indicated Wals with a tip of his chin. "What happened to that one's golden-haired wiya? Does she wait for him in the other place?"

Wolf shook his head and told him about the Prince coming back and reclaiming his love.

"I saw great sadness in his eyes. More than usual. Perhaps Tato Kala can help him forget," the Shaman smiled knowingly as the pretty young woman made sure Wals had something cool to drink.

"Time will tell," shrugged Wolf as he looked back from his friend. "That would mean he would stay here. I don't know if that is the answer for him either."

"So, you have that odd red stone pendant? It seemed to mean so much to the two of you. It is where it should be?" his father asked next, remembering the strange vision of his future that the stone had given him, one that his son had not completely explained to his satisfaction.

Open-mouthed, Wolf could only stare at his father. He had forgotten all about the pendant. They had just been through a small war over that red diamond, and he had left without it. He briefly closed his eyes at his own stupidity, momentarily forgetting he had been under a powerful spell and had not been in any shape to remember much of anything.

Seeing his son's reaction to his question, his father commented dryly, "Let me guess. It is with my canoe."

Knowing the small boat in question was safely stashed behind the Settler's Cabin, the corner of Wolf's mouth turned up slightly as he shook his head. Unfortunately, it wouldn't be that easy. "No. It is buried. Back in the wiya Rose's time." *I think it was near a tree….*

"Ooh," Mato grimaced, handing his son his beaten-up, empty quiver, motioned for him to take to their tent. Once the boy ran off and was out of earshot, he added, "Do we have to retrieve it? Is it so important that we must go back there again to get it?"

Wolf just nodded, and then realized what his brother had said. "No," he corrected, "*I* have to go back and get it." He fell silent as he thought about the trip he must soon make, unconsciously rubbing the wound in his side, and mentally chastising himself over his forgetfulness.

Leaving his brother to work out the newest problem, Mato handed their father the snapshot Kimberly had taken before they left the twenty-first century. "This was made for you. If Wolf wants to explain how it is done, I will leave that to him."

"I guess all their gadgets are not worthless after all," the Shaman muttered, looking at the front and the plain back of the photo. "This is very special. I will keep it in my tipi. But I would rather have my own son in front of me to see for all time." The hint was broad and obvious.

Wolf just gave him a half-grin as he stood, trying not to grimace from the pain. "I need to pay my respects to the rest of our people and to the Cooking Woman."

"Have her look at your wounds," his father called after him as he limped off. Once Wolf was over by the fire, the Shaman had his other son sit. "Now, Mato, tell me all that really happened. Why do you three appear to have been in a battle and had a hard time of it? Did you travel back in time as well? What was wrong with my son that he forgot something so important to him? Tell me now the story. I will want to tell it to our people around the fire and hand it down for generations to come."

Taking a deep breath, Mato settled in and complied. It would be a long tale.

Sitting back, drawing the wolfskin closer around his body as the coolness of the night surrounded him, the Shaman silently listened to his son as he began to weave this marvelous story. Leaves swirled unseen through the camp and wisps of the cooking fire wafted over them as he listened. Darkness fell and a torch was lit and set noiselessly in place next to the father and son. In silence the Shaman sat, staring at Mato, rapt in the tale.

When, finally, Mato had done justice to their journey, the Shaman released him to go join his family in their tent. Wolf then came to his father's side and sat quietly next to him, the flickering firelight playing across his handsome angled face. The older man couldn't seem to take his eyes off of the face of his son. There was happiness and relief on his lined, weathered face. "I am glad you are here, my son."

"As am I, atewaye ki."

CHAPTER TEN

England — 1291

"Here we go again, Wals," Wolf muttered as they got to their feet on the sandy beach.

"I just hope it is a little easier than the last time we were here," he commented, rubbing the sand out of his eyes and removing his red cape to shake out the sticking granules. "I'd hate for your wounds to open again."

Nose in the air, Wolf was taking a survey of the surroundings. Once the ocean had returned to its normal ebb and flow, he could hear the usual sounds on a deserted beach at early evening, as was apparent by the position of the sun near the horizon and the blazing reds and pinks streaking across the western sky. The prickling along his spine also was not present, which was a relief. Like it or not, he hadn't fully recovered from the last fight and the effects of a deep sword wound. "Me, too," he finally agreed with Wals, shaking his thick coat to rid himself of the dripping water and clinging white sand. "Ah, that's better."

"Hey!" Wals yelled, quickly turning his back to the wolf as the spray of water and sand again coated him.

"What? Oh, sorry," he glanced over, having been unaware that Wals was in his line of fire. "Let's get to the trees and out of sight. Then we can determine what to do next."

Giving a final adjustment to his brand new princely costume and polished sword, Wals looked up. "Next? I thought we were just going to grab the pendant and get back home as quick as we can."

As Wolf started trotting towards the edge of the forest, he said back over his shoulder, "That would be ideal, but we have to make sure of a couple of things first."

"You do know where it is, don't you?"

"Yes." *More or less*, he muttered in a low undertone. *Amazing how alike trees all look….*

As they walked on, Wals thought to ask, "I see you are talking now, but will you continue to do so? You didn't want to be known as a talking wolf before."

Wolf had to think about that. At the wrong time, it could be deadly. "Well, I think it will be all right for now. If we are spotted by Nimue, she can just assume her 'spell' to make me talk is still working. We'll have to play it by ear the rest of the time."

"All right."

Nighttime was quickly setting in and darkness was starting to take over the already gloomy woods. Lost in his own thoughts, Wals found he was falling behind the fast moving wolf whose black coat blended into the shadows too well. Picking up his pace, he called to his companion, "By the way, just so you know: I'd appreciate it if you would fill me in on details that I need to know. Your brother didn't think it was necessary to tell me, for instance, that we were being tailed by a pack of wolves on this very same trail. I'd prefer to know what is going on around me."

"Noted," Wolf replied. "I'll give you the same consideration."

"Thank you." After a few moments, Wals realized what the wolf had said. "Hey, that's not funny!"

The low chuckle told him otherwise. "We are not being followed. I am somewhat surprised, but we are not at this point in time. Hopefully, we will continue to be unobserved." *However unlikely that is to happen.*

"Agreed." Wals knew the path on which they were traveling, but Wolf seemed to have a different destination in mind. The route they were on would not come out in the village where Wals had stayed the last time they were here. "Where are we headed?"

"The castle."

"Which castle would that be?" Wals sounded a little nervous, wondering if the wolf was still somehow under *her* power and was leading him into a trap.

Wolf heard the worried inflection in Wals'

voice and decided not to torment the man. "Rose's castle, of course."

Wals wasn't too sure he wanted to go to that castle, either. In the weeks they had been gone, he had started the healing process of putting his love for Rose behind him. While he wished her well and happy, he still wasn't keen on seeing her and being reminded, yet again, of her kindness and beauty and the love he had lost. Even the beautiful Tato Kala, whose name meant Antelope, in Wolf's village hadn't been able to distract him. It had been too soon, too sharp a loss at that point. Perhaps, though, as he thought about the dusky black eyes and long raven-black lashes that framed them, there might be something in the future. Not yet, though. Not yet.

Wolf, unaware of Wals' feelings of apprehension, continued his steady pace and course to the fair castle of King Stefan. He was glad of the silence as he could keep a stronger feel on what—or who—was around them.

"**O**h, Wolf! Wals! It is you!" The good Green Fairy clapped her hands in delight. "I am so happy to see you again! Just wait until I tell the others you're back!"

Before Wolf or Wals could say a word, she was gone in a puff of green smoke.

Still on the path to the castle, but very close, they had been startled by the green sparkles that suddenly appeared before their eyes. As it had become completely dark in the close trees, they both had instinctively taken a defensive position. Relieved it was Flora, they had opened their mouths to greet her but, by then, she was gone.

"Think she'll be back?" Wals wondered out loud with a chuckle.

"Well, she was one of the ones I especially wanted to see, so I hope so," Wolf admitted, his mouth open in a wolf's version of a grin, as he continued on his previous route. "Ah, there they are."

Wals looked up in the direction Wolf was indicating. Three glitter trails were heading towards their position. The lead color was red, followed by the green, and Merri was bringing up the rear with her special blue. The surrounding trees and hanging moss reflected back the bright colors as the trio popped into view.

"Sir Wolf, and Wals, too! I hadn't believed Flora when she told me you both were back," Fauna smiled.

"Now you know I cannot tell a lie, Fauna!" Flora insisted. "Why wouldn't you have believed me?"

"Oh, she didn't mean it that way," Merri started to say.

"Of course I know you never lie! I was merely surprised...."

"Ladies!" Wolf almost yelled, getting their attention before they dissolved into a long, drawn-out argument on who meant what.

All three conical hats turned in his direction. "Yes, Wolf?" asked Flora in her kindly way, as if unaware there had been any contention mere moments before.

"We are likewise happy to see you. Is it possible to get inside out of sight? I have something to ask of you."

The Red Fairy gave Wals a look-over. "Well, as before, he can only go so far in the castle."

Even in the darkness, it could be plainly seen that the embarrassed Wals turned a dark shade of red.

"Now, I meant no offense, Wals," Fauna hurriedly told him. "We are forever grateful to you for all you did. But," she sighed, "that doesn't extend to the King. He still hasn't forgotten you stealing Rose away into the night for that clandestine rendezvous. Most improper, you know."

Not wanting to go over that same argument that they had had before, Wals just remained silent and let Wolf handle whatever it was he wanted to cover. Considering that his lady love was now with another man made it all a moot point anyway.

Seeing his arms folded over his chest and looking away, Fauna considered the matter closed. "Now, Sir Wolf, if you two will follow us, we can use the same passage as before."

Wolf had never been to the secret entrance into the castle wall, so he was quite intrigued. Wals merely gave a heavy sigh as the solid oaken door closed quietly behind them. There would be no happy greeting from Rose this time. The complete darkness was broken by torches that suddenly sprang to life. Wolf could see stone stairways leading to the upper great towers, and a few blackened doors that led to other, secret chambers in the lower realms of the castle. Instead of the expected layers of dust and cobwebs over everything—as in another, darker castle—this typically unused section was spotlessly clean, though undecorated.

"Will we be disturbed down here, ladies?" Wolf asked, subtly trying to find out if Rose knew they were here.

"No, no, we will be quite comfortable...," Flora broke off, putting a hand to her mouth as she looked around. "Dear me, it isn't too comfortable, is it? Perhaps this will be better." Her wand jumped into her hand and suddenly four elaborate chairs and a rather large green embroidered pillow appeared on the floor. "I embroidered that myself," she said proudly with a small blush.

They all admired the neat stitches and intricate floral pattern. "It is almost too pretty to sit on," Wolf told her, preferring to sit on the floor anyway.

"No, no, I insist! What is the use in having pretty things if you don't share them?" the Green Fairy exclaimed, gesturing for Wolf to get comfortable.

Turning around three times, he was finally able to get into a place on the lumpy cushion that allowed him to face the others and still be in a somewhat dignified position. "Yes, very nice," he murmured as he felt his hindquarters slipping off the satin fabric.

"Now," Merri started, after she had handed around tea and cookies, "how have you two been? It has been almost two years since we have seen you."

"Two years?" both the travelers echoed, shocked.

"It's been just a matter of a month or so in our time," Wolf explained.

The three fairies nodded. "Yes, it was that way when I was in your time," Merri pointed out. "Many more years had passed here than the number of years Rose and I were actually gone. Oh, I'm sorry, Wals. I shouldn't have mentioned her." The Blue Fairy had seen a fleeting look of loss pass over the man's face.

"No, it's all right. I...I do hope she is well and happy. I really do," he insisted at the three faces turned at him.

Fauna recovered the quickest. "Oh, she is just lovely! And the baby looks just like her, too!"

"Baby?" Wals and Wolf echoed together again.

Hand to her mouth, Fauna looked over at Merri, "Oh, dear. Perhaps I shouldn't have mentioned that."

Flora told Wals, "She is well and happy, Wals, and we thank you for asking. Yes, she and the Prince welcomed a new princess to the family. They were married soon after Phillip came back, you know. She's a wonderful mother," she sighed happily as she thought about the new life and new adventures to come for all of them.

"Please give them our kindest regards," Wolf took over when it seemed Wals was too stunned to speak.

"Oh, yes, thanks," Wals thought he should add when he could. He then lapsed into silence as he realized the relationship was now completely over for him.

Wolf knew it would be best to bring the discussion to the real reason they had come. "I have two reasons for coming back. The second is to thank you," he looked pointedly at Merri, "for the gift you gave my father. And me," he added. "You have no idea how much it meant for him to see my face again. I do believe that is the first time he was ever speechless!"

Merri briefly bowed her head. "I was glad to do it for both of you. How did you know it was me? I tried to be discrete."

Wolf gave a small grin. "The boy Peter told me after I returned that he had seen a funny blue sparkle follow me into the vortex. I knew it had to be your doing."

"What was the other reason for you two coming back?"

Wolf turned to face the leader of the three. "It is for the pendant. Did you realize we went back without it?"

Her mouth turned down in a brief frown. "Yes, we thought so. It was none of our business, though. Rose was our concern—and helping you as we could." She looked away at one of the far, dark walls. "*She* knows it is still here, as well. There has been a lot of prowling out in the woods over the last two years. She is still weak, but she does know it is still here."

"Obviously, from what you say, Nimue has not found it then."

"That's right, Wolf. That last fight took almost everything out of her." Merri gave an unladylike snort. "Too bad it didn't finish her off…. Her Dark Castle has been very quiet, which is good for everyone round about. Trying to keep you, Wolf, under the effects of her spell, all the wolves she commanded, and with all the spells she had to weave, they were just too much for her. She used too much of her power all at once."

"Then, perhaps I will not be assaulted this time when I fetch it."

"Oh, you can bet that she will be watching," Fauna told him pointedly. "Make no mistake about that. I doubt that she will be able to do much of anything about it right now. It would not be wise to think she is gone for good, wolf. Never assume that."

Wolf nodded quietly. This was good news for him on this trip, but it could mean danger at some further point in time. "I will remember that, Fauna. Thank you for telling me."

"Now, what can we do for you two? Do you require anything of us?"

The large dark head swung around to Merri. "Now that you mention it, there is one little thing you can help me with."

When Wolf told them he couldn't remember exactly where he had buried the pendant, the three good fairies all broke out into delighted laughter. "Oh, Sir Wolf! That is too much! 'All the trees look alike!' Oh, don't tell them that. They would be devastated."

"Who would be devastated, Flora?" Wals

asked, torn between being irritated that Wolf lost the pendant and wondering about the curious statement the fairy had just made.

Flora wiped a tear from the side of her eye. "Why, the trees, Wals! They take their appearance quite seriously. Don't they in your time? They just love spring!"

Wals and Wolf looked at each other. How does one answer that? "We aren't sure," was all Wolf could come up with to say.

"Well, we'll put out the call and let you know what we find out. I think your specifics on what you do remember will help narrow it down quite significantly."

"Uhm, how long do you think it will take? We don't have anywhere to stay the night," Wals pointed out. He wasn't too keen on going back to the dreary tavern where he had stayed before and he figured he wouldn't be allowed to stay in the castle for a moment longer than necessary.

"I'll see to it," Flora waved as she disappeared from view.

"She has such a way with the flowers and trees," Fauna sighed. "I, personally, like the creatures better. But, to each their own."

"Found it!" the Green Fairy happily declared a moment later as she reentered the room. "That delightful elm family in the glade has been keeping watch over it. Such a nice grove of trees. They said the...," she broke off, looking confused. "Now, what was that word they used? Oh, let's just say 'creature' had been looking all around the glade, but they wouldn't let her see it."

"The trees can do that?" Wals asked slowly as they all stood up, preparing to leave the castle.

"Why, yes," Flora flew over to him and retrieved the tea cup from him. "The elms are really pleasant. Now, the maples can be quite forgetful, so it was good you didn't use them. The walnuts are rather grumpy when the squirrels take over. But the thorn bushes, oh, they are rather nasty creatures, I do hate to say." She lowered her voice before she continued, "You all know what they did at *her* bidding, don't you? Quite nasty business," she finished with a shake of her head.

Not sure what to say in answer to any of that, Wolf and Wals wisely remained silent and followed the trio out of the castle into the dead of night. They headed in the direction Wolf thought they should go, as he began to recognize more of the area the further they walked.

When the path widened, he could tell they were in a lovely glade brightened by the full moon shining overhead. The leaves of the elms were edged in silver as a gentle breeze drifted through the air, turning them this way and that.

"Yes, this is the place," he declared, trotting over to an impressive elm on the edge of the clearing. "This is the tree."

The breeze must have gotten a little stronger, because Wals was sure he saw the lowest branches of the tree dip down to graze the back of the wolf. Too far away, he couldn't hear the wolf give his thanks for the protection of the woods.

"I can't believe you couldn't remember where you hid it!" Wals was saying to Wolf as they approached the beach. "That's almost too funny!"

"It's not like I didn't have anything else on my mind," Wolf muttered in self-defense. "Let's see how you do under a spell like that."

The smile left Wals' face. "You're right. I forgot that part of it. Sorry," he said sincerely, though still planning on sharing it with Lance when they got back.

The three good fairies decided to accompany them to the beach for their final good-byes. They assured the wolf they would take the well-wishes and congratulations to Rose and Phillip on the arrival of the new little princess.

All five of them came to an abrupt halt when they neared the location where the portal would appear. There was a thin gray wolf sitting at the edge of the water. She looked emaciated and exhausted as she sat with her head drooping. Her eyes were now a dull gray, not the fiery red they had been during the battle. Nimue was almost unrecognizable.

"What do you want, witch? We are done with you," Wolf declared, stopping just out of what he considered lunging range in case she decided to turn on Wals.

"Ah, my pet. I have missed you, my wolf," her voice creaked. She tried to sit up taller, but it was too much for her. "I came to offer you my hand to join me once again. Once I am myself again—which shall be soon," she promised with a hint of the same fire, the same delusional air she always kept around her.

"I will not fight you again, witch. We are done."

"Fight?" she asked, feigning surprise. "I am not offering to fight. Join me, Wolf. We could rule these lands together."

"Never. Leave me, or I will finish this," Wolf snapped, his fangs bared and his head lowered.

The gray wolf slowly got to her feet, causing all of them to tense. She smugly chuckled at their reaction. "Fools. I will leave you now, Wolf. Because I choose. You are being so unreason-able." She gave a deep sigh, her ribs showing in the process. "And we had such fun together."

The five watched as the thin wolf slowly walked down the beach a ways. It seemed as if the effort was too much and she had to drop heavily into the sand to regain her breath. Turn-ing her head, she glanced back when she heard the commanding howl. The vortex was coming. And she could do nothing about it.

The three good fairies took a defensive stand around Wolf and Wals, just to make sure there were no tricks as the pink swirled behind them and the waves crashed heavily to shore.

Nimue could only watch as the burst of light neared the shore, coming for her wolf.

She might not be able to stop them from leaving with her pendant, but there was one last thing she could do. Getting slowly to her feet, she called out, "It will take me a while, but I will come for you again, Wolf! The pendant will again be mine!"

As the powers of the whirlpool closed over them, both Wals and Wolf heard her one last cry. "Wherever you go, I will find you. Wherever you are in time, I will follow you!"

CHAPTER ELEVEN

Disneyland — 1961

"Hey, there's the Jungle ride! Can we go on that, Mother?"

Standing in the shade of the souvenir stand, Walt's ears perked up when he heard the young boy's question. Glancing around the pole of the Tropical Imports hut that sold realistic-looking rubber snakes, shrunken heads and straw purses, he could easily pick out the family in question.

Wearing a full-skirted floral dress, wide white sunglasses, and a large brimmed straw hat, the mother in question pulled the sunglasses down a ways on her nose to look over at the entrance to the ride in front of them in Adventureland. Her son, his brown hair parted in the middle and a broad spread of freckles across his nose, was about ten years old. Carrying a red felt pennant that said Disneyland in bold white letters, he used its thin, green bamboo pole as a pointer to indicate a round sign up above their heads. The words Jungle Cruise were printed in red on what looked like a stretched leather drum extending out from lethal-looking spears and being guarded by smiling skulls. The ride's bamboo-lined queue was winding around under a thatched roof similar to the one that shaded the unrecognized Walt. Once the people in the queue were in the welcome shade, the scaffolding of the nearby Treehouse that was being built would be unseen. The boy's father, dressed neatly in a white pressed shirt and black trousers, was fanning himself with his dark fedora. He looked around obviously fascinated with the architecture of Adventureland, his glance passing over the shaded builder of the Park as he took in all the intricate features of each and every building.

Pushing her sunglasses back into place, and patting her hair to make sure her hairdo was still neat, the boy's mother, Louise, shook her head. "Mark, dear, we already went on that last time we were here. Remember? There were a couple of alligators…."

"Crocodiles," her husband corrected with a smile as he looked up at the nearby scaffolding that was artfully concealed with a flowering vine.

"Fine. Crocodiles, a big elephant, a lion eating a zebra—which I think was completely unnecessary, Russell—and some dancing men in grass skirts. We already saw it. I don't see any need to go on it again. It's not like the animals are doing anything different. Don't you agree, dear?"

Neither of the males knew to which of them the question was being directed, so they both muttered a non-committal, "Mmmmm."

Recovering quickly from his disappointment, Mark eagerly asked, "Then, let's go on the Pack Mules again! The sign out front said they added a whole bunch of new stuff on that mine train ride!"

The mother scrunched up her nose. "Those mules are pretty smelly," Louise sniffed. "But, I can shop in those cute Western stores while you two ride, if you want. Russell?"

"Hmmm? Oh, sure, dear. I'll take Mark on the mules if he really wants to go on them." Russell tried to sound nonchalant, but she could tell he was just about as excited as their son.

"How do we get there from here? I can never find my way around."

"I know! I know!" Mark jumped excitedly into the conversation. Holding his pennant out in front of him, he pointed to their right. "We can go around these buildings here and into Frontierland. Hey, can we go see that show in the Golden Horseshoe Review again? I want to see if I can get hit by the water pistols again!"

"That's a good idea, Mark," his dad clapped him on the shoulder.

Louise gave a knowing smile as they headed off. "You just want to see those Can-Can dancing girls, Russell."

Walt didn't hear the rest of their conversation as they slowly walked through the rest of Adventureland before turning right into the

Frontierland section of Disneyland. Head down, he was thoughtful as the mother's words—"we already saw it....no need to go on it again"— played over and over in his mind. He looked over at the sunny wooden dock where the *Irrawaddi Woman* with its green and white striped canopy was unloading another boatload of smiling guests. *Would they come and ride it again?* he wondered to himself. Pulling out a small notebook, he made a couple of notes as he walked off. His earlier frown had been replaced by a wide smile. He had heard the boy's name and it reminded him of exactly who he needed on this job—Marc. He would get Marc on the expansion right away and hopefully be ready for the next summer season. Hearing a couple of pistol shots from deep within the ride, he tugged his own hat a little lower as he headed out onto Main Street.

Disneyland — 2008

"I'm sorry, Wolf, but we have a bit of an emergency right now," Lance was telling his partner as they quickly walked through Adventureland, coming in from the New Orleans Square side.

Wolf frowned as he glanced down at his silent walkie-talkie. "I hadn't heard anything since I got back. What is it?"

Lance glanced around to make sure none

of the guests were near enough to hear him. "There was a big problem a couple of nights ago. I'm still not sure if it was a backhoe, or what, but someone set it on top of Schweitzer Falls to continue some work they were doing. Apparently it was too heavy for the aging Falls, and," he stopped to look around one more time, lowering his voice, "the Falls collapsed."

Wolf merely grunted at the news. "That's too bad. Is that why you can't go with me to Columbia again?"

Giving his security partner an unbelieving look, Lance replied, "Yeah, that's why. This isn't a good thing, Wolf."

As they neared the boarded up entrance to the popular ride, Wolf gave a shrug. He couldn't see why Lance was so upset about the Falls. "So, they'll fix it. They always do when something goes wrong."

Lance stopped in his tracks, almost causing the unimpressed guard to run into him. Lance lowered his voice even more. "You don't understand, Wolf. There was another capsule Walt had hidden somewhere in Schweitzer Falls. Another branch of the Hidden Mickey quests that we didn't know about."

Letting that sink in for a moment with Wolf, he was rewarded when a look of understanding came into those sharp blue eyes. Nodding now at his partner, Lance continued, "We were alerted to the problem when Kimberly was in the War Room last night. Sometimes she can't sleep because of the pregnancy...." He clamped his mouth shut at the get-on-with-it look on Wolf's face. "Anyway, one of the green lights on the map of the Park was now blinking yellow, indicating something was wrong. When she called the Park, they were surprised we knew already—even though they don't really know who 'we' are," he smiled, still amazed at the intricacy of the system Kimberly's father—and Walt—had sent into place so long ago. "After rather reluctantly telling us about the collapse, Kimberly immediately put a stop on the work—which they knew we would do—so I could check it out. They didn't like it, but there's nothing they can do. You know what's funny?"

Thinking about his upcoming trip, Wolf had been only half-listening. Now he realized he was supposed to give some kind of an appropriate response. He merely grunted, knowing that would be enough to satisfy Lance.

"What's funny," his partner continued, knowing Wolf wasn't really listening, "is that I walked over those Falls when I was chasing down the second El Lobo hidden in the ride."

At the mention of the carved wolf-shaped rock formation, Wolf's attention came back to the problem at hand. He and Lance had found the original El Lobo in the jungles of Columbia when Lance had been on his second Hidden Mickey quest, the one apart from Adam and Beth's. Knowing he had to go back there soon, Wolf looked more interested. "What about El Lobo?" he asked.

"I knew you weren't paying attention," Lance grinned and received the same narrowed-eyed frown that had stopped quite a few teenagers from doing something stupid. Unperturbed, he continued, "I said I had walked over the top of the Falls and, in the darkness, never saw the **W E D** that had been engraved into a couple of the rocks up on top. You know that was our indicator that we were in the right place...," he broke off when he was given the same get-on-with-it look he had received moments earlier. "My, are we a little testy today, Wolf?"

The blue eyes narrowed even further. "Would you care for me to reiterate what I have just gone through and what is now coming up next?"

Lance held up placating hands. "No, no. I know you have a lot on your mind. I was just teasing. You know, you *really* don't have much of a sense of humor. Wals and I were just talking about...," he wisely stopped and continued with his former line of thought. "Long story short...."

"Too late for that," Wolf mumbled as they pushed aside one of the barriers that blocked the exit to the Jungle Cruise.

"Long story short, there is an undiscovered capsule somewhere in the debris and we need to find it before the backhoes and dump trucks carry everything off. Isn't that amazing? There's another piece to another Hidden Mickey quest right here!"

"Amazing. And what do you mean 'we?' I just came by to see if you wanted to take the pendant back with me."

"You won't help me?" Lance's propensity to

not get dirty was well known by all his friends. But now his curiosity overcame the necessity to move quickly on the missing capsule. "When are you flying out?"

Wolf looked at Lance with a penetrating gaze. "I'm not flying."

Lance's eyes got wide as he finally understood what Wolf was going to do. "Oooooh. So you aren't just going to bury the pendant again under that El Lobo." As the other man's head slowly shook side to side, Lance added, "Right. We already found it so there's no point in that…. Wow," he ran a hand through his hair. "You know where to go? How to get there?"

Giving a single nod, Wolf answered, "I know how to get there. Apparently I've done it before." He gave a frustrated shake of his head, remembering the words of the local native De Tribu who met them deep in the jungle last time. *You've been here before. The future*, he had said. "It's confusing, even for me. But, I know what I have to do to get things back on their right course. In fact, it could be very interesting for you if you came with me. You might get to meet Walt," he threw in as an added incentive, dangling a fascinating possibility of a carrot in front of Lance.

It worked. Lance looked torn. He had always wanted to try that *thing* Wolf did, but knew Kimberly would kill him if he did. And meeting Walt? Wow. After a few minutes of mental deliberations of the pros and cons, he had to finally, reluctantly, realistically shake his head no. "Not this time, buddy, but thanks for thinking of me. Perhaps someday we all can go with you.

Maybe after the new baby. After meeting your brother, Peter would love to go back to see the rest of your family."

"Let me know," was all Wolf said. He, too, knew it would never happen.

"So, are you going to help me look for the capsule?" as they walked to the edge of the silent dock. Three boats were sitting in the slip, waiting for skippers and passengers. Since the water had been drained, it looked odd to see the boats being propped up with wooden beams to keep them centered between the two docks.

Wolf looked down at the mud in the riverbed. The water hadn't been drained long enough for the bottom to dry. "I really didn't come with you for that reason."

"Two hands make for quick work," Lance quoted. Kimberly had requested a couple of shovels be left on site. There should have been some there anyway, but they wanted to make sure Lance wouldn't have to improvise with whatever he could find.

Wolf let out a chuckle at Lance's feeble attempt. Well remembering who was on the business end of the shovel when they had to dig in Columbia, he was sorely tempted to turn around and go back to his security patrol. Instead, he gave a small sigh. "How much time do you have to find it?"

Grinning internally, Lance didn't let it show on his face. "Only a little while." Kimberly had actually shut down the site for two days, but no need to tell Wolf that little tidbit.

"Fine," was the grumbled acceptance. Wolf

lightly jumped down from the end of the unloading dock into the muck. Saying something unpleasant in Lakota under his breath as his spotless shoes sunk up to their laces, he headed for the opposite bank where the mud wasn't so deep.

Lance let himself down a little more gingerly and followed the footsteps of his partner. As they turned the corner and went past the silent Trader Sam and little Ellie, the baby elephant, Lance started his favorite trivia game again. "So, Wolf, tell me: Who were the first people who actually lived at Disneyland?"

Wolf was following the rail between the mechanical piranhas. They didn't seem quite as menacing when seen on their wires, stopped in various positions on the rollers. The water buffalo and the huge python didn't even glance in the men's direction as they headed for the huge mound of fallen earth, framework and pipes. "You mean Owen and Dolly Pope? Nice couple."

"Now, how would you know that? They could have been mean as snakes?"

"If you are talking about the first animal handlers, they were really nice. They had quite a job getting the horses and mules ready for all the sights and sounds they would have to face every day. If you remember, I knew them," he glanced back at the carefully walking Lance.

"Oh, yeah, I keep forgetting how far back your history goes here. Do you know the burro story?"

"Which one? The miniature burro that Walt

loved? He didn't believe it when he was told it snapped at people until it tried to bite him."

Slightly deflated that Wolf knew this tiny tid-bit of history, Lance mumbled, "Yeah, that burro story."

"I thought you were going to ask me some-thing difficult, like: what ride in Fantasyland was supposed to be a roller coaster?"

Lance gave a quick grin. "You mean the en-trance to Storybook Land."

"Nope. A full ride."

Stumped for once, Lance's attention was drawn to something else. Coming to a sudden stop, hands on his hips, Lance let out a low whis-tle. "Wow, look at that mess! I'd hate to be the guy who was running that backhoe."

Not even stopping to admire the destruc-tion, Wolf pointed with the shovel he had picked up off the bank. "Where was the marked stone? What part of the Falls?"

"What? Oh, it was about in the middle on top."

Wolf stepped back a few paces, into what would have been the path of the oncoming boats. Taking some visual measurements and walking forward again, he dug in with his shovel, silently getting to work in what he thought was the most promising area. He figured the capsule would be well covered with debris.

Ducking out of the way of the flying dirt, Lance went to Wolf's other side and finally started his own digging. "So, are you going to tell me the answer?" he asked after an hour of shoveling into the never-ending dirt.

"Answer to what?" Wolf didn't even pause.

"Which ride was going to be a roller coaster. I'm so tired that I can't even come up with a smart answer," as he leaned on his shovel to wipe the sweat off his face with his sleeve.

"Mr. Toad. Now get back to work or I'm leaving."

Daylight was fading when Lance's shovel finally hit on something that wasn't a rock or pipe. They had been at it for hours and wondered if the capsule had somehow already been removed at some point in time. Now this sound made him think that they had finally found it.

Squatting down in what looked like a small cavern in the middle of the pile, Lance was carefully pulling dirt away from his find. When the familiar gray color of the hard plastic capsule revealed itself, he let out a happy yell, "Got it!" but he quickly learned that this was unnecessary as Wolf was standing right behind him, curiously looking over his shoulder. It was a longish capsule, almost a foot in length and about six inches in diameter. Holding it up to his ear, Lance gave it a careful shake. Hearing something rattling around inside, he let out a "Hmmm," and held it out to Wolf.

Giving his head a shake, Wolf told him, "Give it to Wals. He earned it." Turning his attention back to the hole they had created, he asked Lance, "Shouldn't we fill that in?"

"Fill it in? Why?" Lance wanted to know. "You think anyone would notice?" He was seeing how tightly the end cap was attached. When he received no reply, he looked up at his partner who was silently glaring at him. Impatience was written all over Wolf's dirt-streaked face. "What?"

"You don't think anyone would notice a large cavern dug into the middle of what was previously just a pile of dirt? I thought you didn't want to be obvious."

Lance was more intrigued with the hidden capsule than what any of the workers might think about the hole they had made. After a moment's thought, he could now easily see Wolf's point. He could also plainly see that Wolf did not intend on filling it back in all by himself. "Fine," he sighed, setting the capsule gently on the grass of the riverbank. "I'll help you fill it in. You didn't happen to see the rock with the **W E D** on it, did you?"

"You don't need any more souvenirs," Wolf mumbled as his huge shovelful of dirt barely missed Lance. He grinned to himself as Lance leaped out of the way and then picked up his shovel to help.

Head down, Lance's attention was focused on their important find as he worked on the disgusting, back-breaking work of filling in the cavern. Darkness had fallen quickly and both men had been quiet, each with their own thoughts.

Lance suddenly started chuckling as he threw another shovelful of dirt into the smaller cavern. Without pausing, he said, "Hey, Wolf, listen to this skipper joke I just heard the other day. 'Those of you entering the Jungle Cruise, please see that there are two lines, one on the right and one on the left. If you want your family to stay together, stay on the same side of the line. But, if there is someone in your family you want to get rid of, just send them to the other line and you'll never see them again.' Isn't that great? Wolf?"

He hadn't even realized he had been working alone, that his partner had silently gone to the island that had been affectionately called Catalina by the cast members throughout the years. Behind the attacking natives, well hidden by the overgrowth of brush and vines, was the smaller rock statue of the open-mouthed wolf. In sight of the passing guests in the river boats, however, was a tall thatched hut, a drape of some indistinguishable fabric hiding its entrance. Wolf hadn't gone to El Lobo this time. He had ducked inside the hut and quickly removed his dirt-stained security uniform. Tilting his head back, he gave a low, calling howl.

Knowing what was coming, he took the red heart-shaped diamond pendant out of his pants pocket and put the middle of the chain in his mouth. The pendant swung slowly near the side of his chin as he exited the hut and stood waiting there in the darkness.

Still looking for his missing partner, Lance was startled when a stiff sudden breeze blew down the empty boat track and blasted past him. Recognizing what was happening, he threw himself to the ground, protectively covering the capsule with his body until the violence around him stopped and the air returned to normal.

Getting to his feet, he looked around once more, but already knew that he was alone. "Well," he drawled, "I guess that answers the 'when are you going' part."

Once the hole was filled in enough for his satisfaction—which wasn't much longer—Lance picked up the gray plastic canister and turned to retrace his steps back to the dock. Remembering something from his past trip there, he halted and turned back to head for Catalina. Going through the dense vines, he used his security Mag light to look around inside the grass hut. The last time he checked inside the hut he had found a pile of clothing had been left there and had wondered what kind of wild party he had missed out on. On further inspection, he had discovered it was a security uniform—only it was different than the one he was now wearing.

Using his light, he saw that the odd uniform was now gone and replaced by another, muddier outfit. He knew it was Wolf's and he knew his security partner was now on his own mission back to the past. Thinking it would be a nice thing to take the uniform and have it cleaned for Wolf, he nixed that idea as quickly as it came. He didn't know how soon the Guardian would be back and didn't want his friend to have to find his way naked through the Park, amusing as that might be to Lance and his other security friends. He gave the clothes a small pat, and silently wished his friend a good trip.

Tucking the capsule securely under his arm, he let the hut's flap close behind him and made his way back to the dock. Picking up his walkie-talkie, he pushed the button that was only present on his and Wolf's machine. His wife immediately answered, and he eagerly told her the latest and asked if Wals was working in the Park just then.

"Here's a gift for you from Uncle Walt," Lance told the confused Wals as he handed over an unopened gray capsule of some kind.

Back at work on the Canoes, the much-relieved Wals and the security guard sat at an unoccupied table at the far end of the Hungry Bear Restaurant. Lance could tell Wals was happier than he had been in the previous weeks. Now curiosity played across Wals' face.

"What do you mean? What is this?" Wals wanted to know as he gently shook the plastic and heard something muffled rattling around inside.

Lance glanced around to make sure they would not be overheard. "You know a little about the treasure hunt Adam and I went on a couple of years ago?"

Wals just shrugged. "A little. I know you and Wolf were involved in something similar. But I've never been told any details," he added hopefully, setting the capsule into his lap in case Lance changed his mind and wanted it back.

Noticing the movement, Lance just smiled, ignoring the obvious hint. "Well, Walt set a few things in motion years ago. We think this is another leg of that journey. And," he stressed, "we want you to have the honors—wherever this might lead."

"You have no idea?"

"Nope, none." Lance thought back on his exciting Hidden Mickey searches. "We never did know where we would have to go. If this follows suit, it will be a clue you will have to solve."

"Clue to what?" Wals was getting more intrigued by the minute.

Lance gave him a noncommittal shrug as he stood to leave. "You'll just have to open it and find out. If you run into problems, contact Adam and Beth." Lance gave a warm smile. "They are experts at this sort of thing. I've got to get back to work." He glanced at his watch. "And you are officially off duty."

"But I have another two hours to my shift."

"No, you don't." Lance sauntered off with a friendly parting wave. He envied Wals right now. The Hidden Mickey quests he had gone on had changed his life. He wouldn't go back to the way it was before for anything.

As Lance disappeared from his sight, Wals remembered the unexplained power he and Kimberly had at the Park. If Lance said he was off work, then he knew he was off work. With a soft chuckle, he tugged at the sealed end of the gray plastic. "Okay, Walt, let's see what you have planned for me," he muttered to himself. The cap didn't budge. "Walt musta had quite a grip." He set the capsule between his feet, gripped it with his knees, and used both hands to work the endcap back and forth until it, finally, gave way.

His heart sped up as he anxiously tilted the

container. A small lump surrounded by some kind of colorful cloth fell out. Untying a knotted, golden cord and carefully folding back the edges of the material, the cloth proved to be a large silk scarf with various scenes around Disneyland printed onto its light blue background. But, it was not the Disneyland Wals knew. This was an older Disneyland with rounded Skyway cabs going through the Matterhorn and oddly-shaped cars poised on the Autopia track.

When Wals was through examining the scarf, he picked up the screwdriver that had been so carefully protected. "Walt wanted me to have a screwdriver?"

Confused now, he set the two items on the table and ran a finger inside the capsule. He could feel the edge of paper. "Ah, the plot thickens." He tilted the container and gently tugged on the heavy paper. It was curled around inside the tube. When he finally got it out, he found there were actually two pieces of paper. One was a small off-white page that looked to be ripped out of some kind of book. The larger piece was a conceptual drawing of the new Tomorrowland of 1959. The Monorails were sleek and streamlined. The sheet was signed by Gurr and also had Walt's approval signature.

When he finally set down the incredible art find, he turned his attention to the small piece of paper and found himself comparing the writing to the signature on the drawing. "This was written by Walt," he whispered to himself. "This was written by Walt!"

Forcing himself to remain seated and not

jump around like a small girl, his hands shook as he read the words Walt had written so many years ago. **"If you think there is a great, big, beautiful tomorrow, just jump on the Speedramp to Progress City. <u>But</u>, watch out for that hand-cranked washing machine!"**

Wals looked back at the small screwdriver, his heart literally pounding. Picking it up, he said to no one in particular, "Carousel of Progress? Looks like I'm going to Florida!"

Columbia — 1940

The moon was cresting full above the tall foliage that surrounded the clearing where the camp fire blazed in the distance. A single beam of moonlight found its way through branches brightening the area as Walt reached the rock formation. Standing about ten feet tall, the rocks seemed to form a crouching wolf, El Lobo, staring straight at him, standing next to the river's edge. He ran his hands along the jagged rocks that were the 'teeth' in the open mouth of the wolf-like shape. His smile faded as his thoughts inevitably returned to his Studio. "What am I going to do?" he whispered to the unhearing wolf, shaking his head in frustration. Walt reached into his pocket and pulled out a small pack of cigarettes from his pocket, thumping the top of the box against his palm. Walt slid the slender smoke from the box. Reaching into his other pocket, he took out his familiar chrome-plated Zippo lighter and flipped the lid open. Turning the flint-wheel once, the lighter emitted a one-inch flame, illuminating Walt's face and hands. He held the flame in front of his face and stared intently into the flickering flame. "How are we going to go on? I don't want to have to close," Walt said out loud, this time speaking into the flame as if it were a crystal ball that could reveal an answer to his question.

He was startled by a deep voice that came out of the forest. It wasn't the voice of any of his friends. "Walt, you don't need to worry about your future. Your studio will survive just fine. You will even find the money for your little Park. It will become a reality."

The unlit cigarette dangled between loose lips before he unconsciously let it fall to the ground. He looked around for a moment, still holding the Zippo out in front of him like a miniature lantern. He turned around, searching for the voice. Was it a voice? Yes, definitely he heard the words spoken. Suddenly, a stiff breeze blew across the jungle floor, rustling leaves and branches, and, to Walt's dismay, blew out his lighter, allowing the twilight to consume him.

Walt was now thoroughly confused. He tried relighting the Zippo, but the wind kept blowing out the weak flame. He finally gave up and closed the lighter with a loud snap and listened to the sounds around him. Was one of his friends playing a trick on him? "Who's there? Show yourself. How do you know about my Park? No one knows…."

He squinted in the dim moonlight, trying to identify what had actually emerged from the trees...a dark shape, a hand, he thought. Clouds moved in, riding the sudden wind and now obscured the moon. He was bathed in complete darkness. He again squinted his eyes, trying to see better, unwilling to take a step closer. Was it a hand? It looked wrong, but it had to be a hand because it was holding something...something that dangled in front of him.

"Take this! Safeguard and protect it. It will be far more important to you than its face value," the voice told him. "It will show you things...about your little magic kingdom...about your heart's desire. But, remember this: How you get it is up to you."

Extending his hand with trepidation, Walt reached out for what appeared to be a pendant on a heavy gold chain. The moon decided to peek through the moving clouds again and reflected off the object; a blood-red glow seemed to radiate from a heart-shaped stone at the end of the chain. Three flashing gold circles could be seen behind the gemstone. Could this be a red diamond, the rarest of all diamonds? Even in the dim moonlight, colors of the rainbow flashed from its red depth.

Walt forgot about the unknown voice. Mesmerized by the brilliant stone turning slowly in front of his eyes, his free hand came up to touch the red fire. For a moment, Walt felt a strange emotion course through his body. His fingers caressed the stone and a vision streaked through his mind's eye. Blinking, he was not sure if the moonlight was playing tricks on his eyesight. Suddenly as his vision became clear, he could see a pink and white turreted castle and there were two swans floating peacefully in the surrounding moat. Across the lowered drawbridge, he saw scores of happy children streaming toward a slowly turning carousel filled with white horses.

"That's it!" Walt whispered. "That's it!"

"Walt?" the voice returned to him once again.

"Y...yes?" he replied cautiously, his hand dropping from the stone and the vision immediately leaving his mind. He felt bereft that the vision was gone, but still excited by what he thought he had seen.

"Walt," the voice seemed to admonish him, "this time? Hang on to it, all right?"

"Wait!" Walt called, "What do you mean 'this time?' Who are...." Before there could be any reply, he was rocked back by a wicked gust of wind that swept down from the north, swirling around the area in which he was standing. Not wanting to lose the pendant in the freakish windstorm, he put it protectively in his pocket and went behind the nearest tree for shelter from the leaves and debris that blew past him. Shielding his eyes from the dirt, he could make out a bright light that suddenly lit the glade he was in. Then, as quickly as it came, the wind and the light vanished.

Somehow, some way, he knew he was alone once more. What had just happened? Who was that? Why? Rubbing his forehead in confusion, he made his way back to the quiet camp. As he found his sleeping bag, the worries about the strike at the Studio had faded from his mind. At first, Walt thought he was too excited to fall asleep, but sleep did indeed overtake him.

After calling the windstorm that had disturbed Walt, at the last minute Wolf decided not to go back just yet. He had felt that he, too, wasn't alone, that he was being watched again.

Going deeper into the dark jungle, he relied on his keen senses to find his way in the thick underbrush. He didn't know where he was going, just that he needed to go this way.

As he quietly vanished like a wraith, an unseen, black cloaked figure stepped out of the shadows behind El Lobo. Her gray eyes slanted in anger. "Too late again!" she hissed. "At least I have one advantage, wolf," she spat in the direction he had gone. "I now know where it is. And I humbly thank you for finally leading me to The Man who has it. I've been waiting far too long." Her beautiful face broke into a smile. The smile enlarged as she broke into frenzied laughter, laughter edged with madness and hatred. The wind picked up that bone-chilling sound and wafted it through the jungle, stilling the animals on the hunt and making them turn this way and that, trying to make sense of the evil now amongst them. Catching no scent, they slunk off into the darkness and became still, hiding in fear.

The Evil One looked in the direction of the sleeping camp near the edge of the Amazon River. Her laughter died, but the smile remained. "Yes, Walt, I know exactly where my treasured pendant is. Those meddling fairies made sure I cannot touch you now, but," she promised with her hand resting on the place where a warm heart should have beat, "the time will come when I can. And I will."

The green orb on her staff began to glow a brilliant green, lighting the clearing and casting an eerie glow over El Lobo. But, before the incandescent light could fade, she was gone.

Unaware that he had been followed, Wolf continued his way deeper into the jungle. He had wondered at the silence of the night hunters since this was their busiest hour. Figuring it was merely because of his unwelcome presence, he dropped the matter from his mind.

His thoughts now clear, his instincts took over as he headed towards something that felt…familiar. As the odd sensation filled him and slowing his steady pace, the sharp eyes could distinguish the light of a campfire, but his nose could not pick up the smell that should have been quite prevalent from all the smoke he could see. Changing course, he noiselessly circled around to the back of the clearing, not wanting any surprises to catch him unaware. Wolf had not even realized he had traveled in a circular route and that he was almost back at his starting point of El Lobo.

There was a lone figure hunched over the fire as if he was trying to catch every flicker of warmth that the fire could produce. His clothes were obviously very old and non-descript as they hung loosely on his body. What caught the wolf's eye was the necklace hanging from around the old man's—for that is what he could clearly be seen to be—wrinkled neck. Eyes narrowed, Wolf recognized the sharp canine wolf teeth and knew this was the same man, the De Tribu—the witchdoctor—he had met before.

As he pondered his next move, the old man's head shot up, his white hair and beard barely keeping up with his sudden movement. With an unexpected large grin and a welcoming gesture, he motioned for the wolf to come near the fire. "There you are. Right on time, I might add. Very good. Very good. Come to the fire. Don't be shy. You never were before."

As the wolf tentatively took four steps closer, eyes narrowed and head down, a feeling of recognition, of familiarity, again swept through his mind. When Wolf's head tilted to the side, the old man gave a small laugh.

"Yes, yes. 'Tis I. Nice to see you again, Wolf."

Mouth open in amazement, Wolf padded up to the fire and sat heavily on his haunches. "Merlin?" Wolf whispered unbelievingly, looking him up and down. "How can you be here? You're supposed to be…," he stopped, clamping his mouth shut. How could he tell the wizard he was supposed to be dead?

"Entombed? Is that the word you are

searching for?" Merlin asked, his eyes twinkling. The whitish film that had covered one of them the last time was noticeably absent.

"Well, yes," stammered the wolf, still not in control of his thoughts.

"I know, I know," Merlin held up a wrinkled hand. Then, glancing at its aged appearance, he shook his head disgustedly. "Anyway," he finally continued, "while one isn't *supposed* to change the course of the future...." He broke off with an unapologetic shrug. "Can't let you young ones have all the fun. This is much too interesting. So, I decided to lay low and do some, uhm, traveling."

Wolf let the 'young ones' comment go by. That wasn't exactly how he saw himself. "What about your apprentice?" he asked instead.

"Nimue?" Merlin gave a heavy sigh as he looked into the burning embers of the fire that wasn't really a fire. The sigh was still tinged with regret and longing. "My dear apprentice," he murmured. "Though I don't believe she still goes by that name just now. Just as I do not necessarily go by Merlin—but, let's just keep that between the two of us."

Wolf's eyes narrowed as he thought back to his previous encounter with De Tribu. "If that was you when I was here last, why all the mystic mumbo jumbo? Why the switching back and forth through the languages?"

"Because, my lad, you...didn't...know...me ...then." Merlin let the intricacies of time travel sink in and was pleased when realization came over the dark face in front of him. "Plus," he admitted, pleased with himself, "I enjoyed slightly vexing you!"

Not wanting his friend to get angry, Merlin decided to change the subject. With a nod of his head, he motioned in the direction of Walt's camp. "I like that one, Wolf. You chose well."

Wolf nodded. "He appreciates the ancients. You will be well remembered."

The wizard perked up even more. "Really? I am honored." Glancing up at the sky, he then said, "Well, I see that we had better part. Your friend is curious and will return to the clearing in the morning."

Wolf gave a wolfish smile. "Yes, that is like him," he nodded. His expression altered and became thoughtful as he asked, "Will I see you again?"

Merlin stood from the fire, which immediately went out. Stretching his back, he grimaced as a pain shot through his shoulders. "Need to get that looked at," he muttered to no one in particular. Ignoring Wolf's question, he raised a hand and simply said, "Fare thee well, Wolf."

Nodding his head once in respect, Wolf answered back, "Fare thee well, Merlin."

CHAPTER TWELVE

Disneyland — 2042

"How could it possibly take the fools one hundred years to get it right? One hundred years since that wolf gave my pendant to The Man. One hundred years! Well, wolf, I have been waiting patiently, but I will wait no more."

Nimue—as she was now known again—continued muttering and cursing to herself as she wandered through the pristine grounds of Disneyland. "What is that awful smell?" she wondered as she passed the Candy Palace where the candy makers were busy preparing fresh English toffee, the vanilla scent piped onto Main Street through hidden vents. "It's so sweet, so sickening. No wonder these mortals die so young…."

Moments earlier, her arrival in a billowing cloud of smoke was obscured by the steam train releasing its own vapor cloud. The sorceress sourly frowned as she looked around. Being denied the grand entrance of which she was so fond, her mood—already dark—dipped dangerously close to being lethal. Finding she was getting too much attention too soon, she had changed her flowing robes and glowing green staff into a high-collared, form-fitting dress of the blackest purple. Now the attention she was getting from the men was more to her liking as she strode through Town Square. Momentarily thinking she had found what she sought, she had to hold back from angrily casting a lightning bolt through the holographic projection of The Man as he gave an ancient speech to a surrounding crowd of people.

Standing now in the middle of Central Plaza, she glared at yet another representation of The Man, inexplicably holding hands with an over-large smiling mouse, this time cast in bronze. When the shoes of the rodent began to melt from her toxic stare, Nimue pulled her eyes away and looked around her. It appeared she had four options to travel. Shaking her head in disgust at the choices, her eyes closed and her mind reached out to find The Man, to see if he was anywhere close.

Frustrated when she couldn't find what she wanted, her anger simmered and seethed behind her gray eyes. As she muttered in an ancient, dead language, nearby mothers pulled their children back from the Partners Statue and quickly left the flower-filled Plaza. They would get their pictures another time. Unaware, and uncaring of the impression she was leaving on those around her, Nimue turned her attention to the castle, its colorful banners fluttering in the breeze that cooled the early evening. "My castle is far better than this pile of rubble," she mumbled as she strode towards the pink and gold anchor of the Park. "This is so…so pretty," she spat out. "How can they stand it?"

Stomping over to the drawbridge, she came to an abrupt halt and stood over the first archway that was built under the walkway. There seemed to be a sort of power or presence lying under those stones in the dark water. She could feel it. Her malicious eyes lit with understanding and she actually broke into a smile. "Soooo, this is how the wolf got through. Well, we can't have that happen again, can we? I don't need my careful plans messed up again by that…that creature." When she had altered her clothing, her powerful staff had been miniaturized into a brooch that more or less held the low-dipped front of her dress together. As her mind formed the action she desired, the brooch glowed green and did her bidding. A stream of lightning streaked out, and she closed the portal forever.

Chuckling to herself, Nimue continued through the castle arches and into the busy courtyard. Her smile quickly faded as the laughing children and happy faces became far too much for her to bear. As she looked at the turning carrousel, she was tempted to turn it into a mass of real war horses stampeding through the crowds. She laughed out loud at her wonderful idea. It was an evil sound, one that filled those who heard it with anxiety and fear. Then, as her face was upturned, she caught a glimpse of movement up in a curtained window overlooking the squalor below. The Evil Queen pulled aside the blood-red curtains and glared down from on high. "Ah, Your Majesty," the sorceress murmured. "At last! A familiar face from home." She was going to go into a deep curtsey but just then the curtains dropped back into place and the Queen was seen no more. "What is this? Fakery? Is there nothing of value that is *real* any longer?" she cried, flinging her arms and gesturing to no one in particular.

The bright music of Fantasyland and the laughter of the people around her were too much. Pushing back through the Castle entrance, she looked at her other choices as the lights twinkled on all the way down Main Street as darkness was falling. "Hmph, if they want a vision of their tomorrow, just wait," she promised, turning away from the high-tech wonders of the Tomorrowland entrance. "I will supply my own adventure, thank you, so that leaves Frontierland. Wonderful," she muttered dryly, almost walking in front of the double-decked Omnibus that had just pulled away from the curb. Its quaint bulb horn gave a good-natured honk at the oddly dressed woman who was glaring at the tall green *thing* that was telling *her* to get out of the way.

A whinny diverted her attention just as she was about to raise her hand. "Ah, something familiar!" she cried out as she walked over to the huge Belgian horse pulling the trolley. The horse snorted and tossed his head, the blinders on his eyes prevented him from seeing the approaching woman. As she walked in front of him, the horse's eyes widened in fear as he sensed her evilness. Making a sudden half-jump, he lashed out with a huge hoof, telling her to get back, to get away from him. The conductor of the trolley hurried to the horse's nose, and pulled the big head down, murmuring to calm the animal. "I'm sorry, ma'am, he usually isn't like this. Something musta spooked him." *And, from the look in your eyes, it was probably you*, he thought to himself, but wisely said nothing else.

The horse started to calm when she turned in a huff and stormed across the wooden bridge that led into the upright logs of the fort-like entrance to Frontierland. Banjo music was playing on the hidden speakers in the area, but she was so engrossed in her mission that she failed to hear the lively tune. What she did hear was the frightened screams coming from the Big Thunder rollercoaster. Not knowing the source of the terror, the screams pleased her greatly. "A dungeon! Finally, the sounds of home," she sighed. "Perhaps they are not as backwards as I thought."

The Rivers of America seemed to be pulling her forward, the same strange pull that she had felt on the bridge of the Castle. Not finding the exact source of the power she felt, the Evil One walked along the fenced waterway until she noticed a large group of people beginning to gather. Here they were sitting on the ground, apparently waiting for something to happen on that small island across the narrow channel.

A presence suddenly appeared next to her, silent and menacing. With a calm smile on her beautiful face, she turned to look into the blazing, angry eyes. "Ah, it's you, wolf. I wondered when you would dare to show your face, now that you have a face and not a muzzle," she added with a sneer. She gave his human body a slow, scrutinizing look. It was obvious she didn't care for this form of Wolf any more than she had liked the form of the animal he had been last time she had seen him.

"What are you doing here?" Wolf demanded in a low voice, restraining himself from attempting to drag her away. When he saw her hand start to make a gesture, he snarled, "Your spells no longer have an effect on me. Go back to your despicable hovel in the darkness. You aren't wanted here."

"And I have missed you, too, wolf," she cooed. "Such bad manners. Have you learned nothing in all this time? I…I just wanted to visit my old friend," she claimed sweetly, her face a mask of innocence.

"You are not wanted here. I want you to leave. Now!"

Eyes wide open in amazement, she put a ladylike hand on her chest. "Leave? I thought the sign out front," waving an elegant hand in the direction of the entrance, "said 'To all who come to this happy place, welcome.' Did I misunderstand something? How embarrassing!" she murmured, managing to look self-conscious. "Why, I just got here to this…this…place," Nimue spat out the last word, showing her true disdain.

"Is *this* what my pendant did? It should shrivel up, ashamed of itself.... I do want it back, you know," she added casually as if chatting about the weather.

"That will never happen."

She reached out to run a black-tinted fingernail down the side of his handsome face. "So serious," she said with a sigh. "You were once mine, wolf," she purred. "You could be mine again. I really do have such a forgiving nature, you know."

Wolf held back from jerking down her arm as he stared unblinking into her malicious gray eyes. "Again, that will never happen, witch."

Taken aback, Nimue gasped, "Witch? Oh, wolf, that is so hurtful. Such an ugly word to hear."

"Then it's a good thing you can't be reading my thoughts."

Her finger now traced a trail down his other cheek, deep enough to draw a thin line of blood. Not once did his angry eyes ever leave her face or blink. "Did you not learn, wolf, that I get what I want?"

"No, I obviously did not learn that, the proof being that I am standing here. And the pendant is safe here with me. And *not now or ever will be* in your possession."

She gave a small chuckle and dropped her hand, her fingers forming an unseen fist in the folds of her dress. "Oh, do not mock me, wolf. I know The Man has what belongs to me. It has escaped me twice before...."

"Thrice," he corrected with a smug grin.

"But this will not happen again," she continued as if not interrupted. "I am here for my property. It took me a...little while to locate all of you together, but I finally have. Being the generous creature that I am, I will give you until tomorrow. I kindly suggest you tell The Man. Or I will," she hissed, leaning her face close to Wolf's. "Tomorrow. Leave me now," she commanded with an elegant sweep of her hand. "I think I will enjoy the festivities," she claimed brightly, indicating the opening music of *Fantasmic!* as the crowd, oblivious to what was going on behind them, began clapping and calling out in delight.

"You will not harm anyone, Nimue," Wolf warned with an upraised finger. "You are not the only one who has learned something in the passing of the centuries."

Snickering as if he were a fool, Nimue turned from her adversary and paid him no more heed. Her message was delivered. He was given the warning.

As the popular music and light and pyrotechnic show progressed, Nimue got angrier and angrier. *How do they stand this drivel? And that mouse! He is everywhere! If they want some fireworks, I'll give them....*

Her disgust at the show halted when *she* suddenly appeared, challenging the oddly-dressed rodent. Her mouth fell open in delight as she watched the forces of evil fly across the spraying fans of water and the skeletons dance behind the waters. *Finally, something to root for*, she thought. She came as close as she ever came to being happy when Murphy, as the thirty-foot animatronic dragon had been affectionately nicknamed by cast members for decades, began to rise from the hidden platform. *So beautiful*, she cried, a tear streaking down her face. *It's been so long.* Just then, when the dragon screamed and fire tore out of her mouth towards Mickey, setting the River on fire, Nimue abruptly turned and left the show. She had seen what she needed to see.

Watching from the darkness surrounding the show area, Wolf's eyes frowned at the thoughtful, unsettling look on the sorceress' face, a small smile playing across her features. By the time he pushed away to follow her, she had vanished.

He knew she would be back tomorrow. He knew from their dealings in the past that she did not give idle threats. He knew he had to warn Walt.

"I always like to look on the optimistic side of life, but I am realistic enough to know that life is a complex matter. But, this…this is beyond anything we have had to deal with before. I just don't understand it at all, Wolf. How could she have come here now? And, why now?"

"Apparently she has learned much since I last saw her," Wolf replied, shaking his head slowly, wondering what they were in for. "She does sense that you are close, Walt, but she didn't seem to know where you were or know about this room. I definitely think you're in danger."

Walt went to the window of his apartment

and stared out over Main Street. A lot of families were leaving now that the hour was so late. Some of the families would not be making that trek towards the exits, though. They were already in their hotel-like rooms inside Sleeping Beauty's Castle or in one of the luxury huts high up in the Treehouse.

"They," indicating all the people flowing through the tunnels under the train tracks, "have to be protected. How could I live with myself if something happened to any of the guests? This is supposed to be a safe, happy place," he commented, turning from the window, a worried frown creasing his eyes.

Wolf nodded. "I know, Walt, and it has been. But, like you said, nothing like this has ever happened before. Do you think we need to talk to Peter Brentwood?"

Still thoughtful, Walt agreed. "Peter is doing as good a job as his mother and father—and grandfather," he added with a sad smile, "did as Guardians. Lance and Kimberly trained him well. Yes, he should be apprised." Looking back out the window, Walt shook his head as he considered the possibilities. "But, I don't know what any of us *can* do. This is way out of our league."

Wolf's blue eyes shone with his anger. "We will provide a united front. I am sure we will think of something."

Walt turned sharply at his words, suddenly angry. "No! There is no 'we' this time, Wolf. This is *my* fight. Just like Mickey and the dragon over there at *Fantasmic!* I will do what I have to. Alone!" he stressed.

Saying nothing in answer, Wolf gave a simple nod of his head. "I'll go talk to Peter."

He got no reply. Head down, Walt was deep in thought, his outline framed by the glowing lights outside the window.

They both knew they had only one day to figure something out.

"This is my dream!" Mickey cried out the next night as the *Fantasmic!* show progressed. Pointing his wand at the tall, fire-breathing dragon towering over him, a shaft of sparkling light left his wand right on cue and streaked towards the dragon.

"Not this night, Mouse!" The dragon suddenly screamed back at him. She turned her huge head and blew a fireball at the nearby Mark Twain depot. The century-old white building burst into flame. Head back, the dragon began laughing in an odd, cackling sound as she gleefully looked at the burning building.

The watching crowd, seeing something new and different, ooh'd and aah'd as the flames climbed higher into the night sky. They applauded the new special effects and cheered loudly as a silent alarm was sent to the fire crew backstage by a panicked crowd-control member.

The cast member inside the Mickey costume froze in place, not knowing what to do. Trying hard to get back to the script, she was too frightened by the laughing, screaming dragon in front of her. In some shows, occasionally the dragon would do odd things, like bend over backwards or not rise fully from the underground storage box. But this…. Something was wrong. Very, very wrong.

Talking into her voice-altering microphone, the female cast member, sounding like Mickey, tried to end the show. "We're experiencing a little technical difficulties, folks, so, that's all for tonight! Thanks for coming! See ya real soon! Bye now!" she squeaked out, trying to cheerfully wave the white-gloved hand good-bye and keep it from visibly shaking.

Immediately jumping into action, Wolf and his Security team tried to get the people who were watching the show moving through the Adventureland exit, away from the hot flames. The guests didn't want the show to be over. Still wondering what was going on, they did, however, finally accept the direction given by an insistent Security team and filed out in an orderly fashion. Some of the guests turned back to look just as the dragon pushed off of the platform, smashing it into a hundred pieces as she took to flight and streaked upwards into the night sky. As the dark form of the dragon disappeared into the smoke-filled sky, those guests began talking animatedly to each other as they were herded briskly towards the exit. "This was a great new addition to the show," they unanimously agreed, and they were hopeful that "the Imagineers would get the bugs worked out before the show tomorrow night."

Over in Fantasyland, the fireworks over Sleeping Beauty's Castle were just getting underway. Wolf radioed in to stop the show and close the Park. Another hurried call to Peter told him what was going on and who was behind it.

The backstage areas of Disneyland were now opening to allow more people to move even faster towards the exits and into the hovercraft trams that would take them to their cars. The guests, once unhappy at the abrupt end of their favorite show and the early closing of the Park, were now engrossed in seeing what was usually behind closed gates and doors and out of their sight. They gawked at what the cast members saw everyday—the plain backside of the stores, lockers, vending machines, and most importantly, the stairs leading up to Walt's old apartment above the firehouse.

Ignoring the beeping of their transmitter and not realizing what had happened, high on top of the Matterhorn, two cast members were still helping Tinker Bell get ready for her nightly flight over the Castle. Her harness was a high tech marvel that allowed her amazing freedom of movement from the old wire they used to use. Now she could even fly out over the audience if she chose to, dropping a handful of pixie dust from a pocket in her costume as she soared above their heads. Just as she was ready to push off, her spotlight was suddenly pulled away from her entry point and shone on something else in the sky as the rockets exploded over their heads. Their curiosity turned to concern as the spotlight illuminated a huge dark dragon slowly circling the Castle. While they were wondering about this new, unannounced addition to the show, the dragon screamed in anger as the fireworks exploded around her. A stream of red-dish/orange fire blew out of her mouth and in-stantly dissolved a rocket that was coming straight at her.

Eyes wide, Tinker Bell quickly started re-moving her harness. "I ain't going out there. If you want Tinker Bell, you be Tinker Bell!"

"I'm with you, Anne. We'd better get out of sight. Hurry up, Ken! Get that door open!"

In mere moments the three cast members were out of sight and in the elevator inside the Matterhorn that would take them to the under-ground tunnel and to what they hoped would be safety.

As Main Street emptied, the scream echoed off of the vacated buildings. Far enough away, the crowd didn't panic, still feeling safe in the Magic Kingdom despite the menacing flames that were rising from the ruins of the Mark Twain depot. Something was *different*, but they felt se-cure in knowing that it was all Disney magic and that it would somehow be fixed if it was out of order.

As the fire department worked to quell the fire that acted differently than any fire they had ever faced, an older man stood in the back-ground, watching, his shoulders hunched as if in pain. Had they seen him, they might have won-dered why a lone tear streaked down his forlorn face as he watched the entrance to the Mark Twain turn into a sodden pile of ashes. *Not this place!* His heart breaking, special memories of a special occasion on that very spot suddenly flooded through his mind.

Disneyland — 1955

Early in the summer of 1955, almost three hundred friends, celebrities, studio heads and executives received this invitation:

"*Tempus Fugit Celebration*

Where: Disneyland…where's there's plenty of room…

When: Wednesday, July 13, 1955, at six o'clock in the afternoon…

Why: Because we have been married Thirty Years…

How: By cruising down the Mississippi on the Mark Twain's maiden voyage, followed   by dinner at Slue-Foot Sue's Golden Horseshoe!

Hope you can make it—we especially want you and, by the way, no gifts, please—we have everything, including a grandson!

Lilly and Walt"

Joe had arrived early on July thirteenth to make sure that his pride and joy, the Mark Twain, was ready to make her maiden voyage all the way around Tom Sawyer's Island. She hadn't been tested on the River yet and he was a little worried about this first sailing that would be experienced by the cream of Hollywood's society.

Once onboard the boat, he was immediately handed a broom by a woman who was busy with her own broom and dustpan, sweeping the sawdust, shavings and dirt off of the deck. Barely glancing at the man, she told him to get busy and help her so it would be clean in time for all the guests who were coming. This was the first time Admiral Joe had met Lillian Disney.

At the front gate, as the anniversary guests began to arrive, Walt happily directed all of them to waiting horse-drawn surreys. With a steady clip-clop, clip-clop, the horses pulled the excited guests down the glittering avenue of Main Street—that was almost finished and ready for the Grand Opening two days later. Once through the open gates of Frontierland, they were directed aboard the waiting ship.

All decked out with sparkling white lights, the pristine ship was filled with happy, mingling people. A Dixieland band entertained them while waiters served an endless supply of mint juleps.

With a blast of the whistle, the ship slowly pulled away from the dock and the huge paddle-wheel in the back provided a soothing *swish-swish-swish* in the green water. There were no lights on Tom Sawyer's Island yet, but the guests still felt like they were transported into another place and time. The Admiral needn't have worried. The trip was smooth and pleasant, a good omen for the new park.

Once back to the dock, the Golden Horse-shoe Saloon had her doors swung open and waiting. Dinner was served within the gilded wallpaper, red and white light fixtures, and carved wooden accents of the showroom. Walt and Lillian cut the beautiful four-tiered white anniversary cake as family and friends looked on, smiling at the happy occasion and having a wonderful time.

Slue-Foot Sue started her show with a song and then introduced her Can-Can girls. When the Irish tenor had done his song, the Traveling Salesman came onstage with his hilarious vaudeville routine. The finale came too soon and Pecos Bill made his appearance, six-guns in hand and shooting at the audience.

Walt had slipped away by then and reappeared on the upper balcony, pointing his finger at Pecos Bill and going, "Bang! Bang!"

The audience loved it and called for him to come down and give a speech. Enjoying himself so much, Walt stayed up on the balcony. When the band started playing again, his family came on stage and began dancing with different guests.

Watching the scene below onstage, Walt seemed to finally realize his dream of an amusement park that the whole family could enjoy had finally come true.

There had never been a more heartwarming, magical party than that night.

Disneyland — 2042

"I miss you," he softly whispered into the night. "I miss all of you."

The memory of that special occasion faded as Walt realized everything he had worked for, struggled for, gave up for was being threatened. It didn't matter to him that *he* was being threatened. He could deal with that. Not his Park, though. This was his Park, and he wouldn't let anyone or anything take that away from all the happy guests who came from all over the world to visit it. He knew it was a magical, special place that meant so many things to so many people.

Walt brushed the tear from his cheek with a determined finality and balled his hands into fists. No, she wasn't going to destroy anything else. He would fight her with everything he had. He gave a wry smile in the darkness. He had fought dragons of different kinds before. Some of them had won.

Not this time.

Anger coursed through him as he resolutely turned away from the charred mess. It was going to stop. And it was going to stop that night.

Hurrying around the corner into Adventureland, he almost ran through the empty street as he headed for the cast member area behind the shops on Main Street that would take him to his apartment.

To fight a dragon you need a sword.

Wolf and a small band stood together, hidden from sight inside the entrance to the Penny Arcade in the middle of Main Street, its white lighted curved entrance a vestige of the good, the positive of all the Park stood for. Looking towards the location of the Train Station, they could see a lone figure, dressed in casual slacks and a limp cardigan, come into view, walking slowly towards the Castle.

Rising further into the air, the dragon circled the silent Matterhorn and came back to the Castle, sitting on the uppermost turret as her claws closed around the spire. Just for fun, she set fire to two of the swan topiaries that had sat on the bank of the moat for over fifty years. "That's better," Nimue laughed, her eyes glowing yellow. "I hate swans."

Seeing Walt casually approaching down Main Street, his hands in his pockets as if he didn't have a care in the world, the dragon screamed again and took to the air, hovering over the bronze replica of the man approaching her. She let out a fireball that immediately melted the metal head and sent rivulets of molten bronze streaming down the statue. "Come to me," she coaxed as she rose into the air to circle the Castle. "Come to me and deliver what is mine, or this fate shall be yours!"

As Walt strode past the entrance of the Arcade, he was unaware of the movement behind him, so intent was he on the menacing figure that filled the sky with the smell of decay and evil. Had he looked, he would have seen some familiar and some not-so-familiar faces march united out onto the pavement and fall into position behind him as an army would behind their general.

Coming in right behind The Man was the first Guardian, Wolf. He matched Walt step for step as they continued down Main Street. Next came Lance and Kimberly, holding hands with set, determined looks on their faces. As they fell into the marching tempo set by their leader, Adam and Beth joined the ranks. Their gray heads were held high as their hands fisted in anger that all they had worked for was being threatened. Carrying his ancient sword, Wals quickly joined in behind them, ready for one last battle. The final Guardian, Peter, kept his green eyes narrowed on the dragon. Matching him step for step was his wife Catie, Adam and Beth's daughter. There was no trace of fear on any of their faces.

Laughing now, an evil sound coming from behind her forked tongue, the dragon surged towards them, flying low to intimidate, her claws just above their heads.

Walt did look back now, and smiled with gratitude at his loyal friends who had fanned out behind him. Resolute, confident, he took another few steps forward and faced the castle.

"Behold The Man!" the dragon called from high above, turning and swooping in low, the tops of the manicured trees swaying in the blast of air. "You have what is mine. I will take it now or you will all die!"

"No."

The word was said in a low, firm voice, a voice that had led animators and directors and artists to do their best. They had listened to that voice and knew the strength and belief behind it. They had listened and had done what everyone told them could not be done. That voice had not changed.

Unaffected, Nimue laughed again and flapped her ragged wings up to a great height. "Then prepare to die," she shrieked.

Turning as if a graceful sparrow and not a huge, lumbering dragon, the sorceress arched back towards the small army. Just for spite, she knocked off one of the spires of the It's a Small World attraction. With a terrifying scream she dove straight at them, leveling off as she opened her huge mouth and blew a steady stream of hot, yellow fire right at Walt.

Walt could feel the heat building as it got closer and closer to him. The tips of his hair and the fabric of his sweater began to singe and smoke. Standing resolute, he brought out the hand that had been in his pocket this entire time. Lifting his hand in front of him, he raised it over his head and opened his fingers. The ancient chain dangled from his fingertips and the heart-shaped red diamond swung back and forth in the blast of air that preceded the inferno.

The red and yellow flames got closer and closer to its intended victim. But, as soon as she saw the diamond in the line of fire, the dragon screamed, "No!" and clamped her mouth shut as her claws reached towards Walt, frantically moving back and forth in her efforts to weave a spell.

The flames were instantly diverted around the band of Walt's people and swept past them all the way down Main Street, the heat almost scalding their skin until, at last, the blaze was gone.

EPILOGUE

Columbia — 1940

Someone must have thrown more wood on the fire during the long night. It was probably to keep the mosquitoes at bay, but the flames blazed up and the smoke drifted over the clearing and those sleeping around it. Some of the animators sleeping close to the fire shifted uneasily in their makeshift beds, groggily turning away from the intensity of the heat, allowing their cold backs to absorb the warmth while their faces cooled in the night air.

Still asleep, Walt twisted and turned, his face bathed in sweat from the extreme heat as it seemed to flow over and around him. As the early morning fog crept up from the Amazon, he jerked once more as if trying to bring his hand up in front of his face. Obstructed by the material of his trousers, the sharp movement caused his hand to unconsciously let go of the pendant he had been tightly gripping all through the night, and it slipped back into the depths of his pocket. Bereft of the touch of his hand, the intense vision that had been playing like a movie through his mind suddenly dimmed. Once the images had faded from his thoughts, Walt's movements calmed, his breathing once again returned to an even pace. The flames of the fire finally ate through the logs, as all fire does. Once its source was used up, the heat started diminishing, allowing the cooler foggy air to creep back into the surrounding area.

Upon awakening in the damp, misty morning, Walt was greeted with a pounding headache and a few anxious looks from his companions. The pain of his headache worked against the sharp images of his dream last night. Or had it been a vision back in the clearing? Did he really see what he thought he saw at El Lobo? Was there really a hand that came out of the darkness and tried to hand him something? It was probably just one of his friends joking around. *Wow, what a dream!* he finally decided with an uneasy laugh. Saying nothing to the others, he silently vowed never to touch tequila again. *But it was only one, a small drink at that*, he shook his head in frustration.

Standing next to the cold fire pit, Walt was unaware of the concern his men had as he stared unseeing into the ashes. His dream seemed so real that, try as he might, he couldn't shake it off. *Well, I guess it's better than see-*

ing pink elephants, he told himself, smiling slightly, trying desperately for it all to make sense. *Magic Kingdom*, he rolled the words over in his mind. *I like that phrase*.

Unconsciously, Walt's hand went back into the pocket of his rumpled trousers. He gave a silent gasp when his fingers touched the cool metal links of a chain. Glancing around, he could see that the others were now fairly preoccupied with loading their impromptu camp back onto the launch they had commandeered. They seemed more anxious to get out of the jungle and back to their ship, the *Santa Clara*, and were barely paying attention to what Walt was doing, especially now that he was up and moving. During the night, however, he had been so restless in his sleep, even calling out at one point, that a few of his animators had been growing somewhat worried about their boss. Now it seemed obvious he was fine, or so they thought, as they got back to the work of packing so they could get going as soon as possible.

Seeing that he was unobserved, Walt turned slightly away from the activity of the camp. His grasp closed around the chain and he pulled it partway out of his pocket. When the wavering sunlight hit the curves of gold and the glimpse of a brilliant red stone, his heart rate sped up once more.

Without a word of explanation to the others, he jammed the pendant back in his pocket and hurried back to the glade where he had heard that strange voice the night before. Feeling assured now that he was completely alone, Walt carefully removed the pendant once again. Holding it up this time by the chain, he examined the beautiful object thoroughly, turning it slowly in front of his eyes. It was indeed a heart-shaped red diamond. It had to be a diamond, he figured, since he saw all the colors of the rainbow shooting off from every facet. "It was true!" he whispered, amazed. "I did get this last night."

Ancient, was his next thought as he examined the way the gold was crafted; the patina gave the precious metal the appearance of age—great age. *Merlin*, he thought. *Could that have possibly been true, too?* The pendant slowly turned and the back of the setting came into view once again. What he had first thought were simply three circles now showed themselves to be an outline in a shape that was unmistakable to him. *Mickey!* he smiled to himself, *a red diamond with a Hidden Mickey*. The familiarity of the shape relaxed Walt after the confusion of the intense vision he had experienced all through the night. Reaching out his hand, his fingers slowly outlined the shape of Mickey's ears. Needing to know if what he had experienced the day before in this very spot had indeed happened, his tentative touch moved to the brilliant red heart. Immediately the same emotion he had felt before coursed through him once again. Jerking his hand back, the feeling running through his body promptly ceased. "That *was* how it happened!" he claimed out loud. Eager now to see what was next, he reached out and boldly grabbed the heart. Not fighting it this time, he let the thoughts and pictures flood through his mind.

He soon realized that this new vision precisely followed what he had been experiencing all through the night. The images of the night and early morning had been too vivid, too fresh for him to forget so soon where it had left off. Clouds of purple smoke swirled around his mind's eye and parted, allowing him to see once again the great dragon that had attacked him and his loyal group. Deep purple she was, a purple so dark it was almost black. It appeared that she was circling the castle to make one more attack, and she started to make her descent down Main Street toward his loyal friends. Then, suddenly, something like a long, silvery arrow hurled straight towards her. With an anguished scream that could be heard by all, she crashed heavily onto the pavement in front of them. As she rolled lifelessly onto her back, there it was, a long, elaborately-hilted sword protruding out of her heart with wisps of smoke trailing from her open, now-silent mouth. All her screams, all her threats and demands were over. She had lost her final bid to regain her pendant and destroy Walt and all that he had built. Standing proudly over her dead body, the sword's owner, Wals, was now surrounded by Walt and their friends, slapping him on his back and congratulating him on the success of his death stroke. Here stood Lance and Kimberly, Wolf and Peter and Adam and Beth. The vision shifted and they were now in Walt's beautiful apartment above Main Street sharing a bottle of champagne. Peter and his wife Catie told them about a new ride that was being developed for Tomorrowland. The vision faded out for a mere moment and Walt saw that he had shifted another thirteen years forward in time to July of the year 2055. A cloud of doves were released over the Main Street train station, followed by colorful Mickey balloons too numerous to count for the one hundredth anniversary celebration....

As Walt's hand dropped from the stone, the vision immediately extinguished, leaving him feeling sad it was gone but excited at the same time. "How could they know?" he whispered out loud, amazed once again by what he had seen. "How could they know my dream? How could they know I want a park just like that?" The words he had been told about the pendant in the darkness the night before came back to his mind as he stood there staring into the depths of the Amazon jungle. *Safeguard and protect it...far more important to you than its face value...it will show you things...about your little magic kingdom...remember this: How you get it is up to you.* There was no way he could answer the questions of 'who was that' or 'how could this happen' at that moment. There was too much for him to consider. He did, however, believe one thing with an absolute finality: This vision, this prelude of his future—however it was that it was given to him—would come true!

Hoping to get at least some kind of an answer to his many questions, Walt placed the mysterious piece of jewelry reverently back into his pocket and turned his attention to the surroundings. The rock formation of the crouching wolf, El Lobo, was more defined but looked decidedly different in the bright sunlight that had finally burned off the river mist. He didn't pay much attention to the rock formation, though. He knew El Lobo itself wouldn't hold the answer he was seeking. Studying the ground around the trees from which the heart-shaped pendant had emerged, he was looking for footprints, boot prints, tire tracks, anything that made sense. There had to be some explanation on who it was who had given him this wonderful foretaste of his future.

There were no footprints to be found. Retracing his own steps, he even walked all the way around the silent rocky figure looking intently at the ground. As he figured, he found nothing. Going back to the edge of the jungle, he spotted the burned-out stub of a cigarette. Knowing this was the exact spot on which he had stood, he dropped down to his knees. Walt brushed a few stray leaves away from the fallen stub. What he saw made his breath catch in his throat. Slowly standing, he stared down at the visible evidence right in front of his eyes. What he had found in the dust was the unmistakable shape of paw prints. *Big* canine paw prints that led partway into the jungle and simply vanished.

Not being able to take his eyes off of the tracks, the pendant's vision once again filled his mind and caused his hands to tremble with excitement at all that he had seen. He brought up a name out of the future—his future, he reminded himself—and a small, knowing smile turned up the corner of his mouth. "Wolf."

Now onboard the liner *Santa Clara*, Walt and his group made their way slowly through the majestic Panama Canal. Still being recognized and feted, Walt was literally pulled off the ship in Panama City to attend the premiere of *Fantasia*.

The last leg of the journey took them up the Eastern Seaboard. Walt and Lillian attended the opening of *Dumbo* in New York at the Broadway Theatre. The *New York Times* newspaper reported favorably that they had never knew they could fall in love with a baby elephant. The animated feature-length film, the fourth from the studio, was a hit.

Once the festivities in New York were over, after being gone for twelve weeks, the small group of nineteen finally boarded an airplane and gratefully headed home to California.

During their long plane flight home, Walt leaned over to give Lillian a kiss on her cheek, telling her he was going to take a nap. Knowing how worn out and tired he was from the trip, she was glad to hear this. Giving him a warm smile, she turned back to her magazine. He might be tired, she thought, but she also knew he was now excited about the future. She wasn't sure when it had happened during the exhausting trip, but she knew her husband had regained a vitality, an eagerness for whatever was about to come. And, she gave a knowing smile, Walt would be sure to fill them all in on it whenever he was ready.

As Walt settled back into his seat of the

plane, folding his arms comfortably over his stomach and closing his eyes, a small grin tugged at the corners of his mouth. He wasn't sure he could actually sleep as the vision of his little magic kingdom played over and over through his mind like the reels of a live-action movie. One by one, he pictured the many faces he had seen. Some of them, of course, he knew from the Studio. The rest of the people who had inhabited this future world of his he knew he had never seen before. As their images paraded past his closed eyes, they were now as familiar to him as if they were members of his own family. Their personalities and quirks fell into place with their names and Walt felt as if he could easily resume a conversation with any one of them.

Giving a little snort of a laugh as he drifted off, Lillian glanced over at the sound, but it looked to her as if Walt was already asleep. Unaware of his wife's attention, Walt snuggled deeper into his seat. He was thinking that he would be disappointed when he went back to the Studio in the next few days and most of those people wouldn't be there.

There was one phrase that kept going through his mind, one that would become something like a mantra for him: *How you get it is up to you*. Exact details in the vision might not match up, he realized, but the possibilities...the possibilities were thrilling! *How you get it is up to you*. Yes, he would realize his dream of a magic kingdom. It *was* up to him. Right then he didn't know exactly how he would get this vision to come true. It was going to take a lot of work.

But, that never stopped me before, he told himself. *Hmmpf, they said* Snow White *would never happen. Showed them. All it takes is belief…and the right people.* He thought of the men talking quietly amongst themselves or sleeping on the plane around him. *And,* he smiled to himself, *I know how to get the right people.*

Walt finally did drift off to sleep. It was a peaceful sleep—one of the first since this good-will tour of South America began twelve weeks earlier. It was the sleep of a man who had finally been given the answers to all of his many questions.

—THE END—

THANKS AND ACKNOWLEDGEMENTS TO:

JIM KORKIS, AN INTERNATIONALLY RESPECTED DISNEY HISTORIAN WHO HAS WRITTEN HUNDREDS OF ARTICLES ABOUT ALL THINGS DISNEY FOR OVER THREE DECADES. JIM WAS ALSO THE ORIGINAL "MERLIN" IN THE *SWORD IN THE STONE* CEREMONY IN FANTASTLAND AT WALT DISNEY WORLD AND HE GRACIOUSLY ALLOWED US THE USE OF HIS SCRIPT. HIS COUNTLESS ANECDOTES ABOUT WALT ARE PRICELESS AND WE APPRECIATE HIS PERMISSION TO USE THEM. WE ALSO APPRECIATE JIM'S ALLOWED USE OF KEN ANDERSON QUOTES FROM THE KEN ANDERSON INTERVIEW WITH JIM KORKIS © JIM KORKIS 1985, USED BY PERMISSION.

WE HIGHLY RECOMMEND TO OUR READERS JIM'S NEW BOOK *THE VAULT OF WALT* AVAILABLE ON WWW.AMAZON.COM

WE ALSO THANK OUR PROOFREADERS AND EDITORS:
ALYSSA COLODNY
KARLA GALLAGHER, ENGLISH B.A
KIMBERLEE KEELINE, ENGLISH PH.D.
WWW.KEELINE.COM

THE LIMITED EDITION
HIDDEN MICKEY HEART PENDANT

FEATURED IN THE HIDDEN MICKEY NOVELS
IN 14K YELLOW GOLD VERMEIL OR ANTIQUE BRONZE ON STERLING
AVAILABLE AT:
WWW.HIDDENMICKEYBOOK.COM

HIDDEN MICKEY HEART PENDANT
COPYRIGHT © 2010 NANCY RODRIGUE
WWW.AWESOMEGEMS.COM

WITH THE POPULARITY OF THE FIRST HIDDEN MICKEY book, "SOMETIMES DEAD MEN DO TELL TALES!" THE HIDDEN MICKEY FAN CLUB WAS FORMED.

FAN CLUB MEMBERS GET A MONTHLY E-MAIL NEWSLETTER CONTAINING BEHIND-THE-SCENES ARTICLES WRITTEN BY VARIOUS PAST AND PRESENT CAST MEMBERS WITHIN THE DISNEY PARKS, AS WELL AS ADVANCE ANNOUNCEMENTS ON FUTURE BOOK SIGNINGS, SPECIAL EVENTS, AND SPECIAL OFFERS. IN ADDITION, FAN CLUB MEMBERS GET SPECIAL PURCHASE OPPORTUNITIES FOR THE NEXT HIDDEN MICKEY SERIES BOOKS AND MERCHANDISE BEFORE THEY ARE RELEASED TO THE PUBLIC.

JOIN THE HIDDEN MICKEY FAN CLUB:
www.HIDDENMICKEYBOOK.com/fanclub

HIDDEN MICKEY MERCHANDISE ITEMS

 HIDDEN MICKEY MUGS

HIDDEN MICKEY BASEBALL CAPS

 HIDDEN MICKEY SHIRTS

HIDDEN MICKEY JACKETS

 HIDDEN MICKEY CLOCKS

AND THE LIMITED EDITION
HIDDEN MICKEY HEART PENDANT
PENDANT DESIGN BY NANCY RODRIGUE
COPYRIGHT © 2010 NANCY RODRIGUE

AND MUCH MORE...
AVAILABLE AT:
WWW.HIDDENMICKEYBOOK.COM

Enjoy all of the Books by Double-R Books

IN PAPERBACK AND EBOOK FORMATS

THE 1ST BOOK IN THE HIDDEN MICKEY SERIES

HIDDEN MICKEY
SOMETIMES DEAD MEN DO TELL TALES!
BY NANCY TEMPLE RODRIGUE AND DAVID W. SMITH

THE 2ND BOOK IN THE HIDDEN MICKEY SERIES

HIDDEN MICKEY 2
IT ALL STARTED...
BY NANCY TEMPLE RODRIGUE AND DAVID W. SMITH

THE 3RD BOOK IN THE HIDDEN MICKEY SERIES

HIDDEN MICKEY 3 WOLF!
THE LEGEND OF TOM SAWYER'S ISLAND
BY NANCY TEMPLE RODRIGUE

THE 4TH BOOK IN THE HIDDEN MICKEY SERIES

HIDDEN MICKEY 4 WOLF!
HAPPILY EVER AFTER?
BY NANCY TEMPLE RODRIGUE

AND
A NEW ROMANTIC FANTASY

THE FAN LETTER
BY NANCY TEMPLE RODRIGUE

Enjoy a Preview Chapter of:

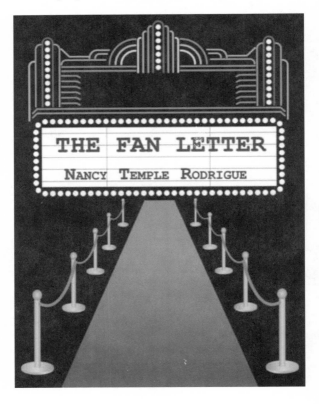

BY NANCY TEMPLE RODRIGUE

CHAPTER 8

*T*he days flew quickly for Jane. There had been so much to learn from Rex during her months at the hidden chateau. Being very happy and very much in love, now knowing him so well, she knew immediately when something was wrong. Rex would come away from the computer console looking tense and uneasy. She knew something was going to happen. Soon.

Whenever she asked Rex to confide what he was thinking, he would momentarily look sad and draw her close to him in a warm embrace. But he wouldn't tell her the reason. Rex would follow her movements around the kitchen with his eyes, or he would stand on the terrace for an hour just holding her without speaking. Studying her face or running a soft hand over her cheek, he was trying to emblazon her features into his memory, becoming more tender and more loving than ever.

One warm evening they stood together on the balcony overlooking the swaying trees.

Rex broke the silence as he stood a step back from her so he could see her face. He held her hands in his. "Jane," he started in a soft voice. "I want to tell you something. I have come to love you more than I have ever felt possible…. No, let me talk," he interrupted her attempted response. "I have been alone for many years. You have been the light to my darkness. Even when you have to go I will still have your light within me."

Jane looked confused by his words. "Go? Why should I go? I'm happy here with you. Is this why you have been troubled lately?" her quick mind picked up. "Rex, tell me what you know," she implored.

His hand caressed her upturned face and he gently kissed her lips. "I can't tell you just yet what will happen, but it will come soon and you will be gone."

Tears came to Jane's eyes at his words. "Are you sending me away?" She had been sent away before, a long time ago in Scotland. The pain in her heart still burned.

The first tear the Professor ever shed now fell slowly down his cheek. "I would never willingly do that. You have to believe me. But, in the next few days—I fear its close—you will choose to go. And it will break both our hearts."

"But, darling…."

He put a soft hand against her lips. "Please, Jane, let me finish. I want to tell you now that my chateau will always be waiting for you. And so will I. I will find some way to watch over you when you are gone from here. Some day, somehow, I will reclaim you. The portal is at my disposal. When your other life is complete, the portal will make you mine again."

"Other life? I don't understand." Her tears were falling again, her face showing her confusion by his words.

"I'm afraid you will understand. Just don't despise me, for I do love you," he finished and his arms reclaimed her.

Jane couldn't comprehend the reason behind his words, but yielded to her love and trust of her dear Rex.

The next day Rex shocked Jane by giving her a small handgun. "I know you hate these, but keep it in your pocket, hidden," was all he told her.

Returning to his computer, he frowned over the readings. It was almost over. His hideout had been located and they were closing in. He programmed the portal and went over to the worried Jane. He took her in his arms one last time and kissed her.

A loud noise startled them. A horrific crash had toppled their front door, and now the sound of running feet could be heard searching the house.

Two men burst into the lab and aimed their weapons. They were shocked when Jane pulled her gun and stood protectively in front of the Professor.

"Andrew! Jack!" she shouted. "Put down those…." Her words trailed off as confusion hit. She knew these intruders. Her memory flooded back in that instant. "I know you! You're my…. Oh, dear! My husband, Jack."

Behind her, unseen, Rex closed his eyes

as if in pain. It was just as he had feared. Her memory returned at the sight of those most familiar to her. It was all over. For now. He could see Andrew was watching him like a fox, but Jack could only see his beloved wife. In these few moments, no one had lowered their weapons. Jane still shielded Rex.

Jane's face was a mixture of happiness at her memory and confusion about the past three months. "Maggie? I killed Maggie. I caused the explosion and Maggie fell. I ran away because I was scared. I remember hitting something and pain and then I was here. I…."

Andrew quickly explained, "Maggie isn't dead, Jane. She was hurt by the explosion, but she is fine. She… We all have been worried about you."

Jane stared at Andrew. "But you...you said you were going to have me arrested for murder."

Andrew looked ashamed. "I was upset and angry. I…I shouldn't have said that."

Jane had turned pale. Her mind couldn't keep up with all these conflicting images. "But Rex, he's always been there. We…I…love…Oh, Jack!" she cried as she fainted and sunk to the ground.

Rex took advantage of the diverted attention and leaped into the portal. He had no fears for Jane. She would be all right and was back with her husband. They had been tracking her ever since he had abducted her and knew this was the way it had to be. He would wait. She would be his once again some day.

Jack and Andrew let Rex go. They gen-

tly lifted Jane and Jack kissed his wife. As her eyes opened, she looked into his concerned face and her arms encircled his neck....

Ring. Ring Ring. Leslie looked up suddenly from her sofa. The phone. Drat, she was almost done....

"Hello?" she demanded shortly.

"Hi, honey. It's Mom. What are you doing?" Bonnie asked, choosing to ignore the sharp tone of her daughter.

"Umm," her mind was still with Jack and Jane. "I'm finishing my last chapter."

"Oh, you're always writing. I'd like you to go to the mall with me. There's a dress I would like your opinion on," her mom requested.

Leslie looked back at the sofa. "I'm almost finished, Mom. I think it's pretty good."

"Of course it is. But we don't get out to the mall much any more. I'd like you to go with me."

"Mom, all the cash registers light up and spell out 'Hi, Leslie and Bonnie' when we walk in the door."

Her mother didn't think that was funny. "Well, if you're too busy...."

Guilt. Lovely, Leslie thought to herself and gave a resigned sigh. "No, I'll go. There are only a few more pages to write. I could use the exercise," she relented. "My rear end is getting flat from the sofa."

She knew Bonnie was smiling into the phone. "Great. I'll pick you up in fifteen minutes."

Leslie looked down at her rumpled clothes. "Okay," she said slowly. "Meet you out front."

Ten minutes later Bonnie looked her daughter over as Leslie slid into passenger seat. "Is that what you're wearing?"

Leslie buttoned her coat to cover her old flannel shirt. "Hey, I only had ten minutes. I brushed my teeth and put on shoes. I hadn't planned on going out, you know."

Her mom became serious and got to what was really bothering her. "Les, between your job at the boutique and your writing, you don't have much free time. Dad and I are worried about you working so hard. If it weren't for Wayne, you probably wouldn't go out at all."

Leslie shook her head and tried to explain. "But I don't feel like my writing is work. I enjoy it too much. And pretty soon it will start paying off...I hope," she muttered under her breath. "When I'm not writing, I feel like I'm in a void. I have all these ideas in my head and nothing to do with them. It keeps my brain active."

"You know we're proud of you no matter what becomes of your little books," Bonnie smiled condescendingly, but added dryly, "Even though we don't understand how you can be so interested in that silly television show! We tried watching it once. Horrible thing! Why can't you write something more wholesome?"

The familiar buildings passing by were unseen as Leslie stared out the window of the car. "Mine are different. They'd make terrific episodes for the show. Mine are more human drama than science and technology."

"What does Wayne think of all this?"

Leslie shrugged. "He seems to like the stories. And, in answer to your next question, I haven't seen him lately. He suddenly had to go to Los Angeles on business, I don't know, weeks ago. He didn't know when he'll be back."

"He's such a nice boy," Bonnie smiled. "He's so polite to us. Renee was asking about the two of you," she told Leslie, glancing over at her. "She says she never sees you any more."

"I still have the same phone number and address," Leslie remarked dryly. "Mom, she's married now. They all are. I just don't fit in. If it weren't for Janice and Wayne, I wouldn't go anywhere," she stated, inadvertently admitting the same thing her mother had pointed out.

As the car pulled into a parking space near their favorite department store, Bonnie turned to Leslie. "We really like Wayne, Leslie. He seems to like you. Has, umm, anything been said?"

The warning bell in Leslie's head went off too late. She should have noticed how many times Wayne's name had come up in the conversation already and been able to deflect what she should have known was coming. "There's nothing to declare, Mom. He's a good friend. That's all right now. Now that my book has sold, I don't know what's going to happen in the near future. I want to be open in case I have to go to New York or Los Angeles."

Knowing when to drop it, Bonnie gathered her purse and keys. "I just don't want you to shut the door on a possibility."

Leslie wasn't thinking of Wayne. She was picturing the cast of "The Time Police" and putting herself in-between Tom and Phillip. "Don't worry, Mom. I'm considering all the possibilities."

"Dizzy blond model," Wayne muttered angrily for the hundredth time as he sat in his surveillance van across from Sarah and Phillip Beck's house.

He had been ordered by Sarah to temporarily stop his watch on Leslie and find out what was going on at her house. All Wayne could piece together from her frantic, angry phone call was that some actress—she was sure it was Cindy Sanders from the show—slept over and Sarah wanted to know what was going on.

Wayne hadn't wanted to return to Los Angeles. He was becoming more comfortable with his life in Amherst and more familiar with Leslie. He spent a lot of time with her and would quietly sit and watch her when she worked on her novels. Immersed as she would get, she didn't even remember he was sitting there. He considered it a victory when he could get her away for the evening to go to dinner and a movie.

What he couldn't comprehend was his lack of progress on a personal nature. She still offered her cheek for a requested good-night kiss and an offer to stay the night resulted in a silent, red-faced shake of her head. He could tell she cared for him and enjoyed his company. But there was some barrier between them that prevented any intimacy.

Wayne found himself reviewing all their times together as he continued his boring watch of Phillip. He could not come up with anything that was said nor done that would explain her refusal to carry things to the next, normal level. He knew she had a passionate side because of her scenes between Jane and Jack or, lately, between Jane and Rex. Leslie had even asked him to try out a certain position to see if a scene would work before she wrote it down. Wayne had enjoyed holding her briefly like that and had received a mild admonition when he failed to let go soon enough upon request.

His occupation as a private investigator still bothered him. While hating to lie to both Leslie and Janice, he couldn't picture their reaction to hearing the truth. Finding he respected them, explanations would have to wait. Perhaps he could find work of another kind in Amherst. *Too bad*, he thought, *that I'm not good at anything else that's legal.*

Contacts of his had provided Wayne with all the details of Phillip's party and the guest list. He had known within the first three days what had happened and who had had to spend the night. He knew what they had to eat and drink and what music had played. He even found out which house Tom Young was going to buy on the beach.

Now he was just wasting time until Sarah was appeased. Phillip led one of the quietest lives of anyone he had ever watched—well, perhaps except for Leslie. At Marty's request he had provided the names of the women guests at the party and of the three who had been in no shape to drive home. The other names hadn't been wanted. Wayne knew Marty's angle and figured it would work on Sarah's jealous nature. Phillip didn't stand a chance with Marty around.

When Phillip finally drove off to the studio, Wayne gave a sigh of relief as he started the van and headed to his apartment. He hoped there would be a message from Sarah sending him back to Amherst.

"**B**eep...Wayne? This is Janice. Hi, how are you? We haven't heard from you in so long. I thought one of us ought to do something. I thought Leslie would, but she is so preoccupied.

"Her agent sent her five copies of her first

book. We're all excited about it. It'll go on sale any day now. I'm sure she just forgot to tell you. She sent two copies to her actor, Phillip Beck. One was for the actor who plays Jack. She kept a copy, her folks got one, and she gave me the last one.

"Well, anyway, that's the latest around here. They keep asking about you at work. Hope you're all right. Give us a call or something. Bye."

Wayne clicked off his answering machine. Hoping that Leslie would have called by now, it was Janice who had to tell him the good news. He could imagine how excited Leslie must be to finally have her book in her hands, but became hurt that she didn't save a copy for him. Instead she sent two to "her actor." *Like Beck really cared. He probably won't even read it*, Wayne snorted. *He was probably still too overwhelmed with his own career. Ha! If Leslie only knew the truth about "her actor" she might be very surprised. He was just a too-bit....*

Wayne stopped his pacing and stood still. It just occurred to him that he was jealous of Phillip Beck. The actor had gotten two novels, probably another letter, and he had gotten nothing. He'd have bet anything that Beck sent Leslie another of his short, say-nothing letters that meant so much to her.

Wayne strode into his bedroom and angrily packed his suitcases again. He had had enough of Los Angeles and Sarah. He was going home to Amherst. Sarah could take a flying leap. And she could take Martin with her.

The Amherst Times

Book Reviews

THE LONER FINDS LOVE

by Leslie Nelson

"Local author Leslie Nelson's first literary attempt has been enthusiastically received by fans of the popular "The Time Police" television series.

Her writing style is simple and direct and has managed to combine the futuristic storyline with old-fashioned romance.

Early predictions indicate the novel is headed for the best-seller list."

Leslie was handed the page out of the newspaper when she entered the boutique. Her boss Mona smiled at her. "Congratulations, Les. Your book seems to be a hit. I'm surprised you came to work today," she kidded.

Leslie glanced at the review that had already been read. Her parents had already called about it. Pretending to yawn, she joked back, "Oh, that. What a bore. What else could the little people say? Bring me a grape. And peel it." Leslie dramatically flung herself into a chair and closed her eyes.

Janice rolled hers. "Brother! Don't tell me we're going to have to put up with this from now on!"

Leslie looked up at her. "Where's my grape?"

"Where's your brain?"

"I don't need one. I'm famous," Leslie sighed.

All the women laughed and threw their coats on top of her before they went out front to get to work.

Leslie dug out from under the pile and fixed her hair in the mirror. "How rude!" she sniffed and strolled over to the pressing machine.

"Seriously, Les, what do you hear from your agent?" Mona wanted to know. "Anything on the second book?"

Leslie started steam pressing some dresses that had just arrived. "Well, he said he liked it and already sent it on to the publisher. He didn't seem to think there would be any problem getting it into print. He does want me to come to New York this spring to meet him and the editors."

"That's great!" Mona beamed.

"Tell her about Phillip," Janice prompted.

Leslie shrugged. "It's nothing really. You know I sent him a copy of my book," to which Mona nodded and waited for her to continue. "Well, he wrote back thanking me for it, and he also sent me a brochure to an up-coming convention. He didn't say so, but he is supposed to be there. I don't know," Leslie said casually, keeping head down so they couldn't see the excitement in her eyes. "Maybe he wants to say hello or something."

Janice looked at her unbelievingly. "What do you mean maybe? Why do you think he sent you the invitation?"

Leslie shook her head as she continued working on the dresses. "It wasn't an invitation, Jan. Just a brochure. All he said was that he didn't know if I had heard about the convention or not. That's all," she stressed, managing to kill her own mood.

Janice wasn't convinced. "He's going to be there and he wanted to make sure you would be, too," she stubbornly insisted, hands on her hips. *Sometimes Leslie could be so dense*!

"Well," Leslie said to end the conversation, "if he is there, and if we do meet, I hope he can tell me how to approach Majestic Studio with the idea for a script."

It took Leslie and Janice two hours to get to the convention site in the Silicon Valley. It was a cold, clear day in February, and there was a long line of cars waiting to get into the Fairington Oaks Hotel's parking garage.

Janice had driven as Leslie was jittery and nervous and quiet. Janice knew Leslie had brought her copy of her novel for the cast to sign. She also knew how many different outfits Leslie had tried on before choosing her blue rayon dress that highlighted the blue of her eyes.

What they both didn't know was that Wayne had followed them in his own car dressed in a disguise of a wig and a fake beard and mustache. He had been hurt that Leslie hadn't invited him to go along. She had told him he would get bored since he didn't like the television show as much as they did. Janice was also disappointed in Leslie's decision as she had wanted him to drive, but Leslie had been firm. Put off, now Wayne wouldn't have missed the meeting of Leslie and Phillip for anything in the world.

When the women finally parked, Leslie again checked her reflection in the car's vanity mirror.

"Your clothes look fine, Les. Don't know why you didn't wear contacts, though. But lighten up. You look like you're going to cry," Janice bluntly told her.

Leslie took a deep breath. "I'm so nervous," she admitted. "I don't know what to say so I don't come off sounding like some tongue-tied teenybopper."

"Just throw yourself into his arms and kiss him!" was Janice's suggestion as she started walking to the elevator.

"Very funny," Leslie scoffed as she looked around. "With all these people I probably won't have time to say much of anything anyway. Just as well. I do better through letters."

"You'll do fine. Wow, this place is great!"

Leslie glanced up at the ornate chandeliers, the glass and brass elevators, and the fern-enclosed grotto. "Close your mouth, Jan. We don't want to look like two geeks from the country who have never seen a grand hotel before."

"We *are* two geeks from the...."

"We are not! Shh!" Leslie insisted as she led them to the back of a long line.

After they stood in line for about ten minutes and had advanced a few yards, Janice started in with her favorite game: "Did you bring Phillip Beck's letter with you?" and "Do you think there is enough room in the front of your novel for all the cast to sign?" and "What did your agent say about your personal appearances?" and "Do you think your book will be on sale here?"

After a few people had turned to look at the red-faced Leslie and the smiling Janice, Leslie hissed under her breath, "Knock it off! This isn't for me."

Janice wasn't bothered in the least. "It will be. Some day."

In an hour they reached the desk and paid their admittance. They received a hand stamp in indelible red ink that read "Enter" and would last longer than the two-day convention. They each grabbed up an information sheet, scanning for the guest star's appearances. The whole cast would

field questions at eleven o'clock and sign autographs from noon until half past two. That gave
the two women an hour to browse.

The room into which they were admitted was
huge. It was lined with display booths filled with
badges, fan magazines, uniforms, dolls of the cast,
lapel pins, posters, postcards, copies of scripts,
coffee mugs, blooper tapes, tapes of each episode,
and anything and everything that could possibly
carry "The Time Police" insignia. Leslie found her
novel mixed in with all the other books for sale.
There were other adventure shows produced by
Majestic Studio that were also represented in the
booths.

All this time, as the pair wandered around,
they never noticed the bearded man who followed
their every move.

At ten-thirty, they found seats towards the
front of the auditorium to watch a slide show that
featured behind-the-scenes looks at the cast and
stills from various episodes. Leslie found herself
looking over at the long white-draped table that had
eight empty chairs behind it. She didn't even notice the elaborate floral spray that extended the
length of the table.

The announcer, Frank, finished the narration
on the slides and again welcomed the conventioneers. He was greeted with loud applause and ver-
bal affirmation.

"Well, I see all of you are in high spirits," he
beamed. "That's great. We're glad each and every
one of you is here. Are you having fun yet?"

Feet were stomped and whistles were heard.

"That's great!" Frank replied. "So are we. And
now, we won't keep you waiting any longer, Silicon
Valley. Here they are! The stars of your favorite

show—Maxwell Marlowe, Eddie Chase, Cindy Sanders, and Tom Young!"

Leslie's mouth dropped open and she looked at Janice. "Where's Phillip?" she yelled over the thunderous ovation the stars were given. Janice could only shrug.

The announcer then introduced the director, Ron Nickles, and two writers for the show. The crowd was still on their feet. Only Leslie and Janice remained seated. Wayne looked over from one row away and could see the obvious disappointment on Leslie's face. He smiled smugly to himself.

The crowd finally quieted down and retook their seats. The stars smiled warmly and waved at some children who ran to the edge of the stage. Flashes from dozens of cameras were still going off.

"Well," Frank cooed into his microphone, "I can tell you know who these people are!"

The crowd went wild with applause again.

Then Frank told them, "I know you all notice the empty chair. That was for Phillip Beck who, as you know, portrays Professor Rex Farrell on the show. Well, he was planning on being here to meet all you wonderful fans, but he was called back to the set of a movie he is filming and had to cancel."

There was a small groan that came from a few of the fans. Leslie looked over at Janice and muttered, "Oh, well, we tried."

The announcer opened the floor for questions and was greeted with a field of waving hands.

"Tom, are you married? Wanna be?"

"Eddie? Will your Andrew and Maggie ever really get together?"

"Cindy, want to go out for a drink later?"

"Has the show been renewed?"

"Can we take pictures?"

"How much money do you make an episode?"

"What is your favorite episode?"

"How long does it take to shoot a show?"

"Who makes the most mistakes?"

"Will The Loner ever get to keep the girl or will you keep killing them off?"

"Mr. Nickles, my cousin directs at a local theater. Need an assistant?"

"Would you accept a script from a local writer?"

"How old are each of you?"

"Which current problems in the world will you be fixing next season?"

"Will you ever do a theater-released movie?"

And so it went for the entire hour. The stars were generous and laughing with their answers or deferments. The writers told about some episodes coming up next season and how ideas are transferred into scripts.

Frank interrupted them all to say there would be another question and answer session later from four o'clock until five, but, for now, the stars would take a fifteen minute break. Then all were invited to the autograph session to be held in the fern grotto. Another ovation was given as the seven panelists exited waving and smiling. There was a rush of noise and movement as the fans streamed out of the auditorium. Some headed back to the merchandise room. Some went to lunch. Some stood around and exchanged fan club gossip. Quite a few—including Leslie, Janice and Wayne—headed for the fern grotto and patiently got into another line.

Janice started in again. "Did you see they have your book for sale?" and "Are you going to send a message back to Phillip Beck?" and "Did you hear what they said about looking for scripts? You're all ready for them."

"Janice!" Leslie pleaded, "Stop! I already told you Phillip probably didn't intend on meeting me. He probably knew about this all along. They'll send him a cut of the take, no doubt. Two extra losers came to the convention."

Janice just smiled. "Oh, sure. Now you're being silly. He was called back to the studio. You heard that. He told you he was really busy."

"He always says that," Leslie pouted, noticing a few people looking back to catch their conversation. "Drop it for now, okay?"

"Do you think he gave your book to Tom?" Janice persisted.

"Doubt it. It didn't sound like he was going to. Maybe I can find out when we go through the line. With all these people I'll only have a few seconds."

"Well, you'd better get that look off your face," Janice told her. "You look like a thundercloud."

Janice finally fell silent, to Leslie's relief and she looked around the crowded hotel. A few fans were strolling around in homemade versions of the show's uniform. Some were browsing through magazines. Janice suddenly nudged Leslie who jumped as though startled. "Hey, look, Les. They're reading your book!"

A couple of conventioneers were indeed re-laxing in chairs reading the opening pages of THE LONER FINDS LOVE. Leslie found her mood lightening as she watched them for a while.

"Well," she remarked to Janice, "that makes seven books in public hands."

"Eight. There goes another one," Janice pointed.

As the line moved forward Leslie took her copy of her novel out of her purse. She felt her stomach tighten as she got closer to the table where the four stars of the show were greeting people. First Maxwell, then Cindy, Eddie and lastly, Tom. There were large eight-by-ten studio pictures to be bought and signed at the head of the table. There were no pictures of Phillip. Most of the fans bought one of each star, Leslie noticed, but she passed them by.

She shyly offered the front blank page of her book to Maxwell, and then to Cindy and thanked them. When it was his turn, Eddie looked up at her and smiled as he took the book. He said hello, and as he asked for her name he glanced at the front of the book at the picture on the cover.

"I don't look very happy, do I?" he remarked as he looked back at Leslie. His smile altered as he again looked at the front cover. It was obvious he was comparing the faces.

Leslie blushed. "I guess it is because Andrew isn't too happy with the newcomer Jane."

"What did you say your name was again?" Eddie asked in a friendly way, his pen poised.

"Just Leslie. That's fine," she mumbled.

"Nice to meet you, Leslie," he said as he handed the book back. He then tapped Tom as Leslie moved down a step and said, "Bunny," in a low voice.

Leslie heard what he had said and saw Tom do a double-take at her. She got all red and flustered again. Janice, who was having the time of her life, prodded her to go to Tom's station.

"I wonder if you could sign this for me," Leslie managed to choke out.

"Did anyone ever tell you that you look like the girl on the cover?" Tom smiled as he looked at the novel's front. "I'll sign yours, Leslie Nelson, if you'll sign mine. Phil told me you might come to the convention when he brought over my copy. I really enjoyed reading it," as he pulled the book out from under his chair.

Leslie looked from Eddie to Tom. She grinned broadly to match theirs. Before she could reply, there was a loud, "You're holding up the line" yelled from the back.

Leslie blushed again. "Oh, dear. I…sure, I'll sign yours."

Tom took her book with the cast signatures and put it under the table. "Tell you what, Leslie," he said quietly, coming to an instant decision without thinking it through—or discussing it with Eddie. "Have dinner with Eddie and me after all this is over. We'd both like to talk about your book. Okay?" he smiled warmly.

"I'm not alone. Janice, my friend, is with me," she stammered, motioning with her hand in the wrong direction from where Janice was standing.

"Great! The more the merrier," Tom grinned, ignoring Eddie's kick under the table. "I'll make the necessary arrangements. See you later," he said as he motioned over an assistant. He pointed out Leslie and Janice, and the aide came over to them, leading them away from the nosey crowd.

"If you two ladies will come to the El Dorado Suite at six this evening, Mr. Young and Mr. Chase will be waiting for you. I do advise you not to mention the suite name to anyone else. Now, if you will give me your names, I will meet you at the door at six."

Leslie and Janice complied. Leslie then remembered, "Oh, I have Tom's book and he has the one signed by everyone else."

The aide told her, "You can exchange them at dinner tonight. It would be best not to say anything here. See you later, ladies."

The two women looked at each other as he walked off. "We're having dinner with Tom Young and Eddie Chase," Leslie murmured, wide-eyed.

"If you scream, I swear I'll slap you!" Janice warned. "I remember your reaction when Phillip called you that time."

"No, no, I'm fine." Leslie was actually stunned. "What did he mean by 'bunny' after he looked at me? Do my teeth look funny?"

"I don't know. We'll ask him at dinner," Janice told her, peering at her friend's white face. "Are you really all right? You're awfully pale."

Leslie put Tom's copy of her book in her purse. "I'm fine. I just can't believe this. Let's have lunch," she said suddenly and started walking towards the hotel's main restaurant.

The bearded man had seen Tom switch the books and then motion for the assistant. He could tell Leslie was shocked and Janice was excited. He just didn't know why. Following them into the restaurant, he figured Janice would soon announce what was going on.

Both women found themselves getting nervous as six o'clock approached. Janice became more talkative, and Leslie became more silent. They had attended the rest of the convention events scheduled for that day and finally entered one of the brass elevators. As they weren't alone in the elevator, they discontinued their on-going speculation on what the evening would be like.

Leslie took off her glasses to clean them just for something to do with her hands. Janice looked mildly disgusted. "You should have worn your contacts," she stated again.

"How was I to know? We would have been home by now."

"Well, we could leave," Janice kidded.

"Yeah, right!" Leslie laughed. Both of them knew nothing on earth could turn them away now.

After numerous stops, the elevator eventually reached the top floor. There were only Leslie, Janice and the disguised Wayne left when the doors slid apart. The view down to the main floor lobby was lovely with all the white lights in the trees and the six-story tall waterfall.

The same assistant met them at the door marked El Dorado Suite, ushering them into a large living area with an L-shaped white sectional sofa, glass and brass accent tables, a desk and chair done in antique white, and a honey oak entertainment center. Their gaze fell on a dining table set for four near the picture window overlooking the lights of the city. Three large fresh flower arrangements, oil paintings, and an Oriental silk screen that half-hid an oak bar did not escape their notice, nor that the room was beautifully tasteful.

From behind one of the three closed doors was the muted sound of male voices conversing. The far right door opened, and Tom Young came out with a grey-haired man who looked like he was in a tremendous hurry.

Tom smiled his greeting to the two women

and brought the man over for introductions.

"Ron Nickles, this is Leslie Nelson, a new author for "The Time Police." And this is...uh..." he faltered at Janet's name which had eluded him. "I'm so sorry."

Leslie extended her hand which was cold. "Hello, Mr. Nickles. This is Janice Woods."

Ron shook hands with each of them and abruptly turned back to Tom. "I need to call the studio. Tell Eddie I'll see him tomorrow. Ladies? A pleasure." He nodded and rushed out of the suite.

Tom explained, "He's the director of the show. But, you probably knew that. Why don't you two go ahead and take a seat. Eddie is talking to his wife in New York. He'll be out in a minute. Can I offer you a drink?"

"White wine would be fine," Leslie answered as she took Tom's book out of her purse. "This suite is lovely," she commented as she took her glass of wine.

Tom looked around as if that was a new thought. He shrugged. "I guess so. In our line of work we travel so much that we get a little jaded. I never really notice."

Leslie took a tentative sip. The wine proved to be excellent. "So, you don't like to travel? I love it. I only wish I could do more."

Tom seemed to be thinking back. "Oh, yes. New York once and the Caribbean twice. And Janice, you have been to Europe."

The women looked confused and a little wary. "How do you know that?" Janice asked him. She looked over at Leslie who likewise didn't understand how he could know that personal information.

Tom smiled a little sheepishly and looked

down. "I *could* say that Phillip told me, but that wouldn't be completely true. I actually found out through your letters, Leslie."

"My letters? To Phillip?" She blushed again. "I didn't think they were anything special to be passed around," she confessed.

Tom grinned again. "Well, he didn't exactly pass them around. Phillip threw a party recently and I needed to use the phone. While looking for something to write on, I came across your letters and a picture of you fell out on the floor. A few lines caught my eye and I ended up reading all of them. I thought they were quite funny," he told her as he looked steadily at her over his own wineglass.

"I'm surprised he kept them," Leslie murmured. "But I am glad he gave you my book. The first manuscript I sent you apparently never reached you."

He shook his head. "No, we don't see much mail," Tom replied, looking disgusted. "We get so much. Then there are the legalities if we read something the general public wrote and it ended up in a show without going through the proper channels. But Phillip..." he broke off for a second. "Well, Phillip doesn't get that much, plus there are different rules for guest stars."

The middle door now opened and Eddie Chase came out. He smiled at the two women with his trademark dazzling smile. He looked as if he was in a very good mood.

Walking up to Leslie first, he shook hands. "It's nice to meet one of our authors," he told her. "I hope Tom isn't boring you too much."

"No, not at all," Janice grinned. "He was just telling us how he came to know about Leslie."

Eddie picked up Tom's glass and took a

healthy sip. "Ah, yes. The snoop! I actually first heard mention of you over a year ago. When Phillip received your first letter. He was quite impressed by the story."

That pleased Leslie. "How come you said the word bunny when you saw Leslie?" Janice asked.

The men exchanged a grin. "That's what Phillip calls you," Eddie told Leslie. "He can't seem to remember your name. Was there some picture or something you sent?"

Leslie looked as if she was trying to decide if she should be hurt or not. Janice immediately knew what they meant and began laughing. "It was that picture! Remember, Les? The one I took when we were at that amusement park together. You were being hugged by a six-foot tall rabbit."

"He calls me Bunny," Leslie muttered. "I guess it could be worse."

There was a knock on the door and Tom arose from one end of the sofa to answer it. "I hope you don't mind. I've already ordered dinner. That's probably room service."

He was correct. Eddie, ever the gentleman when he wanted to be, led them to the dining table and held out the chairs for Leslie and Janice. He took his own seat as Tom brought over the wine to refill their glasses.

Leslie removed her glasses and rubbed the bridge of her nose. When she set them on the side of the table, Tom peered at her face. She noticed his close scrutiny and turned red again.

"You look better without your glasses," he remarked with a kind smile.

Leslie glanced at his face and made a show of squinting. "You look better without my glasses, too," she kidded dryly.

Eddie started laughing and Janice giggled. Tom lifted his glass to Leslie. "Well said," he saluted with a satisfied grin.

As they continued eating their filet mignon, the talk loosened up as the women relaxed more. Tom and Eddie seemed very interested in Leslie's novels.

"How did you happen to develop Jane into a wife for Jack?" Tom asked. "Our writers won't do that."

Leslie looked down at her plate, carefully cutting a stalk of asparagus as she answered. "I really like The Loner character. And…I don't like to see anyone alone like that. I like happy endings. So I wrote one," she ended simply as if the whole process had been that easy.

"I do, too," Tom replied good-naturedly. "I've tried to get the writers to give Jack someone, but they haven't."

Janice gave them a wide grin. "Well, there's always next season. We happen to know of an excellent storyline."

"How many have you written? This isn't the Western, is it?" Eddie asked.

"I've done three so far. The second, the Western, is at the publishers now to see if they will accept it."

"They will," Janice, ever the optimist, stated.

Eddie nodded. "That's good. What's the third about?"

Leslie looked pleased with herself. Her eyes shone as she talked about her work. "It's called CHATEAU REX and Jane is hurt in an explosion she inadvertently caused and gets amnesia. The Professor has been watching her since the time and setting of the second story and abducts Jane.

He takes her to his hidden laboratory in the hills around the Silicon Valley...." She broke off at the looks on the men's faces. "Oh, that's right. You know where that is. Ha, sorry! Anyway, the two of them go back in time to Scotland to discover Jane's past—which she knew nothing about. All this time the squad has been searching for her. Even antagonistic Andrew is worried. Jack is distraught. During the three months she is there, Rex and Jane fall in love...."

"Interesting triangle," Tom commented, intrigued.

"Her memory returns when Jack and Andrew arrive to rescue her, guns in hand," Leslie finished, out of breath and a little embarrassed that she talked so long.

"So, you gave the Professor a love scene? That's a first!" Eddie laughed.

"Actually, he gets three or four and a touching farewell," Leslie explained, turning red again for some reason.

"Does Jack get his wife back?" Tom wanted to know.

"Oh, yes. Jane, of course, is very confused as her memory returns, but she would never leave Jack."

"Of course she wouldn't," Tom declared, lifting his chin. "That Jack is one terrific guy."

Leslie steeled herself to meet his direct look and gave a small smile. "Yes, he is," she responded quietly.

When they were done eating the foursome returned to the sofa and chairs. Tom sat next to Leslie on one end of the sofa as Eddie sat across from them in one of the chairs. Janice sat at the opposite side of the sofa so she could watch everyone easier. She didn't want to miss a thing.

"So," Tom started when they were finally settled. "Tell us about your adventures traveling. I enjoy going to exotic places myself when I'm not filming."

Leslie shook her head slightly and looked at Janice. "I wouldn't call it adventuresome, but it was enjoyable. I've been to seven islands in the Caribbean, and I spent five days shopping in Manhattan, but I prefer shopping in the Caribbean."

"My wife's appearing on Broadway," Eddie told them. You wouldn't go back to New York? She seems to like the pace of the city when she's there."

"Oh, I really liked New York," Leslie was quick to insist. "My agent wants me to come in the spring to meet the publishers. But, I do prefer St. Thomas and Martinique."

Tom looked interested. "When are you going?"

"To New York? I don't know for sure," Leslie frowned slightly and looked back at Janice. "Maybe in April. I'm kind of leery about just Janice and myself going. I was in a group before."

"Take someone else with you," Tom suggested.

Janice piped up here to make a point in Leslie's behalf. "There isn't anyone else, really. All our friends are either married or broke. Or both," she added with a laugh. "We'll just have to stick together."

Eddie glanced at Tom's face and changed the subject. "What are you planning on doing next with your stories, Leslie?"

Leslie looked away from Tom's face. "Next? I'd like to turn them into scripts and submit them, but I'm not sure how."

Tom looked surprised. "Haven't you ever seen a script?"

"Not a real one," Leslie replied and then grinned. "I'm planning on having all my friends send copies of my novel to Majestic with letters extolling the wonderful storyline! I'm hoping there'll be interest in it before I start another rewrite to try and turn it into a script."

Eddie nodded at this strategy, not knowing for certain if she was completely serious. "Public opinion carries some weight. You'll want to contact Richard Avery. He's the head of the studio. If your work is good and enough fans show interest, something could happen."

"It's good," Tom said quietly, studying Leslie's face as she listened intently to Eddie's words. Janice continued to observe Tom and smiled contentedly to herself at his scrutiny of Leslie.

"Thanks," Leslie said brightly. "That's good to hear from a professional." She glanced at her watch. It was almost ten o'clock. "Oh, my, it's getting late, Jan. We shouldn't have taken up so much of your time," she apologized as she stood from the sofa and looked around for her purse.

"No, don't go yet," Tom hurriedly said, standing as if to block her. "We don't often get a chance to talk to people like this."

"We have a two hour drive home," was the reluctant argument from Leslie. She glanced at Janice for back-up. Janice was still seated, her arms across the back of the sofa, settling in for the duration. "Jan?"

"I'm fine. So we get home a little late," she shrugged, knowing this was a once-in-a-lifetime chance for her friend. "No one is waiting for either of us. We both live alone," she added with a smile.

Leslie threw her a "What-are-you-doing?" look and turned back suddenly when Tom picked up one of her hands. "Please stay for a while. If nothing else, we can arrange for you to have a room here. If it gets too late, that is," he told them as he pulled Leslie back onto the seat on the sofa.

It was Eddie who stood next. "Well, after that meal and sitting for so long, I need some exercise. If that crowd is gone, I'm going down to the main lobby."

Janice perked up at this. "I'll go with you," she suddenly interjected, seeing a perfect opportunity to leave Tom and Leslie alone for a few minutes.

Hesitating for a fraction of a second, not seeing any other polite option, Eddie offered his arm. "That would be charming. We'll be back in a few minutes."

Leslie's eyes grew alarmed as Janice strolled out the door with Eddie Chase. "You two are full of surprises. I wish I had a camera. No one will ever believe this," she muttered as she turned back to Tom. He had kicked off his shoes and had his feet up on the coffee table.

He shrugged. "Eddie's the energetic one. He likes to work out and jog and keep active. Plus, he has a son to run after."

"And what about you?"

"Me? No, I don't run around after his son," he teased and was rewarded with a wide smile. "I don't know. I try to keep in shape, but I'm not a fanatic about it. Tell me about yourself, Leslie Nelson. Where are you from? What do you do in your boutique?"

So they talked on and on about their lives and found similarities in likes and dislikes. They told of pranks and jokes at both of their workplaces. Talking about their private lives, there were past loves mentioned and what they were both looking for in a partner. The television show came up and the possibility for Leslie's character in the next season. They went back to traveling and the destinations they would most like to reach. Never once was Phillip mentioned.

Eddie and Janice had returned after an hour only to be quickly, surreptitiously waved away by Tom. Leslie hadn't even noticed the door opening, being so caught up in their discussion and the moment. Somewhat concerned but not wanting to argue with his friend in front of the ladies, Eddie had no choice but to take Janice to his suite as the hour was so late. Always the trooper, she turned on the television and promptly fell asleep on the sofa. Eddie brought in a bedspread to cover her. Returning to his bedroom, he went to sleep himself, wondering what in the world Tom was doing.

Leslie awoke suddenly. There was a man's arm around her shoulder, and she was leaning against someone's chest. Her own arm was encircling a waist. Her shoes were off with her feet tucked up under her wrinkled dress.

She looked up at Tom Young who was still asleep, his head back against the cushion of the sofa. Alarmed, she tried to get out of his arms as quietly as she could without awakening him. However his eyes opened and were momentarily shocked to see someone in his arms. He was quick to recover and quietly murmured, "Morning," with a grin as she sat away from him looking extremely embarrassed.

"I...I can't believe we fell asleep like that," she muttered as she smoothed down her messy dress and pushed absently at her hair.

Tom stretched his cramped arms. "Where's your friend? It's five a.m."

Leslie stood awkwardly and looked around. Her nerves were making her shaky. "I don't know. Maybe in the bedroom?" She checked all three shut doors before she found the right room. "No. Is she with Eddie still?" she gasped at the thought.

"Maybe," Tom shrugged as if he didn't care one way or the other. "She'll be all right. Eddie's a happily married man. Everything's fine. What's wrong?" he asked as her face was far from calm.

"I can't believe this happened! What about your reputation if someone found out? This is terrible," she exclaimed getting herself even more upset.

Tom reached out to her and put his hands on her arms to calm her. "No, it's not terrible...unless you had a really terrible time," he added with a small grin. "We fell asleep on the sofa after a most enjoyable evening. That's all." He put a finger under her chin and raised her face so he could see her eyes. He gave her a sincere smile. "I can't remember the last time I enjoyed an evening so much. You're different from most women I meet. And you're certainly not like most of the fans. You're funny and serious and shy and bold all mixed together."

Leslie didn't know what to say. She was staring into his amber eyes. Her embarrassment had fled at his kind words. He bent down and lightly kissed her cheek. Her hand went up and touched the spot where his lips had been.

"I guess I enjoyed it, too," she almost whispered. "I must look a fright," she claimed wiping at her eyes and looking down.

Tom grinned showing his even white teeth. "Well, you do look like a raccoon."

"Oh!" That was the last thing she wanted to hear and tried to cover her eyes with her hands.

He laughed and pulled her hands down. "I like raccoons," he told her and lifted her face again. This time he gently kissed her lips.

"No, don't," she whispered, turning her head and trying to push away as all the years of brow-beating took over her actions. "I'm nobody. You deserve...."

"Shh," he cut her off, not relinquishing his hold. "You're not a nobody. I think you're special and I'd like to see you again sometime."

"I live in Amherst. You live down in Los Angeles. That's over three hundred miles away. You're just being nice," she argued weakly, her heart pounding at his words.

"Just leave your address and phone number. You'll see. I don't spend the night with just any-one," he added lightly. He was surprised to see her eyes widen.

"We...we didn't spend the night together! Don't say it that way!"

Tom was touched by her protestations. That was all the other women usually wanted from him. He now knew for sure that this one was different. "Okay, I won't. Sorry. Are you going to stay for the convention today? You're already here. We could have lunch together," he offered, hoping.

"No, I have to get home. If my parents knew I wasn't home they would worry." She saw the du-bious look on his face. "I know I'm not fifteen," she smiled, knowing how it sounded. "But they still worry. Plus, I've taken up too much of your time."

"All right," he sighed, relenting. "Do you believe what I told you?" he asked, suddenly getting serious again.

Leslie turned away from his look. "Well, you are a good actor. I think you're trying to make me feel better."

Tom shook his head as he reached for her hands. "My, you're stubborn, too!" he claimed and grinned at the frown she gave him.

"Am not," she sniffed.

"Then kiss me," he murmured, bending down to her lips. He brought her close in an embrace as one hand touched her back and the other dropped below her waist and pushed her even closer.

The ringing of the phone disrupted his convincing Leslie. It was Eddie inquiring what the heck was going on. Tom explained what had happened and asked about Janice. Eddie had already called Cindy to bring over some make-up for the visitors. When Leslie overheard that, she asked for the same help.

When Janice arrived with the needed cosmetics, the two women retreated into one of the bathrooms to make their repairs. Eddie then assaulted Tom.

"Whatintheheck are you doing, Tom!? Are you nuts," he demanded in a low voice.

"It wasn't like that, Eddie," Tom shot back angrily. "We talked all night and fell asleep on the sofa. That's it. Her face is still dented from the buttons on my shirt if you care to check."

"I don't care to check. It was bad enough that you invited them to dinner, but this is terrible. What if the papers pick this up? I'm married, you know!"

"Oh, is that what you're worried about? Yourself?" Tom charged. "Well, this has nothing to do with you. I...I like Leslie. A lot. Her reaction was the same as yours, by the way," he added, trying to end the argument before the women walked into the middle of it. "It wasn't planned. We just fell asleep. Don't worry about Linda. I'll tell her everything if you think it's necessary."

Eddie attempted to smooth his own ruffled feathers. "She already thinks you're a terrible liar. I doubt that would help. I just don't want anyone hurt by gossip. You know how bad it can be."

Tom nodded quietly as he looked at the closed bathroom door. "I know. We've all been burned.... This one is different, Eddie. And she's going home just as fast as she can."

Eddie gazed at Tom but said nothing. He could tell Tom meant what he had said. Tom did seem affected by this woman. Maybe he had been too harsh with his criticism. "Do you know how to reach her again if you wanted to?"

"Not yet," he sighed. "But, I will. Even if I have to ask Phillip."

The bathroom door opened and the two women emerged looking somewhat repaired and refreshed.

"We really need to go," Janice spoke first.

Leslie walked shyly up to Tom. She didn't seem to know what she should do or say to him. "Thank you for the dinner and the...the interesting evening." She extended her hand.

Tom, torn between being amused and hurt, took the offered hand and kissed it. Then he surprised all of them by using that hand to pull Leslie towards him and kissed her on the lips. "No, thank you," he told her. "I meant what I said. I will see you again."

Leslie said nothing as she took up her purse and her signed book. Janice brightly said good-bye to the actors, mentally high-fiving herself. They left the suite without looking back.

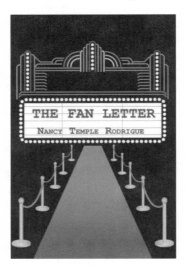

THE FAN LETTER

BY NANCY TEMPLE RODRIGUE

Available in Paperback and eBook formats at Amazon, Barnes & Noble, and Double-Rbooks.com

ABOUT THE AUTHOR

NANCY TEMPLE RODRIGUE

Nancy lives in the small town of Lompoc, California. Besides writing, she is an avid reader and also enjoys knitting and crocheting, she also enjoys showing her award-winning 1957 T-Bird in local car shows. Nancy is just 3 hours North of Disneyland so she visits often, both for research as well as for fun! Grandchildren live nearby and are learning early in their lives the wonders of Walt Disney's Theme Parks.

Writing about her favorite park, Disneyland, comes easy for Nancy as she has been an avid Disney fan ever since she was 6 years old and went to Disneyland for the first time. Her novels show her admiration and respect for the man who started it all–Walt Disney.

The novel, *Hidden Mickey: Sometimes Dead Men DO Tell Tales!* and it's sequel *Hidden Mickey 2: It All Started…*, were her first books in the Hidden Mickey series. In those first two novels she was assisted by her co-author David W. Smith. Nancy has been writing for most of her life, mostly in the fiction and fantasy genre, so when Smith approached her with the idea of a story along the line of the movie National Treasure, but with connections to Walt Disney, she jumped at the opportunity to write it with him. In just 2 months Nancy had penned over 120,000 words of that first novel, once her creative forces started to work she was almost unstoppable. That first book was completed in just 3 months.

With the success of that book and fans demanding a sequel, they got to work to continue the first story. But where do you start? Nancy had an arsenal of unpublished works to draw from so her publisher suggested introducing the material from a book she had written a few months before. The story centered around a wolf and a mysterious pendant that once belonged to Merlin. So, when you read book 2 you'll get the picture. This story allowed her to introduce fantasy. Her publisher sketched a heart shape gemstone and made the pendant into a 3 circled hidden mickey. This pendant is on the cover, and available to fans as the limited edition Hidden Mickey Heart Pendant.

With the completion of *Hidden Mickey 2: It All Started...*, Smith wanted to write his own story so recommended Nancy author the next two novels in the series solo to continue the fantasy element she had successfully introduced. Nancy wanted Wolf to have his own story, so we now have *Hidden Mickey 3 Wolf!: The Legend of Tom Sawyer's Island*, and this novel *Hidden Mickey 4 Wolf!: Happily Ever After?*

Nancy actively participates in book signings and speaking events, and she loves talking to people who enjoy her novels.

When the first book was released in 2009 Disney invited Nancy's publisher to hold a book signing on the *Downtown Disney* property with her '57 T-Bird on site having Mickey and Minnie behind the wheel. This was a huge hit. Since that time her publisher has been able to arrange book signings at many *Barnes & Noble stores*, as well as venues like the *Los Angeles Times Festival of Books,* where a news reporter stated the Hidden Mickey novels were one of the top selling novels at the event. The most recent venue was *Disney's D23 Expo* where Hidden Mickey novels were *"the top selling Novels"* at the Expo. It is noteworthy that the Hidden Mickey novel series are now more popular than ever, thanks to readers like you.

Nancy is planning visits to Walt Disney World in Florida in addition to her regular visits to the original Disneyland park in California, in preparation for even more adventures to come. Fans can go to www.hiddenmickeybook.com and follow the author's blog to learn where book signing event dates and locations are posted.